Bantam Books by Louis L'Amour

LOUIS L'AMOUR'S
Lost Treasures:
Volume 2

LOUIS L'AMOUR'S
Lost Treasures:
Volume 2

*More Mysterious Stories, Unfinished Manuscripts,
and Lost Notes from One of the World's
Most Popular Novelists*

Louis L'Amour
with
Beau L'Amour

BANTAM BOOKS
NEW YORK

2020 Bantam Books Mass Market Edition

Published in the United States by Bantam Books,
an imprint of Random House, a division of
Penguin Random House LLC, New York.

Bantam Books and the House colophon are registered trademarks of
Penguin Random House LLC.

Originally published in hardcover in the United States
by Bantam Books, an imprint of Random House, a division of
Penguin Random House LLC, in 2019.

ISBN 978-0-425-28491-9
Ebook ISBN 978-0-425-28493-3

Cover design: Scott Biel

Printed in the United States of America

randomhousebooks.com

2 4 6 8 9 7 5 3 1

Bantam Books mass market edition: October 2020

What Is Louis L'Amour's
Lost Treasures?

Louis L'Amour's Lost Treasures is a project created to release some of the author's more unconventional manuscripts from the family archives.

Currently included in the project are *Louis L'Amour's Lost Treasures: Volume 1* and *Volume 2*. These books contain both finished and unfinished short stories, unfinished novels, literary and motion picture treatments, notes, and outlines. They are a wide selection of the many works Louis was never able to publish during his lifetime.

In 2018 we released *No Traveller Returns*, L'Amour's never-before-seen first novel, which was written between 1938 and 1942. Additionally, many notes and alternate drafts to Louis's well-known and previously published novels and short stories will now be included as "bonus feature" postscripts within the books that they relate to. For example, the Lost Treasures postscript to *Last of the Breed* will contain early notes on the story, the short story that was discovered to be a missing piece of the novel, the history of the novel's inspiration and creation, and information about unproduced motion picture and comic book versions.

An even more complete description of the Lost Treasures project, along with a number of examples of what is in the books, can be found at louislamourslosttreasures.com. The website also contains a good deal of exclusive material, such as even more pieces of unknown stories that were too short or too incomplete to include in the Lost Treasures books, plus personal photos, scans of original documents, and notes.

All of the works that contain Lost Treasures project materials will display the Louis L'Amour's Lost Treasures banner and logo.

LOUIS L'AMOUR'S LOST TREASURES

CONTENTS

INTRODUCTION

By Beau L'Amour

Not long before presenting this manuscript to Random House, I attended a memorial service for a man named Oscar Dystel. Oscar had been the powerhouse president and chairman of Bantam Books from the 1950s to the 1980s. A visionary when it came to editorial content, art direction, distribution, and inventory control, he had worked at Esquire, Coronet, and Collier's magazines and had been honored for his expertise in psychological warfare during World War II. After Dad had come to Bantam full-time around 1957, and after some initial hesitation, Oscar became a great champion of my father's work and, eventually, his close friend.

The service was a strange experience for me. I recognized faces, voices, and names that I had known as a child or worked with as a young adult. There were people I had lost track of years before, some of whom, though they had seemed mature enough to have been intimidating at the time, must have been fairly young when I first met them—because here they were, older, grayer, but still alive and kicking.

There was a lot of history and a lot of brainpower in that room, men and women who steered the publishing industry through the heyday of the paperback. These were the people who made my father a legend. They were the people who had made

Danielle Steel, Harold Robbins, Irving Wallace, Clive Cussler, Sidney Sheldon, Norman Mailer, Michael Crichton, Barbara Cartland, James Michener, John Grisham, and Ian Fleming household names.

It stirred up a lot of memories, and I found myself mourning Oscar's passing, not only as a child who had looked up to this gruff but kindly man as one of the only authority figures my father ever chose to answer to, but also as a symbol of a passing era.

Louis L'Amour, just after moving to Hollywood.

My father arrived in Los Angeles in the summer of 1946. The bustle of wartime had not yet abated and the rules were such that it was next to impossible to find a hotel that would allow anyone to stay for more than five days. Short-term housing was a constant game of musical chairs. While the primary reason for the trip was the wedding of Dad's niece, the visit also served as a reconnaissance mission.

Louis was thirty-eight years old and possessed of few prospects. Like thousands of other recently returned servicemen, he needed to make a living. The war had disrupted the magazine business as much as it had everything else. Many of Dad's contacts had disappeared and, while he had written a few stories even before leaving Europe, the marketplace was changing. The world had been overwhelmed with the real-life version of the high-adventure tales he had specialized in before going overseas. Postwar, editors were looking for Westerns as a more comfortable and nostalgic alternative.

In the late thirties and early forties Louis succeeded in selling about three dozen short stories. At the time, he had been living with his parents on a small farm in Oklahoma owned by his eldest brother. Now, however, in order to afford the independence he was looking for, he would have to complete more stories each year than he had sold in his entire life.

Writing forty to fifty short stories annually provided Louis with just enough money to live comfortably as long as he kept tight control over his budget. Maintaining his morale was also a reason for the high productivity: "My system was to have so many stories out that when one came back its failure was cushioned by the chances that were left," he wrote to author and editor Ken Fowler, "and by the time they returned I had others out."

For five years, a very nice family allowed him to sublet a ten-by-ten room with a bath in the back of their second-floor flat. In the beginning, he'd sit on his bed and place his typewriter on a folding chair. When he had any extra money, he would send it to his mother or spend it on books.

Eventually Dad got a small typewriter table
and a cabinet for some of his books.

Louis was working full out, as hard as he could. He managed to sell thirty-three out of the fifty-five stories he wrote
in '47, and twenty-seven out of fifty-one in '48. But around
1950 the pulp market began to weaken. Magazines that had
been around for decades were failing, changing their for-
mat, or scaling back from monthly to quarterly editions.
Competition for the remaining space became more and
more fierce.

Some of the difficulties the fiction magazines were experiencing were due to a prewar invention: the paperback
book. The Western "dime novels" and "railway novels" (so
named because they were sold in train stations) of the nineteenth century were early experiments in this form. True
success, however, had to wait until the 1930s, when a pair of
innovations were introduced: an effective glue strip used to
bind the book together and the adoption of a distribution
model invented by magazine publishers.

Before World War II, there were fewer than five hundred real bookstores in the whole of the United States, and
most of those were centralized in a dozen northeastern cit-

ies. The rest of the country was serviced by "book of the month" clubs and libraries. Before the advent of the paperback, at least half of all titles produced by American publishers sold fewer than 2,500 copies. The book industry was staid and predictable, organized around a group of venerable old companies. Its product came from a relatively elite group of writers and sold to a relatively elite group of readers.

On the other hand, the magazine business was a good deal more lively and inventive. While bookstores may have been in limited supply, the country had thousands of newspaper and magazine stands, cigar stores, drugstores, and railway and bus stations. Though the two businesses, books and magazines, eyed one another with a mixture of envy and contempt, it was destined that they should meet.

It was not an immediate love affair. Hardback publishers looked down on the cheap books, and believed that the American masses weren't readers. They allowed paperback publishers to reprint their titles but assumed the arrangement would be at worst an experiment on someone else's dime and at best no more than a passing fad. However, the experiment turned into a breakaway success and led to an explosion of paperback publishing houses in the mid- to late 1940s. The number of copies sold shot into the millions. Mass-market distribution changed the entire concept of success in the publishing industry.

Dad had always intended to become a novelist. That had been his plan ever since his first attempt in the late 1930s, *No Traveller Returns*. But a great many short stories could be written in the same number of months it took to write a novel, and the chance was much better that a few of them would sell.

Ten years later, with rent constantly due and his mom and dad expecting help rather than giving it, the time it took to write—and sell—a novel was an even bigger risk.

Dad was living from paycheck to paycheck, and those checks came only when he was lucky enough to sell a story. Louis wanted to make the move to writing longer material, and, risky or not, the time was right. In the end, though, none of that mattered: Dad *had* to move on to the next step . . . because, with the decline of the magazine fiction business, the one on which he was standing had begun to disintegrate.

In the late 1940s, with some success selling Western short stories under his belt, Louis set out to sell a Western novel. He was still writing a few high-adventure and detective stories, but his sister had sent him a diary containing a brief account of a party of German settlers who had been swindled in a fake gold rush. That section of the diary became the inspiration for *Westward the Tide.*

Years earlier, impressed by a short story published in *New Mexico Quarterly Review*, a New York agent had contacted Louis and offered his services. The man was never particularly good at selling Dad's material, but he did represent some very respected writers and, still a relative newcomer, Dad was honored to think of himself in such august company. The agent initially expressed high hopes for *Westward the Tide.* Louis, writing to his mother, put it this way:

> "Just had a letter . . . on Westward the Tide and [the agent] believes the novel will have an excellent chance with the Post or Collier's, which would mean $6,000 or more for me."

When Louis mentions these two top magazines, he is referring to the possibility of one of them serializing the novel—including a chapter or two per issue until the entire story is printed. This method of publishing was the best money available at the time, and the prestige gave the author an even better chance of selling the rights to a book publisher afterward. It is worth noting that Louis had yet to earn $6,000 in an entire year.

It breaks my heart to know that Dad was so desperate. He was seeing his earnings decline each month as stories became harder and harder to sell, and he wanted to show his parents that he could actually make it as a writer. As the letter goes on you can sense that desperation:

> ". . . I don't believe it will sell to them, although it might. However, I do think it's a fair story. At that, it promises well, for if he thinks it that good, he should know, and it means my next one will be that good . . . I want to double my income this year, but will do better than that, I think . . . Westward the Tide is a fair job that I could have improved a lot with more work. It will sell, but if I get $1,000 for it, I shall be satisfied. And I'll do that one way or the other . . . With luck and no major illness, I'll be a wealthy man one of these days."

Eighteen months later, after rejections from several publishers, his agent finally sold the rights to *The World's Work* in the United Kingdom for a mere $243.68 and mailed away my father's only copy of the manuscript. Dad agreed to the deal because, by then, he was too desperate to wait for anything better. Not only was this vastly less than Dad might have made by cutting the story down and selling it to the pulps, but since he'd lacked the money to have it copied, he could not continue trying to sell the U.S. rights. He would not see a copy of *Westward the Tide* in any form for almost twenty years.

It is only now that I realize how young I was when I first heard about Dad's mysterious missing novel—the book he had never seen in published form, and to which he no longer even had a manuscript. When I was eight years old, the whole family took an extended trip to England and Ireland. The year before, Mom and Dad had made a whirlwind tour of Britain to promote the motion picture version of Shalako. *Both the film's gentlemanly producer, Euan Lloyd, and Dad's publisher in the UK, Corgi, had pulled out all the stops, nearly overwhelming my parents with the best of British hospitality.*

The experience was so extraordinary and Corgi was so enthusiastic about promoting Dad's books that my parents decided to return the next year to do more of the same, except this time they would bring me and my sister along and turn it into a family vacation. It would be the first we had ever taken beyond the American Southwest.

1969 was an amazing time to be in England. The country was blossoming after the grim years of postwar austerity. British music, films, cars, and fashion had taken the United States by storm, and if the acclaim Dad received on our trip was any indication, the English were indulging in American culture as well. In between seeing the various sights, Louis spent a great deal of time autographing books and doing TV and radio interviews.

Corgi did such an exceptional job that when the trip was over my mother marched into Oscar Dystel's office in New York and shoved a scrapbook of all of Dad's appearances across his desk. "This is what you should be doing for Louis in the United States!" she told him. Up until that moment, virtually all of the publicity Louis had received he had set up for himself.

After England we flew to Ireland and saw Tara Hill, the ancient seat of the Irish kings. We saw passage graves a thousand years older than the pyramids and traveled the southern coast in a horse-drawn gypsy caravan wagon. A great many of the Irish locations Louis experienced on this trip would later be used in his novels.

The L'Amour family in Ireland, 1969.

The final success of our great English adventure was that somewhere along the way Dad mentioned to Michael Legat, the editorial director of Transworld, the company that owned Corgi, that he had written a book that had never been published anywhere but England.

By the time we were home in Los Angeles a package was waiting for us. Mr. Legat had convinced World's Work to part with its last copy, discovered in a dusty file in its office in Surrey.

By the early '50s Dad's financial situation had become extraordinarily difficult. He was conning his way onto studio lots to sell television producers episode ideas for the shortest money imaginable and he was going to the park in the mornings so his landlady wouldn't realize he couldn't afford to buy himself breakfast. He was afraid of being asked to leave if she lost confidence in his ability to pay the rent. In 1951 he earned only a disastrous $2,200, less than half the modest amount he made in an average "good" year. His creative output remained high—he produced thirty-eight stories, some of them quite lengthy—but he was able to sell only seventeen of them. In the ledger where he noted which manuscripts had been sent to what magazines, the words *Discontinued Publication* appear again and again; the magazines had gone out of business.

Then, in September, Louis received even more bad news. It was a twist of fate that, over the next two years, would change his life in ways he could barely have imagined. He submitted a short story titled "Gift of Cochise" to *Better Publications*, a magazine outfit run by his friend and long-time benefactor Leo Margulies . . .

. . . and Leo turned it down.

Despairing—and feeling he had nothing to lose—Louis sent the story on to his agent. And at last the man came through, making a sale to *Collier's*.

Dad's fortunes immediately began to improve. In quick succession, he sold a treatment that became the movie *East of Sumatra* to Universal Studios, and another story to NBC's Fireside Theatre. Even before "Gift of Cochise" was published, Louis was able to option it to producers John Wayne and Robert Fellows. The movie, when it was made the following year, was titled *Hondo*.

Louis promptly began paying off his debts and swore that he would never allow himself to get that close to the edge again. Booking a flight to the East Coast, he set up meetings with every editor he knew and probably a few he didn't. Previously, he had relied on his agent or, more often, simply sent his work through the mail in the hopes that an editor might like it. Now, he confronted the publishing industry with the full and considerable force of his personality.

Up until this time, Louis had been a writer working in several genres who just happened to write quite a few Westerns. They were popular and he knew the West from personal experience, so the genre had been a good fit. Writing to Oklahoma author Harold Keith of his early career and the transition away from writing adventure stories, Louis said: "The thing that moved me into the western field was simple economics . . . the market was larger. However I never intended to stay with it . . ."

Using the upcoming movie production of *Hondo* as leverage, and with paperback companies always eager to take advantage of a studio's promotion efforts, Louis pitched himself to paperback and magazine publishers alike as an author who specialized in Westerns. "Success is not a trollop that gives herself to every comer," he later commented. "Success must be lured and trapped . . . Hondo was not my break through, my use of Hondo was."

Within two months he had sold the reprint rights for the magazine novels *The Rider of the Ruby Hills*, *Showdown at Yellow Butte*, and *Crossfire Trail* to Ace Books. In addition, Ace picked up *Utah Blaine*, Louis's first story written specifically for the paperback market.

After the hard times that Dad had just been through— the closest to the edge of abject poverty he had been since he was a kid—this was a major victory. Later that same summer he signed a contract with Fawcett's Gold Medal Books to expand "Gift of Cochise" into a paperback novelization, a companion piece to the release of the movie. That deal included a commitment for one new paperback original per year from Gold Medal.

Dad was ambitious, and concerned about the future. He was getting older and he had lived through tough times, not just the previous several years but the Depression and the rough (for him) decade that preceded it. He figured he could write three paperback-sized novels a year, and he was not going to let up until he could make sure that every month of every year was put to good use. He summarized his goal in response to comments made in *Inside Bookselling*:

"Dick Carroll was then editor at Fawcett,
and I approached him with the idea of three
books per year. He liked the idea but the
powers-that-be at Fawcett did not. I like to
write and I write better when I write all
the time so I went to meet Saul David."

And that meeting led to what must be one of the most
profitable relationships in publishing history.

*The sound of a swimming pool filter hushed in the background,
sunlight reflected off greenish water and cracked cement, a white
glare broken by the outline of a nearly leafless tangerine tree in a
pot. The room where we sat was glass walled, the "family room"
of a rambling 1950s ranch-style home in the heart of the San
Fernando Valley. The place was an indication of the long, slow
purgatory allotted to those no longer in favor in Hollywood. It
had seen better days, and so had the small white-haired man who
sat across from me dressed in tattered pajamas and a faded robe.*

Louis and Saul, late 1950s.

Saul David had once been the producer of such films as Von Ryan's Express, Our Man Flint, Fantastic Voyage, *and* Logan's Run. *He had also once been the editorial director of Bantam Books, a man who, when he left publishing to make movies, had been replaced by a staff—an entire department.*

Saul had many private demons. He could be fiercely vindictive and had never been afraid of giving anyone, from the head of a studio to the lowliest assistant, an identity-destroying dressing-down. In an industry that values deference (let's not call it "subservience") above most other traits, Saul burned many bridges, often well before he even arrived.

The only people who seemed safe from his acid tongue and flashing temper were my parents. His bond with them had been forged in the purer world of books. Neither were intimidated by him, and I think it was their unconditional acceptance that completely disarmed him. Mom and Dad were two of the very few people he actually wanted to be around.

Worried he might decide I was wasting his time, I got my tape recorder rolling and asked him how he had met my father.

Saul:
"I was in a suite at the Beverly Hills Hotel when the front desk called and said, 'There's someone here to see you.' I said who was it, and they said, 'A Mr. L'Amour.' I said, 'I don't know any Mr. L'Amour,' and they said, 'Well, he's on his way up to see you now.'

"I opened the door, and there stood Louis, who was all his life a very large guy. Maybe memory has gilded it, but as I remember . . . the sun was coming in from the doorway and Louis blocked it out.

"He was . . . enormously aggressive, in a soft-spoken sort of way. I mean he had a purpose. He was going to do something, and I was not going to interfere with it. He was going to be pleasant about it, but it was going to happen.

"He said, 'I know you've never heard of me . . .' He had

a sort of set speech which I . . . I'm afraid I can't reproduce
after all these years, but I do remember it came out like,
'I'm the best Western writer even though you've never
heard of me. I want to join with you and I'm going to be-
come the star of your firm . . . and you won't be sorry!'

" 'How do I know this?' I said. He gave me some pages.
They'd been torn out of, I guess, a magazine. And he said,
'Here's some of my stuff. You can read it.'

"So I said, 'Okay, well, uh, what's your phone number?
I'll call you tomorrow or you can call me.'

"He said, 'No, read it now.'

"I considered arguing about it and I decided it was
easier to read it. It was . . . Hondo ["Gift of Cochise"],
and the truth of the matter was that, intimidated or not, it
was terrific! It was so much better than anything we had,
you know? It had a ring to it. It had a personal style to it.
He had a very particular way of using language. The man
himself reminded me of what I thought Jack London must
be like.

"I said, 'Okay, let's talk a deal. What do you have in
mind?'

"And, gosh he was pleased. He didn't fall down and
grovel. He sort of congratulated me, as I remember."

In two years, Louis had gone from the edge of eviction
to signing contracts with multiple publishers. It looked like
his future was set as long as he could keep churning out
books that the public wanted to buy. As a writer who was
rarely at a loss for ideas and who had a powerful will to create, one of the few obstacles he had left was juggling the
needs, and schedules, of his three publishers, Ace, Gold
Medal, and Bantam. More than anything, Dad wanted to
streamline the way he did business, to save as much of his
energy for writing as possible. For all his ambition, he
wasn't greedy. He liked the idea that everyone was making

good money off his work and he eventually pressured Bantam to keep his cover prices low. He wanted his audience to feel like they could always afford to buy his books.

It took Louis four years after his meeting with Saul to bring all of his business to Bantam. The idea of publishing three books a year by a single author was a daunting proposition in the early days of paperbacks. Oscar Dystel, the newly arrived president of Bantam, had come on board to solve the host of issues that had caused the market to become oversaturated with unsold books. Faced with an excess of material being released into an unruly marketplace, he was not initially supportive of an aggressive newcomer writing in what was considered to be a second-rate genre.

But Saul David personally went to bat for Louis. He had known Oscar in Cairo during the war and knew how to be persuasive. It made no sense to lose two thirds of the money Louis's books were making to other publishers. And, *because* the market was chaotic, it made no sense to not be in control of the release of all three books. Louis L'Amour was successful and becoming more so; all it would take was the guts to say yes.

Saul being Saul, he also threatened to quit.

After a successful test in El Paso and a couple of other cities, Louis and Oscar signed a deal that gave Dad the opportunity to sell three Western paperback originals a year to Bantam. For my father, it was the beginning of an era of relative prosperity and stability.

Creatively, however, the pressure to do something different had been mounting. While Louis enjoyed writing Westerns, it was far from the only genre that interested him. With the security of his new contract to protect him, he began to plan an attack on a number of other genres. But it was an effort that did not succeed for a very long time.

———

Before the advent of the paperback, the idea of genres, of different categories within the universe of fiction, wasn't the controlling force that it would later become. When paperbacks first appeared, they were rarely sold in bookshops, and merchants hardly cared what was in the book section of their stores. Paperbacks at magazine stands, drugstores, and supermarkets were primarily organized by publisher, the subject matter casually mixed together.

As the 1950s became the 1960s, bookstores, followed by other outlets, began a process called "integration"—organizing books by genre or category rather than by publisher. Unfortunately for many authors, this meant that publishers developed a keener interest in keeping their writers locked into the category and the specific area of bookstores where the majority of the readers expected to find their work.

In the early 1960s Louis wrote the following in his journal:

```
Oscar Dystel . . . out from NY for a
brief visit. Says my books are selling in
great style but tries to talk me out of
trying anything else, and of course, I see
his point.
```

This conversation was probably regarding material like *The Walking Drum*, a twelfth-century adventure that Dad had just finished. Louis and Oscar had great respect for each other, and Louis understood that once Oscar found a successful author he didn't want to take any chance of disturbing that success.

As much as Dad wanted to stretch his wings creatively, there were similar issues to be considered in his own life. He was fifty-four years old, success was still new to him, and I had been born a year or so earlier. For the first time he had a family of his own to support. Louis knew the Westerns were his bread and butter and, though he had tried, he'd had no luck selling anything *but* a Western in a decade. Yet he still felt like rebelling. A few months later he wrote:

> Starting next month I shall do 5 pages of a western every day, and the rest of the time on other things. Stories I would much rather do. Yet I can't knock the westerns . . . <u>Lando</u> sold 103,000 copies during its first month.[*]

In the previous five or six years, Dad had begun work on a good number of stories in other genres, but the need to cover the costs of his growing family and to save money in case of hard times constantly pulled him away. He had even *finished* two non-Western novels, *The Walking Drum* and the so-far-unpublished *Sky Ring Water*. But *Sky Ring Water* needed a considerable amount of work, and *The Walking Drum* was rejected by a number of publishers. As soon as Dad stepped away from writing Westerns, it seemed like he was starting his career all over again. Something needed to change and, as it turned out, the social upheavals of the 1960s were already creating the opportunity he needed.

In 2012 I was working with artist Thomas Yeates on the comic book adaptation of Louis's story "Law of the Desert Born." I visited his home in Northern California several times during the two years that it took to produce the hundreds of images that went into that project. One evening, we sat in his studio as Tom played the guitar. The sky over the Pacific still glowed bright enough to

---

[*] Given the cover price and royalties of the day, this would have earned him around a thousand dollars. However, that money was almost certainly kept by the publisher to help pay off his advance.

see the horizon. I knew Tom had been an illustrator since the 1970s and I asked him about his familiarity with horses, Western landscapes, and cowboy gear.

He replied by telling me stories of a childhood growing up in some of the more rural areas of the Central Valley. We talked about how we found it odd that many people don't seem to recognize California as the profoundly Western state that it is. "Before I was a hippie, I was a cowboy," he said, and segued from "The Streets of Laredo" into a psychedelic riff à la Jimi Hendrix.

I knew that cultural crossover very well, though I saw it happen the other way around. I spent the 1960s and '70s traveling around the West; my sister, mother, and I went wherever Dad needed to research or promote his books. Even as a child I recognized that the hard-bitten blue-collar cowboys and miners who had once looked down on "longhairs" were suddenly beginning to get a bit shaggy themselves.

On any street in the country, you could spot a guy with shoulder-length locks and elaborate facial hair in the style of Wild Bill Hickok or Commodore Perry Owens. Women affected Indian braids and long skirts and everyone wore Levi's, vests, wide-brimmed hats, and high-heeled pull-on boots. Musical tastes were also drifting, from the British Invasion toward folk and country rock, which had clear roots in rural and Western Americana. In those days, counterculture contained an antielitist bent, regardless of political sentiment. The times they were a-changin' for everyone. The children of the baby boom, the young people of the 1960s, could see that the heroes of Western fiction had a profound anti-authoritarian streak and were seeking relief from the power of the East Coast establishment and the expectations of Victorian conformity. The hippie had met the cowboy, and they'd found they were brothers.

While Louis eschewed the outward trappings of a younger generation, like Woody Guthrie he became an elder statesman to millions of young people remaking their lives in new and rebellious ways. He knew from personal experience what it meant to be a wayfaring stranger, an outsider, a day laborer panhandling his way across a nation that didn't understand his dreams. His characters were often young and adrift, orphans and outcasts, searching for employment and community. I have read hundreds of letters he received in those years, some from girls who were hungry and lost on the streets of Haight-Ashbury, others from lonely and scared boys in the jungles of Vietnam. All discovered freedom and adventure and some sort of comfort and personal guidance in the pages of Dad's work. There are powerful reasons why Louis's greatest growth in popularity was in the 1960s and '70s.

Kathy and Louis L'Amour with original "long-haired country boy" Charlie Daniels, celebrating the inauguration of President Jimmy Carter.

So instead of fighting, unsuccessfully, to make a clean break from Westerns as he had in the late 1950s and early '60s, Louis's new plan was to explore the creative possibilities within the notoriously brittle boundaries of the Western genre. "I know that some of my readers do not like my going away from the straight western, but I must do it for myself," he wrote in his journal. If he succeeded, the next step would be to gently convince both his fans and his publisher to follow him into any genre he wished.

It was a cautious strategy, but Louis knew that it was the right moment. Though as skeptical as anyone who'd lived through the radicalism of the '20s and '30s, Dad also understood what he saw going on around him. From doing personal appearances and book signings, answering fan mail, and just watching the changes in our West Hollywood neighborhood, he could tell that a younger generation was making the world ready to accept a broader definition of just about everything.

Louis laid the groundwork carefully, crafting a vision of himself as a "frontier writer" rather than a man who simply wrote Westerns. He established that he was going to write three interconnected series following the adventures of the Sackett, Chantry, and Talon families. Some of these would be traditional Westerns, but he was going to also carry their stories back to the earliest days of the North American frontier.

The plan was to convince the publisher that he had not drifted beyond their comfort zone, keep the booksellers from feeling they didn't know where to rack his books, and allow his traditional fans to find his work *while* following him into new and interesting territory. With any luck he'd be able to cross over into the arena of swashbuckling adventure and historical novels. Eventually, he hoped to sell longer and more complex novels without rattling too many links in the complicated publisher-to-reader supply chain.

After a series of experiments throughout the 1960s, like the contemporary Western *The Broken Gun,* the attack on audience expectations began in earnest in 1972. THE FERGUSON RIFLE is a Chantry family story and takes place just after the Revolutionary War. *Sackett's Land* spends a good deal of its page count in Elizabethan England. The most significant departure was *The Californios*, which was not only set in a Mexican California slowly being invaded by Yankees, but contained elements of mysticism and science fiction too. "You've really taken a chance with [*Sackett's Land*]," Bantam's Marc Jaffe wrote in a letter to Louis, "but you were always one to take a chance. The story moves as well as any of your conventional westerns."

Chance or not, the impact on sales was positive and meshed closely with the zeitgeist of the 1970s. Carlos Castaneda's *The Teachings of Don Juan* and its mystical sequels had been bestsellers for some time, and the impending American bicentennial had caused historical novels set in years before the Revolution to surge in popularity. On a more negative note, the social unrest of the times, the Watergate investigations, fuel rationing, thousands of domestic bombings, and international terrorism all pushed readers to seek comfort, or a sense of American identity, in genres such as Westerns and historical novels.

The success of *Sackett's Land* and *The Californios* put Louis on course to do more of the same, and eventually allowed him to make the move away from the American frontier and to occasionally publish books like his beloved *The Walking Drum*, in 1984.

That outcome, however, as the following journal entry indicates, was initially far from certain:

I wait warily for the returns on DRUM, out this coming wk. Some of my regulars may desert me on that one but I may recruit new readers. Yet one never knows. Many a writer as well as an actor has broken his back trying to do something different. Several people have commented on my making a change at this [late] date.

In the end, though, the book was a massive bestseller and paved the way for a similar success with *Last of the Breed* in 1986 (a cold war thriller) and *The Haunted Mesa* in 1987 (science fiction). It had been a hard road full of compromise and patience, but Dad had finally proven he was not a writer whose success was tied to just one genre.

In closing, I will return briefly to the memorial service for Oscar Dystel. For me, the most telling moment came when Patrick Janson-Smith, once an editor at Corgi, quoted Oscar saying: "The right to fail is the catalyst of creativity."

I can think of no better phrase to describe the contents of *Louis L'Amour's Lost Treasures: Volume 2.* Yet mostly I believe that what you see here was only a failure of longevity, for Dad intended to permanently abandon very few of these ideas. "Found several good story openings," he wrote in 1976, ". . . and once the opening is written the story is mine forever."

If you read the "bonus feature" postscripts that accompany the new Lost Treasures editions of many classic L'Amour novels, you will notice that Louis started and then set aside quite a few of his best-known works. Whenever possible, he would return to them a few years later and, with typical energy, blast all the way through to the end.

"So much to write and so little time!" he commented in the mid-1980s. "What will it matter if it is not written? Perhaps not at all, yet I think of Nietzsche's Zarathustra: 'I am like the bee that hath gathered too much honey; I need hands reaching out for it.'"

BEAU L'AMOUR
November 2019

LOUIS L'AMOUR'S
Lost Treasures:
Volume 2

THE BASTARD OF BRIGNOGAN

Two Beginnings to a Historical Novel

CHAPTER 1

Alone upon the darkening hillside I wait for the last lights to wink out.

There stands the castle, well-guarded and strong, yet tonight I shall enter that castle. I shall scale its walls, open its doors of oak, walk down its silent halls, a sword in my left hand.

In my _left_ hand?

I have no right hand.

My right hand is gone, struck from the wrist by the order of he who rules this castle, rules it and all the land around.

He will have forgotten me, for to him I was less than the dust beneath his feet, and the sight of my blood dripping to the floor before his eyes will have been drowned in the blood of others he has killed or maimed.

Yet tonight he will remember, and for the brief moment of his life that follows he will swallow the gall of his hatred. He will die slowly and with time for regret.

I will go alone, yet had I an army I would
disdain to use it, for it is a part of my revenge
that he realize my contempt of him, and of the
power he wields. This must be done without help.
Too long he has hidden behind his mighty walls,
behind his armored men, and I will show him what
a hand can do. Only one hand, and the hatred he
fed into me when he deprived me of that which was
all and everything to me.

My right hand . . .

You ask me . . . what is a hand? A hand is a
delicate, yet a mighty thing. It can weave and
weigh and strike and caress. It can grip a sword
or wield a hammer, touch with tenderness or
strike a blow that will crush bone. A hand can
create a tapestry of silk, carve ivory or jade,
create a goddess from raw marble, heal the sick
or bless those who have sinned. A hand can lift a
savage brute to the heights of creative skill.

Was it not the hand that created Man? A lion
walks in the jungle and steps upon a stone, and
from it receives perhaps two impressions, a sense
of hardness, of sharpness? Of something rough or
smooth? But a man stepping upon that same stone
experiencing the same things, can yet lift the
stone, turn it gently in his fingers, feel its
various sides, judge its weight and its balance.

The lion receives perhaps two sensations, the
man receives a dozen . . . perhaps more.

So it is with each thing he touches with the
hand, and with each touch his experience grows,
and with it his knowledge. Truly, man was shaped
and created by his own hands.

Who am I? A man . . . no more, no less.

Except . . . yes, there is a difference, for I am a man with a sword.

Once I was more than that. Once I had a right hand, that could carve, shape, test and create. My hands were born to shape the still wood or stone into things of beauty, and within me there was naught but the wish to create. I asked for nothing but materials and time. The materials were all about me, and the time stretched before me forever . . . I was younger then and there seemed no end to the years.

The will to create is still within me, but the left hand is not enough. The touch is there, as is the mind and the will, but a little something is lacking for the right hand was the master of art, the left only a servant to it.

With my left hand only, I am skilled. With a right hand I was . . . who shall ever know, now, what I was or might have become? Since childhood I had shaped and carved wood into animals and men that could all but speak, and then stone . . .

Apprenticed to an armorer, I learned to handle metal, to emboss, to inlay, to use a hammer with cunning. My skills increased . . .

Then he took from me my hand. He, who rules in yonder castle. Who now drinks his wine, eats his food, and prepares for rest.

His last rest.

Impregnable they say, is the castle. No army has ever taken the castle of Gingee. He sits secure behind his walls, upon his towering peak, high above all that is about him.

My boat lies by the distant shore. My men await me there. Beyond is the Bay of Bengal and a

wide world of which my fellow Europeans know
little.

The artist I once was is dead, but something
was born from the ruins, sired by hatred,
mothered by a will for revenge.

Now I am a warrior.

A warrior with but one hand? Ah, yes . . . but
a warrior trained as no other was ever trained, a
warrior driven by such hatred as you cannot
believe.

He took from me the girl I loved. He took from
me my dreams, all that I had or lived for.

Nor was ever a man trained with the skills
with which I have been trained. The teacher I
had, the greatest master of his craft, a teacher
without another pupil but me, a teacher so
skilled even his former master feared him and
wished him dead. Knowing his time was brief he
strove to pass on to me those skills he had
acquired in a life-time.

My fingers open and close. Soon my time will
come. No army has been able to storm those walls,
or scale the mountain upon which the castle is
built. No elephant has been able to batter down
the giant gates with their steel-spiked doors.
Behind those doors he sits, spinning out his evil
like a great spider, hidden and protected.

Tonight I shall face him . . . and he will be
alone.

Oh, he will have a blade! He will have one or
I shall give him one, and it is said he is a
master swordsman. Yet he will die. He will die
alone with the cold steel of my blade in his
guts, die in a pool of his own blood.

Who am I? I am the Bastard of Brignogan.

My father I saw once only, and well I remember the night he came to us. A night of storm fit to shiver the masts of many a tall ship when he came to our door and rapped on it with a sword-hilt to be heard above the storm.

Ours was a poor cottage though I never thought it so, for beyond the harsh granite of the rocks lay the steep cliffs I loved and the long, lonely beach with the cold Atlantic rollers coming in upon it.

Cold, did I say? Yes. But often indeed they were warm and pleasant for our shore was touched by a current I came to love for upon it were borne many odd things: strange woods, bits of wreckage, fragments of things from afar. There I splashed in the waves, tasted their salt, and there I looked upon the distance.

My father was a tall young man, but he staggered from the wind's force and swore as he slammed the door against it. He removed his cloak with a flourish that scattered drops over the room and draped it across a chair.

He swept the rain from his hat with a gesture and looked at my mother. She was brown and strong and beautiful, but with the fires of Hell in her blood.

"There's nothing for you here," she said flatly, "so why have you come?"

"Nothing for me? Once it was a different song you sang."

"Long ago. I've forgotten the tune. What is it you want?"

"I heard you'd borne a son of mine, and I wished to see what we spawned, you and me."

"He is not your son. He is mine. You've strong lads of your own. Go to them."

"I am his father, am I not?"

"You were the sire. It ended there, and you've no more to do with him."

He looked at her and laughed, from sheer pleasure.

"Ah, girl! What a woman you are!"

He looked at me. "Is this the one?"

"There is no other. That is my son."

The tall man dropped on his knee before me and put his hands on my two shoulders. His face was wet from the storm, and although I was scarcely three, I recall it well, for he was not a man to forget.

"Ah! A handsome lad, to be sure! Look at the shoulders! And the hands!"

"He has good hands, I'll grant you. Already he has taken to weaving and splicing. You'd not believe it, and him so young."

"I'd believe it of your get, lass." He stood up and looked at her. "You know my situation. I've been off to the wars and it was little enough I brought back but the scars and experience. I've a great name, but with three boys and a girl growing, there'll be little enough to divide among them when all is done. I could not take him from you, and I---"

"I would not give him up. He is mine."

"May I be seated?"

She gestured to a chair, and sat down at her loom. "What was it you wanted?"

"I am home for a few days only. Tomorrow I must be off again, I think. I await the word. I returned to bring them what I could, and little

enough it was." From under his belt he took a
leather purse and threw it on the table. "I saved
this for you."

From an inner pocket he drew a sheet of paper.
"Here's a name. The man's an armorer . . . makes
the finest blades in France. When the boy is
seven or eight, take him there. He will take him
on as an apprentice where the boy can learn a
trade and make an honest living.

"Would I could do more, but being born who I
am I have only the choice of going to the wars or
bending a knee at court, and I was never one for
that. Our family land is poor stuff, and scarcely
supports the castle. My sons have a name, lass,
but I doubt they eat better than you do."

"We have the sea."

"Ah? Of course. A fine mother but a harsh
master."

He got to his feet. "They will be expecting
me, and I have far to go. Tiphaine, I wish it had
been otherwise, I wish--"

"No need to waste yourself with wishing. What
was between us was my doing as much as
yours . . . more, perhaps, for you were ever the
gentleman. Do not worry about the boy. I will see
to him."

"What will you do, Tiphaine?"

"For the moment, nothing. The lad has a love
for the sea and the shore, yet one day we shall
go to Paris."

"It is a great city. Yet not an easy city."

My mother laughed. "These shores do not breed
weakness, and I am strong. Paris will do nothing
to me, nor will London, or wherever I go."

They stood for a moment, looking across the

table and into each other's eyes, and I think, for the moment, they each remembered what it was that had been between them.

Then he took me again by the shoulders, and this time he kissed me. "Be a good lad, be a bold lad. Stand your ground."

There was a burst of wind and rain, and he was gone. My mother stared long at the closed door, and then she said, "That was your father. Remember him well. He is a better man than he knows."

Well . . . what would he think of me now? Here? Had I, over the years, stood my ground well enough for him?

One more thing he said before leaving the house, a thing I have never forgotten, for it was my mother's answer that stirred something in me.

"About a name, Tiphaine. The boy must have a name. There's my grandfather's . . . let him take that. I will go to the notary--"

Her chin lifted. "He will need no name until he can make one for himself. What is a name, after all? A thing hung upon you to seal your station in life. Let him name himself when the time comes, and when he wishes. He needs neither your name nor any other."

"It is a proud name."

"It is. And proud men have made it so. Thus it shall be with my son."

We saw no more of him, and I doubt not that after a few days he returned to the wars.

It was the next year I found the figure.

The morning was cold, the sky over-cast. A strong sea was running but I climbed eagerly down the cliffs to the shore and ran along the sand among the great rocks until I saw something white . . . something with a pale sheen.

Cautiously, I approached it. Something in the sand, half-covered. I dug around it, lifted it carefully up.

It was the figure of a woman, carved in what I now know to be ivory, her flowing garments about her, all her features perfectly shaped, her hands, her fingers . . . I had never seen anything so beautiful.

I sat down on the sand and stared, turning it carefully in my hands. Someone, somewhere, somehow, had done this. Someone had carved, taking away a little here, a little there, and so had come from the ivory . . . beauty.

Something created. Something that had not been before had become.

For days I kept my secret. For days I studied it, looked at it, longed for . . . for what?

What was it I wanted? What was that strange excitement within me? Could I . . . could I, perhaps, do such a thing? Could I, with a knife, carve such a thing as this?

I had no ivory, but there was wood. Alone, seated upon the rocks out of the wind, I began to shape a small piece of wood. Days followed. Sometimes I cut too deeply, sometimes I pared away too much. Often the thing I created was lumpy and wrong, and it irritated me, yet always I returned to my study of the figure, and again and again I tried.

One day I came up from the shore with a piece of wood in my hand. My mother saw it, and asked what it was. "It is a man," I said, "an old man

with a barrow. He has sacks upon it, and he is
very tired and old."

She looked at the wood, and then at me. "It is
only a piece of wood," she said, "of driftwood."

"Look!" I held it up. "His head is here. The
barrow with the sacks, it will be here, and--"

"I do not see it," she said gently. "I have
not your eyes."

"Wait," I said, "I will show you. I will cut
away some here. I will shape that curve, I
will--"

"Do it," she said. "I would see what you have
seen."

Days I worked. I ran no more upon the sand, I
showed her nothing. At night I hid it in a crack
in the rocks. I worked and worked again.

Then one day I went to her. She was doing her
hair, looking in the small mirror I had found for
her in some wreckage.

"See?" I said. "The old man and the barrow!"

She took it up, she turned it slowly in her
fingers, then she knelt down and took me by the
shoulders. "You did <u>that</u>? But who could teach
you? How could you learn?"

"I had a teacher. The lady showed me how."

"A lady? <u>Here</u>?"

I took the figure from inside my shirt. "I
found it in the sand. I wondered if I could do
that . . . could do it as well. I have not . . .
yet."

"You will. I am sure you will." She stood up
then, holding the figure in her hands. "It is
old," she said, "it is very, very old."

After a moment, she handed it back. "I think

we will go to Paris," she said quietly. "I think
it will soon be time."

Yet it was two years longer before we left.

Behind me I left carvings of ships and men, of
mermaids and horses, of dolphins, whales, and
strange designs I dreamed of at night or saw
shaped in the sunset clouds.

We went to Paris . . .

My mother, young, beautiful. A girl from a
sea-side village who had never known a city, but
a girl unafraid, a girl very sure, and very
strong, a girl with a few carefully hoarded
coins . . . not including those she had from my
father.

She took with her several of my carvings.

CHAPTER 2

The night was very still. The horses stamped
restlessly, tired of their long wait.

Mahmoud looked at me and shook his head. "One
man? Against a castle? It is mad!"

"Where ten thousand could not go, one man
might. I know what I do."

"You have waited six years, so wait another
year. When the Nayak returns, the Solaga will no
longer be in Rajagiri, the citadel of Gingee. He
will return to his island in the Coleroon, and
you can have him there."

"I have waited too long. I shall wait no
longer. He thinks me dead, drowned in the sack.
He watched me. He saw the sack drawn up around
the girl, and I saw her strangled before my eyes
and her dead arms hung over my shoulders, then

the sack sewn shut. He watched as we were dropped
into the water from his ship. He saw us sink, my
dead beloved and I."

Mahmoud stared. "You got out of that? Your
hands tied? A strong sack sewn tight?"

"It was she. Somehow she had secured a knife,
and in the moment before her hands were tied, she
cut mine free. In the moment she was strangled,
she slipped the knife in my hand, and her one
last word was, 'Wait!' It was whispered, softly.

"I waited, then as the sack struck bottom, I
cut myself free, and when I surfaced it was close
under the stern where I could not be seen.

"The sun was setting, and as the ship moved
away, I dove once more and swam under water, and
was careful to come up with the sun glare in
their eyes.

"I swam then, swam away from the shore where
his soldiers might be. I swam out to sea."

"To sea?"

"There was a ship . . . I had seen it earlier,
lurking along the shore, and when the Solaga's
ship put out from shore, it went further to
sea . . . avoiding us. It seemed to have no wish
to have us draw close.

"Yet when the sack was drawn up, I saw it off
there, a mile or so away and working across the
wind to get more distance still. It was that ship
I swam toward."

"It was a long chance."

"Aye, but I reached it and they took me
aboard, and truly enough, they feared the Solaga.
That night again they came in close to shore and
picked up what it was they awaited . . . some
secret goods, sold without paying the tax to the

Solaga . . . and we sailed off then, far to the
east and were wrecked there."

"You survived?"

"And no other. Of them all, I lived. I was
found and cared for by an old man . . . five
years I lived in his home, and was trained by
him. It is a long story."

I stood up. "It is time, Mahmoud. Do you
return to the boat on the river. If I have not
come in three days, forget me."

Black and terrible the three hills bulked
against the night. Men had called it the
strongest fortress in all India and many an army
had fallen back from its great walls. They were
sixty feet high, surrounded by a ditch eighty
feet across. Beyond those walls, other walls, and
finally the dome of Rajagiri, the highest of the
three hills, a vast rounded head of stone, its
sides almost sheer, great boulders forming a part
of those walls. Within it, temporarily in
command, was the Solaga, Sarbaz Khan, a renegade
Moslem, and the man I sought. It was he who had
ordered my hand cut off at the wrist.

The path to the citadel passed through a
pleasant grove, alongside a reservoir, and by a
shrine, the oldest building in the place, older
than the fort itself. Yet there are legends that
tell of earlier occupation, and not far off is
the ruined city of Padaividu, some sixteen miles
in circumference, a city said to have been
buried, perhaps thousands of years ago, by a
shower of dust and stones.

The main fortress enclosed a triangular space
about three miles around, with citadels upon the
three hills. There were granaries, tanks,

pavilions, barracks, palaces, temples and mosques all enclosed within the walls. There were also more than one thousand highly trained fighting men inside that enclosure, men dedicated to the service of Tubaki Krishnappa Nayaka.

I knew that few of these men admired Sarbaz Khan, who had fled the Moslem forces to serve Krishnappa, for what reason I knew not. What I did know was that he was a cruel tyrant who hated all he could not crush.

Long had I studied design and plan, long had I worked drawing the patterns for gold inlay upon armor, pistol and sword-hilt until I had an eye for detail. For months I had studied the layout of the fort, I had learned it carefully, and now had come the time to make use of my knowledge.

My horse walked along the dark lanes, between boulders, under trees, through thick stands of brush. In the distant jungle I heard the coughing roar of a tiger . . . there were many about . . . but I moved on, approaching the castle steadily, at a pace long planned.

The Bastard of Brignogan . . . so they had called me, and I accepted the name. Yet there was no doubt as to whose son I was, and he was a man much known and much loved in that corner of the coast.

Of my mother's early history, I knew nothing. Nor did I know why she chose to live alone in our thatched cottage of stone near the shore . . . a shore notorious for its wreckers.

There was a man who came often to our cottage. That he was in love with my mother, I well knew, but she would have none of him. He was a great, powerful man, and friendly, yet I knew he was one

of the wreckers. By and large they were a bloody
lot, wrecking ships and then looting them, and no
doubt killing all who survived.

I remembered once, he said, half-humorously,
"What if I took you anyway?"

She said, without any humor at all, "You might
succeed, although I doubt it, and you'd look the
grand fool if you failed, but if you did succeed,
I'd wait until you slept, and then I'd kill you."

He believed her, for he did not mention it
again.

That he admired her still . . . perhaps even
more . . . was obvious. He brought us gifts of
food, clothing from the wrecks, or materials
looted there. These were useful, as my mother
sewed well, exceeding well, in fact.

It was not until later that I began to wonder
about her, for no relatives came to visit. She
had no ties in the village or the country around.
Whoever she was, wherever she had lived before
coming to the cottage, I did not know.

It was a time when few people traveled. Most
of those who lived along our coast had never been
more than a few miles from their homes except
when fishing or going to sea, and the women did
neither.

Nor did my mother ever speak of her past, nor
of anyone she had known before coming to the
cottage where we were. We were much together,
walking along the shore, working in our small
garden, going to Brignogan to sell vegetables or
fish. After it became known that my mother sewed
so very well she was often asked to sew but she
usually refused . . . relenting only when the
task happened to appeal to her.

She made some vestments for a priest, I
remember, and a wedding dress for a young girl
with whom she had talked from time to time. At
night, sometimes, she sang . . . the songs were
not French, yet some were Breton, or some tongue
very like it.

That my mother was a woman of some mystery did
not occur to me. She was my mother. It was that
fact I accepted and no other, yet it did begin to
appear that she was something out of the ordinary
in many ways . . . her independence, her courage,
her strength of purpose. I remembered the way she
spoke to my father with a kind of pride, although
it was not until later that I grasped all she
said.

That I would make my own name was something I
did consider, and once asked her about it.

"Names are important only when you make them
so," she said, as we walked upon the shore. "Men
are named for their trade, for the town in which
they live, for the estate they possess, or
sometimes for some characteristic that is
uniquely theirs.

"You are Brenn. That is the name I have given
you, but in your time you will choose another
when it suits you, or circumstances will confer a
name upon you."

How right she had been! Now I had a name, for
when my hand was cut off I did what must be done.
Always I had been mechanically skillful. I had
designed in metal, worked in metal, wood, stone
and ivory . . . so now, left without a hand, I
designed one for myself, a metal hand that could
be fitted over the stump of my wrist. It was not

only a hand, it was a claw, as well. So they called me the Claw.

The man with the Claw. From that, the man with the Talon. And finally, Brenn Talon.

But when my mother took me to Paris, I was only Brenn.

Etienne Bressy was an old man, yet tall and strong with fierce eyes and a nose like a hawk's beak. It was an early morning when my mother brought me to his door.

He opened the door and glared at us, looking from one to the other. He wore a shirt and breeches, his sleeves rolled up to display powerful forearms. I never forgot them, and envied him his strength, wishing for such arms myself. It was years before I earned them, and it was only after much work, and much use of the hands.

She mentioned my father's name and he stepped back, gesturing for us to enter.

The room was low-ceilinged and relatively bare. There was a table, several wooden benches, and on a smaller table, several books. There was a fireplace and on the far side of the room, a bed.

He looked at her again, and then at me. "He is young," he said.

"But skillful," my mother said coolly. "You will be fortunate to have him as an apprentice. Already," she added, "he can do what you need."

He stared at her then snorted. "Such work needs skill, and skill comes from work, years of work."

She opened the bag she carried and placed

before him the figure of a fisherman I had carved
from bone. He looked at it. "What is that?" he
asked, his voice surly.

"The work is his," she said. "It is good
work."

He took it up then and turned it in his
fingers. As he studied it, she took several other
pieces from her bag, one a piece of inlay done
with shell.

He looked at me again. "<u>You</u> did this? What is
your age?"

COMMENTS: The first chapter of this next draft is missing but we can assume that it also begins in India, with the
hero about to make his attempt on the citadel of Gingee,
before flashing back to his childhood in France. In this version, Brenn is named Dorion and a character much like Etienne Bressy is named Coatlanen.

CHAPTER 2

The year was 1629, and Louis XIII was king of
France.

Of the four years that followed I had only the
most meager of memories, and those were confused,
without focus or direction. They were memories of
swimming in the sea, running over the high,
lonely moors, of fishing, boating, wrestling with

other boys, and of watching the change in my
mother.

At first I was aware of no change. It began
with the books. Gold was scarce, hard to come by,
so greatly valued. My mother had the typical
Breton caution with money. She improved our lot
very gradually, but the books were the first
thing.

My mother could read. How she learned, when so
many people of all classes did not, I never knew.
Now she bought cautiously, also she began to
improve her appearance, so gradually as to make
the change scarcely apparent, yet when four years
had passed my mother no longer was the same.

She spoke quietly, rarely raising her voice.
Guarding herself from the sun, her skin was no
longer brown. Her clothes were plain but
carefully chosen. My mother had become a lady.

With her change in clothing and manner there
had been a change in the attitude toward her on
the part of other people. They accepted her for
what she seemed to be.

Moreover, she had been teaching me. At first
she did the teaching herself, and then she
acquired the assistance of an elderly woman who
had once been maid to a titled lady. She paid the
woman a few coins each month to stop by, and it
was not until later that I realized that while
the woman taught me, my mother was learning also.

She learned by imitation, casual questions,
and by leading the woman to gossip of her former
life.

When I was scarcely past seven years old, we
moved. My mother had prepared the ground well,
but left open an avenue of retreat.

"My uncle in Paris," she told people, "has been asking us to come to visit him. Actually," she would add after a few weeks, "he wants us to live with him, but we shan't do that. Maybe we will visit him."

Then one day the plans were made. She closed up the cottage and we rode with a friend, a driver from the castle some distance off, who was going to Paris. Trust my mother to spend no money if it could be avoided.

I was filled with excitement. I had never traveled except to nearby villages, and to our small village, Paris was a far off place to be imagined rather than seen.

Yet we did see it, and after a few days of getting settled, my mother took me to a narrow little street on the left bank. Louis XIII was in the process of completing the changes Henry IV had begun. Richelieu had completed the Palais Royal a few years before and presented it to the king, and the Ile de la Cite and the Ile St. Louis had been joined by a bridge.

Not too many changes had taken place on the left bank. The old inns that dated back to the twelfth century when the first students began to haunt the left bank were still in existence. And if one knew where to find them there were even Roman ruins, for it was on that bank the Romans had made their station.

The house where my mother took me was of ancient design and in a narrow street. The second floor projected out above the street with heavy timber framing, and there was a sign suspended over the walk.

COATLANEN

I was startled, for even I knew that name. It was the Breton seaman from the Ile of Brehat who had become an admiral in the Spanish navy, and who told Columbus in 1488 of lands that lay to the westward.

The story was an old one in Brittany, and not unlikely, for had not Breton, Basque and Norman fishermen fished off those coasts for generations?

From the sign this Coatlanen was not a seafaring man but an armorer. My mother lifted the latch and entered a long, low-ceilinged room with a few chairs about, and a wide, empty hall to our left, forty feet long and half that wide. A room that had a board floor of amazing smoothness. Two swords lay across a chair.

My mother opened and closed the door again, harder this time, and then we heard footsteps along a passage, and a man appeared who filled the width of the door, a very short but broad and strong man with a large head set upon massive shoulders.

"M. Coatlanen?" my mother asked.

He had looked quickly at us, but he shook his head. "I am Jacques. If you will wait---?"

He disappeared, and a moment later reappeared with a tall, well set-up but much older man with a pointed white beard and keen blue eyes.

"I am Coatlanen," he said.

My mother said, "This is the lad of Brignogan of whom his father spoke to you. His name is Dorion."

Coatlanen looked first at my mother, then at me. He took me in at a glance, then looked again. He took one of my hands and turned it in his.

"A fine hand, a strong hand. Have you lived by the sea, lad? Have you fished? Rowed a boat?"

"I have," I said. "And I swim."

"Of course." He looked at my mother. "The lad has uncommonly fine hands, and strong wrists. He should do well as a swordsman."

"His father wishes him to become an armorer."

"Yes. I believe he said something of that." He looked at me again. "He is the son of a gentleman, a nobleman--he should handle a sword."

My mother looked at him, her eyes cool, her manner composed. "My son has no name, m'sieu. Perhaps he will make it with a sword, but I would prefer he _make_ swords."

They were kin but stern. There was discipline in the shop. Coatlanen believed in basics. He believed in bodily strength, self-discipline, and in knowing the whys and hows of all things. It was Jacques who first took me in hand to show me how steel was tempered, how swords were hammered into shape, how the final point or edge was put on. At first he merely led me around the workshop, showing me the anvils, the forges, the tools and explaining each in turn.

From the first day, I worked. I swept the floors, picked up odds and ends of metal and returned them to their respective boxes, returned the tools to their places at the end of a working day, and worked the bellows. Above all, I was expected to observe.

On my third day as I worked, an object fell from my pocket. It was a bit of hardwood on which I had been carving.

Jacques picked it up, was about to hand it back, then stopped. It was a replica of a ship, not quite so large as my fist, and carved in minute detail. He turned it in his hands, studying it.

"Beautiful!" he said. "Beautiful! Where did you get it?"

"I carved it. I found the wood on the shore . . . among the rocks."

"You? You carved this? How old are you, lad?"

"Eight years . . . nearly eight."

"May I keep this for a few days? To look at?"

"You may have it, if you like. I can carve another."

He left me then and went to the room where Coatlanen worked, and a moment later, opened the door and called me.

I was frightened. I did not know them well and feared they would believe I had carved it when I should have worked.

Coatlanen studied the piece in his hands, with his eyes and his touch. Then he looked at me thoughtfully. "Have you done much of this?"

"I have."

"Only ships?"

"Birds, animals, flowers, people . . . whatever I see."

He leaned over his table and looked at me. "Dorion, you are an artist. You have a gift. Continue this, and show me what you do, but above all, study the basics, lad, the basics. You must know the look of heated metal, must know the sound of the hammer upon it, the sound of it when dipped into water. No matter how beautiful a thing is, it is nothing unless it is also strong.

"Tiny, if you will. Fragile, if you must, delicate as any rose petal, but for what it is . . . strong. Always strong. Men or metals, lad, the strong survive. And be careful of those hands . . . there may not be another pair like them in the world."

What would he think now, that good and gifted man? What would he think to see me standing here, with one hand only? Waiting for the hour when I would go up those rocks, over the wall? But he would know how I did it, for he taught me that, too.

He taught me the art of the <u>ninja</u>, which he had learned long ago, in Japan.

He taught me patience, and to turn each problem into profit. As a boy, cast away upon the shores of Japan, he had learned the art of the <u>ninja</u>, the making of swords, and the using of them, Japanese style.

Like his distinguished ancestor, he had taken early to the sea, his skill with a sword swiftly winning him an honored place, yet he had little money, and no title. He was simply a master-at-arms and a soldier, a man of peculiar skills, respected by all, feared by not a few.

His first voyage to sea at the age of ten had ended with the ship of his father wrecked on a reef in the north Pacific, and Coatlanen himself the only survivor. Washed overboard, he had struck out wildly, trying to swim in the madly churning water. On the second stroke his hand smashed hard against the side of the captain's

gig, and he caught the stern and pulled himself
into the boat.

Hours later he awakened with the morning sun
upon his face. He lay in a small cove, his boat
bobbing upon the waters, the storm clouds
scattered and drifting. The cove was an
indentation in a rocky and beautiful shore,
ragged, wind-blown pines and what he took to be
cedars clinging to the rocks. Not far off was a
small sandy beach.

He was working toward the beach, half-hidden
by an over-hang of rocky cliff, when he heard
shouts, then a clatter of hoofs upon stone and
gravel. Peering out from his over-hang he
glimpsed a party of horsemen clad in strange
armor charge along the edge of the cliff on the
other side of the cove and then into the trees.
Wild and fierce they were and, frightened, he
stopped his boat and crouched down. The men were
circling to find a way to the beach, apparently.

Clinging to the vines, Coatlanen stood up in
his boat and peered toward the beach.

On the white sand, not a hundred yards away,
lay the body of a man. Even as he looked, the man
put out a hand, trying to crawl. No doubt it was
he for whom the riders searched, and in minutes
they would be upon him.

On impulse, Coatlanen urged his boat swiftly
along, reaching the sandy shore. He scrambled
from the boat and caught the wounded man under
the arms. "Quick! You must help!"

Somehow the man mustered strength, and
together they reached the boat. Toppling the
wounded man into it, the Breton sailor boy pushed
off from shore. Swiftly he skulled the boat. The

nearest over-hang was only a few yards away. He
could hear the horses coming, heard angry shouts,
and then he was in the shadows and under the
vines. Once out of sight, he continued to move,
using his hands upon the rocks to move the boat
silently along into a deeper and darker part of
the over-hanging cliff.

Behind him were shouts and angry yells. He
could see only a few of the horsemen in their
strange armor. Most of them carried bows, and a
few had swords as well. They rushed down upon the
sand, whirling about.

Yet their very anger was a blessing, for
charging down upon the sand, even into the edge
of the water, they trampled out any tracks he
might have made.

They scattered out, searching.

Careful to make no sound Coatlanen worked his
boat along the shore. The water was deep close up
under the rocks, and even from the sea his boat
would have been invisible due to the over-hang's
shadow and the vines. The tide was changing and
as he continued to ease the boat along it more
and more often threatened to crash them against
the cliff.

Suddenly the over-hang deepened and he found
himself in the entrance of a cavern hollowed by
ages of pounding seas. The boat was carried
inward and it was only with a quick twist of the
oar that he avoided a rocky barrier where a piece
of the roof had fallen in. As he grew accustomed
to the dim light he made out a sandy shore, but
tied to the rocks was a boat, a boat with round
wooden eyes on the bow . . . Japanese or Chinese,
he knew that at once, and as they had been not

far off the coast of Japan, he knew now where he was, where he must be. This cave was a hidden place, a secret place, but someone had been here, might still be here. Silently he tied his boat to the other.

For the first time, in the vague light reflected from the water, and filtering through a small hole in the roof, far, far above, he looked at the man he had rescued.

A small man, but compact and strongly built. The man was bleeding from several wounds, one apparently a spear-thrust, another a cut that was not deep but had bled much, and the third, an arrow through his side that still remained there.

On the voyage with his father around the Cape and into the Indian Ocean, then along the Malabar Coast and thence to Sumatra, their ship had been several times attacked by pirates or others, and Coatlanen, too young for combat, had helped the cook who was also the most skilled hand with wounds.

He knew what to do and he pushed the arrow on through then bathed the wounds in salt water, and tore pieces from the wounded man's clothing to make compresses and stop the bleeding.

On board the Japanese boat he found dried fish, rice and some vegetables he did not recognize. There was also tea and rice wine. He found many curious things, among them a number of small discs, stars, and swastikas of iron, with edges razor-sharp. There were several kinds of weapons and a number of devices whose purpose he could not guess.

From time to time he paused to listen, but no sound came to this place but the lapping of the

water against the hulls and the sandy beach and
the deeper sound of surf on the breakwater of
fallen rock. He was about four boat-lengths
inside the cave, which was a large, vaulted
cavern. He could see several openings that might
lead to the surface, or might only go deeper into
the ground.

He prepared a small meal for himself and some
hot broth for the wounded man, careful to make no
sound. Then he heard a voice muttering.

The man's eyes were open and he was looking
up, and he said something in a strange language.
Coatlanen replied, "I found you on the sand." And
when the man spoke again in the strange language,
Coatlanen indicated lifting him and helping him.

The man smiled weakly, nodding his head, and
then he lay quiet and Coatlanen brought the broth
he had made and fed it to him, sip by sip from
the edge of a bowl. After a time the man signaled
that he had enough, and then he slept.

Weeks passed. The wounded man slowly
recovered, but their food supply was running low.
Twice detachments of what seemed to be soldiers
had come back to search the area, and finally one
night the wounded man indicated they were to load
all that was left into the boat with the eyes.
When that was done the man went around and
carefully removed every evidence of their being
here. And when they left they towed the gig after
them and set it adrift at sea.

Moving only by night they crept along the
shore, hiding by day in some rocky crevice in the
shore cliffs or tiny cove, each time masking the
boat with fish nets into which they wove vines.

From the first the wounded man had begun to
teach the boy. He touched himself and said,
"Sand-a-yu," and then one by one he touched the
items about him, saying their names.

One day Sandayu touched the discs with the
razor-edges. "Shuriken," he said, and picking one
up he threw it suddenly at a beetle upon the
bulkhead of the cabin. The disc cut it neatly in
two.

Swiftly, his hands a blur of motion, Sandayu
threw a dozen more, several of them in the air at
one time. They struck the target in a rough star.

Coatlanen was amazed. Such swiftness and
accuracy was unbelievable.

It was the beginning. Little by little Sandayu
taught the boy his skills, working with infinite
patience. He also instructed him in the language
of the Japanese.

"I am ninja," he explained finally. "It is my
art to be invisible, to come, to go . . . to spy
and to kill. There were many of us, but there
will be few now, those few scattered.

"The riders were the soldiers of Nobunaga Oda,
a great lord. He sent them to kill me, and to
wipe out all ninja. If he learns I live he will
not cease until he kills me."

"Where do we go?"

"To Kii. It is a place where there are
friends, Buddhist friends. They will hide me and
protect me, and I have a farm there, a hut and
some land near the sea. You will come with me,
you will be my son."

"Is it far?"

"Not too far, and we can go along the coast.

The Buddhists there are militant, and have no
cause to love Nobunaga."

For ten years Coatlanen remained with Sandayu,
and for ten years he was trained in the skills of
the ninja. As they made their own weapons, he
learned the arts of the sword-maker and armorer
at the side of the master. Only when the ninja
died did he leave Kii, and then it was by night,
in the same boat in which he had come.

On the coast of China he found a Portuguese
ship and returned with it to Europe.

Those were the skills he had passed on to me.
The ninja were adept at scaling walls, using
hand-cannon, poison-water guns, smoke bombs and
blow-guns.

COMMENTS: Given the pieces of the drafts you have just
read, I believe that the first section was actually written
later and that Louis intended to take Coatlanen's adventures in Japan from this second section and hand them off
to Talon, creating a narrative that would be both more exciting and more focused on its protagonist.

As many of his fans know, Louis was working on three
interconnected series of books about the Sackett, Chantry,
and Talon families, each following a different family through
the period of European exploration and development of the
North American continent. Though he did not write them
in order, this novel, once finished, would have been the first,
chronologically, of the Talon series.

Below are several sets of my father's notes on the early

Talon stories that suggest how he might have continued on past these several chapters. I have compiled them into one continuum for easier reading:

Begin in India, flash back to Brittany. Illegitimate son. Lonely boyhood along shore. Talon . . . sees animals, fish and other objects in pieces of bone or wood . . . says "I will show you" and cuts away unneeded wood until the thing he sees is there. He has a gift for perception of form and line.

In 1569 apprenticed to an armorer in Paris, he develops his natural genius for design and sculpture, becomes skilled at trade. [He becomes an] Aid to [a] diplomat . . .

Goes to Persia by ship and caravan with Master, master dies, accused of theft by those who rob his master. He escapes into the swamps of the Tigris.

India, Talon in love: meets on the shore with a beautiful girl, is captured, replies fiercely to Solaga, who discovers how marvelous his art, then cuts off his hand, dropped in sea.

Escapes, gets aboard ship, proves useful, learns much about seafaring (use early sailing records), is wrecked in Japan . . . Stern teacher, some take him for Ainu [the Ainu were a native people in the Japanese islands]. Leaves Japan after long training, returns overland to India.

Joins pirates, takes a small boat and reaches Gingee. Using arts of ninja, enters castle and kills man who took his hand, becomes a pirate leader, raids along coast. Visits Tamil country. Stops at Krakatoa.

After capture of town or ship he examines prisoners for knowledge, information, etc. Those who can teach [him something] he keeps, then releases with presents. Finds one gathering info on his ship . . . in order to steal it. All written down. He suggests prisoner develop a better memory, maroons him upon an island. Returns to find prisoner has become ruler. Prisoner now plans to take Talon's ship again. Talon outwits him. They become friends.

Finds Neolithic settlements, old maps, falls in love with Rajput princess, escapes with her. Battle at sea, raids up river, mysterious voyage up the Indus and recovery of treasure at night. Some of his men mutiny but he defeats them, puts them ashore on an island and sets sail across the Pacific.

Crosses Pacific, terrible voyage, many die--1 of 4 [of his] ships disappears at sea. He sails to west coast [of North America], fight with Spanish ship, scurvy causes another ship to be abandoned,

treasure buried or hidden on west coast of
America.

With loyal seamen he sails around horn to
France. He pensions them off, one at a time,
invests some of his fortune there. His
mother has gone on to become a famous woman,
a patron of the arts. Brings the rest of his
treasure to Canada packed among bales of
clothing, etc. To Gaspe [the Gaspe Peninsula
is the southern side of the mouth of
Canada's St. Lawrence River], sees rock
[from] an earlier dream and stays there.
[Perce Rock is a distinctive formation just
off shore from the Gaspe town of Perce.]

After loss of hand, he creates art in
secret, using only the left. Hides work due
to shame as to quality, actually quite good.
Do not show this until close to end or at
end, create mystery, show his secret pain,
discards work.

Next are notes on a possible sequel, picking up after the
fight with the Spanish ship and duplicating or expanding
on the rest of Talon's life. The reference to "Sackett" suggests Louis was thinking of this as an opportunity to inter-
weave this novel with the early stories in the Sackett series.

Down west coast thru [through] [the
Strait of] Magellan, arrives off Gaspe, sees
rock [from] an earlier dream and stays
there. En route north passes another ship at
sea near Carolina coast (Sackett?) then on
to Gaspe with treasure. In a small bay on

east coast attempted seizure of ship
defeated, but some friendly seamen killed.
Talon almost single-handed beats them off,
his wife fighting beside him. On the Gaspe
shore they hide treasure, find signs of
activity on island there, signs of someone
else in the area.

They sail into a small bay and begin to
build a large home. (Jambe de Bois a boy on
this voyage?) [de Bois is a character in a
later Talon family book, Rivers West, and
would, almost certainly, not have lived long
enough to appear in both stories.] Attacks
by Indians? Pirates? Finds remains of
ancient settlement of some sort (tie in with
Oak Island treasure), makes effort to
recover treasure but defeated by storm and
Indians. Beginning of trouble between
colonies & England. Early feeling for
preserving French language. Beautiful love
story.

He builds a home, studies the sea through
a spy-glass, has children, 3 boys and a
girl. One boy sails away to the West Indies.
One becomes a steady man, a ship builder (a
descendant of this child will become the
Character in RIVERS WEST). One travels to
Ottawa and then north. Daughter? Sometime
during this period Talon is in Quebec and
meets his father.

Perhaps when he is an old man a traveler
tells him of carving found in France, the
work of a great genius, someone inspired. He
alone knows he was that carver.

Ends his days, after Indian battles,

pirates, etc., looking off to sea, his wife
beside him. She is a daughter of Rajput
kings.

Louis's first journal reference to creating a series of stories covering several generations of three families was in
1962. Back then, it was possible he was thinking that his
"Three Family" stories would all be set in the nineteenth
century. However, by 1971 he was planning *Fair Blows the
Wind*, a Chantry family novel that takes place a couple hundred years before his traditional Westerns. And in 1972
his journal produces the earliest mention of *The Bastard of
Brignogan* or its sequel when he mentions that he is looking
for a certain location in Canada:

> . . . drove out and spent about ten days
> or more on the Gaspe. I was looking for an
> old village I could use, picked up much
> history, and finally decided that Perce
> itself was the place I needed.

In the summer of 1978 it is clear he is working on the
chapters you have just read when he writes:

> Continuing my reading on pirates and
> piracy for the Talon book. I read much of
> them years ago but want to soak it all up
> now. Too little written about any pirates
> but Europeans or Americans, however most
> piracy was in Asia (and still is!).
> The Talon book, one of those which will
> be done soon requires a good knowledge of
> the life and action in Japan and India in
> the late 1500s.

And then:

Also reading for Talon. He is an armorer
early in his career and I have been studying
methods of work, the work itself, and the
tools. I shall draw upon things seen by
Manucci and other early travelers in India
for his first impressions. I have several
[accounts of people] who were there at the
time. Also reading about Japan, same period.
I am well-established in that history but
one can always learn more. Have been reading
books on piracy most of them of a later
period, to be more familiar with that
aspect. And must brush up on seamanship of
the period. I shall have a bit to say about
Asiatic seamen, too. Most of the books imply
they copied it all from us, or much of it,
which is nonsense. A lot of interesting lore

Perce, Quebec: This photo was taken from the spot where
Louis imagined Talon's house would have been built.

to be weeded from the ARABIAN NIGHTS and
OCEAN OF STORY.

Finally, there is one last slip of paper used to sketch out
some of the Three Families series. On it Louis has written:

1. Talon--India.
2. Chantry--Ireland, England, Newfoundland.
3. Talon--Oak Island.
4. Talon--Huron, Brule, Iroquois.
5. Talon to West Coast after treasure.

Item number one is certainly *The Bastard of Brignogan*.
Item two is partly the novel *Fair Blows the Wind*, but the
"Newfoundland" part suggests a Chantry is going to end
up in Talon's part of the New World. With item three, it
looks like he is considering that previously mentioned connection between Talon and the Oak Island Treasure. Four
refers to Etienne Brule, an early explorer in Canada and a
pretty wild character. For his sins, he was tortured by the
Iroquois and then eventually dismembered and eaten by a
group of Huron. Item five suggests that Talon or a descendant decided to go after a portion of the East Indies treasure Talon had abandoned in order to make it home to
Europe.

MAC ROSS

The Beginning of a Western Novel

CHAPTER I

He was seven or eight miles away when he saw
it for the first time, stark and lonely against
the empty sky.

Upon the wide plain there was nothing else,
only the yellow-brown grass blowing in the long,
low wind and the great square house, lonely in
the evening.

It was autumn, and the wind was chill without
being cold, but it was a time when a man began to
wonder what had become of his summer's wages.

He had been riding three days and had seen no
living thing but a wolf, trotting, head down,
along a far off slope. There had been tracks of
buffalo and of cattle, but even those grew fewer
as he rode deeper into that vast and vacant land.
Water-holes were few, and tinged with alkali, and
it had been a week since he had seen a tree or
brush taller than his saddle.

At first he thought what he saw was an
upthrust of rock, incongruous as that might be,
yet as the sun dropped lower its light glinted on

the far off windows . . . glass windows, in a
place like this.

Uneasily his eyes strayed left and right, but
there was nothing else upon the low hill but the
house, a small shed that could do for a barn, and
a corral. He rode with his sheep-skin coat
hanging open, his gun-butt forward on his left
hip. In his saddle scabbard he carried a
Winchester.

He was still three hundred yards off when
something moved on the grassy slope between
himself and the house, yet he had ridden another
fifty yards before he could make it out.

Someone slight and small, lying in a half-
sitting, half-reclining position, looking back
toward the house. As yet that person's attention
was so strongly upon the house that he or she was
not aware of the approaching rider.

There was a slight movement and he saw the
figure was that of a girl in a faded brown or
yellow dress. She was staring back toward the
great, gaunt frame house as though frightened,
but there was no movement near the house, nor any
sound. From this distance he would have guessed
the house to be empty, for it offered no evidence
of occupation.

By now he was within a few yards of the girl,
but on the prairie turf his horse's hoofs made no
sound to warn her of his approach. When he was
within easy speaking distance, he said, "Hello,
there!"

She started as if to spring to her feet, then
sagged back. The face she turned toward him was
gaunt and pale.

It was also beautiful in a haunted, wistful

way, with great dark eyes and black hair, a wisp of it falling over her brow and stirred by the wind.

She had reason to be startled, for he knew what she saw. His clothes were dusty and he had a week's stubble of beard on his lean jaws, and hard green eyes that had small cause to be anything but cold. His hat was battered and there was a bullet-hole through the brim. His sheep-skin coat was worn and stained. His boots were down-at-heel, his jeans worn thin by many washings. The horse he rode showed none of its fine lines for his winter coat was on, and he was long-haired and ragged, as tired and ill-fed as his rider.

"Something wrong, ma'am?" He strove to make his tone gentle, only partly succeeding. "If I can help--?"

"No . . . no, it is nothing."

She came suddenly and gracefully to her feet. On the ground she had seemed wasted and thin, now she looked lithe and lovely as a young antelope.

"It is a long ride that's behind me. When I saw the house I thought I might find a meal and a place to sleep."

"I . . . I don't know. You will have to ask."

She turned away and walked ahead of him toward the house. Once he had a vague notion he saw a curtain move on one of the ground-floor windows, but it could have been his imagination.

He was uneasy. There was something here that disturbed him, and he liked nothing about the weather-beaten, unpainted house. It appeared to have stood there for quite some time yet he knew that could not be the case for this had been

Indian country until just four or five years ago,
and the only travel through here had been a few
buffalo hunters.

"Kind of a lonely place," he suggested.

"We don't have many visitors." She turned her
head. "You must not be surprised. I mean . . . he
may not let you stay. He does not like visitors."

"I'll be no trouble," he said hastily. "I need
grub and water. I can sleep out."

Anywhere but in that house, he told himself,
and the thought surprised him.

"You came from the west?"

"Southwest." He hesitated, then added
apologetically, "I haven't eaten in three days."

She was shocked. "I'll get something for you.
No matter what he says."

Now what kind of man would turn a body away
without eating? he asked himself. That makes no
sense. None at all.

At the corral he dismounted, hesitated a
moment with his hands on the saddle, then
stripped the rig from the dun. The Hell with it.
You're going to rest, no matter what.

He turned the line-back dun into the corral,
then rousted around the barn. Surprisingly there
were several sacks of corn and oats in a room at
one side of the shed. He dipped up some of each
and took it to his horse.

There was a trough in the corral, and the
water looked good. It was only then that he saw
the pump near the house, and the pipe leading to
it from the trough.

He went to the pump. There was no dipper . . .
at most wells a man found a tin-dipper or a gourd
hanging from a wire, but not here. He worked the

pump-handle and water gushed clear and cold at
the fourth stroke. Cupping his hand, he tasted
the water. It was cold . . . and sweet.

A sweet-water well in this country! Whoever
owned this place, he was shot with luck.

The girl had gone into the house, so he worked
the pump-handle a few more times to send water
gushing into the corral trough to replace what
his horse would drink. Wiping his mouth with the
back of his hand, he started toward the house.

He went up to the door, scraped his feet, then
knocked.

The knock was loud in the silence, but for a
long time there was no response, then the door
opened suddenly and an old Negro stood there, a
tall, fine-looking man, ramrod straight. "Come
in, sir," he said expressionlessly. "Whom shall I
announce?"

"Mac Ross," he said, and saw the Negro stiffen
ever so slightly, then bow and turn away.

At the end of the short hall was a tall door
of dark oak panels. The Negro opened it, and said
quietly, "Mr. Mac Ross, sir."

Mac Ross stepped into the door, and stopped
for a moment, yet nothing in his face revealed
his astonishment.

The room was high-ceilinged and lined with
books. On the wall above the fireplace was an
oil-painting of an austere man in uniform. Before
it, one heel hooked over the edge of a brass
hearth fender, stood a tall man in a black suit.
A singularly handsome man despite his long face
emphasized by the wave of hair above the brow,
somewhat in the Andrew Jackson manner.

"Come in, Mr. Ross. I am General Robinson."

General is it? Well, if you're going to take a title it might as well be a good one.

His immediate impression was that he did not like General Robinson, and his next impression was that the feeling was mutual. He came to the point at once.

"I was ridin' past and I'm short of grub."

"Of course. You are most welcome." There was an edge of sarcasm to Robinson's voice and Mac Ross felt a stir of irritation, and fought it down. He wanted no trouble. The last thing he needed right now was more trouble.

"You came from the southwest? Is that right?" Robinson's tone was no longer sarcastic. This was something he wished to be sure about, and Mac Ross had the feeling that Robinson desperately wanted him to have come from the southwest . . . hence not from some other direction.

"That's right. Been ridin' for a week."

"I was wondering. We are told there is nothing out that way, nothing at all."

"Your information is correct. It's level country for mile after mile. A few dry lakes here and yonder, probably filled up after a good rain."

"Buffalo?"

"Saw some tracks . . . buffalo, and a few cattle tracks."

"Cattle? From where?"

Again he seemed disturbed, although why Ross could not guess.

"No idea," he replied, honestly enough. "I saw nothing but tracks."

"Come! We'll have a drink, then we'll eat."

Mac Ross hesitated. "I'd like to wash up first. It's been a dusty ride."

"Certainly." He turned slightly as the black man entered. "Manisty, will you show Mr. Ross where he may wash up? And you may set an extra place--he will be dining with us."

"Of course, sir. Mr. Ross? Will you come with me?"

He led the way upstairs and to a comfortable bedroom on the second floor. "You will find warm water in the pitcher, sir. Dinner will be served in thirty minutes."

"Is there a whisk broom? I gathered some dust."

"Of course, sir. May I take your coat? I should be glad to dust it for you, and--"

"That's all right," Mac Ross said easily, "I'll take care of it."

"Of course, sir. As you wish."

When the black man had gone, Mac Ross removed his coat and took his second gun from his waistband and placed it on a stand nearby. Then he took off his shirt, and using a washcloth, washed off his face, neck and hands, then his chest. There was a livid scar . . . a fresh scar . . . across his chest and shoulder. He was especially careful around that only partly healed wound.

He put his shirt on once more, buttoned the collar, and with a black string tie from his breast pocket, he made himself appear somewhat more formal as befitted the dining room in a gentleman's house.

He checked both guns as well as the thin knife

he wore down the back of his neck below the
collar.

What was a house like this doing in a place
like this? And who was this "General Robinson"?
And who was the girl?

He had seen no one other than the black man,
but assumed there was further help in the
kitchen. And what of the ranch? Or was it a
ranch?

His uneasiness increased. The girl had seemed
frightened . . . of what?

He brushed his coat carefully, then adjusted
it, trying to smooth out the pockets that had too
often bulged with necessaries. The haunting
uneasiness refused to leave him. Going to the
window, he looked out. It was a sheer drop, a
good thirty feet to the ground, as the house
stood on a knoll that fell away sharply on his
side of the house. The other window was scarcely
better.

He had turned away when something that had
caught his eye claimed his renewed attention. He
went back to the window. Some distance off,
barely discernible now in the late twilight, was
something black . . . a building of some sort,
long and low, nestled in a corner of the hills
and almost hidden from sight.

He let the curtain fall into place and stood
listening. All was very quiet . . . too quiet.

He stood in the middle of the room, thinking.
He had seen but three people, yet there had to be
more. Did they run cattle here? Sheep? Where were
the cowhands . . . if any?

Who built the house? Who supplied it with
food? And from where? There were some Mexicans

settled on the Canadian, but how far away was
that? This was new country to him although he had
hunted buffalo in other parts of the Panhandle
and High Plains country.

As a matter of fact, he did not know exactly
where he was. He had left the Pecos in a hurry,
and had ridden far and fast, changing directions
several times in an effort to elude those who
pursued him. Later, he had changed direction
looking for water as one water-hole after another
proved dry. He knew only that he was in the High
Plains country somewhere east of the Pecos and
still upon the cap-rock.

It was very possible there was not another
habitation of any sort within a hundred miles of
where he now was. He did not know that, of
course, but from his knowledge of the country it
was a logical guess. Certainly, he knew of none.

So then . . . what was this "General"
Robinson, a strikingly handsome, educated
gentleman, whose hands showed no indication of
hard labor, doing out here in the middle of
nowhere? And with a young, and very attractive,
woman, very possibly a sister, niece or even a
daughter.

Or his wife.

For some reason he found the idea distasteful.
He smiled grimly at that. Was he, Mac Ross,
becoming enamored of a girl he had just met?
Scarcely glimpsed?

"Mac," he spoke softly, but aloud, "you've
been away from women too long."

There was a discreet tap on his door.

"Yes?"

"Dinner is served, sir. At the foot of the stairs, sir, in the room on your right."

Careful directions . . . a courtesy? Or to keep him from wandering about?

He glanced at himself in the mirror once more. Excellent mirror, he thought, and beautiful furniture. The house had been done by someone with taste. He opened the door and stepped out into the hallway. He glanced along it as he turned toward the steps. At least four doors opened on the hall . . . yet there could be even more rooms.

The stairs were carpeted. He walked down them carefully, spurs jingling. He did not want to catch a spur in the carpet . . . obviously Persian.

The lower hall was wider, carpeted as well. The library where he had seen the General was on the left as he came down the steps, the dining room on the right. He opened the door and stepped inside.

The table was long. There was silver and crystal, place settings as for a formal dinner. There were eight chairs.

General Robinson stood with his back to the fireplace, hands clasped behind him.

"Good evening, Mr. Ross. Jettchen will be down briefly."

"Jettchen? It is an unusual name."

"Jetta, if you wish, Mr. Ross. It is a Frisian name." Robinson glanced at him. "You have heard of the Frisians, Mr. Ross?"

"An ancient Teutonic people, weren't they? From the Netherlands area?"

"I am amazed. The Frisians are little heard of in these later days."

Mac Ross offered no comment. He was waiting, every sense alert. Something was decidedly wrong here, and it disturbed him.

Robinson took down a cigar box and opened it for him . . . Havanas. Ross shook his head. Excellent cigars, but he was no smoker. "Thank you, no."

"You are traveling far, Mr. Ross?"

He took a name out of a hat. "St. Louis, eventually. Abilene first, as I hear the railroad's there now."

"It is? I had not expected it so soon." Robinson clipped the end of his cigar, then lighted it. "Abilene? I do not know the place although I have heard some rumor of it. Kansas, is it not?"

"It is, and there's nothing there unless McCoy has built something. A few sod houses and dug-outs, and a sort of a saloon, I think."

"You mentioned a McCoy?"

"Joseph McCoy. He's the one who talked them into building the railroad out there. He's convinced them there's money in shipping beef that will be driven up from Texas, now that the war is over."

"Ah, yes. The war. I am afraid some of us suffered very much from the war, Mr. Ross. We . . . my family, I mean . . . lost everything. It was no use rebuilding, no use at all."

"You seem to be doing very well here," Ross said, glancing around.

"A pittance, Mr. Ross, just a pittance. But we manage, we manage. Of course, as we could no

longer afford to work our estates, we were forced
to sell . . . to sell at a very bad time, Mr.
Ross. It was distressing."

He paused, glanced at the end of his cigar.
"Of course, our business had not been in
satisfactory shape for some time. When the
government passed the Non-Importation Act in
1806, it was a blow. Of course, that was before
my time."

"The Non-Importation Act? You refer to the
slave-trade?"

"Of course, and an excellent business it was,
too. We had half-a-dozen ships in the trade, Mr.
Ross. The family saw the end coming, naturally,
as Vermont, Massachusetts, New Hampshire, Rhode
Island, and a number of other states had already
abolished it, but we had ties with the Arab
traders . . . and the help of a few African
chiefs. The Arabs and the Portugese almost
controlled the slave trade."

"You had no doubts about all that, General?"

"Doubts? Why? There had always been slaves.
The Greek and Roman civilizations were built on
slave labor, and the same with the Egyptians and
Babylonians. Race mattered little in those days."

He shrugged. "Labor has always been needed.
Some men, whether white or black, are born to be
slaves."

Ross's irritation was mounting, but the man
was his host, and if such was his viewpoint, he
was entitled to it. Before he could make a reply,
the door opened again and Jettchen entered.

She was dressed in white, and she was
breathtakingly beautiful. She crossed the room to

him. "How nice that you could stay. We have so
few visitors, Mr. Ross."

She went to the table, and he held her chair
for her to be seated. Momentarily as she moved up
to her chair her body pressed against him,
pushing his gun against his side. He was
embarrassed by the gun, yet when the General
moved to his chair he was no longer embarrassed.

He was also wearing a gun.

COMMENTS: At this point a page is missing. The narrative picks back up, for just a moment, after the first course of dinner:

Manisty entered and took up the soup plates.
He moved silently and smoothly, his skill that of
years of practice, but there was an assurance
about him that disturbed Ross, an assurance that
went beyond the fact that he knew his business
and was, perhaps, an old retainer. There was in
him a sense of power, of strength that was not
only physical, but something more.

COMMENTS: I have always wondered if the early images in this story weren't inspired by the famous painting by Andrew Wyeth, *Christina's World*. In the early 1960s a friend of my mother's had a print of it hanging just inside the door to her apartment. I remember it, and I was just five years old, so Dad could hardly have failed to see the picture every time he visited. Then, as now, it was known that Anna Christina Olson, the inspiration for that work of art, had been paralyzed by an undiagnosed muscular disorder. That fact and the pathos that goes with it adds an interesting tension to what could be seen simply as a pastoral, if somewhat mysterious, painting. The concept of the distant house with nothing else around and of a woman trapped in some strange and unknown way is at the core of the initial moments of this oddly Gothic-seeming Western novel.

I love the creepy atmosphere Louis created, and I wish I had more information about when it was written and what my father may have intended.

DAM AND TIMBER

Notes for an Adventure Story

COMMENTS: This project was probably intended to be a short story aimed at the men's adventure magazines of the 1950s. The men's adventure genre was one of the last gasps of the once dominant pulp magazine market, and the various magazines, like *Argosy, Saga, Real Men*, and many others, were cheekily referred to as the "sweats" or "armpit slicks" (some were published on slick paper like the more upscale magazines). They focused on "true" stories of crime, war, and often quite bizarre man-against-nature encounters. I have always suspected that they were an expression of a rather odd postwar/cold war–era psychology that I have never completely understood. In general the subject matter was fairly graphic and the art pretty kinky.

I've always considered the "sweats" to be a macho version of our supermarket tabloids, with their lurid half-fact, half-fantasy feel and their somewhat voyeuristic tales. Louis was never completely comfortable with the operatic cartooniness of the genre, but in the years prior to his breaking into the paperback market, he was forced to give it a try.

Regardless, Dad's notes for the following story channeled some recognizable aspects of the men's adventure genre: blue-collar manly men doing manly things in a challenging natural setting.

Use puff formula for story —
(re-tells logic?)

Often: Hero arrives from freight train. He is surprised at ease of getting sub-contract
Heavy sends things after time
He begins looking for help
there is none.
He begins taking bums, drunks, etc. The fight with things

More grief — perhaps the dealer calls back his equipment. So hero goes to mean character and gets equipment from him. Make this good. —

The location of "Dam and Timber" seems to be Arizona or Nevada, someplace very hot and remote from civilization. A dam is under construction, and the protagonist of the story is the winner of the contract to clear what is about to become the bottom of a large lake of brush, trees, and other debris. The corporation or local government must have the job done by a certain date, so there is a lot of pressure to finish quickly, and not too much concern for worker safety.

From hearing Dad talk about it, I believe he was planning to incorporate a conflict in which a group wanted to stop the hero from finishing the job, or from finishing on time—but from these notes it's not completely clear why. The equipment being used to clear the brush and trees includes heavy chains stretched between bulldozers and a huge steel ball that is dragged over areas to crush the vegetation flat.

Don't be thrown as you read through—Louis experiments with a couple of different names for the female characters . . .

The first set of notes:

Open: Hero arrives from freight train.
He is surprised at ease of getting sub-contract.

Heavy sends thugs after him
He begins looking for help, there is none.
He begins taking bums, drunks, etc.
The fight with thugs

More grief--perhaps the dealer calls back his equipment

So Hero goes to a really tough character and gets equipment from him.

Make this good -

Perhaps use cloud-seeding stunt. [Cloud seeding is a process that uses chemicals spread by aircraft or fired into the atmosphere from the ground to create rain.]

Second set of notes:

Opening scene: he arrives and there is tough talk, then he bids for contract--gets it-

Heavy sends two thugs after him. Heroine sees it [the fight] and afterward her friends tell her he is not a man a nice girl would be interested in--she answers that even a nice girl likes a little red blood in her men. Gleason overhears this and comments--then the tramp [Louis is talking about a "trampy" woman] joins him [the Hero], and takes his arm possessively.

One of workers is knocked down in front of steel ball and Hero goes to rescue -

At climax logs fail to burn as rain, increased by cloud-seeding, stops fire. [This may refer to the debris piled up by the crew clearing what will become the lake bottom behind the dam, or it might be something completely different.]

Then Hero has pay-off fight with Heavy-- terrific.

Fight between girls: Heroine knows judo-- she takes off her stole and coolly beats the hell out of tramp.

Build for 8 high points and in about 30 pages.

Humor--Gleason & others [Gleason seems a
bit like a comic-relief, sidekick sort of
character.]

Strong character--different

Make girl unusual--simply wants her man--
Gleason advises--"She's [the trampy woman]
got no brand on him. Move in if you've got
the guts."

So battle is joined

The job is man-killing and brutal--it
goes on through rain and sun in the roughest
kind of country -

Man falls before steel ball -

Perhaps a fight between two men with
bulldozers to deflect tumbling ball, or to
push logs in its way

Sub-contract from a guy who wants him
[our hero] whipped, broken, dead. This man
broke him on [the] last job--wants to finish
it. Gives him sub-contract where he can't
win--but he takes his misfit crew and does
win--two women--one a lady, the other a
tramp, but the lady beats hell out of the
tramp

Strictly a fight for a man. Cathy
remarks--older man tells her she must fight
with all her weapons. She does and wins.

The third set of notes:

Part cliff, part swamp, all hell -

Use fire scene, steel ball, fight scene--
make this a honey--two really tough mugs--
scene where 2 are sent out to beat up
Hero--He whips them both, takes them to boss
and throws them across his desk at him--

1. Jim Tyler.
2. Tom Bassett, of Bassett Demolition &
   Construction Co.
3. "Larry" Lorraine, a sexy babe with Tyler
   on her mind and Bassett on her trail.
4. Ruth Sheridan, visiting in vicinity of
   project, who falls for Jim. Wealthy but
   unspoiled, quiet, but determined. Her
   father had been a contract mine boss and
   she had spent her early years in mining
   camps.
5. "Doc" Cassidy, stew-bum but old friend of
   Tyler. The first of his new crew. [This
   might be the same as the Gleason
   character.]
6. Jack Helms, Bassett's straw-boss and
   muscle man.
7. Swede, the ex-con; Milligan, ex-Seabee;
   John, the half-breed; Lee, the coward;
   Laramie, ex-contest rider (all bums
   picked up by Tyler for his misfit crew.)
8. Louise Butler and Dave: Friends of Ruth,
   who entertain Tom Bassett and later, Jim
   Tyler.

Some of the inspiration for this story may have come from accounts Louis heard in the 1920s from a girlfriend's father, a man who was working on a dam project near Klamath Falls, Oregon. I also suspect that this concept later evolved into the Western novel *Guns of the Timberlands*, but I have only my sense of my father's career and methodology to suggest that.

THE QUEST FOR THE BEAR

A Complete Adventure Story

Night and the cold . . . four men crouching
above a tiny fire in a shallow cave, hollowed by
the wind.

Black and glistening peaks towering into the
silence of the night . . . a frozen surf of
glaciers. Sixteen thousand feet . . .

Far off, miles away through the night, an
avalanche rumbles, tearing the brow from a cliff,
hurling its thundering mass of millions of tons
of ice, frozen snow and rock into some vast,
unknown chasm.

A lonely, prowling wind moaning along the
pass, a wind seeking out every crevice, every
fold, every tiniest crack among the mountains, a
wind that creeps up close to the fire and
flattens itself above the flames, that huddles
close to the warmth of men, a shuddering wind
that has known no living thing . . . a lost wind
in a lost land.

These are mountains unpeopled and still, these
are haunted canyons, unclimbed and unattempted
peaks, these are the pillars that loom above the
Roof of the World, above the silent and somber

Kuen Luns, backbone of Asia . . . lonely as the ranges of the moon.

Three of the four men are mountain Ladakhis, skilled guides and hunters, men of the caravans, wanderers of the highest mountains on earth . . . but they are afraid now.

The fourth man stretches his hands toward the tongues of flame, watching the fire as it curls lecherously about the few chilled sticks and yak chips gathered from the long-unused trail.

"Sir?" The Ladakhi with the scar speaks carefully. He wears the scar as a badge of bravery, so it is he who speaks, for the Ladakhis would not be thought afraid. "We will go back? The season is long past. There will be another year for the bear."

"No." The tone was flat. "We will find him now. I cannot hope to come this close again. It is a miracle that we have found him, and he is near . . . I can feel it."

No man among them spoke, but within them stirred fear. The great white bears of the mountains possessed, it was said, the souls of evil men. Some said they had the souls of the wicked black lamas of the land of Bod, which white men call Tibet. This man had come to them, hunting a certain bear, just one bear in all these vast ranges . . . and he had found it.

Frightened they were of the late season in the high passes, knowing as they did the dangers of remaining too long, and frightened as they were of the bear, they were even more frightened of the man who sought the bear. They were frightened, and yet they were filled with admiration. First among mountain men, the

THE QUEST FOR THE BEAR   63

Ladakhis had found in this man their equal if not
their superior. He had been able to find one
trail out of the many trails, one bear out of the
hundreds of bears.

Had he not described the bear to them? Had he
not told them of the great scar across muzzle and
jowl? A scar burned by a torch in the hands of
this very man? Had he not shown that it was his
destiny to find this bear? Already the Tibetans
had deserted, the food supply grew short, and the
Ladakhis knew but little time remained. Yet the
man had found his bear.

Sanju Pass was far and away to the south. The
pass upon which they camped was nameless and
little known. It was but four days before that
Morgan had come upon the trail.

They had ascended a valley, walking on crusted
snow. They had picked their way across a recent
slide, and seen other slides poised above them.
They had come down upon the new fallen snow
covering a glacier, and there on the snow were
gigantic tracks.

The Ladakhis were aghast when they saw
them . . . they looked away and then looked
again. How could the tracks of any living thing
be so huge? And across one of them was the old
mark, a scar like a rope across one huge padded
foot.

"He is big." The Ladakhi looked from the track
to Morgan. And Morgan had nodded grimly. "Yes,"
he had said, "this bear is big. He may be the
biggest bear that ever lived. He is bigger than a
Kodiak grizzly. He is bigger than a yak. He will
weigh well over two thousand pounds. He stands

more than six feet high at the shoulder. He is
The Bear."

The Ladakhis looked again at the tracks, and
they avoided each other's eyes. This was a tale
they would not dare to tell. No man would believe
there was a bear of such hugeness. This was The
Bear. Now they understood why Morgan spoke of it
as he did.

They had tracked him across the glacier and
down into the forest, and they had tracked him
across the rocks and soon they became aware. The
Bear knew he was being followed. He knew!

On the second day the Ladakhis pointed this
out to Morgan. "Sir, he knows we follow him. See
where he stopped to look back? See where he swung
wide to go up the hill and look down upon this
trail? He has seen us. Now he will kill."

On the third day The Bear circled back and lay
down beside his trail. This a Kodiak will also
do, but when they wait for their hunter they
attack. The Bear did not attack. He watched.

It was afternoon of the third day when they
found where The Bear had circled back to watch
them. The Ladakhis shook their heads and looked
all about them, superstitious and frightened. Yet
the Ladakhi is a man of the mountains, proud of
his reputation for bravery.

And then The Bear moved away from the forest.
He climbed the long glaciers, moved over the
rocky slopes, mounting higher and ever higher
into the bleak, cold fastnesses of the mountains.
The sky flattened into endless, monotonous gray,
the tops of the peaks were lost in the clouds and
overnight their flanks took on the blinding white
of new snow.

"We must go back now," the Ladakhis said, but Morgan did not seem to have heard. Bowed and steady he stayed upon the trail, and on the fourth day they came suddenly upon The Bear.

He was standing on the slope above them and they were almost abreast of him before he was seen. He reared up then, a gigantic beast, so enormous as to defy calculation, his great nose thrust toward them, his little eyes blinking as if to ask what manner of creature this was who stayed so relentlessly upon his trail.

A full minute they stared and then The Bear turned. Morgan jerked up his rifle but The Bear was gone!

Like that, he vanished . . . but when they reached the spot, there were no tracks to be seen . . . of course, it was rock where he had stood. Nevertheless . . .

It had been a forced landing, that first time. The plane had been lost on a flight from Chungking to Iran, and it had crashed in a remote valley high among the peaks of the Kuen Luns. There had been four of them left alive and they had started to walk out.

From the beginning it had appeared hopeless but they were men and men must act. Carrying what food they could, they started north for Sinkiang proper, hoping to strike one of the old caravan routes and to find people. None of them knew the country and only Morgan had a vague idea of where to go. Their navigator had been killed and none of them had ever been over this country before.

By the night of the fifth day they were well

broken in to the walking. Their food was holding out, and they had supplemented it by killing an ibex that very day. At night they camped near the foot of a black column of rock, and it was there The Bear had come upon them.

Drawn, no doubt, by the smell of fresh blood from the ibex, The Bear appeared. Yet at first he had not seemed dangerous. They had seen him some fifty yards off, a gigantic creature, so enormous as to make them doubt their senses. He had his nose to the wind and was sensing their body odor . . . seemingly puzzled.

Ryerson had been broiling the meat over a fire. Smith was dozing, half-asleep. Gordon and Morgan had seen The Bear at the same moment.

"Harry . . ." Morgan's voice had been muted, low with astonishment. "Look at that."

They stared, and then The Bear had started toward them. Lumbering forward curiously he seemed more curious than anything else . . . but Gordon was suddenly stricken with panic.

No outdoors man was Gordon. He was city bred and city stifled. To him a wild animal was an immediate danger, and when The Bear started toward their camp, instead of giving him a chance to satisfy his curiosity and leave, as he might have done, Gordon grabbed up his carbine and fired.

A .30 caliber carbine is no weapon, as either Ryerson or Morgan could have told him, with which to tackle two thousand pounds of bear . . . or any bear.

The bullet struck . . . they all heard it strike, and then with a muffled roar, The Bear charged. Perhaps he had only been curious, but these strange creatures had lashed out at him, they had stung him, and red-eyed with fury, he charged, thinking only to annihilate them. And he very nearly did.

When the huge beast lunged for them, instead of holding his ground and emptying the carbine into it, Gordon cried out, dropped the gun and fled. Ryerson sprang for his own carbine and Morgan rolled over, grabbing up the fallen gun. A huge paw smashed at him, caught him a glancing blow, and he was knocked rolling.

Poor Smith never had a chance. Startled from his sleep by the sudden crack of the gunshot, he lunged to his feet squarely in front of The Bear. With one smashing blow it broke his neck, and then crunched his skull between great jaws. Gordon fled and fell, and the charging bear was upon him. Gordon's scream was to ring in Morgan's ears all during the months that followed, and the memory of it never died.

Ryerson tried one wild shot, and then as The Bear rushed him, he crowded himself into a narrow crack in the rock. It snarled and muttered, reaching for him with huge paws, biting angrily at the edges of the crack, but Ryerson was out of reach.

Morgan lay perfectly still. The beast turned to Smith's body, and not knowing he was already dead, Morgan could not stand to see the helpless man mauled again. Lying within a yard of the fire, it was easy for Morgan to reach over and grab a burning brand. The Bear saw the movement and swung around. Morgan's flaming wood was a heavy stick and it was filled with pitch and

burning with a bright flame. Swiftly he struck,
and the blow caught the beast across the face.

For an instant, everything seemed to stop. The
flame seared the face and Morgan smelled burning
hair, and then the monster cried out, an almost
human sound, and struck, knocking the stick from
Morgan's hand, but the pitch on his face still
blazed and the eyes of the beast seemed to stare
down at Morgan with a wild sort of horror. Then
The Bear wheeled and lunged away, stopping every
few yards to rub his face in the snow.

Slowly, Morgan got to his feet, then sat back,
shuddering with nervous reaction, thinking of
that final, awful moment when The Bear had looked
down upon him with that wild, helpless, tragic
fear as if wondering what sort of creature had
done this to him.

Ryerson edged his way out of the crack, his
body shaking as if from fever. "Good God, man!
Did you see that creature?" His voice was shrill
with shock and fear. "I never imagined . . . !"

Gordon was dead and Smith was dead. They
buried them there with the towering black
pinnacles as marker, then left their two carbines
beside the grave, and went on. And somehow,
ragged and worn, half-starved and half-frozen,
months later, they reached warmth and
civilization.

Only their knowledge of the wilderness, their
skill at hunting, their physical condition could
have gotten them through. They were a good team,
and they made it. And the first night Morgan had
glanced around at Harry Ryerson. "I'm going
back," he said, "and kill that brute."

They told their story and people smiled, as

inexperienced people always will. They smiled
that smile that every traveler knows, the good-
natured tolerance of polite skepticism of the
person who believes he is being subjected to a
wild tale, but who listens politely, anyhow. And
then they stopped telling it. They stopped
because nobody would believe, nobody could
believe. The people they knew had nothing by
which to judge such a story, for each judges by
his own limited experience.

Ryerson was discharged a year later. Morgan
remained on a bit longer and then he too returned
home. They no longer told the story of The Bear,
but to them both he had become just that. He was
no longer just a bear, just any bear. He was The
Bear, the personification of all bears, the
undying spirit of Bear.

And to Morgan he was something else. He was an
obsession.

Gordon had been relatively a stranger,
although a crew member on the plane. But Smith
had been Morgan's oldest and best friend. Perhaps
it was some primitive lust for revenge, perhaps
it was his own memory of that awful instant of
horror when he looked into the eyes of The Bear.
Perhaps he believed that if he returned, found
The Bear and destroyed it, the memory of those
eyes would fade.

Perhaps it was because he remembered his own
awful fear. Perhaps if he had managed to
fire . . . after all he, Morgan, was the real
hunter of the lot. Time and again he told himself
that he could have done nothing, yet a sense of
guilt remained. If only . . . well, if he had
done something sooner those two might have lived.

He worked, and he did well. He married, and he was relatively happy, but the memory wouldn't leave him. It became an obsession. He talked of it to his wife . . . he no longer mentioned it to others . . . and she listened with understanding. On the subject of The Bear, Morgan decided, he was touched. He was a little insane.

It is given to no man to judge the depths of horror with which a certain experience may strike another. Time often wipes away all scars, dims all memories, yet it was not so with Morgan. The memory of The Bear rode him and he could not shake it off.

Finally, one night as they lay in bed, he said to his wife, "Ruth, I'm going back there. I'm going to find that bear and kill it."

"How could you? In all those mountains? There must be hundreds, even thousands of bears."

"Yes," he agreed, "but I'll find him. I'm sure of it."

After that she offered no objections, but helped him prepare for the expedition. The revolution had swept over China and there were dangers other than mountains, landslides and bears. Nevertheless, he had made it.

At first, he had scouted around for their old trail. Between them, Ryerson and himself, they had worked out the approximate location of the crashed plane, and surprisingly, Morgan found it rather easily. He was sorry Ryerson could not have come along, for his memory would have been an added help, but finally Morgan found the pinnacle where his companions had been buried. The graves were there, undisturbed. It was evidence of the loneliness of the mountains that

the carbines stood, covered with frost, where
they had been left.

The season had drawn on, their Tibetan
carriers deserted them and only the Ladakhis
remained. Not until after the Tibetans had left
did they find the tracks of his bear.

Morgan added another stick to the fire in the
wind-hollowed cave. He no longer thought of home.
He scarcely thought of Ruth. He did not consider
the lateness of the season, the impending
awfulness of the winter nor the difficulties of
travel. Now he thought of nothing, dreamed of
nothing, lived for nothing but The Bear.

Even now, as he huddled above his fire, he
knew it was out there. And he was remembering
something his friend had said after they had
returned home. "You know, Morg," Ryerson had
spoken quietly, "if you think back, I don't
believe that bear intended to attack us until
Gordon fired that crazy shot. I think he was just
curious.

"Think of it. It's possible the creature had
never seen a man before. If you remember, he
didn't seem angry at first, he wasn't frightened,
he was just curious. After all," Ryerson had
added, "he was a king in his own land, and we
were invaders. He had a right to look us over."

Maybe. But he had killed Smith and he had
killed Gordon, and he had given Morgan those
awful minutes of fear and horror. Minutes that
could, Morgan believed, only be washed away by
the blood of the monster that inspired them. Or
was it simply that he used this as an excuse? He
did not know.

———

In the morning it was colder. An icy wind
whined off the glacier. Frozen snow rattled upon
the rocks and the hard crust underfoot. Morgan
got to his feet, the heavy rifle cradled in his
arms. "Let's go," he said, and they went.

He had been right. The beast had been outside
during the night. With slow care, he unwound the
skein of tracks, ferreted out the mystery of The
Bear's actions. And then they started to follow.
All morning they worked their way through the icy
mountains, descending into a deep valley,
crossing a frozen stream, mounting at an angle a
long, steep slope above which towered the
beetling brow of a cliff.

Down a vast gorge they followed the trail, and
then up the face of a great declivity, a
precipitous slope wind-swept and bare for five
miles, looking always upward toward the brutal
mass of rock that towered above them. Yet now The
Bear seemed to be going somewhere, and not only
away from them. He seemed to have a destination,
a certain goal in the unbelievable vastness of
the mountains.

The icy wind gnawed at their exposed flesh,
the snow crunched under foot. They paused to rest
and made hot black tea and ate, and then they
pressed on.

No vegetation now, only black rock . . . and
ice. No soft, gentle snow, but blades and anvils,
frozen and jagged, under their feet a crunching
blanket of it, like broken glass. And then,
suddenly, The Bear stopped.

Wherever he had been going, the trail was

blocked by a vast slide of rock and snow, bigger
itself than a mountain in a lesser range. But The
Bear had stopped and then The Bear turned.

The Ladakhis drew back, their faces stiff with
fright, and the great bear lifted himself to his
hind legs, towering above them, vast, yellowish
white, with open jaws. The heavy rifle in his
hand, Morgan inched forward, alert for the
slightest move. Now he had him! The Bear! The
killer of Smith and of Gordon! Now . . .

Across its face was the blackened scar of the
burn, the hair scorched away from one side of the
muzzle, from the great jowl, one ear partly gone,
and the flesh around one eye snarled and wrinkled
and black. And from that scar peered an eye, a
still seeing eye, but with the lid burned away.
And it was from that strangely wide-open eye that
The Bear watched him.

For a long moment they stared, fascinated,
each at the other. No Kodiak bear had ever been
so huge, no gaze from man or animal had ever been
so appalling as that strange, quizzical stare
from the one, wide-open eye, the other lidded and
small.

The Bear was the first to move. It was a
sudden, flicking movement of the great head,
turning slightly away from Morgan, as if
sniffing. And then one of the Ladakhis called
out.

"Slide!"

It was a scream rather than a yell . . . and
then Morgan heard it himself. The distant, faint
whispering that suddenly began to rumble, and
then became a roar. He took one swift, frightened
glance upward and saw the whole side of the

mountain was coming down upon them. He wheeled, and threw himself down the path after the Ladakhis.

The closest of them stumbled and fell. Morgan tripped and sprawled over him, then scrambled to his feet. The Bear had turned and was charging at the cliff! For one startled instant, Morgan hesitated, then he grabbed the Ladakhi. "This way!" he said, and lunged after The Bear. He had a tight grip on the Ladakhi and the man had no choice but to follow.

And then The Bear vanished. Yet they were so closely behind him as to see him rush into a cave-like crack in the cliff. It was all of sixty feet high and how deep they could not see. It was almost covered over at the top, yet they rushed in just as the slide roared above them and swept off down the mountain. For endless minutes it seemed to roar on, like a dozen express trains running abreast. Then it was over and there was a vast and awful silence.

Morgan looked at the Ladakhi. The man's face was sickly pale under the dark, drawn skin. Above them the crack was closed over. They got up and climbed over the snow that had fallen through and reached the entrance. It took them only a few minutes to push out into the day.

The trail they had followed was gone. Before them the slope was swept clean of snow, swept almost smooth of all projections of ice or rock. There was no sign of the other Ladakhis.

"They couldn't have made it," Morgan said.

"No." The Ladakhi looked at him. "The Bear saved us."

Morgan started to reply irritably, but could

not. After all, they had followed The Bear to
safety. Not that The Bear intended it so. The
very idea that he might phrase such a thought
irritated him. Was he becoming as bad as the
natives? Thinking of a bear intending to save a
man? The Bear was his enemy.

Where was it now? The thought drew Morgan
back. The Ladakhi was looking at him. "We must go
now," he said, "we can delay no longer."

But he turned back to the crevice, and then
stopped. The Bear had emerged. It was not over
twenty yards away. Morgan lifted the rifle,
steadied it against his shoulder, and looked over
the sights at the great beast.

It stood there, head lifted slightly, staring
at him. One shot from this rifle and The Bear was
his. One shot? No, it might require several to
stop him, but even if it charged it would die. At
this range Morgan could not miss.

The Bear would be dead.

The king of this lonely land slain. The
thought came strangely to him, and with it,
hesitation. Suddenly . . . no, he did not want
The Bear dead. Not this way, at least.

The Bear deserved his chance. The heavy slugs
of the rifle would smash the life from him, and
he would be slain by a machine from the outer,
unrealized world. Morgan put his rifle down
carefully. Then he took out his hunting knife.

It was an eleven-inch weapon, razor sharp.
With this he could meet The Bear on his own
terms. After all, as Ryerson had said, he was
king in this world . . . this was his land . . .
and maybe he was only curious.

And maybe he, Morgan, was a little insane. The thought flickered through his awareness and died, lost in the greater urge. Knife in hand, he took a tentative step forward. The Bear would rear up, and he would close in. Mentally, icily cold, he calculated. The Bear would strike and in that instant he would step inside, like a good boxer, and drive his blow home to the body. He would rip open the soft belly. Slashing swiftly and wickedly. He would get clawed, but he would kill The Bear. He would fight him hand to hand, on The Bear's own terms, and then . . .

"Sir?" The Ladakhi's voice was calm. "Why should you kill him now? I do not believe he wishes to fight."

Morgan advanced another step, the knife ready. The Bear looked at him, sniffing the air toward him, still more curious than aggressive.

It was possible his memory did not recall that other day, those years ago, when he had been fired upon, that day when in a red surge of fury he had killed and killed again. It was possible The Bear did not even conceive of these humans as a threat. In its world they were something rare, something different.

Morgan gripped his knife tighter, holding it low, cutting edge up, as does the trained knife fighter. He advanced another step, and then another.

Now The Bear seemed to sense danger, for he swung a little, then reared up, sniffing toward Morgan, studying him with that curious, wide, unblinking stare.

Morgan sought out the spot for his knife. He

studied with a flick of his eyes the snow over which he must cross, for to slip might be fatal.

But possibly the thought that this creature might attack him might never have entered The Bear's mind. Probably, with the exception of that one time, long ago . . . and who is to judge the length of an animal's memory . . . this bear had never been attacked by anything save another bear. Suddenly, even as Morgan poised himself for another cat-like step, The Bear dropped to all fours and turned away.

Lumbering, slow, he walked away over the slope. Once, fifty yards farther on, The Bear swung his huge head and glanced back over his shoulder. A long minute he stood there, studying these strange invaders. Then ignoring them, he walked slowly away.

Morgan stood still, knife in hand. A chill wind moaned down the barren, icy slope, and he shivered a little. Morgan stared after the retreating bear, and suddenly he felt a desperate sense of relief . . .

Frozen snow rattled on his stiff garments, needled his raw skin.

"Sir?" The Ladakhi's voice seemed to come from far off.

"All right," Morgan said, "we'll go now."

Once, far down and away along the slope, he paused to look back. Up among the high black rocks where the icy winds prowled, he seemed to see something moving, something white, something . . .

It could have been his imagination.

COMMENTS: I've never known quite what to think of "The Quest for the Bear." I was on the verge of adding it to more than one of our past collections of short stories but always decided not to.

I have a fairly strict set of rules for myself when I'm editing or rewriting one of Dad's stories. The goal is always to help the story live up to its potential. Thus a story idea that wasn't the best to begin with might get a quick once-over to make it read quickly and easily, while a better story, one with a concept that had more potential, would get considerably more attention.

The first phase is straight editorial work—spelling, punctuation, phrasing, and the like. After that, if additional work is needed, the next thing I do is some judicious cutting. If the cuts become significant, occasionally I will add material to bridge the trimmed sections. If you know what you're after, it's pretty amazing how much can be improved with a very light touch. There was only one time when I felt the need to truly do what in the film business is called a "page one rewrite." In that case, there were so many overlapping requirements that there was no other way out. Dad wrote so much material in his life, to this date I have never felt the need to create something entirely "new" in his name, nor have I considered finishing anything of his where I did not feel I understood the direction he intended to take the story.

I considered many alternatives with "The Quest for the Bear." I felt it had so much potential and I wanted to do something special with it, yet figuring out exactly what was a real challenge.

I started to revise it to be a bit more realistic, cutting out the avalanche and Morgan's weird (and sort of hollow) impulse to try to kill The Bear with his knife . . . then I stopped myself. I started to try to build more material into The Bear's stalking of the downed airmen, trying to create a longer period of trauma for them in order to justify Morgan's near-suicidal mission into what could be considered enemy territory in order to get his revenge on this bear, which, to a great extent, was simply defending itself.

I even thought I might have The Bear lead Morgan and his Ladakhi guides somewhere more important, to a magical place of some sort that would be better at justifying this amazing bear's existence or would be more helpful in explaining Morgan's final change of heart. And I even got a few pages into a complete rewrite that reset the story in Alaska in the very early twentieth century. I tried to apply the best interpretation of the mythic and character-building aspects of this story to something that was more believable and that commented on Man's desire to hunt for sport.

In the end I did none of the above. All of that seemed to be too much of a change from Louis's original intention, even though I could tell he was struggling with many of these same issues.

I'm not entirely sure when "The Quest for the Bear" was written. The text tells us that Morgan's return takes place after the Chinese Revolution of 1949, but some evidence for the date of the story's creation lurks in an interesting connection to a couple of other L'Amour works.

Dad used the mechanism of an airplane crash to transport a modern man (or woman) into a world of adventure a number of times. The simplest of these stories was "Crash Landing," which was published in 1952, but the concept also appears in "Beyond the Great Snow Mountains," "With These Hands," and the "Ben Mallory" section of this book. I'm sure that my father, who was born just five years after the Wright Brothers' first flight, could sense the irony in using a modern aircraft as a way of transporting his heroes and heroines "back in time."

Dad's earliest notes on this story contain the following passage:

```
   They come . . . to a high cirque [a
glacial valley or hollow] and corner the
Bear at last in fading afternoon and
mounting wind and the man fights the Bear,
hand to claw in a deadly combat. The man
wins.
```

Later he wrote a rough description of a slightly more realistic version. That description ends like this:

```
   The bear at last, cornered, ready to
fight. Wounded by previous shot. Man closes
in to end it with a knife.
```

The political conditions mentioned in the story seem to indicate a date between the earliest days of "Red" China and the 1959 uprising that caused the Dalai Lama to flee Tibet a decade later. That was the era of the previously mentioned "sweats." They were famous for their over-the-top man-against-nature themes but, because Louis's hero finally allows The Bear to live, this story seems to be trapped somewhere between the ethos of the sweats and something potentially greater. I'm still convinced that there is an even more interesting and meaningful story locked up in "The Quest for the Bear," but it will just have to exist, flickering and half-formed, on the edges of our imaginations.

———————————

KILLS BEAR

The First Three Chapters of a Frontier Novel

CHAPTER I

For the third time in as many days they had
lost the trail and the two Delawares were casting
back and forth along the hillside.

The four white men who were the Company
trappers directing the chase stood together, the
Bannocks gathering nearby. Kills Bear stood aloof
as befitted the lone Nez Perce among them.

Kills Bear liked the Delawares well enough but
was disdainful of their tracking ability, and now
they wasted time. The white man they followed had
tricked them again and Kills Bear was amused.

When they found the white man they would kill
him, but Kills Bear respected their quarry, and
it gave him real pleasure to follow the white
man's trail, for undoubtedly he was a warrior fit
to walk beside the greatest.

Although Kills Bear was half white, he thought
of himself as Nez Perce and he had no liking for
the Company trappers. They lived among the
Bannocks, friends and neighbors to the Nez Perce,
and Kills Bear had been visiting when the

trappers came looking for trackers. He had joined
for the chase, but what the trail revealed
excited him in a different way.

Every action or reaction of a man is an
indication of his character, his training and his
experience, and this his trail will reveal. The
path left by a Sioux is not that of a Blackfoot,
and that of a Shoshone is different from that of
a Crow. So it is that a trail left by one man is
different from that of another, and to a skilled
tracker not only is the path revealed but the
maker of the path as well.

The four Hudson's Bay Company trappers were
slovenly, untidy men, careless on the trail, and
dirty about their camps. Left to themselves they
could scarcely have followed a buffalo bull.

He whom they pursued was a man of another
sort, for even before he knew he was being
followed the man left no trail to speak of. He
disguised each camp before leaving and only a
shrewd tracker, after careful study, would
realize that someone had indeed stopped there.

Kills Bear permitted himself an icy smile. He
was nineteen, but a warrior for the past four
years. And he had already been a famous hunter by
the time he took his first scalp, that of a
Blackfoot. Before he was sixteen he had also
stolen ponies from the Crow and taken the scalp
of a Sioux warrior.

"What you grinnin' at?" Higgins demanded.

"He knows he is followed."

"What do we care?" Higgins asked. Then struck
by the comment he asked, "How do you know that?"

"The trail has changed. He will be dangerous
now."

"So he knows we're behind him. How does that make him dangerous?"

Kills Bear liked this white man the least of all. "The man you follow," he said contemptuously, "is a great warrior. To know what he knows, to move as he moves, one must have followed many war trails, made many hunts. Soon he will circle to see who follows him, then he will decide what to do."

"One man against twenty? I hope he decides to fight."

"The twenty must see before they can kill, and he will choose the time and place of battle."

"Maybe," said Higgins, skeptically.

"Only he," Kills Bear replied, "knows where he goes, and you must go where he wishes you to go, or give up the chase."

Thinking of it from that aspect Higgins began not to like it so much. The Company wanted no free trappers in this country of fine fur, and spies in St. Louis warned them of any likely party. This man had gone to the Big Horns with a party of two dozen other free trappers but had left them for some unaccountable reason and was pushing westward alone.

Why the Company was making such an issue of one man Higgins could not guess, unless they feared he might somehow break the control they held.

"When he decides to fight," Kills Bear said, "there will no longer be twenty to face."

Higgins threw the young Indian an irritable glance. He was too smug, Higgins decided, too know-it-all. But there'd be time.

———

Kills Bear was himself curious. The Indian, in company with the wild animals among whom he lived, was curious to a fault. He knew the ways of the wild creatures because he had studied them, often following an antelope, bear, or wild horse until all traits were made plain. And this man they pursued was westward bound. He rode a better than ordinary horse and had three pack horses with him, but he did not pause to trap although they had passed several streams where there had been beaver sign. Only now, when aware of pursuit, did he deviate from his path toward the setting sun.

The ways of the white man were confusing. Many seemed obvious fools, while others deserved great respect. Unlike many Indians, Kills Bear did not think of them as just another nomadic tribe. Their existence and their origins were a mystery and, because of that, because his father had been one of them, so were his own.

His father had first come to their village when they were in great need. Illness had been among the Nez Perce and many had died. The white man had come with meat and had shared it among the lodges as an Indian would share. Then he had gone back into the hills to hunt.

In the snow-covered Bitterroot Mountains he had killed a grizzly, and later found several elk trapped by winter snows. All this meat he had brought to the lodges of the Nez Perce. And so it was that in a time of sickness and starvation their village had survived and grown strong. Against the Blackfeet he proved a great warrior and took scalps like any Indian. Eventually, he took a Nez Perce wife and lived among them for some time.

Kills Bear could not remember his father but had grown to manhood hearing stories of him. Like his father, he had begun by killing a bear in the Bitterroots, and among his people it was taken as an omen that he was favored as his father had been.

The training of Kills Bear had been the training of any young brave. Among the tribes the words for stranger and enemy were synonymous. A stranger who came willingly into a village might remain there unmolested, would be fed and lodged, yet that same man might be killed immediately if seen again. There was no question of right or wrong in this. One did not kill a guest within the village, nor did one steal from his own people. To steal from enemies was merely warfare of another kind, and a sport as well. To steal successfully was a matter of pride.

Kills Bear found nothing strange in the pursuit of the white man for the purpose of killing him. Had Kills Bear come upon the white man and found it possible he might have killed him himself, although he had never yet killed a white man. The four horses, rifle and goods the man carried constituted a considerable wealth to an Indian.

From his mother Kills Bear knew the customs of the white man were different and that white men often consulted books before deciding what should or should not be done. Several books had been left behind by his father and Kills Bear had examined them closely, but learned nothing. The

mystery of the talking leaves was beyond him.
They were his father's medicine, and surely his
father had been a great hunter if he could
decipher even these small and complicated signs.

Kills Bear watched the Delawares. He knew
where the white man had gone but he had not been
asked, nor was he paid as were the others. He had
come along simply because he was interested in
the chase, yet he was sorely tempted to join in.
To find and kill such a man, even to simply count
coup on his body would be something of which to
tell in the lodges.

Humility was not a trait to be admired among
Indians. A man was expected to tell of his
victories, even to enlarge upon them, for such
was the poetry of the Indian, such were his
songs, his stories, even his history. Poetry was
ever the language of memory, and victory alone
was not enough; the story must be well told about
a fire in the lodges. From such stories the young
boys learn to be warriors and the girls what to
expect of a man.

Suddenly Kills Bear lost his patience. He
turned his horse and walked him away at right
angles.

"Where do you go?" a Bannock called. "Do you
leave us?"

"The white man went there!" Kills Bear
indicated a low saddle in the hills in front of
him. They were not so far behind the white man as
they believed, and this hill was exposed to view
for a great distance. He believed the white man
deliberately led them over this ridge so he might
see them clearly, count their numbers and see who
it was who followed him. And the low saddle at

which Kills Bear pointed was the one place where
he could cross the opposite ridge without being
sky-lined for all to see.

After much debate the others followed. When he
had found the vague tracks Kills Bear sat waiting
for the others to come up and see for themselves.

Higgins threw him an ugly glance. "I'll kill
that one," he muttered to Johnson, who rode
beside him. "He's too high an' mighty."

"He's the best of them," Johnson said. "If you
want to collect that money the Company has
offered, save your killing until this is over."

"We got trackers of our own," Higgins replied
brusquely.

Johnson thought Higgins a fool, but did not
say so. Higgins was the best shot with a rifle
that Johnson had ever known.

"All Indians are not good trackers any more
than all white men are good shots. The Bannocks
say Kills Bear is the greatest tracker among his
people."

Kills Bear was searching the ground but he was
also thinking. It was not enough to simply follow
the indications on the ground but the trail must
be followed in the mind of a man. From sign upon
the earth one might learn what manner of a man it
is who is followed, and some indication of the
pattern of his thinking, for only then can a
trail be followed with success.

This man knew he was pursued. By this time he
knew how many they were, and he had some idea of
their purpose. Yet the white man had been going
somewhere, changing direction as soon as he knew
he was followed. Therefore he did not wish to
take his pursuers to his ultimate destination.

What could that destination be? It was not a
lodge, for no white men had lodges out here.
There must be something else, something important
which he wished them not to find.

The white man would try to escape by tricks
and devices, and if that failed he would fight.
He would fight as a lone man must, by surprise
and escape, by taking a shot here, another there,
by whatever means he could find for he was one
and they were many.

The white man knew the country. For some time
this had been obvious to Kills Bear, hence he was
leading them somewhere of advantage to him,
perhaps a trap for them. Kills Bear considered
the country that lay ahead.

Much of it was unknown even to him although he
had wandered farther afield than anyone of his
village. It was a region of wild snowcapped
ridges and towering peaks. Of deep, pine-scented
canyons and rushing streams. Not far away was the
place the white men had called Colter's Hell, a
vast area of hot springs, geysers and
fantastically colored rocks. It was a lonely,
broken, desolate area, but if one knew where to
find it there was game, and in some of the
streams there were beaver.

The Delawares were on the trail again, moving
swiftly. He watched them go, then started after
them, in no hurry.

Higgins watched Kills Bear, making no effort
to mask the malice in his eyes. "He's got
somethin' to learn, that young un has. I reckon
I'll be his teacher."

Johnson glanced at Higgins. He was an ill-
smelling, dirty man given to sly brutality, and

Johnson trusted him not at all. There were men
who might not have trusted Johnson, and with
reason, but there are degrees in all things. He
was suspicious of Higgins, wary of his plans. If
they killed the man they sought there would be a
reward from the Company. But how many would live
to collect that reward? Had Higgins thought of
that?

"Remember this, Hig," Johnson said, "we've got
to trade with the Nez Perce, and the Bannocks and
Flatheads are their friends. That Kills Bear is
already a big man among them and his father was
bigger, so be careful what you do."

From under his straight black brows Higgins
shot Johnson a hard glance. "That's the joke."
Higgins' grin was cruel. "Kills Bear doesn't know
the man we're huntin' is his own father!"

CHAPTER II

Tom Patrick lay on a grassy hillside near a
clump of aspens and studied the group through his
glass. It had been a fortunate buy. A drunken
steamboat captain had sold it to him in St. Louis
on his last trip, and the captain himself had
picked it up in New Orleans. It was battered and
old but the lenses had been ground by a man who
knew his craft.

He had lived in wild country too long not to
watch his back trail, and he very soon realized
he was followed. The presence of the four white
men and the Delawares told him all he needed to
know. These were Hudson's Bay Company men, and

the Company did not want anyone trading with the
Nez Perce.

Higgins he recognized with no pleasure. A
thief and a back-shooting killer who had been
suspected of murdering more than one trapper and
stealing his furs. The others he did not
recognize but he knew that Company men had seen
him outfitting in St. Louis and he had worried
there might be trouble.

The Delawares he knew by sight. Their tribe
had been dispersed and many had come west,
selling their skills as hunters and trackers. The
Bannocks he knew by their style of dress and the
only one who surprised him was the tall young Nez
Perce.

The Nez Perce were his own people and twenty
years ago he had left a wife among them. It had
taken all that time to get back as far as he was
now.

Twenty years ago he had gone down the Missouri
in a hide boat with a fortune in furs. He reached
St. Louis after a bitter fight with Arikaras with
his furs intact but a festering wound in his
thigh and another in his side.

It had been almost three months before he
could walk, and then he had gone home. His
parents were old, poor, and times were hard. He
bought them a small farm, some pigs, chickens, a
few head of dairy cattle as well as a team of
horses. By the time they were settled in the
house he built for them two years had gone by. He
out-fitted in St. Louis intending to return to
the Snake and Salmon River country.

There was trouble on the Missouri and the
river was low. It was a year in which few fur

traders or free trappers wanted to attempt the
long push up the Missouri. So he had gone
overland to Santa Fe, trapped successfully and
then had his furs seized by the governor and was
thrown into prison, a Yankee interloper in New
Spain, a foreign land. It had been another year
before he was released and made his way back to
Missouri minus his furs and with no money for a
stake.

The years that followed had been a brutal
struggle against impossible odds. Three times he
lost his furs, and twice the years were bad and
he took few pelts and those were of poor quality.
Trying to return to the Salmon River country he
had started up the Platte with a free company of
twenty-three men.

Two were killed near the Sweetwater, another
trampled by a wounded buffalo, and they had
fights with the Sioux and the Crows. With only a
few furs to show for their efforts they returned
to St. Louis and there Tom Patrick talked to a
man who had recently come from the Yellowstone.
His Nez Perce wife was dead.

Rumors abounded that the Hudson's Bay Company
had ordered their trappers on the Snake River to
kill every beaver they found, not for their fur,
but to keep Yankee trappers from occupying land
the Company considered its private domain. There
were fewer and fewer reasons to return to his
adopted people.

Tom Patrick had gone west again, to California
where he remained several years. He fought the
Modocs, traded with the Choloquins in the Oregon
Territory and returned to St. Louis. And there he

encountered a man just in from the upper
Missouri.

For hours they talked of trapping, of the Nez
Perce, and of their splendid horses, the
Appaloosas. "Kills Bear has become a great hunter
and warrior. You would be proud of him, Tom."

"Kills Bear?" He did not recall the name. "I
should be proud of him? Why?"

The trapper turned on him, astonished. "You
mean you didn't know? He's your son!"

Two days later Tom Patrick had started for the
mountains with a party of free trappers and the
Company men noticed their departure, for they had
spies everywhere. Now scarcely a week's journey
from the hunting grounds of the Nez Perce the
Company men and their allies were on his trail
and he did not want to bring trouble to his own
people.

For several days he had been playing with
them, testing his skills against theirs. And Tom
Patrick knew that someone among them was a first
class hand at reading sign.

He looked again at the tall young Nez Perce.
He studied the face through his glass. That young
man could know his son, could be his son . . .
they would be nearly the same age. Certainly,
whoever he was, he was a splendidly built young
man and without a doubt he was the tracker who
held them to the trail. He was watching when he
saw him turn and point toward the saddle.

Tom Patrick slid back from his position and
led his horses down to the creek. Mounting up, he
rode into the water. It was a shallow stream and
he walked the horses down it for a mile, then
turned up a branch that he remembered and left

the creek at a shelf of rock where he tied elk-
hide moccasins on his horses' hooves and rode
with them for a half mile by a twisting, turning
route before dismounting to take the moccasins
off. He rode at once into the edge of a small
lake and walked his horses along the curving
shore for half a mile, then up a deep, sandy
gully into the hills. This was all country he
knew and where he had trapped more than twenty
years before.

The old trail was blocked by blow-downs but
they were young stuff and light. He dismounted,
lifted the fallen trees clear and rode his horse
through, leading the pack animals. Once through
he walked back and shifted the trees, like
closing so many gates. He straightened the grass
where he could and taking up a handful of leaves
he let the wind drift them down naturally.

Only then did he ride on.

He had cut the odds. There were too many of
them, but they were hunting him and he had no
compunctions against what he intended to do.
Only . . . he did not want to get into a shooting
affair with any Nez Perce.

The young Indian seemed to be with, but not
of, the party. Time and again he had held aloof,
watching the others blundering about. Once he had
seen Higgins seemingly have words with the Nez
Perce . . . the young brave should be warned.
Higgins was dangerous, a bitter and vengeful man
who hated Indians of whatever kind.

Yet Higgins and the others were but tools. Tom
Patrick knew very well the man who stood behind
them. It was a dour and hard-featured Scotsman, a
close-trading man and a cruel one.

Tom Patrick camped among the aspen where he could watch his back trail. With a few dry sticks he prepared a hot meal, ate it, wiped out the few signs he had left and rode on for another hour before camping.

At daylight he was up, chewing on a bit of jerky, and riding down to a rushing cold mountain stream. It was all of a hundred yards wide and deep, but he knew of a ford. Again he resorted to the moccasins and rode down to the ford before taking them off, then into the water.

He would never have dared enter such a stream with an Indian pony but his own horses were strong stock, heavier than most and accustomed to rough going. He crossed the stream, wiped out his tracks and disappeared into the forest where he wove a tricky way through the trees, doubling back from time to time. He had an idea he was not fooling that young Indian, but he had been thinking about that, too. Suppose it was Kills Bear?

Tom Patrick was worried. He dared not lead Higgins or those with him to his village. Unless matters had changed much over the years it was short on man-power, and Higgins and those with him were thieves and worse. Most mountain men were solid, hard-working men of above-average intelligence. Often they were very shrewd businessmen who knew the quickest way for a man of small capital to get ahead was by trapping fur or trading for it.

Higgins was another matter. Without question he was a skilled hunter and trapper. He was an excellent rifle shot, and he often boasted of killing Indians. Every mountain man had his

brushes with Indian war parties, as Indians did
with each other, but when they killed it was to
protect themselves or those with them, who often
enough were other Indians. It was a custom as
well as a matter of survival for a mountain man
to affiliate with one or another of the tribes,
which automatically made their enemies his
enemies.

He knew what he must do, and with the young
Nez Perce with them it would not be an easy thing
to accomplish. He must lead them into an area of
little game, he must stampede their horses, try
to get their Indian allies to desert them. There
was no time to waste.

The Nez Perce worried him . . . he did not
want to kill or be killed by anyone from his
adopted tribe. Even worse what if it was Kills
Bear!

How much, if anything, would Kills Bear know
of his father? What if anything might be left of
him in the lodge?

Suddenly he remembered the scrimshaw and
knots. As a boy when he first left Ireland he had
gone to sea and as many deep-water sailors did,
he took up the habit of carving and making belts
or ornaments from string, weaving them into all
sorts of intricate patterns. Having time on his
hands, he had developed considerable skill. He
had made a belt for his wife of strings with
stars of red and blue. He had also made a sailing
ship of string and hung it on a tipi pole.

At daybreak Tom Patrick loaded his horses and
started south along the Yellowstone. It was as

beautiful a country as man could wish with the river running swift and clear over a mostly gravel bottom. There were springs all about and fine grass. "Someday," Tom Patrick said to his horse, "you an' me will come back here an' settle down." The horse flicked a doubtful ear and Tom chuckled.

He left the Yellowstone at what somebody had called Sixmile Creek and followed a dim trail along the watercourse to the high mountain that loomed against the sky. Skirting the mountain he camped in a lovely basin southeast of the peak. In the twenty years since his last visit it did not seem to have changed. He bedded down near a spring well back from the lake.

He let his horses graze until well after sundown when he brought them in and tied them in the aspen close by. He checked the load on his rifle with the ramrod, and pulled the old charges from his pistols, tightened their flints, and reloaded them. He got the shotgun from his pack and loaded it with buckshot.

They would find him, he was sure, but not yet. They would have trouble with his trail on the other side of the Yellowstone and by the time they worked it out his horses would be rested.

After he brought the horses in he prepared a good meal, hoisted what meat he had left high into an aspen where the bears could not get it, and relaxed by the fire.

To think, that after all these years, he had a son!

Never had he even dreamed of such a thing, and certainly if she had known, his wife had said nothing to him before he left. Suddenly, he

swore, deeply and with feeling. To think of the
years he had missed! Of the times they might have
had together!

He lay back, supported by a log, and watched
the slow smoke rise from the coals. His fire was
dying, and he would let it die. This was Crow
country but he had seen no Indian sign and for
the moment he felt reasonably secure . . . a
dangerous feeling, he knew, for over-confidence
breeds disaster. Yet he needed these quiet
moments.

The trouble was people took too little time to
savor their existence, to breathe the cool air,
to walk the quiet ways, to enjoy the simple
pleasure of living. The Indian did this better
than the white man although the pressures, social
and survival, were just as serious for him. The
fisherman, the shepherd, the sailor and the
wagon-men lived closer to nature, they had time
to feel the air, to know the stars, to live in
their world.

The basin in which he rested was not quite a
half mile long and somewhat less wide, with a
small lake from which Bear Creek flowed steeply
down to the Yellowstone. He knew by the plant
life around him that the altitude was around nine
thousand feet, and the peak behind him went up a
good fifteen hundred feet higher.

The last firelight flickered on the slim white
trunks of the aspen, overhead the stars seemed
very near. He got out his pipe and stoked it with
tobacco. He rarely smoked, and when he did it was
beside a campfire.

Kills Bear . . . it was a good name, a strong
name. The bear was always big medicine. A noted

warrior at nineteen, that spoke well of him.
Well, his mother had been a fine woman, a woman
with strength and pride and hunger to know of the
life beyond the mountains. A hunger to know, to
understand. It had been that as much as her
beauty and grace that had drawn him to her.

He smoked quietly, listening to the horses and
the night sounds, enjoying his recollections of
the past. Finally, he knocked the ashes from his
pipe and stowed it away.

The moon was coming up, and the great peaks
stood icy clear against the sky.

Before the sun was warming the hills he was in
the saddle, riding directly for the head of Bear
Creek. He started down the trail then doubled
back and took a dim path that curved above
timberline and past the forks of Horse Creek.

It was sliderock country and his horses' hoofs
would leave few tracks, nothing but here and
there a scar upon a piece of rock already scarred
by tumbling and falling. He found the trail in
good shape as most of the higher mountain trails
were inclined to be and followed it for several
miles until he came to a still dimmer track that
led north toward the head of Passage Creek.
Leaving his pack horses he rode along that trail
for perhaps a hundred yards, leaving tracks in a
few sandy spots, then returning through the
sliderock.

His pack animals in tow once more he rode on
to the head of Grizzly Creek, following it down
until it joined Hellroaring Creek which he
crossed and started down the far side, putting

the deep, narrowing Hellroaring Canyon between
himself and pursuit.

The high, bare ridges lay above him now and
from where he paused he could see anything that
moved along the way he had come.

He built a small fire under a spruce where any
smoke would be dissipated among the branches, and
he made coffee and fixed a hot meal. There would
be few of those in the future, he suspected.

From time to time he glanced up along the
mountainside or studied it through his glass.
There were several points along that trail where
a rider must skirt close to the edge and at such
times would be easily visible from below.

While his horses rested and grazed on the rich
grass and wildflowers, Tom Patrick dug through
his duffel and got out a ball of string.

He chuckled to himself. Oh, they would find
him, soon enough, but he'd lead them on a merry
chase in the meantime. They would see some mighty
fine country, climb a lot of mountains and run
into a lot of trouble, a part of which he would
cause. The rest would come naturally.

And if that was Kills Bear back there he would
find out soon enough.

CHAPTER III

Higgins reined in and looked down the slope
ahead of him. "Where the Hell is he goin'?" he
demanded irritably.

Kills Bear was curious, too. An amusing idea
had occurred to him. Was the mysterious white man
they followed taking them only to view the

strange and beautiful? Or was he leading them on,
lulling them into over-confidence until they fell
into a trap?

Kills Bear knew something now of the type of
man they pursued and he was very careful not to
be first in line . . . nor last. Not being a
regular member of the party it ill-befitted him
to take the lead, anyway. There were times when
it needed all his skill to pick up the trail, and
several times he let them wander astray when he
knew how they should go.

At least he knew where they were being led,
for he had twice been into this land of smoking
ground. It was a place bewitched where not many
Indians cared to go, and many refused to even
look upon the land . . . but why was he taking
them there, of all places? And where had he been
going before he discovered he was being followed?

Higgins had grown more and more irritable.
Kills Bear, who knew enough English to
understand, heard him grumbling to Johnson and
the others. "Figured to be back afore this," he
grumbled. "I figured to be back in St. Louis by
now."

Shang Draper looked across the fire at him.
"Hig, the way we're goin' it'll be months before
we get back. Why don't we just forget it an' trap
some fur? There's beaver all about here."

"You crazy?" Hig demanded angrily. "I was sent
to kill a man and that's what I aim to do. He'll
be trappin' our fur, gettin' the best of the
tradin', buckin' those Canucks and the Company
all the way. He's got to be got rid of."

Kills Bear understood the sense of what they
were saying but cared little what white men did

to each other, or why. He tired of the bickering and walked down to sit by the fire of the Bannocks. He listened to their talk with sympathy. They were growing weary of the protracted search and had bad feelings about the land into which they were going. They muttered among themselves and he listened with only part of his mind. He was thinking of the white man . . . where was he going? Why had he turned aside so quickly when he realized he was being followed? An Indian might do that to lead enemies away from his village but there was no white man's town except for the fort where the great west-flowing river ran into the sea, and that was many weeks of travel from here.

Kills Bear was himself feeling uneasy and he did not know why. It might be that he was putting himself too much in the place of the man they pursued. It was necessary to do this in order to read the trail at all, and it was such feelings as this that had helped Indians to identify with the wildlife that lived all about them.

He was dissatisfied with himself, also. He was accepted as a successful hunter within his small branch of his people, and few surpassed him as a warrior and yet his heart was not right. Perhaps it was what his mother had told him of his father, or what Running Wolf had told him. Running Wolf was also a white man like Kills Bear's father, and he had been a prisoner of the Blackfeet when Kills Bear had succeeded in freeing him.

"Don't know your pa," Running Wolf had said, after looking over the books Tom Patrick had left behind at the lodge, "but these," he tapped the books, "show he was an educated man."

It was Running Wolf who taught him the little English he knew. Few of the tribes knew any language but their own, even that of others living close by, and Running Wolf, whose name was John Ryland, did not expect Kills Bear to listen, but he did, and showed an easy affinity for languages.

Ryland read the books, reading some passages aloud to Kills Bear, and explaining them. Much about them puzzled him for their thinking was so different from what he had known. Kills Bear said as much and Ryland agreed.

"Worries a body," he commented. "Here's two sets of folks, my people and yours, each with different ideas and different languages. I don't see how they will ever get together. Even with the best intentions. The words may seem the same but the meanings are different. When an Indian thinks of land that land is separate from him, its own thing rather than a possession. It's an area to hunt like a wolf or cougar or maybe a place to gather or plant. A white man thinks of building or ownership, clearly defined farms and towns. Both of them are honest but they mean different things when they say 'em. In language there's the words and then there's the deeper meaning."

Kills Bear had puzzled a long time about that. Then he tried even harder to learn the language for he had heard the old men among both Nez Perce and Bannock talking of the increasing numbers of the white man. If they were to deal with this stranger they must understand him.

His father had become like an Indian, living
as an Indian and accepting the Indian ways. So
had Running Wolf, or Ryland, as Kills Bear now
thought of him. Could the Indian learn to live
with the white man just as easily? He did not
know.

At daybreak they were on the trail. At first
it had been clear enough, then they lost it many
times, but now the tracks were plain again. He
was leading them south and Kills Bear only
occasionally took a hand in the tracking, for he
did not like the white men and was thinking of
setting off on his own.

They followed along the river of the yellow
stones, crossing and recrossing it, then they
came near to a falls, and went up among the
mountains from which the falls appeared and took
a dim trail that led between that river and the
river of the yellow stones. The winding trail
took them higher and higher along the ridges
until suddenly there lay before them a vast basin
more than fifty miles in diameter and surrounded
by peaks and ridges. Far away the sun glinted
from what must be a large lake.

"Man, oh man, would you look at that!" Draper
exclaimed. "Ever see such a stretch of country?"

"Smoke down there," Johnson said. "Somebody's
got 'em a fire."

"More'n one smoke," Draper agreed.

"Hot springs," Higgins said. "I heard tell of
them."

They rode on, more cautiously now, through
clumps of scattered pine. There was much sulphur
rock around and Kills Bear did not like the odor.
The tracks led straight along, pointing toward

the basin to the south. East was the tremendous gash of the canyon of the river of the yellow stones.

They had skirted a clump of pine and started down a steep declivity when the horse of the Indian who was in the lead seemed to stumble. Instantly there was a roar and a rush. Kills Bear's horse leaped forward, frightened, and the horse of the Bannock who followed reared up and turned . . . only just in time.

There was a rattle and rush of boulders and rocks bursting across the trail and many of the bigger boulders rolling and tumbling down the mountainside. There was a moment of sound, a moment of dust and then silence. The trail was blocked.

Perhaps three or four tons of rock and debris would have to be moved as the cliff edge allowed no room for skirting the pile.

"That was no accident," Draper said.

"A trap," Johnson agreed. "We've got to expect it from now on."

"It wasn't much," Higgins scoffed.

"A warning," Kills Bear said. "He is telling us what is to come."

Higgins' expression was unpleasant. "Since you know so much, maybe you better ride up front."

Kills Bear sat very tall in the saddle and he looked calmly at Higgins. "I tell you what I know. I am not pay by you. I am Nez Perce."

Higgins' rifle started to move. Johnson put a hand on it. "You shoot him an' they'll all leave. And like he says, he's just along for the ride."

Kills Bear had not moved. For the first time Higgins saw that Kills Bear's rifle, lying across

the crook of his elbow, was pointed directly at
him, and Kills Bear's hand was on the action.
Higgins would have been shot from the saddle
before his rifle got into position. The knowledge
infuriated him, yet he simply shrugged. "Forget
it. I'm gettin' touchy, I guess."

But he made up his mind . . . at the first
chance he would kill this Indian. The first
opportunity when no one was around to pin it on
him.

Dismounting they began clearing the rocks and
debris from the trail. Draper scrambled up the
exceedingly steep slope to see how the trap had
been arranged. It was unclear, but somehow a thin
piece of rawhide tied across the trail had
triggered it. The lead horse tripped over the
string, which had pulled a stick and that had
caused the slide of rocks, no doubt already
precariously perched, to come tumbling down.

An hour was lost before they cleared the
passage, for as one boulder was moved another
rolled into its place. Frustrated and angry, they
mounted at last and started down the trail again,
yet now they rode with caution, uncertain as to
what might come next. This, too, slowed their
pace. When they made camp at the head of a small
stream that flowed toward the Yellowstone they
had covered but a half dozen miles.

The ashes of old fires told them they were not
the first to think of this as a likely place to
camp. They staked out their horses on a wide,
flat stretch of grass, and Higgins straightened
up from his picket-pin to look toward Kills Bear.
The Nez Perce rode a blue roan Appaloosa, a
splendidly built animal that moved through the

miles without effort, seemingly as fresh when the day ended as when it began.

Higgins wanted that horse, and he meant to have him. He said as much, low-voiced, to Johnson.

Johnson shook his head. "Hig, you better think on it. The Company wants the Nez Perce trade. Kills Bear is a big man among them, and if anything happened to him they'd be mighty upset."

"Who's to know?"

"Them Bannocks, for one thing. If he dies and you show up ridin' that horse you've got a problem. It ain't only them, but what if the Scotsman finds out? And he will. He knows everything that happens in these woods."

"It's the Injun's pa we're killin', ain't it? An' he was a bigger man among them than his son. I'll just say he found out who we were trailin' and I had to kill him."

"You want my advice, I'd say let it lay. Besides, that one won't be so easy to kill. He moves through the trees like a ghost."

"Uh-huh, an' I'm better than him. You'll see."

Kills Bear had known only a few white men and had trusted but one. He had seen Higgins' eyes upon his horse, and he knew about horses. Stealing horses was an even quicker way to rise in influence in the tribe than taking scalps or counting coup. Stealing horses called for an inordinate amount of skill and among Indians it was not accounted a crime or an evil thing, but a test of ability as well as a means to wealth. Already Kills Bear had over fifty horses, stolen from the Sioux, the Blackfeet and the Crows. Ryland had taught him something about selective breeding.

"Don't let them all run loose," he advised. "Get your best stallion and keep him up with your best mares. In a few years you'll have the best and fastest horses around."

Beside the fire Kills Bear listened to the talk and then said to Black Beaver, "This one we follow. His medicine is strong. He understands much."

"We will find no more tracks," Little Hatchet said. "He has brought us here, now he will go."

Kills Bear was making new moccasins for the ones he wore would soon fall apart. "Where will he go?" he asked.

Black Beaver shrugged. "Where he was going. To your village, I think."

Kills Bear wondered. What else was there unless the white man went on down the great river to the place called Astoria. But nobody went there. It was too far.

He glanced at the fire of the white men. Higgins was standing up and he had the coffee pot in his hand. He was talking.

Suddenly the pot seemed to burst, splattering him with hot coffee. The report of a rifle hung in the air.

Kills Bear was in the darkness, moving swiftly. The man they sought was near. He paused to listen. He heard nothing, but then he expected to hear nothing. He went to the horses and they were standing with their ears pricked.

He glanced back toward camp. The fires still burned but nobody was about them. He waited, watching and listening, but wherever the man was, he was far from here by now, or well hidden at least. To go seeking him in the darkness would be insanity.

When all was quiet again he went back to camp.

"Horses all right?" Johnson asked.

"Yes."

"Scared Hig," Johnson commented. "Never seen a man get himself lost so fast."

Shang Draper moved up beside them. "I was all fixed for some o' that coffee," he grumbled. "Now we got to do it all over."

"No," Kills Bear said.

"What?"

"He is still out there I think. I think no more hot meals by night. He will shoot."

Draper swore, slowly, viciously, "If I get my hands on that--"

"We got to catch him first," Johnson said, grimly. "Like lookin' for a single flea in a sand hill."

Higgins came out of the shadows and stood near them. "Injun," he said to Kills Bear, "you get me that man's scalp an' I'll get you a new rifle and a hundred rounds of shot an' powder. You get him, do you hear?"

A new rifle? A hundred rounds? It was a treasure. Yet he did not trust this man. He had never trusted him.

"Got me a brand new rifle right in my duffel. Ain't never been fired. Canucks give it to me for the man who killed this gent. You go get him an' the rifle is yours."

Kills Bear had seen the rifle, had looked upon it with envy, yet he hesitated. Elusive as the

white man was, Kills Bear believed he could track
him down, yet something within him shied from
doing so.

Nevertheless, that was a beautiful rifle . . .
a beautiful rifle.

COMMENTS: My father was a master of the device of
having one character track another as a way to reveal a
story. Other examples would include the short stories "Law
of the Desert Born" and "Dutchman's Flat," and the novels
The Key-Lock Man and *Last of the Breed*, to name just a few.
I found it amusing to see Dad subtly extending the cast of
characters from his Sackett series by using a Higgins as the
heavy. In the Sackett stories, the Higgins family is often
mentioned as being engaged in a long-running feud with
the Sacketts, though this does not mean that all of his Higgins characters are portrayed in a negative light.

Dad wrote these chapters in the middle to late 1970s,
during his second attempt to broaden his appeal and move
away from constantly writing traditional Westerns. In this
case, the time period is that of the true frontier, prior to
both the Civil and the Mexican wars.

Early in the 1800s, what we now consider the North-
west United States was a territory disputed by the British
and Americans. The Hudson's Bay Company administered
the area for Great Britain and was concerned that more and
more Yankees would be drawn to Oregon (which, in those
days, was the name for quite a large area) by the agricul-
tural possibilities in Willamette Valley and by the rich fur
trade. The fear was that a critical mass of settlers from the
United States would cost them control over the territory

and, more important, over the rendezvous point for shipping at the mouth of the Columbia River.

The company used many tactics to keep interlopers out, including some of those mentioned in this story. At times there were worries that war might again break out between the United States and England. In 1818 and 1846, treaties were signed in an effort to resolve the issue, finally splitting the Western United States and Canada along the 49th parallel. I have always found this to be the most interesting time in the history of the West, the classic era of manifest destiny and of confronting many of the issues that created the modern United States.

BEN MALLORY

Seventeen Chapters of an Adventure Novel

CHAPTER 1

Sunlight and the shadow of trees lay across a
road that had never known a wheel. An ancient
road, forgotten in the passage of years by all
but the people of the remote mountain villages,
itinerant traders or occasional pilgrims.

Over much of its distance the trail was a mere
succession of stone slabs proceeding in single
file through the dark forests or along the brink
of impossible chasms. From time to time it
mounted to heights shared only by the wind or the
Yeti, called in some parts of Tibet the Migeu,
and known elsewhere as the Abominable Snowman.

Occasionally, caravans passed along this road
carrying goods from India, Nepal or Assam to the
farthest reaches of Tibet, Sinkiang or the region
of the Tsaidam marshes, just as they had for more
than four thousand years.

Upon this day among the trees flanking the
road sat a row of horsemen. At that point the
trail lay along the bottom of a narrow defile
whose tree-clad slopes rose steeply but not

abruptly, and among the trees the bodies of men and horses were dappled with sunlight and shadow until virtually invisible.

Each rider held in his hand a rifle, butt resting upon his thigh, muzzle pointed skyward at an angle from his body.

The horsemen were dark and savage men with high cheekbones and narrow eyes, most carrying the scars of combat. They wore bulky knee-length sheepskin coats with the wool on the inside. Each wore a bandolier of cartridges across his chest and carried a broad-sword slung between his shoulder blades, the hilt in a position to be grasped over the left shoulder. Many wore a pointed cap with flaring ear-flaps.

The air, as is the case at such heights, was astonishingly clear and there was nothing to be heard but the sound of far-off wind among the trees.

The riders were motionless as stone-carved figures, their eyes upon a Red Chinese soldier on the trail below.

The magnolias lining the trail were heavy with immense purple blossoms, a variety rarely occurring below 8,000 feet. The soldier, unaware of their beauty, hurried on, intent only upon some goal of his own. Over his shoulder he carried a sack, in his hand a rifle.

He was obviously worried. This far from his command he might be a deserter, but more likely was a scout or forager who had slipped away from his detachment in search of food or loot. From time to time he glanced over his shoulder.

Suddenly, as if aware of some sense of danger, his eyes swept up the slope.

Until that moment he had been secure, but that upward flick of the eyes cost him his life. He came to an abrupt halt, staring as if unable or unwilling to believe what he saw . . . and then he broke into a run.

Mallory spoke then, and the rider at the end of the line lifted his rifle, almost negligently. An instant his aim held, and just as the soldier was about to disappear around a turn of the trail, he squeezed off his shot.

The rifle seemed to leap in his hands and, caught in mid-stride, the running man put down his stiff, advanced leg and catapulted over it, falling on his face. He made one lonely, involuntary movement, a dying spasm, then lay still.

The report of the shot hung suspended in the still afternoon air, then lost itself in futile echoes against the surrounding hills. After it faded there was no other sound, and for several minutes, no movement.

Mallory was a lean, powerful man with dark, weathered features and green eyes. He spoke, haltingly but effectively in the Go-log dialect, "I do not want him found."

Three riders detached themselves from the rank of horsemen and walked their mounts to where the dead soldier lay. Bending over, the first rider hooked the fore-sight of his rifle under the dead man's collar, lifting him within reach of the second rider's grasp. Trotting their horses to the rim of the gorge that flanked the trail on one side, they dropped the body over the edge. The third rider recovered the dead man's sack and rifle, and then all three fell into place in the column now forming on the narrow road.

Mallory lifted a hand and the column moved out in the direction from which the soldier had come. Behind them the ancient road lay empty once more, sleeping in sunlight and shadow. Only a single slab of rock bore witness to their passing, for upon that rock lay the shadow of war, the shadow of blood.

Thirty miles away and nearly a thousand feet lower, the defile down which the detachment of Go-log rode opened into a narrow mountain valley. It in turn descended into a deep gorge and thence to the Yellow River.

Near the opening of the defile stood an inn, if such it might be called in a land where such things are nearly unknown. Incredibly ancient, its buildings were a patch-work of addition and repair, surrounded by a rough wall. Massive wooden gates, closed except when admitting the rare traveler, gave access to the courtyard. There was but one other opening in the surrounding wall, this being behind the inn, and of a size to permit the passage of one man or one rider at a time.

The structure was low and rambling, seeming to crouch warily behind its palisade as if fearful of being seen. Nearby were a few acres of cultivation, and on the rich meadows along the stream two dozen yaks grazed in company with a few horses and fat-tailed sheep.

At one time the entire ground floor had been, as in most Tibetan houses, a stable for yaks and horses, but the demands of travelers in some far-off time had caused half the stable to be made into the inn. Within this ground floor a third of the area was given over to a k'ang. This was a raised portion of the floor, some three feet higher than the remainder, and built of stone slabs. On the exposed side were openings through which fuel could be thrust to heat the k'ang, and generations of travelers had slept upon it until their twistings and turnings had worn hollows in the stone.

The ceiling of the room was low, the huge, time-blackened timbers grimed with the smoke of centuries of cooking fires or charcoal braziers.

The k'ang was a relic of years when the inn had been occupied by a Chinese from Shensi, a Chinese who found the atmosphere less than congenial and abandoned the area in the wake of a Chinese army badly used by the fierce Go-log horsemen.

For many years the inn had not functioned as such, being alternately occupied and abandoned, then finally chosen by Mohammedan merchants from Kansu as a stopping place. The Kansu merchants were a wild and hardy lot who established a friendly relationship with the Go-log for purposes of trade.

The trail that led past the inn joined with the main caravan trail that led from Koko Nor, that fabulous blue lake, crossed the Yellow River, skirted Tossum Nor on the south and Oring Nor on the west, avoiding the vast marshes of the Karma Tang to proceed westward by way of Ulanergi to a crossing of the Yangtze at Baga Kokoser.

Of this ancient track no known map existed,

although upon some maps there were thin red lines that suggested that the way might be traveled. Of the track coming up from Choni to join the main trail there was not so much as a suggestion. No record remained except that in the memories of men.

Before entering the valley of the inn from the south the trail mounted steeply for some distance, so the valley itself remained invisible until the traveler was upon its very edge.

It was a place of quiet beauty, steep mountains lifting to high peaks where glacier-clogged hanging valleys and cirques surrounded it and the mountains were clad thickly with forest.

Renata Bernard, riding beside Marty Wells, drew up as she topped the rise. Nothing on the road from the south had quite prepared her for this, although there had been much that was beautiful.

At the moment the valley was bathed in sunlight along one side. In the green meadow yaks grazed beside the clear mountain stream, the mountains soaring above in snow-crowned serenity. At some distance the inn waited, a study of picturesque decay.

Dr. Martin Wells, whose somewhat boyish face belied the official title, reined his horse around. The view was beautiful beyond belief but he hoped any Red Chinese officials they met could read enough to comprehend the documents they carried. So far all had gone smoothly, guided and guarded by Gunther Hart's wealth and Gunther Hart's diplomacy, yet Marty Wells had found himself growing increasingly skeptical and increasingly wary.

"How can anyone think of war when there are places such as this?" Renata wondered.

"They don't all live in places like this, Nata. We haven't seen a human being for three days."

"I'm glad we're stopping here."

"We are?"

"There's an inn. A very old place. That must be it over there . . . across the valley."

"First I've heard of it. Of stopping, I mean. Hart never tells anybody anything."

The red and gold banner proclaiming in English, Chinese and Tibetan characters that this was the Gunther Hart Expedition to Tibet and Tsaidam was a good half mile behind them.

"I hope he really has it fixed. I'd hate to come this far and wind up in a Chinese prison."

"There's nothing to worry about, Marty. We're here, aren't we? Gunther is very friendly with many of the Red Chinese. He knows Chou En-lai himself. They were friends in Paris, years ago."

"I'd like to know who he knows in the State Department. How could he get permission to go into Tibet with things as they are?"

"Gunther went to school with the Under Secretary or somebody. But you should know that. He has friends everywhere."

"I'm still surprised. As for having friends everywhere, I'm skeptical."

"Marty!"

"I mean it. I've never known anyone less likely to win friends. To influence people, yes. He has all that money."

"He's a bit eccentric, I know, but he knows people everywhere, and people know who he is."

"A Fellow-Traveler?"

"You've no right to say that. Once you get to know him you'll change your mind."

"How long does it take, for God's sake?" Marty shifted his seat in the saddle and looked back at the expedition which was slowly over-taking them. "He hasn't said three words to me yet."

"He does keep to himself. He meditates."

Marty scoffed. "If you ask me, he sleeps. I still haven't grasped his purpose. The rest of us are obvious enough. We are all working scientists willing to risk our necks to collect data. I will admit that without him there might not have been another chance in this century to get into this part of the world. That explains you, your uncle, Roy and the rest of us. It does nothing to explain Gunther Hart."

Renata hesitated, then said, "Marty, don't breathe a word of this, but Gunther believes he can locate a great store of manuscripts, Tantric manuscripts from the Bon period . . . pre-Buddhist. He is quite sure he is on the track of an important find, something to compare with Stein's discovery at the Caves of the Thousand Buddhas."

Marty was silent. It could be the truth. He had seen enough of Gunther Hart and heard him talk just enough to believe it. The man claimed to be a Buddhist . . . well, a pseudo-Buddhist, in Marty's books. The more he saw of Hart the more he believed his old friend Doc Whiting.

"I had no reason to say the things I did," Marty said, "and if he makes any kind of discovery at all I'll be the first to say I was mistaken. I know you like him, and you know him

better than any of us. All I know is pure hear-
say, but in the past few days I'd come to believe
most of what I'd heard."

"And that was?"

"That he was a pseudo-Buddhist, a pseudo-
scientist, a pseudo-philanthropist, and a pseudo-
pacifist."

Renata's eyes sparked with anger. "You didn't
have to come you know."

"I was advised not to."

"You were? By whom?"

"Milne Whiting. He warned me that Hart was
unstable."

She was surprised. "Milne Whiting?"

"He's a very good friend. Hart had classes
with him."

They started on, and Renata was more disturbed
than she would have admitted. At twenty-eight,
Marty Wells had achieved a considerable
reputation. He had specialized in the search for
useful and medicinal herbs, had written an
important paper on plant physiology, and another
on the occurrence of metallic poisons in plants.
He had been one of those consulted when soil from
the moon had proved toxic to some earth bacteria.

When the opportunity to accompany the Hart
Expedition to Tibet and Tsaidam had been offered,
he had accepted at once. Everyone agreed it was
the chance of a life-time. Everyone, that is, but
Dr. Milne Whiting.

Marty was no novice when it came to
investigating wild country. At nineteen he had
spent four months on the island of New Britain
off the coast of New Guinea.

He chuckled, remembering the expression of

distaste on Whiting's face when he informed him
of Hart's proposed expedition and his acceptance.

"It will be an experience," Whiting
acknowledged, "but you can have it."

"Do you know Hart?"

"He was in one of my classes, and the first
time he submitted a paper, I knew I was in
trouble."

After a moment, he continued. "It was written
in long hand, script as precise as any machine,
each line as if ruled, each letter of exact
height, the grammar and punctuation faultless.
Each point of argument was advanced in the most
bloated and complex language imaginable. Yet,
although you had to struggle to follow it, the
logic was always impeccable. At first I wondered
if he was having me on, but if it was a challenge
to my intelligence or a joke of some sort there
was never any indication. He seemed utterly
devoid of humor, emotion or imagination."

Whiting was stuffing papers into his brief
case as he talked. "My advice is to forget the
whole idea. There will be other expeditions."

"Not to Tibet. And probably not in our life-
time to eastern and northern Tibet. It may well
be a generation before any western scientist
enters the region again, and I simply can't
afford to pass it up."

After a moment, he added, "It could be the
beginning of a career!"

"Or the end of one. Oh, I'll admit if there
was a chance to come up with some ancient
Sanskrit or Karoshthi manuscripts, I'd be
tempted."

"You're damned right you would."

"Tempted, I said. I did not say I'd go."
Pausing on the steps outside the building,
Whiting had offered one last bit of advice.
"We've been friends a long time, Marty, so just
listen. Don't ever cross him. Keep your opinions
to yourself. Better still, don't let him even
realize you have any opinions, and above all,
don't get in his way!"

Marty was shocked. Milne Whiting was a scholar
of international reputation, and a tolerant man.
Admitting Hart was an eccentric, it still seemed
intemperate advice. If the man was eccentric it
was his privilege, and by all accounts he could
afford to be.

"Well, Hart may be difficult at times, but who
is not?"

"I am not referring to day to day irritations,
Marty. I believe the man is a dangerous
psychopath."

"You can't be serious."

"But I am. Completely serious." Marty had no
idea what to say. For the first time his respect
for Whiting wavered. What was it with him? Was he
jealous of the man? Gunther Hart had an
international reputation for scholarship as well
as for his wealth.

Whiting seemed to sense Marty's doubt. "For
nearly two years I spent four hours a day with
Hart. My opinion is based on an accumulation of
details, few of which amount to much in
themselves.

"Gunther Hart is an extremely egocentric
individual who never, so far as I am aware,
suffered the slightest frustration. His father

died when he was young and his mother adored him and catered to his every whim.

"There was never any reason to give the slightest consideration to the rights and feelings of others. He was born with a gold spoon in his mouth and left it for an ivory tower of his own construction. He has a brilliant mind, but if he merely imagines something, he assumes it is reality.

"All you have heard is part of a carefully constructed public image that represents what he believes himself to be. Pay close attention to it, and remember that Hart is completely convinced of his own rightness on every score."

"But he was an athlete, Doc! There must have been some frustration there. He did compete, did he not?"

"After a fashion. His decathlon score was among the best, and he won an inter-collegiate championship in boxing, but to understand that you must have the complete picture.

"As a boy he wanted to be an athlete. He was naturally strong and active. His mother promptly hired the best coaches, and believe me, I mean the best.

"He was beautifully coordinated, and they did their job well. Every event in which he was entered was carefully prepared in advance. His coaches and trainers were paid for results, so they found reason to enter him only in events he was sure to win. When he was entered in the inter-collegiate tournament it was only after his prospective opponents had been well scouted and he had been carefully trained to beat them.

"He was good, believe me. How far he might

have gone on his own it is hard to say. He was
facing a bunch of boys who had learned their
fighting with busy trainers with little time to
spare for any one boy. His coaches had trained
the top professionals."

Marty had nothing more to say. He liked
Whiting too much to argue with him, and his own
knowledge of Hart was too limited to permit
discussion.

Looking over the valley his thoughts returned
to the present situation. "Nata," he asked
suddenly, "have you looked at the maps? The
government maps?"

"No. Not since we came into this wild
country."

"That river down there is the Ba. It is a big
river and it flows into the Yellow not far west
of here, but it isn't even on the map."

"Gunther has a map. Marty, you should see it.
I've no idea where he got it, but it is very old,
and very strange. He told me once that most of
the names on the government maps are simply the
names of monasteries or sometimes only of
temporary camps used by caravans."

"You've seen his map?"

"Not to examine it. It is like no map I ever
saw, even in a museum. Nobody else has seen it,
I'm sure. Unless it was Hank Carpenter."

"You can have him."

"Oh, he's all right, I guess. He's very
efficient."

The sky was a deep, impossible blue. They drew
up at the foot of the trail and waited for the
caravan to catch up. Aside from the yaks, horses

and sheep grazing on the meadow there was no evidence of life anywhere, and it was very still.

Now the sun touched only the high slopes of the mountains, for the valley was deep within the hills, and the day was drawing on.

"It has an eerie feeling," Renata said suddenly, "being so far from civilization. I wonder if anyone outside has any idea where we are?"

Marty shrugged his shoulders, then hunched them against a brief, chill wind. "If we do get into trouble there just isn't anything anyone outside can do. All the State Department could do would be to ask discreet questions. From all I hear even the authority of the Communists means little in some of these remote sections."

"There's nothing to worry about. Gunther has the connections to handle any sort of trouble, and Uncle Ralph and Dr. Penfield have friends everywhere."

Marty thought back to that first meeting with Gunther Hart at the Beverly Hills Hotel. The members of the expedition had been invited for a briefing, and it was a distinguished company.

Aside from Hank Carpenter, Hart's secretary, Marty knew none of them except by reputation.

Dr. Ralph Bernard, archaeologist, was a handsome, white-haired man of distinguished appearance, his skin darkened by the years of exposure to Middle Eastern suns where he had conducted digs or scouted areas for future investigation. He was the author of a half dozen books on those lesser known cultures fringing the Fertile Crescent.

Renata Bernard was his niece, with a growing

reputation as an anthropologist whose most important work had been a study of the Tochari tribesman.

Dr. Grant Penfield, accompanied by his wife, Mary, was a noted physician and surgeon. He had contributed time to the organization of a clinic for the Tibetan refugees at Mussoorie, and had organized medical research projects in Vietnam, Tanganyika and New Guinea.

Of Roy Lewis, geologist, Marty knew nothing beyond the fact that he had written a number of popular articles on earthquakes, had photographed some hitherto unknown ruins in Peru, and had conducted surveys for the government of the United States in various areas.

Others, not present at the briefing, had joined them en route.

At the briefing no time was allowed for getting acquainted. No sooner were they seated than Carpenter arrived and presented the details. Whatever else might be said, he kept the meeting moving. He presented a good deal of information . . . and deflected many questions.

He would personally handle all luggage except carry-on bags. He would handle passports, visas and clearances of all kinds. If there were complaints or discomforts all should be brought to him. Under no circumstances was Gunther Hart to be disturbed.

The briefing completed, Hank Carpenter stepped to one side and drew a curtain, revealing Gunther Hart, seated in profile, wearing the robes of a Buddhist monk.

They were allowed to study his profile in absolute silence for a long, long minute.

Undoubtedly, the profile was magnificent. Then
Carpenter spoke. "Sir? Do you have any comments
at this time?"

One might have counted a slow ten before Hart
turned to face them. He looked at them each in
turn.

"You will be granted," as he spoke he arose to
his full six feet and four inches, "every
facility for the work you wish to do. If there is
anything that would contribute to a better
completion of your work, please speak to Mr.
Carpenter.

"I have one small request. Interfere as little
as possible with those among whom we visit,
taking care not to offend their customs or
religious beliefs.

"Above all I must insist there be no
discussion of politics with the Chinese or other
peoples with whom we come in contact." He smiled
a warm, magnificent smile. "We must remember we
are guests in their country, and we must act as
we would wish them to act if they were guests in
our homes."

"One question, Mr. Hart," Dr. Penfield asked.
"We are entering a country that has recently been
not on the best of terms with ours and there have
been threats--"

"Have no fear, Doctor. None whatsoever. The
way has been cleared for us and every facility
will be granted.

"I would suggest," he addressed them all,
"that you dismiss from your minds all you have
heard of Red Chinese. You will find them warm and
friendly hosts. Much of what you have heard was
mere propaganda written by war-mongers.

"There are those who consider the Red Chinese as potential enemies. I cannot allow myself to be guided by such prejudices." He paused briefly. "Mr. Carpenter will provide you with mimeographed instructions. Among other things you will observe that all statements to the press, under whatever circumstances, are to be cleared with Mr. Carpenter, and he is to be present at all interviews. Any unauthorized statement will lead to immediate dismissal."

He took one step back, bowed slightly, and the curtain was redrawn.

Carpenter resumed his place before the curtain. "That will be all--thank you for coming. We shall meet again at the airport on the fifteenth. You may pick up your instruction folders at the door as you leave."

Marty recalled he had been amused by the so obviously stage-managed meeting, but whatever doubts he had were forgotten in preparations for the trip.

"What," Renata said suddenly, "are you thinking of?"

"Of that day in Beverly Hills when we first met Hart."

"When you first met him, you mean. I already knew him."

They started on. "I shouldn't be riding with you, Nata," he commented. "I don't think he likes it."

"Gunther? Don't be absurd."

"No . . . I mean it."

Suddenly, as if played on a tape, Whiting's warning sounded in his ears. "Above all, don't get in his way."

The man took himself very seriously, seriously
enough to think that the show he put on was
impressive rather than amusing. Back in
California, Marty had thought he was just an
eccentric but now, off all maps and on the other
side of the world, he was beginning to realize
that Gunther Hart was a dangerous narcissist.

CHAPTER 2

Mallory squatted on his heels beside the small
fire. Built beneath a huge, wide-branching
rhododendron, the rising smoke was thinned and
dissipated by the leaves and branches until
invisible but a few yards away.

He cupped a bowl of yak butter tea in his big
hands and listened to Gomba.

The sixty men of his command were scattered
along the side of a small ravine. All were hidden
from observation among the dense growth of trees
and shrubs.

"I do not know him. Obviously, he flees from
the Communists and from how he is treated it is
plain he is of great importance, an Incarnation,
I think. He has good men with him, but I am
afraid he will not escape."

"He is an old man?"

"A young man. He speaks your tongue, it is
said." Gomba spilled a little yak butter tea into
a bowl, added a double-handful of barley meal,
and mixed it slowly with his fingers. This was
tsamba, the staple diet of Tibet and the lands
adjoining. There had been a time when Mallory
doubted his ability to swallow another mouthful,

but he had come to like it as he did the yak
butter tea. A lot of habits can change in ten
years.

"They won't permit him to escape if it can be
helped," Mallory said. "There is too much unrest
as it is."

An Incarnation, such as this young lama
reportedly was, would be too important for the
Chinese to allow him to slip through their
fingers. To control him would enable them to
influence the Go-log, the Lolo, the Na-khi as
well as other minor tribes along the difficult
borderlands of Tibet, an area where the authority
of China had always been doubtful, under whatever
regime was in power.

"Do you think the Chinese will pursue him?"

"They will." He recalled the soldier they had
killed. "They may already be here."

Gomba waited, popping a ball of tsamba into
his mouth. Gomba had been a mere boy when Mallory
first came among them but he remembered Mallory's
father, too, and had seen the father win his way
from abject slavery to leadership among the Go-
log. Now he was curious, wondering what Mallory
would do about the Incarnation.

"We must help him," Mallory said at last,
"although it endangers our mission. Where is he
now?"

"Tonight he sleeps at the Inn of the Three
Hawks in the Valley of Pleasant Winds. The valley
lies before us." Gomba paused, then added, "His
strength among us is equal to the soldiers of ten
thousand tents."

It was very cold. While the others slept,
Mallory huddled over the fire considering the

possibilities, yet even as he weighed the reasons for and against siding with the Incarnation, his decision was a foregone conclusion.

The Go-log would say nothing, yet if he failed to attempt a rescue they would think the less of him. They would follow and obey, but he would have lost prestige among them. Besides that, his own inclinations were to aid the escaping lama.

Already he was out of Go-log country as such, moving into an area where they were both feared and hated. A war-like, raiding people who had changed little from the days of Genghis Khan, they lived by the sword, and their neighbors had suffered from that sword.

He had proposed the trip to India, hundreds of miles through some of the most forbidding terrain on earth, much of it, for safety's sake, over trails unused a century or more.

The Go-log had fought the Chinese since before the memory of man, and had held their homeland in the bend of the Yellow River inviolate. They were a nomadic people within their own vast area, but aside from their flocks their chief source of income as well as their greatest pleasure was in raiding caravans from China to Tibet. Now the Communist Chinese were determined, better armed, better led than before, and they planned to put an end to the independence of the mountain tribes.

Mallory argued the need for better rifles, grenades, mortars and machine guns. He argued that if he could talk to certain people in India he could arrange for periodic drops of medicine, weapons and ammunition. Reluctantly, they agreed. Their every instinct was to remain in their own country, trusting to no one but themselves. He had convinced these few otherwise. Now, to maintain that trust, he must risk everything in an attempt to save a man he had not seen, a man who meant nothing to him.

If he succeeded in reaching India he anticipated no such easy time as he had led the Go-log to believe. The government of India wanted no trouble, and contacting the proper officials of either the British or American governments would not be easy.

He was considered dead, as his father had been. They must search their records to prove he even existed, and that would take time.

Yet in the back of his mind was the thought: this was his chance to escape.

He owed these people nothing. He had come into their country of his own free will and had succeeded in staying with them partly because of his own strength and will to survive . . . and the reputation his father had won before his arrival.

Mallory had been nine years old when his father's plane crashed in China while flying the Hump from India. Two years later there had been a rumor that some American pilots might be held as slaves among the mountain tribes. The Army investigated and, years later, stated it was untrue, but by that time Mallory had been reading everything he could find about the borderlands of Tibet and decided there was no way the Army could have been sure of that in the time their investigation team was in the area . . . or the out-skirts of the area.

He had grown up on a ranch in Montana,

punching cows, hunting, and living a rugged
frontier life. His mother had died when he was
ten, and he had continued to live with an uncle,
and together they whiled away many hours studying
maps of China and speculating on his father's
chances of survival.

In the back of his mind there had always been
the thought: someday I shall go there. Someday I
shall find out for myself.

He had gone and he had found his father alive
and an important man among these people . . . but
since his father had died he had continually
thought of escape.

Once they arrived in India he would fulfill
his promise. He would obtain guns for them and
see them off for their homeland, but he would
then be free. He could return to the States.

The home of the nomads with whom he lived was
around a great mountain called Nyambo Yurtse,
20,000 or more feet in height, a lovely limestone
range, honeycombed with caves and with several
beautiful lakes fed by glacial waters.

For months following his capture by the Go-log
he had slowly but steadily won a place among
them, yet the event that finally freed him from
servitude and permitted him to ride among them as
a warrior might have turned out very differently.

From his boyhood he had known much about the
handling and treating of animals and the horses
he had ridden as a boy were bigger and fiercer
than these. First, he had captured their
admiration by riding an outlaw horse and next
when he repaired a broken rifle, then a captured
machine gun. But it was his single-handed taking

of a Chinese truck containing food, weapons and ammunition that really won him his place.

He had seen the truck veer sharply from the road and disappear into the hills while another tribe of the Go-log were attacking the convoy. Following it, he watched for his chance. He had thought of the truck as a means of escape, so he came from the rocks and offered to help the four Chinese get their truck out of the sand.

They agreed, and he over-heard one Chinese say, "Let him help. Then kill him."

Which left him simply no choice at all.

The officer was in the cab with the driver. One man was behind the truck with Mallory, pushing. Another was on the far side. As the wheels dug in and began to spin Mallory slipped an arm beneath the chin of the man beside him, and strangled him.

When the truck failed to move, the man at the side came around behind and Mallory met him with a bayonet in the stomach. The man screamed, and the officer and driver leaped from the truck. Mallory was ready, and shot first.

Using their coats and some brush for traction, Mallory jockeyed the truck out of its hole and drove it across country and hid it among the rocks. Armed with a .45 Colt and a Russian sub-machine gun he returned to the Go-log to bargain.

He made his point, but among the fighting, brawling Go-log one victory was not an end. He had three brutal fights before he was at last accepted as one of them. It was only then that he learned that his father was alive, with another band.

Now, while the others slept, he traced their

route in the sand and studied it. He was uneasy about their proximity to the Inn of the Three Hawks. Their safety lay in the fact that their presence was unknown, and Mallory hoped to keep it so.

The man responsible was old Shi-lo. In his younger years Shi-lo had been a trader, living his life along obscure trails from the Tarim Basin to Choni, from Choni to Darjeeling, from Darjeeling to Mount Kailas and Leh. It was his knowledge of the ancient trade routes that enabled them to slip across the country like ghosts.

Yet there had been accidents. A few days earlier, crossing the headwaters of a river, they had come upon a Chinese patrol. Challenged, Mallory had attacked immediately, and the Go-log, always ready to fight, had cut down the patrol to the last man.

The attack had been sudden, totally unexpected, and the Go-log had suffered only a few minor wounds. The bodies of the dead were dumped into the river after being relieved of their weapons, ammunition and food supplies.

Of course, the disappearance of the patrol would bring about an investigation. Forty men do not easily vanish from the earth and no doubt some of the bodies would be found down-stream. Twice, in the days following the battle, planes were observed circling above the country, but each time the sound of their motors warned the Go-log and they were swiftly under cover.

Mallory had taken time to eliminate what tracks they had left, yet now they were nearing the Inn of the Three Hawks and there was no possible way to avoid passing through the valley unless some secret trail could be found along the ridges above the timberline.

Assigning some men to this task, Mallory decided he would take seven men and visit the Inn. If the Incarnation was there, as rumor had it, they would offer him their protection and aid in escaping to India.

Mallory got to his feet. India! And after India, Paris, London, and New York! Baseball, movies, the bars, the restaurants . . . ten years was a long time to be away, and aside from the fifty thousand dollars in gold he carried for the Go-log, he carried evidence of his father's death and the twenty-odd years of back-pay that would be forth-coming.

His excitement was touched with an odd reluctance to think of it. He would be going home to his country, but to nothing else. His uncle had died long ago, his brother Tom had been killed in Korea.

The Go-log had no doubt he was returning with them. That could mean trouble. He liked these people—his life among them had been like an exotic dream, occasionally a nightmare—but it was time to go. Whether they would understand or not he did not know, but once they were in his world he had no doubt he could get away.

After the tents were pitched on level grass near the Inn, Renata went inside the largest and set up her uncle's portable desk. Dr. Bernard had strolled away toward the head of the valley to examine the step-like road.

Her conversation with Marty had brought into focus her own doubts. They had been there from the beginning, yet why should she be uneasy?

Gunther Hart was a striking figure, with a smile he knew how to use, although he used it rarely. A romantic part of her wanted to attribute his aloofness to an innate shyness and reserve. The theatricality was something else, something she didn't have an answer for.

Straightening from the desk she looked off toward the Inn. Something about what she had just been thinking bothered her. "A smile he knew how to use." Was that it? That he used his smile instead of smiling because he felt like it.

She had gone out with him but three times before the expedition, and everywhere they were received with flattering deference. Gunther had few friends and no intimates and by the third date she began to see how completely he was insulated from all outside contact. Sometimes she thought it was sad but it worried her that he might actually like it that way. Certainly, no one else thought anything about the multi-millionaire was sad . . . in fact some of the scientists thought he was a pretentious ass. Well, she had lived among scientists and academics her whole life and she knew it took one to know one.

Stepping outside she breathed deeply of the cool mountain air. Beyond the gorge the mountain dropped so steeply from enormous heights that it seemed impossible anything could grow there, yet the entire face was covered with the deep green of forest.

Roy Lewis strolled over, taking out his pipe.

"Gorgeous country. When I was a youngster I used to dream about Tibet, but never imagined it like this. Everything a man reads makes it out to be a cold, windy country, all high plateau, mountains and yaks."

"Pen says much of it is that way. He's learned a lot from treating his patients at Mussoorie."

Lewis was a well set-up man in his late thirties, with an open, pleasant face. "Let's walk over to the Inn? I'd like to see what it's like inside."

She glanced around. "Where is Mr. Hart? He might like to go with us."

"He's meditating. I spoke to Carpenter, but he just said 'The Master does not wish to be disturbed.' So I came away."

She glanced at him to see if any sarcasm was implied, but Lewis' features were innocent. "Let's go then," she suggested.

They crossed the spongy grass to the gate, which stood open, and for the first time she saw it was crowded with the horses and yaks of a caravan, as well as packs of goods and equipment. Lewis paused, striking a match to light his pipe, taking the moment to study the packs.

"Looks like company," he commented. "Somebody from up country."

"They might be going in, as we are."

"No. Those packs aren't from the outside. I am sure of that."

As they crossed the courtyard two wild-looking men emerged from the Inn. Both were armed. They glared and lifted their rifles threateningly.

Lewis stopped and took the pipe from his teeth. He smiled, but he lifted the hand holding

the pipe and gently tried to push the muzzle of
the rifle to one side. "It's all right," he said,
"we're just going inside to look around."

A voice spoke from within and the rifles were
lowered. Then in English the voice said, "Please
to enter. I am regretting my soldiers."

The room was shadowed and still, the only
light that which filtered through the open door
and the reddish glow from a charcoal brazier. On
the k'ang, cross-legged, sat a slim young man
with a pleasant Asiatic face.

"Come in. Please do. I am Lagskha-tsang."

"Miss Renata Bernard," Lewis said, "and I am
Roy Lewis. We are with the Gunther Hart
Expedition."

"You are British?"

"American," Lewis said. "Our mission is
scientific."

"It is so? Forgive me. I did not think to see
Americans in my country. It is an awkward time."

"Gunther Hart is a friend of Chou En-lai,"
Lewis explained, and then added, "Miss Bernard is
an anthropologist. I am a geologist."

"Ah?" He indicated they should be seated. "I
regret I cannot invite. I am traveling now. My
position is no longer official." He hesitated.
"Many things have been changed in my country."

He was wary, Renata thought, and since the
mention of Chou En-lai's name, a little less than
warm.

"My uncle hopes to examine some of the ancient
sites," Renata said. "He is an archaeologist."

"We find few archaeologists in Tibet. I
believe they think my country too young." He
glanced from Lewis to Renata. "It is very old, my

country. Particularly the part in which we now
are."

He looked thoughtfully at Renata. "Your uncle
is Bernard also? He is distinguished man."

"You know of him?"

"I see American journal." He smiled suddenly.
"Very strange. You come to my country, I go to
yours."

"You are going to America?" She was surprised.

"I think yes. I like very much American music.
I like American film."

Roy Lewis chuckled, and at Renata's glance he
explained, "I was thinking of Hart. He despises
American films and music, and the first lama with
whom we come in contact likes them."

"You like films?"

"Very much. I am a regular fan."

"Fan? What is it . . . a fan? Is it not to
brush air?"

"We use it in another sense as well, as
someone who is very appreciative, and who knows a
lot about the subject . . . movies, jazz music,
rock and roll, baseball . . . whatever it happens
to be."

"Good!" His grin was boyish and friendly. "I
will be fan."

"You will have to talk to Marty. He knows more
about films and music than any of us."

"He is with you also?"

"He is our expert on botany. He will be
looking for useful herbs."

"Good! He will inform me of music and films, I
will tell him of plants. It is my education to
know such things."

He sat silent as a servant brought beautifully carved bowls of yak butter tea.

"This Gunther Hart. He is a Communist?"

"Gunther?" Renata asked. "I think it is unlikely though he may admire their goals. He is a very wealthy man--wealthy men are rarely Communists."

"So? It is different in America, then. In China some wealthy men become Communist to protect riches or power. They think to do so."

"Gunther Hart," Renata explained seriously, "is a very gentle man. He is a Buddhist. At least, he follows the teachings of Buddha. To him this is a sacred pilgrimage. He comes to learn, to visit the shrines. He wishes to visit Mount Kailas and Lake Mansorovar."

"These are sacred places. Much respected. Forgive me. I did not know there were Buddhists in your country."

"There are few, I'm afraid," Lewis said, "although there would be more if they understood what Buddha taught. I know very little, but I hope to learn more."

"Is it a good time to come?" Lagskha inquired. "I think there is much unrest."

"Gunther . . . Mr. Hart," Renata said, "wished to come now. He . . . he is not a man to wait. He is impatient, sometimes."

"I should like to meet this man. This impatient Buddhist."

"We were fortunate to get the opportunity to visit your country," Lewis said. "Hart is the man who has made it possible."

"Yes, you are right. Who can know? The chance may not come again." He smiled gently. "The

Peking government does not accept me into its
confidences."

There was a stir behind them, and Gunther Hart
spoke, his tone deeply reverent. "Greetings. I
hope my people have not disturbed you, Master."

CHAPTER 3

Lagskha's face was innocent of expression. "It
is to my pleasure. I have much to learn."

"So have we all," Hart replied. "I come to
your land a pilgrim, seeking truth."

"The truth you seek lies within you."

Hart inclined his head. "I seek a guru,
Master. I seek one to lead me upon the Eight-Fold
Path."

Lagskha's eyes were shadowed and his
expression unreadable. "My land is no longer
free, Mr. Hart. You might with better success go
to India." His tone was edged with bitterness.
"Our great teachers do forced labor on the roads,
and many die. Often they are old men, unsuited to
such labor."

"I am sure," Hart replied smoothly, "the
Chinese will do what is possible to preserve the
ancient beliefs."

There was a moment of silence, and then
Lagskha said, "Your journey to my land will no
doubt prove informative."

He turned to Renata then, ignoring Hart. "Some
of my family have been fortunate. My sister, whom
you shall meet, has spent much time in Paris,
London and New York. She had sent me many films
of your country, and much music."

"Your sister is with you?"

"I am here."

She stood in the doorway, a slender, graceful girl, eyes slightly oblique, skin a pale ivory, her face delicately but beautifully boned. Renata Bernard, who had been called a beautiful woman by many, felt suddenly awkward and plain.

She stepped into the room. "How do you do? Miss Bernard, I have read your paper on the Tochari. They are ancestors of ours . . . in part. It was very well done."

Turning her head she measured Hart with a glance. "I am afraid my brother is much too polite, Mr. Hart. You will find little of what you seek, and I know what you seek. The only teachers who might instruct you in the Tantric learning are hidden far back in the mountains where we hope they will not be found."

"If you could tell me where I might find them . . ."

Her smile was brief and cool. "I would tell you nothing. I am afraid those who arranged your visit here are not among those we can trust."

"You are abrupt," Gunther Hart said politely, "and mistaken. I am not what you would term political. The affairs of the world about us are temporary, transitory things. All this will pass. The eternal truths will remain."

"Nevertheless, this is a world many must live in. Your very presence in this part of China implies the permission of the Chinese government and permission implies recognition or friendship and that implies you are an enemy of our people."

She paused, ever so briefly. "If you will recall, Mr. Hart, our land was occupied by force of arms. Our leaders must flee or be used by those who have occupied our country. I am afraid you will find me neither a forgiving nor a tolerant person."

"If I am to incur dislike," Hart replied gently, "I should prefer it to be by a woman as lovely as yourself. At least, you are not indifferent."

"You are mistaken, Mr. Hart. I am completely indifferent!"

His face stiffened a little, but he turned to Lagskha and bowed. "If there is any way in which we may be of service, feel free to call upon me or any of my people."

Hank Carpenter appeared in the back of the room. "Sir? There's a party coming down the trail. I don't like their looks."

The sister of the Incarnation moved swiftly to the door. She shaded her eyes, looking toward the mountains.

"Who are they?" Carpenter's voice was sharp.

"No reason to get the wind up," Lewis prodded, "they are probably just bandits."

The Incarnation's sister spoke quietly. "I would suggest you be very, very careful. I have no idea how they come to be in this place, but those men are Go-logs."

"What?" Hart's tone was high. "What did you call them?"

"Go-logs." There was a kind of triumph in her voice. "And they are savage, completely without mercy. They come from the big bend of the Yellow River and are nomadic herdsmen and yes, they are often bandits."

"What are they doing here?"

"That," she admitted, "is a very good question. They are farther from home than ever before."

"How can it be that I have never heard of these . . . these Go-logs, as you call them?" Hart inquired.

"A question I cannot answer, but there are people in both Tibet and China who have never heard of them. They've lived off the beaten tracks of history and they prefer it so. They permit no travel through their country, and when China has sent armies they either found no one or were sent back bloody and beaten."

Lewis touched Renata's arm. "Nata! The man on the black horse! I'd swear he was a white man!"

Mallory drew up some hundred feet off, and instantly three men broke away on either side to ride around the Inn and make sure there was no ambush. He was, however, expecting no trouble. The Inn had been watched for several hours.

Two parties were in residence. The Incarnation had but six Khambas as escort, and two dozen others handling the yak train. Of the Gunther Hart Expedition he knew nothing, but there were several women along and they did not at all resemble an armed party.

"Gomba," Mallory said, "my compliments to Lagskha-tsang and request permission to approach him."

Gunther Hart stepped out, a tall, arresting figure.

"How do you do? Do you speak English?"

Mallory swung down. "I speak American, if you

call it English. You picked a lousy time to come into this country."

The sister of the Incarnation spoke from the gateway, using the Lolo dialect. "I am Brikhuti, the sister of the Lagskha-tsang. Be careful of what you say. I do not trust this man."

Mallory looked at her again, feeling a flush of warmth at the very sight of her. "I know who you are. Tell your brother we are going his way. I will gladly escort him . . . and my people wish it."

"Thank you. I shall speak to him." She hesitated an instant. "Major Mallory, whether you realize it or not, you have become a famous man."

Mallory started for the gate, rifle in hand. Hart spoke, his tone brusque. "Look here, my man. I asked you a question."

"And I answered it. What more do you want?"

"I want to know who you are, and just what you are doing here. I know of no one . . . no one, you understand . . . who has permission to be in this area."

Mallory merely looked at him. "Looks to me like you missed something somewhere. If you don't know about me maybe I'm not even here, so forget about it. You ignore me and I'll be glad to ignore you."

His riders dismounting, he strode into the Inn. Roy Lewis looked after him, his eyes alive with curiosity.

There was no nonsense about the Go-log. One rider raced off in the direction from which they had come, another toward the road up which the expedition had marched. The others dismounted,

several taking the horses to water, the others
clustering about the gate.

Gunther Hart had not moved. Then he started
after Mallory, his face flushed and angry. He
motioned to Carpenter. "Hank, I want to know who
that man is and all about him. I want to know at
once, do you hear?"

"Yes, sir. At once." Carpenter hurried away
and Hart turned sharply away and walked to his
tent.

"Well," Lewis commented mildly, "he could've
asked me."

"Do you know who he is? How could you?" Renata
said.

"When Hart gave me the chance to come with him
I went to the library and read everything I could
find. There's a lot published in magazines and
newspapers that never got into the books."

"During World War Two a number of flyers were
reported to have crash-landed while flying the
Hump. Some were reported held as slaves by
various peoples that border on Tibet.

"About ten years ago there was an article
about a young fellow who went back in here
looking for his father. He never came out. He
served in Korea and then was among the first
advisers sent to Vietnam."

"You believe he is that man?"

"Who else?"

"He rides well," Renata admitted.

Mallory paused inside the door to let his eyes
grow accustomed to the deeper shadow within.
Outside the last of the light was fading and the

stars were out. Brikhuti came up beside him.
"Major Mallory, we believe Marshal Chu is not far
behind us."

"We killed a Red soldier up yonder. He could
have been one of Marshal Chu's men."

He indicated the courtyard. "What about them?"

"The tall man is Gunther Hart. He is the
leader of a scientific expedition. I know some of
the people by reputation and they are well-
established in their fields. Dr. Penfield has
done a great deal of work among the Tibetan
refugees, so we have a particular interest in
him.

"Hart is very wealthy and he is used to
getting what he wants. The geologist said Hart
was a personal friend of Chou En-lai." Her
fingers touched his sleeve. "Major, we need help.
Help to get my brother out of this country."

"That's what we came for. The Go-log have
great respect for him, and that's saying a lot.
I'll do whatever I can, but that means we haven't
much time. We've got to get out before Chu's men
get here. And soft pedal that 'Major' bit. I'm no
major and never have been."

"That's what they call you."

"Forget it."

"The trail is open . . . the Americans came in
over it."

"No good. They'll have planes scouting that
trail." He looked down at her. "Ma'am, I've got
to see your brother."

The k'ang was empty. Brikhuti disappeared up
the stairs, returning after a moment. "He is
meditating and we cannot disturb him."

"All right. Be sure that your people eat

something, and without making any fuss, have them ready to pull out."

"I never thought to see a foreigner win a place among the Go-log," she said. "They are a difficult people."

"I like them."

He seated himself on the k'ang. He had some meditating of his own to do. He had learned much since coming to the borderlands of Tibet, and one was to exclude all else from his mind but the problem at hand, and he did that now.

He and the men with him had slipped through the country unobserved until now, but their efforts were to be rendered useless by this American expedition, whose people would surely talk.

The trail up which Gunther Hart had brought the expedition was out of the question. It was vulnerable to attacking aircraft, offering no concealment. They must continue along the ancient tracks, even if it meant rebuilding them in places.

In recent years most travel was by well-known routes, and many of the old ways had been left out of use. At the end that might lead him through Bhutan or Nepal, and neither country was eager to incur the displeasure of the Chinese.

One by one he examined the possibilities, and one by one he tested the problems offered by each. He avoided no issues, thinking ruthlessly, favoring no idea, allowing himself to be convinced by none of them until he had studied their every aspect.

A trail must be found, and they must move by

daylight, if at all possible. Every instant of
delay brought added danger.

Renata and Dr. Bernard entered the room.
Renata glanced at Mallory, then said, "If I were
you I'd not make an enemy of Mr. Hart--he might
be of help to you."

"We do not need his help."

"He has great influence."

"Obviously."

Renata flushed at his sarcasm but Dr. Bernard
said, "If you have the time I would enjoy
discussing the Go-log country, and the country
you crossed in getting here."

"It's rugged." He paused. "I wish, Doctor, you
could have the time and the opportunity to
investigate the situation here. The country we
passed over shows indication of very ancient
habitation.

"There are caves in the mountains of the Go-
log country where grain has been stored from very
ancient times. I have seen characters carved in
rock, almost obliterated by time, and these are
often in sheltered areas."

"That is very interesting. I have suspected
something of the kind."

"What are your plans now?" Renata interrupted.

"To get away from here before your friends
close in on us."

Renata stifled her anger. "If you refer to the
Red Chinese as my friends, I suppose you are
right. They have done nothing to cause me to
regard them as enemies."

"Not being a Tibetan, I suppose that may be
true. You must forgive them if their reactions
are somewhat different. After all, they have been

a peace-loving people for more than a thousand
years and did not wish to be invaded."

"This lama is making a mistake. He should
remain with his people."

"His people," Mallory replied brusquely, "have
been forced into a way of life they did not want.
They have been killed, enslaved or have escaped
into the mountains to fight. The Incarnation of
whom you speak will be of much more use to his
people on the outside. Here he would be held in
restraint, bulletins would be issued in his name,
and he would become a puppet of a regime he does
not admire."

"I cannot accept that," Bernard replied.

"Nobody asked you to. A question was made and
replied to. You can believe whatever you damn
please."

Renata was furious. "You are not polite."

Mallory smiled without humor. "It is simply
that I have a quaint, old-fashioned idea that a
people should be allowed to choose their own
government, and to make their reforms in their
own time, in their own way."

"You do not believe that China can help?"

"If you were a Tibetan at this moment, Doctor,
you would either have become a mouthpiece for
Chinese policy or you would be doing hand-labor
on the roads, working in all kinds of weather,
regardless of your age or health.

"China can best help Tibet by leaving it
alone. I have every respect for the Chinese but
they have problems enough in their own country."

"You do not deny they have made great
strides?"

"Compared to the period before World War Two?

Absolutely. Almost anything would be better than that sort of anarchy, communism included. When several hundred million people are organized into labor units they can accomplish a great deal, even if enthusiasm is lacking. That is their business and I wish them luck. However, Tibet did not have the same problems and I know few Tibetans who would choose to be like China, let alone be a part of it.

"Make no mistake. The Chinese are an energetic people, a great people. No man on earth admires them more than I. But their present methods I admire not at all."

"Perhaps it is as well that you are leaving," Renata said, coolly.

Roy Lewis had come into the room with Marty Wells. Both sat on a corner of the k'ang, listening without comment.

Mallory glanced at them. "Either of you guys a baseball fan?"

"I'm a Dodger fan myself," Lewis said, "but since Koufax quit we haven't had much to yell about."

"I've had a short-wave radio," Mallory explained, "but the only baseball news we got was an occasional Armed Services broadcast from Vietnam. Most of what we picked up was from China, India or Japan."

Mallory glanced at Renata. She was a damned pretty girl. Too bad they'd gotten off on the wrong foot. It was almost like old times to see an American girl. He'd lost touch with women and how to converse with them, and he wished these people would stop talking to him and talk among themselves. He could learn more that way. He

found himself grasping for words . . . his
English had grown weak over the years.

He had a few books and he often read aloud
just to hear the English words. The Go-log
respected that, oddly enough. They believed he
was making magic. Only priests read, so far as
they knew.

Gomba entered and whispered to Mallory.
Mallory glanced over at Bernard. "Take a tip from
me and get back down that trail fast. The Red
Army has sent a detachment after the
Incarnation."

"I am sorry for him," Bernard replied, "but
that cannot affect us."

Mallory shrugged. "Better tell Hart, anyway.
It's your funeral."

"You don't seem to understand," Renata said.
"We have personal letters from Chou En-lai."

"Bully for you," Mallory said dryly, "and
where is Chou En-lai?"

"In Peking, I expect."

"Exactly . . . and he might as well be on the
moon. If anything happens to you up here nobody
would ever know or care. When you're in this
country you're clean off the map."

Mallory walked out and stood for a moment in
the gateway. Too many memories were aroused by
hearing their voices and he was uneasy. A
premonition of danger? He had learned, like a
wild animal, to trust his instincts.

His countrymen were fools to come here at such
a time. Command decisions were made here, not
Peking. Marshal Chu was a soldier first, a

Communist second. He would do what was necessary
to survive and prosper politically, and whoever
or whatever got in the way would be brushed
aside.

Mallory considered the situation. His
knowledge of trails across Tibet was limited, and
so far he had gone by what he had picked up and
by what Shi-lo had told him. Lagskha might know
more. His ties with the old Bon religion were as
close as with Buddhism. He was an Incarnation and
few secrets would have been kept from him . . .
if he had ever found reason to inquire.

Mallory's father had told him over a campfire,
when they had one of their few times alone, about
the old monastery and about the secret trail, an
ancient trail used by Bon monks in traveling to
Kashmir and India before the time of Buddha.

Ten years of discreet inquiries had brought
him little knowledge. Some said the trail had not
been traveled since used by Kesar of Ling, the
great Tibetan folk hero. Padma Sambhava and
Sambhota were said to have traveled it in coming
to Tibet from Nalanda.

Rumor had it that the trail was beset with
traps for the unwary, and that it was a way known
only to the Bon priests. Mallory discounted much
of this, but over the years many trails had been
abandoned due to slides, changing river courses
and other reasons.

Yet legend said there was a trail, and if
Mallory had learned one thing in his life it was
that most legends contained a core of truth.

He must talk to Lagskha, and to Brikhuti.

There was no time to be wasted.

CHAPTER 4

Cook fires blazed at the two camps, the camp
of the expedition and the smaller camp of the Go-
logs. No light showed from the Inn, squatting as
it did behind its palisade.

Brikhuti crossed the grass to the Go-log camp.
"Mallory, I must talk to you."

He stood up. The Go-log looked at her, their
cold faces showing nothing. "I was coming to see
you, and your brother."

"The geologist . . . Mr. Lewis . . . told me
you had some word of the Chinese."

"They are near. I'm afraid whatever is done we
must do quickly. We should leave before
daylight . . . if possible."

"We will do it." She looked at him. "You do
not need to help us."

"Six Khambas? They are good men, but not
enough. I can help your brother, but I need help
also. That trail," he indicated the way the
expedition had come, "is a death-trap for either
of us, but there is another."

"I know of none."

"I was hoping your brother did. I know a
little, but not enough. It is an ancient trail,
no longer used."

"I suppose there are old trails," she was
dubious, "but my brother is not widely traveled.
I am not sure he would know much."

"This one he might know."

She looked at him suddenly. "But that's just a
legend! That is, if you are thinking of the one I
am. You mean Kesar's route."

"It has sometimes been called that."

"I don't know. I don't believe he knows anything about it." She accepted a bowl of tea from one of the Go-logs. "You say you do?"

"I know where it begins. I know a little of the way it follows, but there are said to be traps, places one cannot pass."

"I will ask him."

"I had heard Lagskha had a sister who lived in Europe. It was you?"

"Yes. My father wanted his children to study there as well as at home. He saw conditions were changing, and he wished us to be prepared, yet I was the only one who had the chance to go. I am afraid I was gone too long. I am more of a European now."

"Your name is a famous one."

She was surprised. "You know our history?"

"I remember Brikhuti was the Nepalese wife of the king who brought Buddhism to Tibet."

"He had two wives. The other was Chinese and also a Buddhist." She looked at him curiously. "Do you miss your own country? All this is so different, so strange to you."

He shrugged. "I don't know, really. I have no idea what I'd be doing if I was back in the States. Ranching, I expect. I hadn't made up my mind when I went into the Army, and of course there was always that obsession to find out what happened to my father. I was afraid I'd find him somewhere, crippled and helpless."

"But you did not."

"No, he'd made a place for himself with the Go-log. God knows what he must have gone through first."

"But you went through it also?"

"Some. They knew I was the son of my father long before they let me know he was alive."

"I liked the West . . . loved it. Capri, St. Tropez, Deauville, Cannes, Paris, Acapulco, Mexico City, New York . . . it was exciting at first, but there was always so much to learn, and it was so . . . different."

"I knew nothing of such places. I ran a trap-line from the time I was ten. I punched cows and I went to school."

"You can go home now. When you get to India, what is to prevent you?"

"Nothing . . . I hope. But I've come to love this country. There's so much of it unknown to the world outside. There's been a few plant-hunters in here, but not many. I hear the Lolo country is lovely, too. There's a valley over near the Min-shan somewhere, it's called Choni . . . I hear it is close to paradise."

She gestured toward the tents of the expedition. "What do you think will happen to them?"

"Who knows."

"They have faith in Gunther Hart," she commented.

"He'd better live up to it," Mallory said grimly.

They walked back to the courtyard. Large as it was, it was crowded now. The yaks lay with hoofs doubled under calmly chewing their cuds. The only brightness came from a little thread of light around the door.

Lagskha was seated on the k'ang in the lotus position when Mallory entered. Facing him from a

dozen feet away in Buddhist robes was Gunther
Hart. The others from the expedition were
gathered around.

Mallory and Brikhuti entered. Renata glanced
at them, then away. They seated themselves just
as Hank Carpenter entered. Mallory noticed
that . . . where had he been? At the tents?
Mallory had seen nothing of him as they passed.

"If you wish," Hart was saying, "you may come
with us, under our protection, but I am sure your
fears are without foundation. The leaders of the
new China would welcome you among them."

"I am sure they would," Lagskha quipped.

"And you would be assured of your position,"
Hart added.

"It is not my position that disturbs me, Mr.
Hart. It is the position of my people."

"I believe your fears to be without base.
These men are striving to rule China with science
and intellect, the best choices made by experts
for the benefit of all. Naturally, there will
have to be some reorganization at the labor
source, but your religion will remain
undisturbed. Chou En-lai himself assured me of
it. After all," he added, "I am a practicing
Buddhist."

There was a very long moment of silence during
which Hart's ears began to grow pink.

Dr. Penfield broke the silence. "I have heard
stories about you but know little for certain. Do
you come from Lhasa?"

"I was there briefly, Doctor, as a very small
boy. I know of your work at Mussoorie, and am
deeply grateful. My people are lonely, Doctor,
and they know not which way to turn. Their homes

are gone, their herds are taken and their temples have been bombed."

"Come with us," Hart insisted. "Then if you wish to leave, I will arrange it."

"You are confident," Lagskha murmured.

"Mr. Hart," Brikhuti interrupted, "you do not know what you suggest. If he went to Lhasa he would be imprisoned or killed . . . or held in what is termed 'protective restraint.'"

"You need not be alarmed. If you are under my protection no harm will come to you."

Mallory put down his bowl. "That," he said emphatically, "is a lot of damned nonsense."

There was a startled, unbelieving silence. Before Hart could respond, Hank Carpenter leaped to his feet. "You will apologize to Mr. Hart, or leave the room."

Mallory ignored him, taking up his bowl and sipping tea as if Carpenter had not spoken. Carpenter gestured, and on the far side of the Inn a huge man got to his feet. "I said," Carpenter repeated, "you will apologize or leave the Inn."

"Oh, sit down!" Mallory said tiredly. "If you don't like my being here you're free to leave. Hart was talking of something he doesn't know the least bit about. Obviously, he is accustomed to having his wishes respected. He had better begin to realize he is a long way from home. In a democracy people might listen; here they do not."

"You do not understand," Dr. Penfield said. "Gunther Hart has a clearance from Chou En-lai. You may be sure his wishes will be respected."

"Not by me," Mallory replied cheerfully, "or by anyone unless it suits their purpose. You've much to learn, gentlemen, and what happens in these mountains need never be heard of outside them. All your influence isn't worth a plugged nickel unless the officer in command is amused by it.

"Chou is a very competent man, and has a greater understanding of world power relationships than any of the others. But he and Mao have a . . ." American English was coming back to Mallory. ". . . a 'good cop, bad cop' routine going. And when they are not busy playing their power games, he's as worried about getting stabbed in the back as anyone.

"I also know a good bit about Marshal Chu, who is in command in this area. He is a tough, competent soldier, a military man first, last, and always. No matter what regime is in power, Marshal Chu will be listened to and respected. His mission is to bring this area under control. For that he needs the Incarnation under his control so he can issue orders in his name. The Dalai Lama got away and they'll be damned if they let it happen again!

"Anybody who creates trouble will likely be killed, and if it happens to be your expedition he will simply eliminate all of you, report you had been killed by bandits or wiped out by an avalanche, and who is to say he is wrong?"

Carpenter faced Mallory. "You have one minute to apologize or leave the Inn. If you do not you will be thrown out bodily."

There was a murmur of protest, but Mallory merely smiled. "You wouldn't try that yourself, would you?"

"I wouldn't soil my hands." Carpenter stepped

aside, gesturing to the big man who had come up
behind him. "He will do it for me."

Pulaski had been a professional football
player until recruited by Gunther Hart. He
weighed in at two hundred and sixty pounds, in
condition.

Mallory ignored him. "I was under the
impression you good people did not believe in
violence. Particularly Mr. Hart, who is a
practicing Buddhist. Can I be mistaken?"

"You are not mistaken." Hart spoke sharply.
"Hank, tell Pulaski to remain where he is."

"Don't disturb yourself." Mallory had not even
looked up. "He isn't going anywhere."

Pulaski was standing rock-still, his face an
ugly white. Three Go-log stood around him, sword-
points denting his flesh.

"The Go-log," Mallory explained, "pride
themselves on disemboweling a man with one twist
of the blade. Pulaski is in an excellent position
to put the matter to a test."

Mallory lifted his bowl again. Hart had made
no move to stop Pulaski until it was obvious the
big man would have been killed had he moved. Was
the delay deliberate? Or had Hart been distracted
by their argument?

"Mr. Hart's protection means nothing at all
here," Mallory continued calmly. "Administration
is at the field level, in the hands of field
officers. Whatever report Chu turns in will be
accepted in Peking."

"You under-estimate me," Hart said mildly.

"Actually, I am not concerned with you.
Anybody fool enough to come _into_ this country at
this time cannot concern me. However, Lagskha-

tsang and his people want to get <u>out</u> and so do we. If he wishes, he may accompany me."

"He will, of course, do as he wishes," Hart replied. "I want nothing but his safety and happiness."

Mallory was tired, tired as a man can be. For days they had followed dim trails through the roughest country on earth, traveling often by night and in the worst possible weather, yet they must move on at once. He had an uneasy feeling, a premonition of trouble.

Carpenter worried him. The man was cool and efficient. Admittedly, he was secretary to a man of power and influence, but there was still something more. Gunther Hart might be guilty of fuzzy thinking. Hank Carpenter would not.

He got up, took his bowl of tea and walked outside. To the Go-log on guard he said, "There may be trouble."

"The more who come," the Go-log said, "the more we will kill. Let them come."

He handed the bowl to the guard. "I will ride now."

"A horse stands ready."

Mallory gathered the reins and stepped into the saddle. He turned toward the upper end of the valley to check the guard there. He had an instinct for the night, and knew that in these gorges there could be no movement without sound. He drew up, hearing a rider coming up behind him. It was Renata Bernard.

"Do you mind? I wanted to ride."

"If you wish."

They rode on in silence, and after a bit she said, "You talk very little."

"I have lived with the Go-log. They speak when there is something to say."

"That would be dull. Don't they ever talk for fun? I love to talk, and to listen to people who talk well."

He offered no comment, but she persisted. "You could be more diplomatic, you know. After all, why antagonize a man like Hart?"

"I don't trust him. He's a poseur and I think he's going to get you and maybe me in trouble."

Renata rode on in silence. She wanted to retort, but was bothered by the similarity of Mallory's comment to that Marty Wells reported made by Dr. Milne Whiting.

"He has his own way of doing things, I expect. He is a multi-millionaire and has always been wealthy."

"That explains a lot but excuses nothing. In any event he's not a topic I would choose on a night ride with a pretty girl."

"I wasn't aware you'd noticed."

"It's obvious, isn't it? Not that it matters, because you are riding into Tibet and I am riding out. If I decide to return there's small chance of our meeting, even if you are alive."

"You're not very cheerful."

"Only honest . . . and if I come back I'll be fighting, helping the Go-log or somebody."

"Is that all you think of? Fighting is brutal, disgusting, and cruel. I should think a man of your intelligence--"

"Don't give me that. You've no idea whether I am intelligent or not. Fighting is all the things you say, yet the world isn't going to change . . . or stay the same because some

professor wrote a critical essay. Would you even
want to live in a world where people believed in
things so . . . lightly that they wouldn't risk
everything for what they cared about? You
couldn't talk freely if men hadn't bought the
right with blood and death. They can't do that
here . . . not even someone like your Mr. Chou
En-lai."

"Gunther Hart doesn't believe that way;
neither does Dr. Penfield or my uncle." After a
moment, she added, "Neither did Mahatma Gandhi."

Mallory snorted. "The Mahatma used violence
more intelligently than any man in history, he
just used it on himself. The British, who for all
their faults have an ingrained decency, couldn't
take it. He confronted them with their own
hypocrisy and they blinked. More power to him.

"Had he been non-violent against the Nazis,
the Imperial Japanese, or any one of fifty
governments of the time or of now they would
simply have shot him or thrown him into prison
and he wouldn't have lasted long enough to be
known to anybody but his mother. I'll bet this
country has seen fifty Gandhis in the last fifty
years and none of them lasted long enough to
speak out more than twice!"

"I believe Mahatma Gandhi was a great man,"
she insisted.

"So do I. I merely maintain that he was
fortunate to live and protest in a country, and
against an empire, that would listen to protest,
and where there were enough people willing to
hold back those who wouldn't.

"Just be careful. The only thing between you

and disaster is good fortune and whatever flimsy
influence Hart is supposed to have."

"I have seen what his influence can do, Mr.
Mallory," she said stiffly.

"Just remember, his influence is in banks, in
trust funds, in stocks or real estate, and all
that is far away. Little of it could even be used
if it was here . . . we are in the feudal
borderlands of a Communist country. You can still
buy influence but you have to do it with what you
have today . . . they don't take checks. If you
want to impress them you have to talk in terms of
gold or yaks or horses or sheep, or the number of
rifles at your command."

"You believe we really are in danger?"

"In danger? Right now I'd say you've one
chance in a hundred of escaping death, ransom or
a local prison somewhere."

He turned to her. "What does Hart want,
anyway? Why did he come here? I can understand
the rest of you--a scholar in pursuit of an idea
will go where a normal man wouldn't dream of
going--but why Hart?"

"Why, to learn! To study! He wishes to know
something more in the field of yoga."

"Lady, with a very few exceptions, the
greatest masters are refugees in Kashmir or
India."

"What does that mean?"

"You're being led down the garden path. The
purpose of the expedition is something else
entirely. Or else--"

He stopped, startled by the thought that came
to him. "No . . . no, that's unlikely."

"What?"

"Oh . . . just a random thought, but don't forget what I told you."

They had come to the end of the valley. A Golog emerged from the darkness, and Mallory conversed with him in low tones.

"We have to walk," he said. "Horses' hoofs make too much noise on rock slabs."

She fell in beside him. He carried a rifle and he walked easily, as a woodsman walks, rather than a rider. When they had walked about a half mile from where they had left their horses, he whispered, "Stay here on that slab. I want to look around."

He moved away from her and disappeared into the dark, then she saw the outline of him at the rim of the gorge and off the rock-slab trail. He knelt and seemed to be touching the ground. Behind them the whole valley lay open and she could see a faint glow from a light within one of the tents.

Then he was beside her again. "You won't have to wait long to see what the Red Chinese are like," he said. "There was a small patrol here, just about sundown."

"How can you tell?"

"Horse tracks. Mud that fell off their shoes is still soft. They picked up that mud crossing the stream about a hundred yards back up the trail. They stood there looking down toward us and some of the mud fell off while the horses were moving about. The cold stiffens the mud, and by midnight it would have only a soft center."

"What will you do?"

"Wait until daybreak. I'm stretching our

chances but my men are tired, and so are their horses."

"And if they come before then?"

"You'll have a chance to see what war is like."

As they rode up to the Inn gate a dark figure materialized before them. It was Gunther Hart.

"Renata," his tone was cool, "I do not like this. Your safety is my concern."

"It was my idea, Gunther. Mallory had left the Inn. It was a beautiful night for a ride, so I followed him."

"Nevertheless," Hart's voice lifted, "I will not have it. The behavior of this group is my responsibility."

"Don't worry," Renata replied, "I shall do nothing to embarrass you or the expedition."

Suddenly furious, he held his tongue, his eyes following Mallory as he walked away. When he spoke again his voice was calm, reasonable.

"He is not important, Renata, except that his presence endangers us all. He is an enemy of the people, and if our hosts believe we were consorting with him our invitation might be withdrawn.

"I am sure," he added, "the others would not appreciate that. Their work has been planned for months."

She was contrite. Gunther was perfectly right. Mallory infuriated her but there was something electric about him, something that demanded one's attention.

She returned to her tent. Her uncle, beyond

the canvas partition, was asleep. The only tent
now showing a light was that of Marty and Roy.

Mallory found Lagskha seated on the k'ang; the
only light was from the brazier. "I have waited,"
the young lama said. "You have a plan?"

"To leave before daybreak. You must be away
from here, Your Eminence. You must escape."

"You go to India with Go-log? That is
curious."

Mallory lowered his voice. "They will fight,
as you know, so I will try to arrange an air-drop
of guns, machine guns, recoilless rifles,
grenades."

"You will return?"

"They expect me to. They even might kill me if
they believe I will not return. I do not know. I
am alone here."

"You have no woman?"

"No. At first I was a slave. My father was
with another tribe. To have gone among the Go-log
women when I was a slave would have meant my
death. Since then I have been wary. I like them,
but . . ."

"You would be missed."

"Maybe. I think of staying sometimes but the
world has moved on and maybe I'm kidding when I
pretend their problems are my own."

"What of the Americans? Will they aid us?"

"Officially, no. Unofficially, perhaps. Some
fear involvement, some believe in diplomacy. But
diplomacy only works if you have something to
trade . . . or if you are backed up by active
force."

"Our people were unprepared to defend themselves against a modern army. Had we begun preparing earlier nobody would have risked invading our land."

Fire-light played on the time-stained walls, and the Incarnation studied Mallory with thoughtful eyes. "You have lived many lives . . . even in this one life you have lived many lives. You are a trukka, one of those who reached the threshold of eternity but chose to be reborn, to live on among men. Will you return to your Montana?"

"Where can a man go who has been dead for ten years? I have nothing there . . . nothing here. I have to figure it out . . ."

Mallory and Lagskha talked a bit longer. Mallory felt himself strangely drawn to this troubled young man, scarcely more than a boy, wise beyond his years, yet eager for the things any young man would have wanted.

Lagskha returned to the upstairs room and Mallory rolled up on the k'ang, his rifle beside him, a pistol-butt within reach of his fingers.

Long after he fell asleep, he awakened briefly, hearing the distant rumble of an avalanche.

And then, for a long time, there was silence.

CHAPTER 5

The Valley of Peasant Winds offered no other sound to the night. Mallory, lying on the k'ang, felt the urge to change position and sat up. Except for the faint crimson glow from the

brazier, the room was in darkness. The Inn
offered faint, old-building creaks, but there was
no other sound until just as his eyes began to
close he became aware of a sporadic, metallic
tapping. After a moment it stopped . . . and then
began again.

He swung his feet to the floor and tucked his
pistol behind his belt. Taking up his broad-sword
he moved toward the sound, on tip-toe to the foot
of the stairs. The sound seemed to come from
behind the steps.

From a crack in the wall came a suggestion of
light. He peered through.

In a cubby-hole of a room, his back to
Mallory, a man sat at a radio; there were
headphones covering his ears and he was working a
Morse key. He began the pattern of taps again--
evidently he was calling a station.

Mallory felt for a door but there was none--
the wall was bare except for the crack where age
had crumbled the mortar between the stones. But
beyond the man at the radio Mallory could see the
edge of a door evidently opening to the outside.
He turned quickly, his eyes seeking the front
door to the Inn. The darkness, even after the dim
light that came through the crack, was profound
and in his haste, his elbow touched a bowl left
on the edge of the stairs and it fell with a
clatter. Swearing under his breath, Mallory ran
through the door to the yard, out and around the
building.

The wing of the building extended far to the
side and by the time he rounded it the small door
stood open, the room empty. Both the man and the
radio had vanished. There was a thin smell of

smoke and a glow of red from a recently blown out lantern wick. The rarely used gate at the back of the Inn yard was open, and Mallory ran to it.

The meadow was empty. He went through cautiously. Nothing lay beyond but the dark, silent tents of the Hart Expedition.

Sword in hand he crossed to the tents, and hearing a movement within one, he ripped back the flap.

Renata Bernard stood before him, in a negligee. Startled, her eyes went from the naked blade to his face. "Really, Mr. Mallory, isn't this a bit much?"

"Did you hear anyone? Anything? I am looking for a man."

Roy Lewis emerged from the next tent, buckling his belt. From another tent, Gunther Hart emerged. "Just what is going on here?" he demanded.

"Somebody was operating a radio at the Inn. He got away."

"And why shouldn't he? Whoever he is? I don't understand what disturbs you."

"Don't act the fool. The only thing the Chinese would like better than to wipe out my people and me would be to take the Incarnation. I can permit no communications that would endanger our security."

"You are mistaken. No message can be sent from here without my authorization and I have not given it. Now have the goodness to put that . . . that . . . object away."

Mallory checked their feet. All wore slippers or untied boots, or were bare-footed. None showed any indication of a run through wet grass. Yet

Bernard, Carpenter, Penfield and his wife were missing.

"Do you have a radio?"

"Of course. We maintain communication with New Delhi, Hongkong and Peking."

"You are sure no message was sent tonight?"

"Our radio has not even been set up. You may see it if you wish."

"All right."

The set was larger, more powerful, altogether a better outfit than the compact set he had seen. And it was still packed for travel.

Nothing was to be gained by delay. The set he had seen must be carried by someone who had slipped into the abandoned storage room to send out messages unheard by the people in the tents.

Lagskha-tsang was sipping tea when he re-entered the Inn. "We must go," Mallory said, "there is little time."

"I know." He put down the bowl. "I think even now it is too late."

There was a rush of hoofs, a shout of warning, and the Go-log from the entrance to the valley rushed in. "They come," he said, "they come quickly."

"How many?"

The Go-log grinned. "Only ten fours," he said. "We can beat them."

"Do not fire. Let us see what talking can do."

The sky was turning gray, the mountains were deep in shadow. He could see the column of horsemen but could not make out their number.

They rode smartly, a tough, disciplined lot of men.

Mallory called out to Bernard. "You had better come inside the wall. All of you."

"We have nothing to fear," Hart said.

Gomba had moved up beside Mallory. "The rifles! Look at them! Shall I ride for the others?"

"Wait."

"But we can have their guns!" Gomba protested. "If we get the men from the hills--!"

"Wait. We must think of the Incarnation. Close the gate and stay out of sight."

The first troops in line headed at once for the lower end of the valley. Now both ends of the valley would be blocked . . . did they know of the other route?

These were no raw recruits. These were soldiers. As for Marshal Chu, he was no commissar, no bureaucrat, no party functionary. He was a fighting man. Accompanied by two soldiers he was approaching the Inn. It was apparent that he anticipated no trouble, which meant that he knew nothing of the presence of the Go-log.

Gunther Hart, in his robe, stepped away from the tents and walked out to meet him, a tall, austere, and impressive figure. Bernard and Penfield walked beside him, Wells and Lewis remaining near the tent, with the woman. Suddenly a tent flap was pushed aside and Hank Carpenter emerged. He went quickly to Gunther Hart and stood a half-step behind him.

Chu drew up before the closed gates, glanced toward the tents, finally at Hart.

Hart stated his name as one who expects it to be known, and so it was, over much of the world. Chu merely glanced at him, then at the closed gate. "I want that gate opened," he said.

"We have nothing to do with those inside," Hart replied, "except for the lama. He is under my protection."

Chu was a stocky, well set-up man of forty, every inch the soldier. He looked at Hart again. Slowly, carefully, he looked him up and down, then at the others.

His eyes rested on Penfield. "Who is in there?" he demanded.

"A lama, whose name seems to be Lagskha-tsang. Also, there is an American named Mallory and a party of Go-logs," Penfield replied.

"Go-logs? Here?" Chu was startled.

Hart tried once more. "Marshal, I am Gunther Hart. This is the Hart Expedi--"

"Be still!" Chu said impatiently, then to Penfield, "They cannot be Go-logs . . . not here."

"They are Go-logs," Renata said. "I know their physical type, their dress, their customs."

"Miss Bernard is an anthropologist," Carpenter explained.

Chu looked thoughtfully at the palisade. No sound came from it, no evidence of movement, yet Chu was disturbed. At such point-blank range he could be killed. "How many are there?"

"Ten?" Penfield suggested. "I don't know. There might be less. They scattered out very quickly, and I was not counting."

The palisade, old as it was, patched though it might be, was still strong. Anticipating only the

capture of a fleeing lama, of a religion that did
not advocate fighting, he had brought only
riflemen. No rocket propelled grenade launcher,
nor machine gun, or mortar. The weight would have
slowed him down on the steep, narrow passes, and
no need for them was foreseen.

Hart started to speak again, but Chu pushed
his horse past him, brushing him aside. "You I
will talk to later. Stay out of the way." His
eyes swept the tents. Roy Lewis had come forward
with Renata and his eyes slid over him, paused on
Dr. Bernard, then returned to the palisade.

"You have seen the lama?"

"He is there," Carpenter said.

Marty Wells threw Carpenter an irritated
glance. Why help him? Let Chu solve his own
problems.

Chu turned to the soldier nearest him. "Open
the gate," he said.

The soldier hesitated the merest second, then
strode to the gate and grasped the handle. The
gate opened easily. The soldier leaned to peer
inside . . . and disappeared. Then the gate
closed, and again there was silence.

"Open that gate and release that man!" Chu
shouted. "Or I'll break it down!"

Mallory appeared on the palisade near the
gate. "I wouldn't try that. You haven't men
enough."

"Come down here! I want to talk to you!"

"It will be my pleasure, Marshal Chu," Mallory
replied, "but if you move out of your tracks
before I get back inside the gate you will have
six bullets in your belly."

The gate opened and two Go-logs appeared, each

armed with a Soviet PPSh machine-pistol. Chu's
glance identified the weapons and his manner grew
more cautious.

"I want the lama who is inside. Give him to me
and go your way."

"You are amusing yourself, Marshal. If you
consent to ride out of here right now we will let
you go."

"I did not come to joke," said the Chinese.
"You have ten minutes."

Mallory stepped forward. "You'd better
reconsider. If you try to signal your men you
will be shot to bits. The truth of the matter is,
Marshal, we've got you."

Chu's features revealed nothing. In a career
that began as a child on the Long March,
continued in warfare against the Japanese, then
against Chiang Kai-shek and finally in Korea, he
had faced many difficulties.

He had no intention of allowing himself or any
of his men to be killed to no purpose. The weight
of power was on his side and the escape route to
India was long. Peking did not appreciate failure
and he did not permit failure to himself nor was
there need to think of that now. He had six
hundred men within call and, within hours, his
radio could bring planes to strafe any escaping
party.

His mission was to capture the Incarnation,
for that young man had already given evidence of
judgment and intelligence far beyond his years.
Moreover, his name carried great weight among the
hill tribes, never subdued under any Chinese
government. He could be a powerful weapon in the

hands of Mao but if allowed to escape he could become a formidable propaganda tool.

The presence of the expedition was an annoying complication, for if the Incarnation was not captured, he must be killed, and there must be no witnesses who could take the story to the outside.

Undoubtedly, the expedition had come with official sanction or they would never have gotten this far, but what were they doing here? This was no known route. In fact he himself had known nothing of this inn until forty-eight hours before. Their presence was one of the things that had thrown him off guard.

Chu had not met the Go-log before, but he knew all about them, and had a wholesome respect for them as fighting men. This Mallory . . . he did not look old enough to have been here for nearly twenty-five years but his name had been known that long.

"Do you mind if I smoke?"

"Suit yourself," Mallory replied.

Chu took a cigarette case from his pocket but took his own time in lighting up. "We are at a stand-off, my friend. You have me but I also have you. No doubt you can order me killed, but you would never escape alive."

Hart interrupted. "Marshal, this man is no concern of ours. He arrived after we did. We have a permit from Chou En-lai and--"

Chu spoke directly to Mallory. "These civilians will be killed if I am killed. You would not want that on your conscience?"

"You trust to my conscience?"

Chu shrugged. "You Americans are sentimental

people. Conscience is important to you. To me it is nothing. I think of results."

"I have read Confucius," Mallory said. "He was more ethical, I believe."

"But scarcely a Marxist, would you say?" Chu was enjoying himself. "I respect Marx but when it is inconvenient, I ignore him. I don't care that men are taught to think the right thoughts, I just want them to obey and help me carry out my orders."

He drew on his cigarette. "Let us make an end to this. I do not know what you are doing here, nor do I care. I am a single-minded man and my problem is that young lama. You can surrender him and ride away freely, or you can try to help him and all die together. It is as simple as that."

"Chou--" Hart began.

Chu glanced at Hart with contempt. "Comrade Chou is a very important man for whom I have great admiration. He also has many duties. If you interfere with me I will have you shot and then I will explain my actions. He will be understanding, particularly as I am in a position to be very useful to him, and a dead American, even several dead Americans, means nothing to anybody."

Chu turned in his saddle and spoke to the soldier beside him. "If that man," he pointed at Hart, "speaks again, strike him in the mouth with your rifle butt. After you do it, if he has any teeth left in the front of his face I will have you shot."

Dr. Bernard spoke, "Sir, Mr. Hart wishes to cause no trouble. We are concerned with the welfare of the People's Republic of China, and came here to study the ancient life of your country, its plants and its geology. Our reports will be submitted to Peking, and are looked for there. We are, sir, men of peace. Hence Gunther Hart was concerned that our expedition not be confused with whatever Mallory and his men are doing."

"And what is he doing?"

"I . . . I don't actually know, sir. We have had no opportunity to talk."

Chu's expression was icy. "But time to use a radio? There was time for that, was there not?"

"Radio? I do not know. Mallory was very concerned about somebody using a radio. I believed it was a mistake."

"It was not a mistake. A radio message was sent . . . or attempted . . . just recently." Chu looked over at Mallory. "You know something of this?"

"You're damned right I do. Marshal, if a message was sent from here it was somebody with a hidden radio. I do not believe more than one of this expedition knows anything about it but I could be wrong."

"It was sent by one of them?"

"Unless there is somebody here whom none of us know. I believe that message was being relayed to Peking . . . or Moscow."

"Ah?"

Chu considered the matter. He was not surprised. The Party had its people everywhere and they could be reporting his actions. He had friends in Peking but enemies also. He was not sure who all of those enemies were but they were

concerned with his growing strength, his
autonomy.

The leaders were old, none of them in the best
of health, and soon there would be changes, new
faces. Marshal Chu had long had it in mind to be
one of those new faces. A radio message was not
only possible but probable. His own operator had
picked up a signal, and from its strength it
could have come from nowhere else . . . in this
area there simply wasn't anywhere else. Of
course, it might also be an agent of the
imperialist West.

Even as he used the phrase he rebelled at it.
He was a party member in good standing, but that
did not say he accepted all the pap used for
propaganda purposes. The Party had been an
effective means to seize control and if some of
the older members and young idealists still clung
to the vision of International Communism, it was
their privilege. For himself, party slogans were
simply a means to seize power and to hold it.

He was quite willing to deal with the so-
called capitalist powers but he wished to deal
from strength. And, soon enough, there must be
such deals; there must be arrangements. They had
much China needed and could get in no other way
except through Russia . . . and there had been
enough of that. His eyes shifted to Mallory,
weighing the man. This was the one with whom he
must deal, this was his enemy, and yet he was the
man Chu respected most.

"You can hold me, Major Mallory, or release
me. It grows late and I am tired. If you intend
holding me, by all means let us go inside. If not
release me to return to my command."

"We shall go inside, of course. Come, Marshal Chu. Will you be first?"

Chu hesitated only a moment. "Not first. If my men decide I am a prisoner, they will attack." He smiled. "I have a second in command who is very ambitious, Major."

CHAPTER 6

Marty Wells walked back to the tents. Chu had gone inside with Mallory, walking side by side as if they were old friends, but that was window-dressing for any of his men who might be watching.

Renata had started toward the tents but she waited for Marty to over-take her. "You're worried?"

"I'm scared."

"Of the Chinese? Gunther will manage. Just wait and see."

He gave her a sour glance. "Chu couldn't care less about him, or about us."

"Wait. Gunther will be in touch with Peking and Chu will get his orders."

Marty glanced at the mountains. "I'm still trying to figure out where Gunther Hart was going. He was never very explicit, you know, except that we should be in eastern Tibet, perhaps the Upper Mekong area or the sources of the Huang-Ho, but all that covers an enormous stretch of country. People outside do not realize the vastness of all this. Tibet is about twice the size of Texas, and this area . . . some of it used to be Tibet . . . . is almost as large.

"Hart is using a map that we have never had a chance to examine. When we were permitted to come here we were given a prescribed route to follow. That was part of his agreement with the People's Republic of China. I heard him discussing it with Hank and Hank was very upset when Hart turned off the designated route."

Lewis joined them. "I like this man Mallory," he said. "He doesn't take any guff from anyone." He glanced at Wells. "How'd you come to make this trip, Marty?"

"A friend of mine recommended me to Hart. Of course, I jumped at it. This area has been gone over lightly . . . I say this area, but I mean this part of China. Ward covered some of it further south, and Wilson, Forrest and Rock worked through here some, but none of it has been done as thoroughly as one would like.

"There have been some old documents turning up lately, their origin is uncertain, but they are extremely old. The thing is they describe plants quite accurately, some of which we know, and some we've never catalogued."

"When you say 'old' what do you mean, Marty?"

"Renata, I simply mean old. You know about the Bower manuscript, of course? These were similar except the thin strips of wood on which they were written had been treated with some kind of preservative."

"Didn't you have a carbon-14 reading on it?"

"That's just it. And the man who did the reading was one of the best, but he flatly refused to issue a statement on it. He said the reading had to be wrong . . . it was far too old.

He believed the way the wood had been treated had made a difference in the reading."

"Who knows?" Lewis said. "They've just found some rice in Thailand that proves man was cultivating grain long before anybody dreamed they could.

"There's been too much of a fixation on the Near and Middle East, Egypt, Sumer and all that. Most of the studies have been made there and without anything more than that many European scientists jumped to the conclusion that those were the first civilizations.

"Most of the money goes into the Mediterranean area or Sumer. We know damned little about the rest of the world. It's fairly obvious there was a great belt of civilizations stretching across the great land masses from the Sahara through Egypt, Sumer, southern Arabia, Dilmun, the Indus Valley and Southeast Asia. I believe trade and travel were as active as in Europe of the Crusade period."

"I wonder what's going on inside?" Marty suggested.

"Let's go see," Renata offered.

Lagskha-tsang sat on the k'ang, Brikhuti beside him. Mallory and Marshal Chu faced them with Gunther Hart and Hank Carpenter at one side.

"You would be wise, Your Eminence," Chu suggested, "to return with us. Your former position is assured. You may be sure your opinions will be listened to and respected."

"And ignored?" Lagskha asked.

"The Dalai Lama is no longer in Tibet," Chu

suggested suavely. "It is important your people have someone to speak for them. By leaving the country he has, in effect, abdicated. It is important he be replaced by someone suitable."

"Ah? That is a possibility I had not considered." Lagskha's face was innocent of guile. "I must have time. I must meditate. For such a decision . . . I must have a day and a night."

"Of course. Shall we say twenty-four hours? I regret I can allow no more time but my government is impatient. Someone is needed in Lhasa, someone with authority."

Lagskha frowned thoughtfully. "Yes . . . yes, of course. You understand, however, that a Dalai Lama cannot, as you put it, abdicate? He is an Incarnation, and the only way such a man can abdicate is by dying. He is not the first Dalai Lama to leave his country temporarily. Such a decision has been forced upon several . . . all have returned. I think the people understand very well why he left, and in fact, they tried to persuade him to leave long before he finally did. And a Dalai Lama cannot be appointed by Peking."

Chu smiled. "We understand, Your Eminence, that a Dalai Lama is born . . . a regent is not. In his absence, the government must continue, conducted by a regent."

"Yes, of course. That might just be the thing. Twenty-four hours, please?"

Marshal Chu turned to Mallory. "You will abide by his decision?"

"Of course. I have no interest in kidnapping. He will do as he sees fit."

"And you, Major Mallory? What will you do in that case?"

Mallory smiled. "I want to settle down with a good bottle of bourbon and a cigar. You can have this country." His words were calculated to disarm Marshal Chu, as much as he might be disarmed, but Mallory had spoken with the awareness that few of the Go-log could follow the nuances of the conversation. Only a couple of his men understood more than the most basic Mandarin Chinese. It always came as a surprise to Europeans or Americans that so few people in the outlying portions of China actually spoke Chinese.

What he needed was time, and if Chu believed he was leaving, he might not be so quick to follow unless he discovered Lagskha had gone with him. Chu was a pragmatist. To capture or kill Mallory and his Go-log was a possibility, and a desirable one, yet if Mallory would leave of his own accord, Chu and China were well rid of him, and without him the Go-log might never get back to their own land in the bend of the Yellow River.

To attempt a capture now would mean a battle, the loss of time and undoubtedly many casualties . . . one of whom might be this young lama that Chu was so interested in. That fear might work to all their benefit, Mallory thought.

"All right," Mallory said, "you can go. I have no idea what the Incarnation wishes to do. He will make his own decision."

"My interest," Chu said bluntly, "is only in him." He smiled. "As for the Hart Expedition, they are Comrade Chou's problem. Not mine."

Nothing was to be gained by holding him. That
he had an ambitious second in command was
probably true, and such a man might be likely to
precipitate a fight. What Mallory needed was
time, and Chu was confident enough to give it to
him. After all, did he not have both ends of the
valley blocked?

When Marshal Chu had gone Mallory immediately
dispatched a rider to get word to the rest of his
men, holed up in the mountains only a few miles
away. He had a feeling he would need them all,
and the time was near when a move must be made.
Both of the armed camps would be gathering
reinforcements. In the short term the numbers
favored the Go-log, but that could not last. As
soon as Marshal Chu felt he had the advantage the
truce might be over.

There was nothing for it but to attempt the
secret trail, hoping he would be able to find his
way.

Renata was awaiting him inside. "What will you
do? You realize, of course, that anything you do
will involve us?"

"I am not concerned with you. My only interest
is getting to India with my men. You are Hart's
problem."

He went on up the stairs after the lama.
Renata looked after him. "He's trouble, Marty,"
she said wryly. "I wish he had never come here.
We're going to be in all kinds of trouble."

"That's one way of looking at it. Personally,
I wonder if we're getting a last chance to get
out of here while the getting is good. Gunther

was so sure of himself, but the Marshal obviously
didn't care who he was or what connections he
had. What they say is true. Peking is a long way
off."

At the top of the stairs Lagskha awaited him.
Mallory seated himself. Brikhuti appeared,
offering them both bowls of tsamba.

"Do you trust the Marshal, Mallory?" Lagskha
asked.

"No."

"Nor do I. I am afraid you are better at what
comes next, Major. I place myself in your hands."

"Chu's men bar the way on the traditional
route. If we broke through, Chu could call upon
planes to bomb and strafe the road. The route
through the valley is wide--we would be an easy
target for aircraft."

Lagskha waited, his eyes bright and attentive.

"There is another way. I believe you know it,
and I do not. At least, I do not know all one
needs to know." He paused. "If we could vanish in
the night . . . suddenly."

"You talk of miracles."

"I talk of a road. A secret road."

"It is not possible. We would be leading
them--no, it cannot be done."

Brikhuti started to speak, then was silent.
Her brother spoke then. "This way you speak
of . . . how do you know of it?"

"I found a map on the wall of a cave temple. A
very intricate, difficult map, by the way. It was
like nothing I had ever seen, but then, quite
suddenly it began to look familiar and I
recognized it for what it was.

"Marked on this map was a road, beside the

road a monastery, further along a temple and a
fort. There was even a city, hidden among the
peaks."

"Who has seen this map?"

"So far as I am aware, only myself. It is
hidden beyond finding. In the land of the Go-
log."

"He is one of us, My Brother," Brikhuti said,
"is that not plain enough? This must have been
the cave of Kesar . . . and who could find it was
he not guided there?"

"I know the way is a sacred way, but you are
an Incarnation, so what better use for such a
road?"

"Give me time. I must think of this."

Mallory got to his feet. "Between this time
and the noon sun, I must know."

Brikhuti followed him down the stairs. "He
will go. I know it. But you must tell me how you
found the cave."

"It was an accident. I was climbing in the
mountains."

"I do not believe in accidents. You found it
because you were meant to find it."

"Well, you may see it as some sort of destiny.
I'm just happy to have a way out . . . and to
have someone who understands at least some of the
path and can help me follow it."

Her eyes were dark and lovely. Mallory found
himself groping for words. How did a man talk to
a woman? It had been so long, and this girl was
infinitely more lovely than any he had known.
"You'll be going back to Europe?"

"Wherever we must. I hope so, however. I love

the cities, the music, the gaiety . . . and the books."

"Books?"

"Here there are so few, and I like to read."

"What of you, Major Mallory? That is your world, too."

"I am not so sure. I fear I have become a savage."

"A savage who reads the Upanishads? Perhaps not so savage as you would have us believe."

He looked at her quizzically. "Now who could have told you that?"

"You have been too long among the mountain people for there not to be stories, and you are a curiosity. Many of the people you've met had never seen a European or an American before.

"Long before I went away to school there were stories about you, how you rode like a demon and fought like a tiger. A Bon priest stopped at our house for a few days and he told us about the mysterious white man who reads books. He said you were a man of great wisdom."

"That was my father. But a man does need exercise for the mind."

He was tired, tired as ever he could remember. He wondered about Gunther Hart. The man was accustomed to authority. How would he react when his word was no longer obeyed?

"Stay with your brother," he told her. "If there is trouble, call me."

After she had gone he finished his tsamba, drank another bowl of tea, and looked up as Roy Lewis came in.

The geologist sat down. "I hope I am not disturbing you, Mallory, but you know this country. Why would Hart choose to come into this valley?"

"Hasn't he told you?"

"We were told nothing. Renata was the only one who knew he planned to stop here for a few days."

"He had planned to stop here?"

"So Renata told Marty Wells. He's off the route prescribed by Peking."

"He's taking a chance. When the Chinese give you a route you'd better stay with it."

Lewis shrugged. "You've been out of touch, Mallory. Gunther Hart has a name for doing what he damn well chooses and with his money and his connections he gets away with it. He is a heavy contributor to both the Republicans and Democrats and nobody wants to cross him. He has the reputation of being a bad enemy."

Mallory stretched out on the k'ang and clasped his hands behind his head.

"He must be looking for something and I suspect he knows a lot more than he's letting on," Lewis said. "The man values his life as highly as anything. I'll bet he's not taking this risk lightly. I heard he has a map. Could he be looking for something archaeological? The Bernards were brought in on this thing very early."

"That depends on where he looks. In most of the high plateau country he will find little, but in the valleys . . . there are places here, Lewis, that are older than man's measurement of time.

"It is very easy to lay down rules for the ages of history when you examine only one small

corner. It is quite another thing when you look
further and dig deeper."

"Just this afternoon I was saying something
like that. We must have a talk."

"It would be interesting," Mallory said,
closing his eyes, "but I'm headed out of here as
soon as I can figure out how."

Roy Lewis walked from the room and Mallory lay
one last moment awake, staring up at the smoke-
blackened beams. This inn was more Chinese than
Tibetan, an odd thing, at this remote place. And
it was old, so very, very old.

He closed his eyes again. The inside of his
lids seemed raw from sleeplessness, yet they
remained shut, and in a moment, he slept.

CHAPTER 7

Over the Valley of Pleasant Winds there was an
avenue of stars, and within the valley there was
silence. The lights in the tents had gone out and
within the Inn men slept upon the k'ang in the
faint red glow of the charcoal brazier.

Back in the lost canyons of the mountains
there were the small, lonely sounds of the
mountains breathing, and of the forest. A rock
fell, gravel trickled after it, and the
contraction of cold caused a branch to creak.
Here and there some small nocturnal creature
rustled among the leaves of the rhododendrons.

Here in these lonely peaks, these dark,
mysterious canyons, here on the edge of the vast,
grassy plains of the Chang-tang, here begin
several of the greatest rivers on earth, all

finding their sources within one comparatively
small area.

Out of great gorges in the mountains flow the
Yellow, the Yangtze, the Mekong, the Salween, the
Brahmaputra, the Irrawaddy . . . and others, all
with names like incantations.

In her tent Renata lay awake, staring up into
darkness. She, who always fell asleep easily, was
sleepless, and it was not the altitude, for they
were but little higher than yesterday.

Was it fear? She searched herself and found
nothing that resembled fear. She admitted she was
no longer so sure of Gunther. Chu had brushed him
aside as though he were an annoyance rather than
anyone to be considered seriously.

Mallory was the disturbing element. She was
not accustomed to such a completely masculine
man, and with it was the realization that she
seemed unable to reach him, to affect him in any
way. He was single-minded to a degree to which
she was unaccustomed.

Men had always been attracted to her
physically, and had come to respect her
intelligence later. If Mallory was attracted it
did not seem to matter very much, and as for
intelligence, he simply took it for granted if he
realized it at all.

She had been immediately aware that Chu
respected Mallory, and vice versa. The two men
were enemies, but in a sense they spoke the same
language, and had come to an immediate
understanding, yet she was quite sure each of
them was now planning to out-wit the other.

What had they gotten into? For the first time
she began to realize the vast distances involved

here, and her total irrelevance as a person in the light of international complications. For the first time it dawned upon her that this whole venture had been foolish. Scientists too easily considered themselves, or perhaps their work, to be the center of the universe.

Gunther Hart moved in such an aura of his own that he had seemed immune from the petty bickerings of nations. Now she began to wonder if he was inconsequential once removed from the world that his money and influence had built. Well, he still had the radio with which to communicate to the world outside. He could put himself in touch with Chu's superiors if he needed to.

Yet what if the rules were different here even if they were able to speak with Gunther's connections? What if Chou En-lai or his lieutenants behaved differently now that Gunther was in their world? They might seem more than polite and helpful when Gunther Hart was treating them to dinner in the West but what would they be like when Hart started asking them for favors here . . . in a place where he might not know the rules? Just what could Gunther mean to them, anyway? Could a Communist in a land of Communists be seen to allow a person whose position was based on wealth to influence policy or goals?

They were a long way from home. Lhasa, the capital of Tibet, was at least four hundred miles away from their present position. On horseback, in this country, that could be a trip that took weeks. The nearest Tibetan city, if such it could be called, was Chamdo, several days travel from where they were now.

Moreover, Gunther Hart, on some mission of his
own, had taken them off the designated route.
This in itself was enough to land them in prison
in any Communist country where travel was
restricted.

Worried, she remembered Carpenter telling
Pulaski to throw Mallory out. It had been a
hasty, ill-considered action, and suddenly she
was trembling, remembering that naked display of
power when the three Go-log had moved so quickly
with their blades. An instant more and if there
had been no word from Mallory they might have
killed Pulaski . . . would have killed him.
Mallory and the Go-logs, even Lagskha and his
sister, were armed and their survival was
threatened. Her people must not forget that.
Academics often chose to live in a world of
abstractions, but here life could be terrifying
and immediate.

A long time later she fell asleep, and it was
not until day was breaking that she awakened,
suddenly. For an instant she lay still, hearing
low voices outside, then the swish of feet
through the grass. The tent curtain drew back and
Mary Penfield came in.

"Now they've done it." Mary's hands were
shaking as she tried to light her cigarette.
"Somebody got into the packs last night and
smashed the radio . . . smashed it to bits."

Renata sat up, her mind blank. She could only
stare. Realization came over her slowly. The
radio smashed! Then how--?

"Oh, Mary!" she whispered. "The radio! What
will we do?"

Mary drew on her cigarette and glanced at her,

then smiled, wryly. "Make friends with Mallory. What else?"

There was a scratching at the canvas. "Come in," she said, and Marty lifted the flap and stepped in.

"It's early but you'd better get dressed. Somebody got into the supplies, smashed the radio, stole some extra batteries, and Hart's fit to be tied."

"We'd better pack up and get out," Mary commented. "At least back to a city or town where there are communications."

"That's a good idea," Marty agreed, squatting on his heels, "but we've come a long way to quit so quickly. Why, I haven't done hardly anything, and I'm sure nobody ever worked this valley before. Or the country around here, for that matter."

Marty Wells left and she dressed quickly. Marty was waiting outside with Dr. Penfield and Renata's uncle. The morning was bright enough, but the sky was not the clear blue she expected.

"The weather's changing," her uncle said. "I think it's going to rain."

"Have you seen Gunther?"

"Only for a minute. He's been talking to Carpenter." He glanced at her. "He's not going back, if that's what you are thinking. He's going to send a man out with a message. He'll have an air-drop of a new radio . . . two of them in fact."

"A messenger? Where to?"

"I don't know. He didn't say."

"Why, he would have to ride for days!"

———

Mallory opened the gate and stepped out,
looking around. His Go-log had returned only an
hour before, having made contact with the rest of
his command in the hills. Chu had attempted to
prevent anyone from leaving the valley but most
of his soldiers were city men, unused to the ways
or the skills of the Go-log. His messenger had
slipped by within a few feet of a watching
soldier, and returning had done the same thing.

"If you like," he said to Mallory, "I bring
them all in . . . every one. These are stupid."

"Don't take them lightly," Mallory advised.
"They aren't hunters and woodsmen, but they can
fight, and they will. They also have damned good
weapons."

"Which we will have soon," the Go-log said
grimly. "I have seen them." He slapped his long
Mosin Nagant rifle. "But I prefer this."

Roy Lewis walked over. "Know anything about
Tantric Yoga?"

"A little."

"I think that's the bee in Hart's bonnet."

"Well, if he's looking for a teacher he'd do
better to look somewhere that isn't in so much
conflict. These gurus up here are independent.
They don't care who you are or what you are, and
they will only accept you as a student if they
feel the urge. That is if they haven't fled or
gone into hiding. He's going to a Hell of a lot
of trouble if he's not looking for something in
particular."

"Those Go-logs of yours," Lewis said

tentatively. "Old enemies of the Chinese, are they not?"

"They are enemies of almost everybody. Aside from their raids on Tibet to China caravans, they want to be left alone."

"I've heard they hit the Reds pretty hard, even shot down some low-flying aircraft. Is that true?"

Mallory glanced at him. "The Go-logs mind their own affairs, and so do I."

Lewis chuckled. "No offense intended, Mallory. I am interested, however. I was just thinking how lucky it is that these Go-logs don't have modern equipment. With somebody to instruct them they could be welded into quite a force. Something the CIA might appreciate . . . even pay for, if the situation was right."

Mallory stretched. "You know something, Lewis? I'm going to get some breakfast."

"Why not join us? Hart might be more willing to listen to reason now that his radio is busted. We can offer you bacon and eggs, good coffee--?"

"I'll take it," Mallory said. "The change might do me good." He turned back into the gate and conferred briefly with the Go-log sentry. "All right," he said to Lewis. "I hope Hart doesn't resent my coming."

"Talk gently," Lewis advised. "After all, why antagonize the man?"

Renata watched Mallory talking to Roy Lewis. How strong he was! It was a strange face, a brooding, unrevealing face. It was the face of a man who had lived with mountains. She irritably pushed the thought away; some part of her mind seemed bent on making him seem more attractive than he really was.

Brikhuti came up beside her. "Without him," she said, "we will die here . . . all of us."

"You are mistaken." Renata lifted her chin. "Our expedition need have nothing to do with him. Gunther Hart will communicate with Peking and everything will be all right. Another radio will be flown in, and perhaps an official to act as an intermediary."

"How strong is your Mr. Hart when he faces adversity? How would he react to a knife? Or a gun?"

"Gunther Hart," Renata replied coolly, "is not my man. As to facing a knife, I doubt if that will be necessary. He is a man of peace."

"To be a man of peace is very easy when one is protected. My country was a land of peace, yet we have been invaded several times, and now we have been enslaved, our homes and our religion destroyed. Would it have been so had we been better armed? Had we had alliances with other countries? Your country, perhaps? You have an example in your own world . . . the Swiss. They are men of peace, but every Swiss has a rifle in his home, and he is prepared to use it. Other nations know this, and know the cost of invasion would be too high. In being so prepared the Swiss have no need of greater, more immoral, weapons."

Brikhuti smiled slightly, at Renata. "I saw how you looked at Mallory. He is very much a man."

Renata felt herself tense. "I really wouldn't

know," she said politely, "he isn't my man. Is he yours?"

"Like you, I never saw him before yesterday, but I've heard of him, of course."

Renata was eager to hear what Brikhuti had heard, but could not bring herself to ask. The morning was very still. The yaks grazed in the meadows and all was peaceful. Above them the mountains towered, the peaks icy and alone, the sunlight sparkling on their snows. She could hear the rustling of the water in the small creek that crossed the meadow.

Brikhuti held out her hand. "I have enjoyed the chat, Miss Bernard. You know, if you want him you will have to fight, because I want him, too!"

CHAPTER 8

Breakfast was a pleasant meal, served in a long tent, and at a long, folding table. Gunther Hart was already seated when Mallory entered.

"Mr. Hart," Lewis said, "I took the liberty of inviting Mallory to join us."

"Of course, it will be our pleasure. Will you be seated? I am afraid our menu is somewhat limited, but from all I understand yours has been even more so."

"You're right," Mallory said, "and an American style breakfast will be a treat."

"In fact, we could spare you a few odds and ends, I believe." He turned his head. "Hank, see that Mallory has a few jars of marmalade from our supply, will you?"

"Mallory," Marty said suddenly, "I don't

suppose you are a botanist, but you undoubtedly are familiar with a lot of the plants. Can you tell me anything about them?"

Mallory watched his coffee-cup filled, then said, "This is the Chala Shan where we are now . . . shan meaning mountain range. I think you'll find it listed among the unexplored areas, if at all. As near as I've noticed the growth is somewhat similar to that in the Yunnan mountains.

"From seven thousand feet to ten thousand there's a variety of trees and shrubs, many fine hardwoods, and the lower-level types of rhododendrons. Many of them are fair-sized trees, and not just the shrubs you've probably seen.

"Above ten thousand feet is mostly evergreen, several varieties of pines, for example, and delphiniums, anemones, and the usual plants you find growing at that altitude anywhere. The best stuff for you will be found above twelve thousand."

"Are you as familiar with the local history?" Hart asked. "I mean the very ancient history?"

"You're in the midst of it, Hart. This inn has been a stopping place for centuries. Before it was an inn it was a farmhouse, before that a minor fort or castle.

"This trade route that runs through here, part of which you followed coming in, and all of that you would follow if you continued on, is thousands of years old."

"Thousands?" Dr. Bernard asked.

"I know. The usual story is that Tibet began when Rupati, a Kaurava prince or commander, escaped here after the defeat of the Kauravas by

the Pandavas in the great war in northern India.
But it is foolish to talk of beginnings.

"Whenever one tries to find a beginning, one
finds there was still something before that and
Tibet has been no different in that respect than
others. There is a place not far from here where
long ago the river cut deep into the hill that
supported a deserted monastery . . . a very old
one, dating from the first years of Buddhism in
Tibet. That bank reveals seven layers of
habitation, Dr. Bernard, with a three-foot-thick
bed of silt between the fourth and the fifth
layers."

"Could you take me to that place?"

"Another time." Mallory smiled thinly. "When
it won't cost me my life. There are ancient
places all around you. If you live long in this
country and are of a curious mind it does not
take long to understand how much has taken place
here.

"Major trade routes from India to the Tarim
Valley led across Tibet not far from here. In
those days there was a great civilization
there--"

"You have some basis for this?"

"Observation, careful listening . . . I'm not
trying to prove anything or threaten anyone's
theories. There were trade routes that led from
here into Burma, and others that went into
Thailand. Our world is old, Dr. Bernard, so much
older than the caution of scholars will allow
them to admit."

Gunther Hart studied Mallory thoughtfully as
Mallory talked, and after a moment, he said,
"These old monasteries . . ." He paused. "Are any

of them left? Wasn't this area a stronghold of
the Bon religion?"

"It was." Mallory refilled his cup and waited
a moment. Then he said, "It was also a stronghold
of the belief from which the Bon religion
derived. Unfortunately, all religions eventually
end in superstition, losing their purity with
time and with the ignorance of the followers.
What became the Bon religion grew out of
something infinitely stronger, deeper, and more
real than what preceded it. Are you familiar with
the logical theories of Dignaga and Dharmakirti?"

"No."

"They had some similarity to ideas of Bergson
and Leibniz. I'm not an expert but they seem to
share something with contemporary physics. In
part those ideas are very ancient, such as the
theory of instantaneous being, the idea that
change is constant and immediate. Our senses
betray us in being unable to record the changes
rapidly enough to perceive the alteration that
has taken place. Therefore we speak of things as
being the same when they are no longer so. Every
minute is lost in that minute."

"What you are suggesting," Hart said, "is a
civilization advanced enough to conceive of such
ideas, a civilization of which we have no
record."

"We had no record of the Indus Valley
civilization that any scholar would accept until
about 1928, and it was one of the greatest of the
ancient civilizations. Actually, most of the work
there has been done in the past ten to fifteen
years. Are we constantly to assume there is no
more to be discovered?"

"I had no idea you were a scholar, Mr. Mallory," Renata said. "You surprise me."

"I am not a scholar, but I had ten years with several hours of each day, and sometimes months, with no demands on my time, no interruptions. I had very few books, but the ones I had were excellent, and I had access to the old men, and the old men love to talk, and I to listen."

Mallory got up. "Look, this is all well and good but it is not worth our lives. There isn't much time, so let me make you an offer. Come out of here with me. Come now . . . you may not have another chance."

Gunther Hart shook his head. "No, Mr. Mallory. We will persist. We are not frightened. You see, I suspected something might happen and I have arranged for planes to scout certain routes. One of those planes will be coming soon. We can make our wants known with ground signals."

"Very well then." Mallory paused in the opening. "Be sure you do not miss what you came for, Mr. Hart. It is easy to be blind, very hard to see clearly."

He went out, and Renata looked after him, watching him cross the meadow toward the Inn.

"Well," her uncle said, "we have a philosopher among us!"

"Words come easily to some," Hart replied carelessly. "If the man had anything, would he be wasting it here?"

Mallory crossed the meadow, mentally cursing himself for a fool. He had no business making such an offer, for the last thing he needed was

to be saddled with a party such as this:
scientists who would find fifty reasons for
stopping by the way, and coddled Western women.

Speed was the essence of escape, speed and the
immediate necessity for covering their tracks. He
need not worry about the lama or about his
sister. They were Tibetans, accustomed to travel
under much worse conditions.

Yet one thing had happened in there, for even
as he talked he had made up his mind. He would go
today . . . within a few hours. He would not even
wait until night.

They would be suspecting nothing now. After
dark tonight, as his time was growing shorter,
they would double the guards. With any luck by
night he would be on his way and moving fast but
to do that he was going to need a lot of luck.

At the gate he turned and let his eyes sweep
the meadow. Gomba moved up beside him. "Tell the
Khambas to drive their yaks to water." He
pointed. "Over there where there is low ground
along the stream. Drive them slowly, let whoever
is watching see them go down to the low ground;
after they've had a drink, bring them back up on
the meadow, but close-herd them, understand?
Later, drift a couple of them down to the low
ground, then more, and more.

"I want them to disappear. Now in the Inn
there are several yak hides. Kick some brush
together or find standing brush and drape them
with the hides . . . while the yaks are feeding.

"The soldiers watch from a distance. They will
know there is low ground along the stream, and
hopefully, they will think nothing of it when a
few yak drift off to drink."

He scowled suddenly, remembering the radio. If Hart knew who that operator was, he wasn't saying, but Mallory had a hunch he did not know.

And somebody had destroyed Hart's radio--nine chances out of ten that had been Chu's men. Whatever Chu had to do now he would do himself; he wanted no interference. Once it was all over others could say little, but he obviously wanted no one talking to Peking, providing ammunition for his enemies there.

His thoughts returned to the conversation at breakfast. Gunther Hart was fishing for something. He wanted information but he was reluctant to come right out and ask yet something had brought him here in the first place.

Lagskha came down the steps, Brikhuti behind him. "Mallory?" He paused on the lowest step. "I have decided. I shall go with you."

"It will be very hard."

He shrugged. "When was travel not hard? At least, the cold will not be so great as on the Chang-tang." He seated himself on the k'ang. "If anything happens to me, Mallory, you will care for my sister?"

"I will. With her permission."

"Thank you. What do you think of the man Carpenter?"

"Very cold, very intelligent, very dangerous. He is not to be trusted, never, not under any circumstances."

"I agree. And Lewis?"

Mallory hesitated. "We'll wait and see. I am not sure about Lewis. He was suggesting a drop of guns and ammunition might be helpful."

"Was he fishing?"

Mallory considered that. "Maybe. And perhaps he was just talking. Lots of men do. Or--?"

"Yes?"

"Suggesting. That might have been it. He might have been seriously suggesting."

"You spoke of a way out of this valley, Mallory? Do you know it?"

"The general direction, but what I do not know are the problems peculiar to that trail, the special problems there might be. The stories of those who have traveled the route might save our lives."

"I shall be of little help, I am afraid. Mallory, do you have any idea what it means to be an Incarnation? My studies began when I was very young. Each day there were many hours, and some lessons I learned very well, and some not so well. Do you remember all you learned in school?"

"Very little, I'm afraid."

"It was the same with me. I am afraid I liked the stories best, and stories of Kesar of Ling, of Dikchen Shenpa, his minister, and of Kurkar, his enemy. I also liked the stories of Chang Shambala." He chuckled. "My sister told me you have a story of it, too?"

"Yes, Lost Horizon. A very popular novel-- there was a film made of it, which was also very good. Only they called it Shangri-la."

"A good name. Do you believe that story, Mallory?"

Mallory shrugged. "We all like to believe such stories."

"Some say Shambala is only in your mind," Brikhuti said, "and it is just as well if that is so."

"The map in the cave of Kesar, Mallory? Did it
show the way to Shambala?"

"I don't know. The map was very intricate, not
like any map I ever saw."

A Go-log came in with tea. Mallory sipped his,
waiting for a moment to feel the warmth of it in
his stomach. And then he said, "This afternoon,
Lagskha."

"All of us?"

"Your people and mine."

"And the Hart Expedition? Do we leave them
here?"

"It is their choice, and anyway, I do not
think we could all go as we are going. It will
have to be done as a magician does it,
distracting attention and then disappearing
before their eyes."

"I do not like to leave them. They are very
innocent, I think. They have not seen blood,"
Lagskha said.

"They will. This is not a land in which one
keeps one's innocence. They have heard of violent
things, evil things, read of them, but it always
occurs somewhere else, happens to somebody else.
They have been protected by traffic lights,
curbstones, policemen and soldiers for so long
they scarcely believe them necessary."

"Is that the way your country is?"

"That depends. The world of academics and the
wealthy is often very protected . . . they go to
great trouble to insulate themselves and then
they forget what they wanted protection from."

"Yes. I understand. In Tibet we did that too."

They were quiet, drinking their tea. Then

Lagskha said, "Mallory? The way the map showed?
Where did it end?"

"At the sea?"

"No further?"

Mallory hesitated, then reluctantly he added,
"At an island in the sea."

CHAPTER 9

The Chinese had a saying that he who could
concentrate upon any particular problem for three
uninterrupted minutes could rule the world.
Mallory didn't believe it was true but he had at
least learned to focus his attention upon one
problem at a time.

Now with a bowl of yak butter tea, he sat on
the k'ang, and considered the problem before him.
A problem well-stated was a problem half-solved
and his problem was simple indeed.

He must move approximately thirty people and
as many animals from under the eyes of watching
guards in broad daylight.

With luck, his method would work, but he must
consider alternatives, sudden changes that might
be necessary, and the probable moves of the
enemy. Two things were in his favor. The natural
negligence of any kind of a guard, and the sheer
unexpectedness of attempting an escape at such a
time.

The moment he had seen the yak hides he had
realized their possibility, and they could be
carried into the fields on the backs of yaks,
draped over shrubs or rocks when the yaks went to

drink. Each time some of the yaks went down to
the creek, some would be allowed to wander back,
but those belonging to the train of the lama
would remain hidden.

Three of the Go-log and two of the Khambas who
accompanied Lagskha had been in the creek bottom
since his order. It was they who after allowing
them to drink, carefully led the lama's yaks away
into a hidden hollow. All of this movement was
barely out of sight behind the banks of the small
stream.

Another advantage was that ever since the Hart
Expedition arrived there had been a constant
movement around the tents, into the meadows, back
and forth from the tents to the Inn. The
attention of the soldiers on guard would be
naturally drawn to the Hart Expedition. First,
their activities, clothing, tents and all
connected with them were strange, even
extraordinary by the standards of Chu's troops.
They would be distracted and exactly which horses
and yaks belonged to the scientists and their
porters, which belonged to Lagskha, Mallory, and
the Go-logs, and which were the property of the
Inn would be hard to determine.

The guards would also be watching the women.
Renata and Mary Penfield wore clothing strange to
them. Brikhuti wore the clothing of a Tibetan
woman traveling, and that, too, they had seen
many times. It might work, and it might forestall
a fire fight.

Marshal Chu, encamped near the head of the
valley, emerged from his tent from time to time

to watch the activity. All was normal. Possibly, he reflected, they were trying to put him off guard before an attempted escape under cover of darkness. More likely they had simply given up.

"Could it be anything else?" Colonel Shih was a young officer, but very stiff, very correct, very much a party man. "How could they escape?"

Marshal Chu glanced at him, his expression bland. "Do not under-estimate the imagination. A man of imagination is a dangerous antagonist."

"The American? Bah! He is as weak and degenerate as all of them! Why else would he be in such a place, living with animals?"

"Animals who can fight, Colonel. Our armies have been defeated in their country, many times. Or when they go into that country they find nothing . . . simply nothing at all!"

In the late morning Marty Wells rode up to the tent. Chu stepped outside at the sound of the horse's hoofs. "Sir? Mr. Hart presents his compliments and wishes you, and any of your officers who are free, to join him for lunch."

"Yes, of course. You may tell him we will be there."

Wells lifted a hand, and turning his horse rode away. "You are going?" Shih said, lifting an eyebrow.

"I am going," Chu said quietly, "and so are you. It is your duty," he said, "to know the enemy. At his meals he is often off guard. You will come with us, Colonel."

Mallory was pleased. The invitation could have come at no better time. Dinner, for example,

would have been fatal. Lunch gave them a chance
to appear casual, unworried, unhurried.

Lagskha was seated on Hart's right, Chu
opposite him. Brikhuti was seated beside Chu,
Renata beside the lama. Dr. Bernard and Dr.
Penfield faced each other across the table, and
Mallory was seated opposite Mary Penfield with
Lewis, Shih and Wells close by. Hank Carpenter
sat at the foot of the table.

Mary Penfield looked across the table at
Mallory. "There are stories about you, Mr.
Mallory. When we were working with the clinic in
Mussoorie I heard things that sounded like pure
fantasy."

"No doubt they were," he said, "or perhaps
some of them were actually about my father."

"You must know a great deal about this part of
China."

"Ten years is nothing, even ten years in the
saddle. The country is too big, too diverse."

"We are building roads," Colonel Shih said.
"Soon there will be good roads everywhere. Soon
the entire country will be working as one toward
the great goal of communism. It will be an
example to all but especially you in the
imperialist West."

"I'm sure everyone appreciates these
advances," Mallory said. "Lucky for you that
China's enormous size has been achieved through
something other than imperialism. How
astonishing, when one recalls that China was once
only a tiny nation on the Yellow River."

He turned to Mary Penfield. "Are you
interested in poetry, Mrs. Penfield? The Chinese
poets are as eloquent as their historians. Some

time you must read 'The Chariots Go Forth' by Tu
Fu. It is very informative. There was an emperor
of China named Wu-ti, also. A very interesting
man. His armies spent a great deal of time in the
Tarim Basin protecting trade routes . . . or
something."

"That is part of China," Shih said stiffly.

"Well, perhaps you are riding on the coat-
tails of previous empires. Still, perhaps they
should be able to choose independence."

Mallory looked away and taking up his cup
said, "By the way, Mrs. Penfield, where was your
home in the States?"

Shih had started to speak but the abrupt
change of direction stopped him.

For several minutes they talked of Texas,
California and New York, but Mallory's attention
was only half present. He was picking up the
discussion between Hart and Chu.

The food was good, and he ate as he listened.
Colonel Shih seemed to have nothing more to say
to him and Mary Penfield talked, lightly and
easily, of many things. She was a charming woman
and she knew how to make conversation.

"You speak Chinese, Mr. Mallory. Did you learn
it here?"

"In Montana. When I heard my father was lost
over China when his plane crashed, I told myself
someday I would come here.

"There was a small town near our ranch and
there was a Chinese restaurant there. I used to
drop in quite often, drink coffee, and get them
to tell me about China. Most of the Chinese in
that part of America are from Canton or its

environs. But this family spoke Mandarin. They
offered to teach me.

"In the winter I delivered newspapers in the
town, and I started dropping in every night after
I'd finished my paper route. By the time I was
twelve, about two years from the time I started,
I could speak enough to be understood. Because of
that, the Army put me in a crash course for
officers headed for Korea."

"Did you know anything about this part of
China?" she asked.

"I'm afraid I got over into Mr. Wells's field.
I found some of the best books were written by
plant-hunters. I also read Ssu-ma ch'ien's
history, The Art of War, and some of the Chinese
novels, The Dream of the Red Chamber, The
Scholars, and of course, The Romance of the Three
Kingdoms."

Chu glanced down the table. "And Chin P'ing
Mei?"

Mallory smiled. "Yes, that, too."

He took his time eating and with his coffee,
yet inwardly he was eager to be out and going.
From time to time through the tent door he saw
somebody cross the grass walking toward the
creek. Most of the Khambas and many of his own
men would be ready.

Yet the most important, the most noticeable
ones were trapped here keeping up the illusion.
He must not be the first to leave the table, yet
Lagskha could do that . . . he had his own ritual
of living and none of those at the table were
familiar enough with his life to guess what was
his custom or was not.

A slow half hour went by, with talk that moved

from archaeology to Tibet to China proper. "The
Tsinling Mountains," Marshal Chu suggested, "are
the least explored area in China."

"Where are they exactly?" Marty Wells asked.

"In Shensi, near the border of Kansu. Very
rugged. Once, as a boy, after the Long March, I
had occasion to be in that area. Even the people
who live nearby know little of them."

At last Lagskha excused himself, and rising
from the table, started back for the Inn,
accompanied by his sister. Shih, obviously
impatient with socializing, also arose and left,
accompanied by Chu's aide. Chu lingered, dawdling
over his coffee.

Mallory refilled his cup, sitting back in his
chair as if time were the least important of all
things. Yet even now he knew his men would be
moving the stock away; only the Khambas would be
waiting in the hollow near the stream for the
lama to join them.

It was growing darker, clouding over a little.
He glanced outside. "Looks like rain," he
commented.

"This place you mentioned," Dr. Bernard said
suddenly, ". . . could you guide us to it?"

Mallory chuckled. "Now, Doctor, our very
civilized meeting here at this table is one thing
but that is quite another. I'd be glad to show
you . . . some time.

"You see," he explained, "when the Incarnation
announces his decision, the good Marshal will no
longer have to restrain himself. A party can
escort Lagskha toward Chamdo and the Marshal will
still have a considerable number of soldiers
left. I think he will make a move to detain us,

to restrain our movements. He would like to have me for a prisoner . . . or dead . . . and the same for those men with me.

"Marshal Chu is a gentleman, and conducts himself as such, but he is also a soldier. In his place I would do as he will do. I am afraid, Doctor, that you and your friends are about to see what war is like. It will be a small war, but the Go-log do not surrender and neither shall I.

"None of us wish to endanger the Incarnation but when he is safely off the stage we all know what will happen here. I suggest you all keep down and out of sight. A bullet doesn't care who it hits."

"I am sure you exaggerate," Penfield protested.

"Major Mallory could surrender," Chu suggested. "If he would surrender, I do not think his Go-log would last long."

Mallory chuckled. "You know I'll not surrender, Marshal, and I shall not suggest that you do so."

"I?" The Marshal was suddenly wary.

Mallory smiled. "Your position is but little better than mine. Even, if I may say so, a little worse. You have a career at stake. I do not.

"The trail out there, it runs two ways, north to the Magnung Chu, and south along that stream to the Yalung River.

"Now if the Marshal takes Lagskha and retires without any fanfare, he has every chance of making it back to his headquarters at Chamdo. But supposing he decides to move against me?

"My men are few, but they are very tough men. They are well-armed and determined . . . even

eager. The Marshal is going to have to pursue us
down the trail your expedition came up. It is a
very difficult trail, ideal for a guerrilla
action.

"I am sure as distinguished an officer as
Marshal Chu, and as high in the ranks of the
followers of Mao, is familiar with his maxims for
guerrilla war? I say 'his' advisedly, for the
principles have been known and used for years.

"Now I suspect the Marshal is an excellent
chess-player. As he knows there is a point in
every game where further moves are useless . . .
but there is always another game. Especially when
he has gotten what he came for, the Incarnation.
He can return to headquarters a success or with a
devastated command and little to show for it
beyond what he would have anyway."

"You are right, Mallory. There is always
another game. My only regret is that you are not
Chinese, Major Mallory, we have so many ideas in
common."

He got to his feet. "Mallory, you pleased me
very much a little earlier when you mentioned Tu
Fu's poem. Colonel Shih is a very efficient man,
a very excellent soldier, but he should also
paint . . . or write poetry.

"Did you know, Mr. Hart, that many of our
greatest military men were poets? I understand
that your own General Patton was also. That he
wrote at least two volumes of poetry. It develops
the imagination, opens the avenues of thought.

"I particularly like that part of the poem
that is something like this: 'Today they send me
again to the wars, Back to the north frontier, By
whose gray towers our blood has flowed In a red

tide, like the sea--And will flow again, for Wu
Huang Ti is resolved to rule the world.'"

Chu paused at the opening of the tent. "I will
return in the morning for our lama's decision and
I will watch closely by night." He walked swiftly
away, and Bernard looked after him. "An
interesting man," he said, "a very interesting
man."

"And a dangerous one," Mallory said. "Anyone
who under-rates him is a fool."

"What do think he will do?" Renata asked.

Mallory shrugged. "Probably he will do the
unexpected. He might gracefully pull out, taking
the lama with him, knowing, as I suggested, that
there is always another day. He is shrewd enough
to retreat from an untenable position.

"What is even more likely is that he will seem
to retire, but will actually detach a portion of
his men to destroy us." Mallory smiled then. "And
he will probably offer Colonel Shih the command."

CHAPTER 10

Mallory paused on the grass, glancing toward
the Inn. All was quiet.

Lagskha and Brikhuti were strolling together
upon the meadow, Brikhuti pausing from time to
time to pick a flower from the thick grass.

Mallory hesitated a moment longer, then
strolled after them. In the distance thunder
rolled, and Lagskha turned as if to start back
for the Inn, but his sister tugged at his sleeve.

It was as beautiful a bit of impromptu acting
as Mallory had seen, and he smiled as he walked,

yet his mouth was dry, his heart was beating heavily. If they were stopped now--

But nobody did stop them and the rain that might have ended their little performance held off. They paused on the bank of the stream, then walked down into it.

Mallory, who had gained on them, followed.

The moment they were hidden below the bank, which was scarcely high enough to conceal them, both started to run.

Lagskha gathered up his robe and ran well. They paused to catch their breath, and Mallory over-took them. "It's now or never," he said. "The horses are right ahead!"

Six Go-log awaited them with their horses. They all rode into the water and swiftly along the creek bed. But Mallory knew that despite all the stories one read, running water would not immediately wipe out the tracks of horses or men. The water was crystal clear and the indentations of the hoof tracks would remain an hour or more.

For a half mile they followed the stream, then Mallory led them out at a low cut where formerly another stream had joined this one. The surface was rock, and they rode up the small draw and into the mountains.

The ancient stream had cut down to bed-rock, leaving no soil. Here and there leaves had fallen, and there was much scattered debris of rock, small slides, dead branches. Here they paused a moment to listen.

"Nothing yet," he said, at last. "Now follow me." The banks of the stream were high, and here and there an old slide permitted a climb up the steep, tree-clad hill.

Turning his horse suddenly, Mallory rode up the bank, and ducking his head under arching rhododendrons, disappeared. They all followed.

"Keep on along the trail," he said. "You'll catch up with the yaks soon." Dismounting, he walked back. The horses' hoofs had torn the earth of the slide, so using a branch he loosened more dirt from the slope above and allowed it to cascade down to the water's edge.

The dim trail was heavily shadowed by the trees and brush. Riding swiftly, Mallory overtook the convoy and with Brikhuti beside him, rode swiftly ahead. Gomba looked at him curiously. "It is not old," he said, "old, but not yet that old."

"No." He pointed back down the way they had come. "Hundreds of years ago a slide washed down there, wiping out the road, turning the stream. This is a cut-off. You will see."

He led the way. There were no tracks on the trail. The canyon was narrow, thickly covered with trees, and the trail would be invisible from the sky. Only one could go at a time, except in rare places where two might ride.

The trail dipped down between two massive boulders allowing scarcely room for passage. The trail kept on, but Mallory, consulting notes he kept in an inner pocket, turned sharply right and scrambled up a rocky trail that showed no evidence of passage. Riders and yaks followed him.

Not even a mountain goat can excel the yak as a climber. Huge, long-haired and horned, but sure-footed, the yaks with their packs followed him.

Soon it began to rain. At first a few big scattered drops, then a down-pour.

From time to time through breaks in the trees they could see towering snow- and ice-covered peaks looming before them in a gigantic wall. "We aren't going over that?" Brikhuti exclaimed.

"Through it," Mallory said, "but not yet."

They emerged from the trees and before them lay slopes covered with alpine grasses and flowers. More and more their movement made breathing a conscious action. "We'll walk now. This altitude is too much, even for these horses."

The rain fell steadily then turned to snow, gathering in a thin white sheet over the rocks. For a little way he held to his upward course, then turned sharply right and eastward along the flank of the mountains.

Vast drums of thunder rolled in the canyons, and lightning leaped from peak to peak. By the time darkness began to close in they had traveled nine miles since leaving the Valley of Pleasant Winds.

Mallory led them down into the trees and into a hollow among some rocks. There were wind-hollowed caves there, not deep, but shelter of a sort. "We'll camp here."

Lagskha turned in his saddle, concerned, "It is soon to stop, if it is for me or my sister--"

"We can't see in the dark. I'm guessing the trail from here on is a nightmare."

"You mean this one hasn't been?" Brikhuti looked down at the fire a Go-log was kindling. "How much of this do we have?"

"Weeks, perhaps months. It is a long way to India."

They sat together in the shallow cave and watched the gray curtain of rain slanting down, metallic and cold. Mallory held the bowl of tea in his hands, enjoying the warmth. When he had first come to Tibet he had been astonished at the capacity the Tibetans had for tea, drinking as many as thirty bowls in a day . . . and often even more.

A Go-log came in, a slender, powerful man in a weather-darkened sheepskin coat. The man spoke rapidly.

Mallory said, "This man says there is a place nearby where one can see the trail far, far below. Would you like to come?"

The caves where they had taken shelter were just below timberline, and leaving them they climbed up between some boulders to the alpine meadows which slanted away for miles upon miles toward the south, the icy gray peaks and ridges rearing proudly up on their left.

A few dwarfish, wind-barbered trees straggled up the slope, then even these disappeared. They walked on, following their guide for nearly a hundred yards, then went out on a rain-wet rock, and their eyes followed the Go-log's pointing finger.

Far below, caught in a momentary island of slanting sunlight, they could see the shine of the rain-wet inn roof, the white of the tents, and the distant sheen of the stream in the meadow.

"Do you think they have found our trail?"

Mallory had been wondering about that. "I

don't know, but they would have to look. The dry
creek bed up which we came is over-lapped by the
mountain. From the valley one cannot even see
that an opening exists. They would have to ride
up the bed of the stream, as we did."

He waved a hand. "All of this is unexplored
country. Tomorrow morning we will be riding the
old trail, but don't expect much. So far as
anyone knows it hasn't been traveled in
centuries.

"I said earlier that we would go through those
mountains. You see, far ahead of us this range
jogs somewhat, and in that jog there is a saddle.
The old trail went over that saddle and follows
down the back side."

Mallory went out into the night and moved away
from the small sounds of their camp. Despite his
doubt that Chu had so quickly located their line
of flight, he dared not risk the possibility that
the contrary was true.

It was very dark, and in the silence of the
mountains he could hear only the whisper of the
rain. He walked among the horses, talking to them
gently. He was uneasy. Brikhuti's presence was
distracting, and now, if ever in his life, he
needed to concentrate. He was under no illusions
as to what lay before them. Aside from the
pursuit which would soon be augmented by aircraft
there were all the risks of travel in the high
country. At this altitude even their rough
mountain horses must be handled with care. He had
seen passes but little higher than this marked
with the bones of animals that had died in the
crossing.

The trails would be bad. Never very good, they

had been untraveled in many years, and undoubtedly other ways must occasionally be found or repairs made. Yet within a few days their only way would lead them down from the peaks. They must cross the Yalung river, and it would be necessary to get additional horses at Dzogchen Gompa, one of the largest monasteries in this part of Tibet.

Without a doubt Marshal Chu would anticipate both the crossing of the river and the possibility they must pass by Dzogchen Gompa. He would have troops at both places, or spies, at least. And they could expect troops eventually.

On the other hand the grape-vine would probably alert the monks at Dzogchen to the fact that the Incarnation would be coming their way. With luck they would be ready to help.

Both the Incarnation and his sister seemed strong, and so they must be. The march ahead was to be desperate and grueling.

When at last he returned to the caves, all were asleep. He added a few heavier sticks to the small fire, drank one more bowl of tea, and thought longingly of the coffee enjoyed with Hart's expedition. He also thought of Renata, the American girl. She was very lovely . . . well, no matter. They had little use for him. To them he was a renegade, a drifter whom they were better off without.

The night wind moaned in the trees, and slow drops fell from the drooping branches of the evergreens. He finished his tea and went to his bed, rolling up in a couple of yak hides to sleep until morning.

A time or two he awakened, as always, to

listen to the night, but there was only the
whisper of rain, the falling of an occasional
drop into the coals, and a faint stirring among
the horses or yaks. Again he slept.

CHAPTER 11

Renata Bernard was awakened suddenly by a
thunder of hoofs and angry shouts. The canvas
flap of her tent was ripped open and a soldier
rushed in. She got to her feet and, prodded by a
rifle, was driven to the main tent.

Hart was already there, his face white with
anger. Dr. Bernard stumbled in, a cut over one
eye, and then Marty Wells. Of them all, only Hank
Carpenter and Roy Lewis seemed calm.

In the other tents there was shouting and
confusion. Horses raced by, and then Colonel Shih
entered the tent.

"Where are they?" he shouted.

"Where are who?" Hart's manner was icy.

"The lama!" Shih shouted again. "Where have
you hidden him? Where is Mallory?"

"I assure you," Hart said calmly, "I have no
idea what you are talking about. I have seen none
of them since lunch . . . when you were present
as well."

"Lies! Lies! You are all together in this!"

"What has happened?" Hart asked. "If you could
tell us then we might be able to help you."

"You know what happened!" Shih's tone was
ugly. "They are gone. Gone!"

"How can that be?" Dr. Penfield said. "Haven't you guards at both ends of the valley?"

"They saw nothing," Shih said irritably. "They heard nothing. They are fools."

"As I explained to the Marshal," Hart said coolly, "their activities are no concern of ours. It merely happened that they arrived here at the same time we did. We entertained them, as we did you."

"We will find them," Shih threatened, "and in the meantime you may all consider yourselves under arrest."

"I am afraid that Chou En-lai will not appreciate this," Hart said calmly. "I shall have to notify him of my treatment."

Colonel Shih turned very slowly, measuring Gunther Hart with a careful glance. "Do you know Chou En-lai?"

"Of course. We are good friends. He was the one who arranged for our permission to enter this part of China."

"I see."

The change in manner was subtle, but it was there. The anger went from his tone, and Hart, who could see the obsequiousness in a man quicker than most, recognized the tone for what it was.

"Chou En-lai and I were friends in Paris," Gunther Hart said quietly, "and I have been able to be of some small aid to him from time to time. You know," he suggested, "how it is. One man can often help another in reaching the seats of power. There were occasionally people whom Chou wished to talk to off the record. I was in a position to arrange this.

"When all communication is through military or

political channels a very competent man can often
be prevented from doing those things he is best
able to do. Take yourself, for example," Hart
said suavely. "I doubt if the reports of your
efficiency and skill always reach the ears of
your superiors."

He paused. "I am always glad to recommend
those who help me. And I have been a good friend
to the People's Republic of China." He smiled his
beautiful smile. "If it were not so, would they
permit me to come here?"

"I am ordered to find the man Mallory and the
monk."

"Of course. I hope you do find him, but I
assure you we have no knowledge of his
whereabouts. As you may have heard, Major Mallory
and I were not friendly."

"I have been ordered," Colonel Shih said, "to
place you under arrest. You are not to attempt to
leave this valley. These are my orders, do you
understand?"

"Of course, Colonel Shih, and we shall do our
best to obey. When you again see Marshal Chu I
wish you would give him my respects and suggest
that I should like to talk to him. In the
meanwhile, the best of luck to you. We must talk
again, Colonel, but if there is anything I can do
to help, would you tell me? I would take it as a
favor."

When the Colonel departed, Hart suggested, "My
advice would be for us all to dress, as promptly
as possible."

"But how could he have escaped?" Carpenter
protested. "There is no other way out!"

"For a clever man, there might be--also for a

man who knows much of the history of this region.
My friends, I have erred. I should have
cultivated the acquaintance of this man Mallory.
I think he knew the very thing I wished to
know . . . I had some inkling of his knowledge
but . . . well, there simply wasn't time."

When they were back in their tent Mary
Penfield said, "Gunther Hart isn't the only one
to miss their chance."

"What do you mean by that?"

"If I'd been a single woman I'd never let the
most exciting man I ever saw slip through my
fingers. And now look what's happened. He's off
on a long trek through the mountains with another
woman."

"I had not thought of him in that way," Renata
said primly.

"You're a liar, Nata," Mary said cheerfully,
"or woefully under-sexed. Any red-blooded woman
who could look at that man . . . well, honey, had
I been your age I'd have moved in . . . fast."

"I wonder how they got away?"

"Talk to Jalu about it . . . you know, the
herdsman. The Doctor and I were talking to him
last night . . . he knows a thousand stories
about your man Mallory. Jalu says he can walk
over mountains . . . or through them. He says
this is enchanted country. Most outsiders won't
even think of coming here, and as far as going
back into the Chala shan, forget it."

Renata dressed hurriedly and met the others
outside. Marty was waiting for her, Roy Lewis
beside him. "Roy suggests we not stray away today
and I think he's got something, although I do
want to work the banks of the creek."

"I'll come with you."

"Just don't get out of sight," Lewis warned. "Just because Hart soft-soaped the Colonel doesn't mean we're off the hook."

"I'm armed," Marty said. And Renata glanced at him, surprised.

"Don't use it or even show it unless there's no other way," Lewis warned. "No matter what Hart says or does, Chu is in command here. He can issue any kind of a report he wants and spin any kind of a story. He could shoot the lot of us and merely say we were trying to stir up a counter revolution."

Marty Wells and Renata walked toward the stream. The rain of the previous night had ceased but lowering clouds shrouded the peaks. They walked along the banks of the stream but the plants he saw were ones he had previously collected or which were well known . . . he would note them in his journal for the trip but there was no need to collect.

They had almost reached the mountain wall when Marty stopped. What he saw was an odd color on a white-flowered gentian, and a closer look showed him the petal had been bruised. He squatted on his heels, looking carefully around.

The growth along the opposite bank was willow and birch; farther back the birch was mixed with juniper. Two kinds of willow . . . he got up and moved along the bank.

Renata, who was picking flowers, turned to watch. "Found something unusual?"

"It isn't the plant," he said, and the tone of his voice brought her to him.

"What is it, Marty?"

He had picked the bruised flower. "This," he said.

"It's been stepped on or something."

"Exactly . . . by whom?" He walked along the bank and discovered a place where a little gravel had been caved off. He looked at it, then along the stream toward the mountain. "Well, I'll be damned!"

"What is it?"

"Don't you see? There's a break in the mountain, right where the stream curves."

"I'm not sure . . . it may be the way the light falls."

"No, there's a break. This near wall over-laps the other and from a few hundred yards you can hardly see it. I'll bet there's a water-course there . . . run-off from the mountain. And that's how they got away!"

"Marty? Don't tell anybody."

He looked at her. "Glad you feel that way. I wasn't going to." He glanced at it again. "That must be the old route they were speaking of."

"We'd better start back--they'll come looking for us."

When they had walked back a little way Marty said, "Nata, the way I see it, let the lama make up his own mind. If he wants to stay, he will. If he wants to go, it should be his choice."

"Did you ever talk to him about music? Brikhuti said she brought him a lot of records-- jazz, swing, rock and roll . . . even the classics. But he really likes the modern stuff."

"Sure. We talked about an hour the other night. What he really likes is country-western. I was telling him about Johnny Cash."

They were silent. The night had become
suddenly dark with the heavy clouds over the
tight little valley. A light glowed through the
canvas of the tent Lewis shared with Wells, and
they could see him moving about. Then another man
entered the tent. Marty hesitated . . . the head-
gear the newcomer wore looked like the ear-flaps
the Khambas wore.

A Khamba visiting Lewis? It was unlikely. So
far as Wells knew, none of them spoke English.

Gunther Hart was standing outside when they
approached, and he glanced from one to the other,
no pleasure on his face. "A moment," he said,
"before you go in."

They paused. The man in conversation with Hart
was Dr. Penfield. "In the old stories," Hart
said, "they called it a council of war. Keep
yourselves prepared for a quick move. We may be
forced to take a page from Mallory's book."

"What has happened?"

"Nothing . . . yet. I shall speak to Marshal
Chu tomorrow and request permission to go
forward. He will tell me I cannot go forward and
so we will go back."

"Back?"

Gunther Hart smiled. "At least as far as that
monastery we passed by on the way in. We will go
into the hills from there, but I want no talk of
this.

"I believe Chu wishes to be rid of us, and he
will be, but not by our leaving the country. Once
on the hill trail you shall study and research to
your heart's desire."

He looked at Renata. "Did Mallory give you any

idea which direction he was taking? Did he speak of a way out?"

"No . . . no, he didn't. Actually, I talked to him very little."

Mary Penfield was combing her hair before Renata's mirror. "It's better than mine. Do you mind? Your uncle was working in the main tent, so I took the opportunity."

"Come any time." Renata sat down, her hat in her hand. She should be doing the work her uncle was doing for himself, but she had been unable to settle down to anything. And now they might move again, at any moment.

"I'm worried," she said suddenly. "Sometimes I wish we had listened to Mallory. Gunther is conniving to use Colonel Shih to circumvent Marshal Chu in some way. I don't like it."

"Neither do I. Shih isn't shrewd enough to match wits with Chu and neither is Gunther. Well, we're here. All we can do now is sing the song the way the notes read."

Dinner was a silent meal. Gunther Hart had little to say, eating and retiring to his own tent to dictate to Hank Carpenter.

Lewis and Wells stayed on in the main tent. Of them all, Bernard was the only one excited. "I've been checking the Inn . . . you know, Mallory made some comments about the age of it and he was right.

"There's a part of the wall on the far side . . . a whole corner, in fact, that is very, very old. But the stones themselves are even older. I can just make out some inscriptions . . . no language I could recognize, but I'm sure the inscription was turned on its side.

"Obviously, that stone was taken from some older site to be used in this building. The place is a patch-work . . . a regular cross-word puzzle of a building, and I never saw so much material from different periods put together into one structure.

"Back about two hundred yards behind the Inn there's an old stone water-trough they use for washing clothes . . . not too often, I'm afraid.

"It stands on the edge of a tilted stone platform, tilted by some upheaval in the earth, I imagine. A shrine, perhaps, or a part of a fort or castle such as the ones mentioned by Mallory."

They sat over their coffee and talked until nearly midnight, discussing mutual problems and points at which their various disciplines might be of service to one another.

"I never thought of it as anything but an exploration," Bernard said. "There's been no serious work under-taken in this area. Not even a good canvass that I'm aware of. I have no doubt there were trade routes of a sort . . . even the American Indians had them . . . but not to the extent Mallory implies."

He smiled suddenly, a little embarrassed. "You know, a good many years ago . . . oh, twenty-five, perhaps thirty years ago, I stumbled on a translation of a book by a man who claimed to know something about the Tantric beliefs. It was a wild, unbelievable sort of account, purporting to be the truth.

"He told of the track, route or trail, whatever you wish to call it, that could be

followed only by those of particular courage or
virtue, a route beset with dangers . . . all
manner of evil . . . but which led to ancient
monasteries where the old secret knowledge was
still studied by people who came there from the
ends of the earth . . . chosen people.

"Oh, it was a ridiculous story but I loved it.
I had less discrimination then, and that book was
something right out of Rider-Haggard or Pierre
Benoit."

He stood up. "It is late. I think I shall be
off to bed."

Lewis stopped him. "Doctor? Who wrote that
book?"

Bernard paused, frowning. "You know, I've been
trying to remember. It has simply escaped me."

He shrugged into his coat. "You know how it is
when one is young. The imagination is there and
anything is possible. It was my dream then . . .
I really think it was what got me started in
archaeology . . . it was my dream to follow that
road. To find it, no matter how, and follow it."

"You may yet, Doctor Bernard." It was Gunther
Hart standing in the opening of the tent. "You
may yet, indeed."

CHAPTER 12

Among the icy peaks and across the alpine
uplands there was silence. Only the soft hoof-
falls of horse and yak, only the creak of saddle-
leather and occasionally the moan of the wind.
Mallory rode ahead, his rifle at hand.

Occasionally he looked back. There was nothing. But he knew they were not alone, for no matter what else was back there, his Go-logs would be following, the band that he left in the hills when he went down into the Valley of Pleasant Winds. They would follow and they would also form a rear guard, maintaining a moving ambush for any who pressed too closely.

The travelers talked little, for the silence about them bred silence within. Something seemed to listen . . . and they listened in turn.

Now, from time to time, they found artifacts. An ancient fire circle, and once a magnificent axe-head shaped from obsidian, beautifully worked and polished. And here and there the trail, brief sections of it that even the snow, ice and wind of these altitudes could not erase.

"How high are we?" Brikhuti asked, during one pause for rest.

They were almost two miles ahead of the slowly plodding caravan. The yak moves at a speed of a camel, about two and a half miles per hour, when on long treks. This allowed time for Mallory or one of the Go-log, usually Gomba, to ride on ahead and scout the trail.

He glanced around, then shrugged. "One can usually judge from the plants, although I'm not Marty Wells. The tree limit is about twelve thousand feet, and vegetation of all kinds except moss and what they call cushion herbs disappears at about sixteen thousand.

"I'd say we were around fourteen thousand, maybe a little less." He pointed. "I've seen those red poppies growing on up to almost fifteen

thousand feet, and that dark blue, purplish
flower . . . I don't know what it is . . . grows
in the scree up to well over fifteen."

He indicated the raw-backed peaks above them.
"They probably aren't over sixteen thousand, but
I'd be guessing. This is all new country to me."

They huddled together at night in a rock
basin, a kind of miniature cirque hollowed by a
glacier. There was water from melted snow, and
timberline, with a straggling growth of cedar
lying not far below. Two of the Go-log took a yak
and went down into the juniper for fire-wood,
returning with ancient juniper logs and chunks
from dead growth, of which there was plenty.

They were settled down around their cooking
fires when suddenly there was a shout and the Go-
log scattered into the rocks, rifles in hand.

"What is it?" Mallory asked.

Gomba pointed across the alpine meadow. It was
not quite dark, and out of the shadows came
riding at least fifty horsemen.

They were obviously Go-log, wild, fierce
horsemen carrying thirty-foot lances as well as
their rifles and broad-swords. But they were not
the men of his group; this was a raiding party of
the Ri-mang, largest of the Go-log tribes, whose
home-lands were east of the Chala Shan and south
of the Yellow River.

They drew up in a tight line, lances gripped
in their fists.

Mallory and Gomba walked out to meet them.
Speaking quickly, Mallory asked who they were and
where they were going.

Their leader looked down at him coldly. "We

have heard of you. You are the foreigner who
rides with the Khang-rgan."

Mallory had lived too long among the Go-log
not to know that when no one else was available,
they fought among themselves, and he had neither
the time nor the men to waste in fighting for
sheer glory.

"I am that foreigner. I ride with my people on
a far mission. I escort the Lagskha-tsang and his
sister, who go to India."

The Go-log respected few things, feared
nothing. They were considered Buddhists, though
religion sat lightly upon their hard shoulders.

"Not far behind us," Mallory continued, "are
fifty of the Khang-rgan who will soon join us.
And," he added, "in the Valley of Pleasant Winds
are six hundred soldiers of China . . . unless
they are following us."

Several of the Go-log had come down from the
rocks. They also knew the temper of their people,
and each carried his machine pistol in plain
sight. The weapons were better than any the Ri-
mang carried . . . at least, in this group. Some
had modern rifles, some only had old match-locks.

"The soldiers of China have good rifles,"
Gomba suggested slyly.

"We will see," the chieftain said. He started
to turn the horse.

"One moment," Mallory lifted a hand. "How is
the road?"

For a long moment there was silence, and then
the chieftain said, "For some it is not bad, for
others not good. We did not travel far, coming up
from Ch'ang-ning-ha." A kind of ugly smile came

to his lips. "Ride carefully, Foreigner, this is not a road to be easily traveled."

And then they were gone, a clatter of hoofs, one last derisive yell, and the sound faded.

They returned to their fires then and Brikhuti handed him a bowl of tea. "You know," she said, "I have lived away from my people so much that I feel a stranger. So much of this is new to me . . . or just barely remembered from when I was a child.

"When I came to Europe there was so much I did not understand, and I felt I must know something of their history, so I began to read. I already knew English . . . I had learned it at home from a teacher who had lived in Sikkim.

"I read a book called When Knighthood Was in Flower, and then Ivanhoe. The ceremonies and the tourneys were so much like those in my country that I was astonished. Do you know our Festival of the Great Prayer? When there are horse races, foot races, wrestling and all? It was like that.

"My father was an official, so we had to send many horsemen to the festival . . . all in armor just like in the Middle Ages in Europe.

"I remember, my father often would ride himself to demonstrate. They would charge down a course at full gallop, shoot at a white disk hanging about five or six feet from the ground, then put the rifle away, and shoot at another target with a bow and arrow. Father was very good, and he rarely missed. There were booths where one could buy food or something to drink, and it was fun.

"The Go-logs have such games, too, but theirs

are rough. My military training was pretty easy
when compared to what they think is fun."

The fire dwindled. The Go-log had gone to
sleep except for one man, who was on guard.

Mallory added a few sticks to the fire and
walked out into the night. It was very still but
the guard moved over to him as soon as he
appeared.

"We are watched," he whispered. "There is
something out there."

"What have you heard?"

"Nothing . . . only, I know. There is
something there."

"Go get some tea. I will watch until you have
finished."

Mallory moved out a little farther from camp.
The moon was rising and the shoulder of the
mountain lay in vast tilted ledges, grass-covered
except here and there where they were
exposed . . . great smooth, almost polished white
ledges, shining in the night.

After awhile his eyes became accustomed to the
night, and he could see more clearly. The moon
lifted higher, and the great flat shoulder of the
mountain stretched away into an infinity that
ended in darkness. There were shadows here and
there . . . had the Ri-mang come back? He doubted
that.

Yet he felt it, too. There was something out
there in the darkness. Behind him the camp was
hidden. From here there was not even a glow of
the fire, for they had chosen their site well. He
put a hand into the folds of his shuba and
touched the butt of his gun, to make sure it was
ready to hand.

He waited . . . he thought he detected a
sound, but it was not repeated. He strained his
ears to hear, and all was quiet.

A yeti? He had heard the stories of the
mountain creatures but he had never seen one.
Many of the Go-log had . . . he no longer
doubted the existence of something though he
would not speculate on what it was. After all,
who should know better? A scientist who spent a
few weeks in the mountains? Or the people who
lived there?

There had been a time when he spent nearly a
year in the desert without ever seeing a rattler.
Of course, he knew they were there and the
Indians had told him so . . . then, on his last
day, he saw three. Yet anyone coming into that
desert might have gone away and said there were
no snakes because that person had not happened to
see one.

The people of eastern Tibet had known forever
of the giant panda, but it was not until about
forty years ago that the first was seen by a
white man.

He moved out into the night. If the yeti lived
in the mountains there could be no better area
than this . . . lonely as it was.

He heard and saw nothing. Like his guard, it
was rather something that he felt. Something
intangible, elusive . . . yet perhaps it was
simply the loneliness, the emptiness, perhaps
some primitive suspicion that there ought to be
something out there. Man had always peopled his
wilderness with shadows, werewolves, gnomes and
the ghosts of things departed.

Was thought only a mechanical function of the brain? Or could it become, under proper guidance, a tangible thing bringing tangible results by its very being? By some force within itself?

He shook his head irritably; he was tired and he wanted to sleep. He hadn't the capability of solving such problems--he'd be lucky to avoid a bullet in the back. Looking out over the moonlit wastes, he thought that the Buddhists were right. Each instant lives only in that instant. Out there before him nothing could be in any two successive minutes the same.

The Go-log returned, moving silently. "You have listened?"

"Do not sleep, my friend. We live in a world of darkness and enemies."

"I shall not."

Mallory pushed the charred ends of a few sticks into the fire and loosened his clothes for sleep. There could be no thought of undressing. Not upon this night.

The Ri-mang were gone . . . but what else remained?

Were the shadows in his own mind? Of his own creation?

He hunched his yak-skin about his ears. He would think of that in the morning.

Only he knew he would not, for morning brought sanity, or at least freedom from the imagination which loved to create monsters in the shadows.

He slept . . . and long after the moon had passed behind the mountains something came silently out of the night and squatted by the fire, watching him.

CHAPTER 13

By daybreak they were moving again, Mallory in the lead. Until now the ancient trail had been vague, often broken, and sometimes faded out entirely. Far ahead he could see the break in the line of the ridge that was the pass toward which they were headed.

They rode across a vast slope of the most impossible green. The alpine grass was thick with wildflowers, for the ridge was high enough to catch a few extra rain clouds . . . perhaps the last gathering of moisture before the great desiccated bowl of Central Asia.

Here and there the ice of winter had polished the limestone ledges until they were smooth as glass and white as marble. Overhead the sky was a dark blue and the sun was warm.

From time to time they drew up to let the horses breathe. Accustomed as they were to high altitudes, this was higher still and the horses could suffer and die if not handled with extreme care. The air was very clear and sounds carried for great distances.

Brikhuti came up beside him. "Mallory, did you say you had more men?"

"They are behind us. We will await them before we cross the pass."

"You are not worried? I mean by what we might find on the other side of the range?"

"Mountains do not worry me. People do. When I am sad or in trouble, I always go to the mountains. We had a poet in the United States named Robinson Jeffers, and he said, 'When the cities lie at the monster's feet, there are left the mountains.' I believe that."

He thought ahead to the river crossing. If only there were another spot, some place not known or no longer used. But an unknown crossing was unlikely in an area where travel was thousands of years old. He checked his notes and tried to recall the details of the map, closing his eyes to bring the picture into focus. The river crossing on the ancient and forgotten trail they traveled had seemed to be at the same spot where the main trail crossed, but was that true? Might there not be some older or more difficult crossing that had fallen out of favor?

He was dreaming. The Go-log might know of such a place. They often raided this area, and if anyone knew, they would.

Lagskha-tsang rode up beside them. "This I like!" he said with enthusiasm. "I envy the man with sheep! He lives always among the high mountains!"

Brikhuti talked for awhile with her brother, in Tibetan. Mallory rode on ahead, swinging his horse this way and that, checking every available place for tracks. Much of their travel was over stone, where no tracks would be left, but there was much also of grass and some spots of soil. Yet he found no tracks.

Marmots whistled from the rocks nearby, and a kite soared lazily overhead.

Tomorrow they would make the pass . . . and after that?

————

In the Valley of Pleasant Winds, all was
still. The soldiers were gone and the way of
departure was open, yet Gunther Hart made no move
to leave.

Today he had gone out alone, on horseback,
refusing company. Renata watched him go, watched
him as she typed her uncle's report on the Inn
and the stone ruins behind it.

Hart circled around toward the gorge and rode
along its edge. Was he looking for something he
expected to find? The way taken by Mallory, for
example? Or was he looking for something he had
known of before he came to the valley?

Marty had gone into the hills searching for
samples. Roy Lewis was writing up his notes on
the geology of the region and her uncle was off
across the valley, casting back and forth to see
if there were any other remains or surface
indications.

Renata had done a little work of her own. She
alone had come along with no definite project
beyond that of learning all she could of the
myths, legends and mysteries of the Sino-Tibetan
borderland. Hart had been pleased at the thought
and had promised her some rather spectacular
results. Her own wish was simply to gather what
information she could. She hoped to contribute
something to the origin of the Tibetan people
through a study of those myths she was seeking.

She had discovered that the easiest way to
learn was simply to ask, to ask anybody,
everybody. One never knew who possessed the
information she needed and the idea that such
information could only be obtained from officials
or scholars was mistaken.

To learn the plants, the animals, the geology or the stories in an area, ask the man who lives there. Invariably in each village or area there is one man who has specialized in its history, or one man who is the storyteller.

In the Valley of Pleasant Winds she had talked a little with the inn-keeper, who was manifestly impatient with the whole idea. He was worried about his unexpected guests, about the Red soldiers, about Mallory and his Go-logs. The old stories, he implied rather definitely, were for women and children. Men had no time for such things.

But on the day that Mallory departed with Lagskha-tsang, another man appeared in the valley.

He was a slender man, of indefinite age, yet obviously no longer young. His face was European rather than Asiatic, but that was a quality she was accustomed to, for many of the Tocharis appeared Caucasian, as did many of the Lolos. The old man had sat alone on the k'ang, talking to no one, ignored by all. The inn-keeper avoided him. The old man seemed to have no place to go or at least no particular time in which to get there.

Now, as she turned to look for Hart, she failed to find him. Instead, she saw the old man coming toward her across the meadow from the Inn. He paused a short distance away, obviously listening to the sound of the typewriter. She spoke to him, and he smiled slightly. "It is a good sound," he said.

She was astonished. She had no idea the man spoke English, but she said, "I had not thought of it in that way. It does get the work done."

"Yes. Of course." He paused a moment. "The stylus was much slower."

In spite of herself, she laughed. "I should say it was. Thank Heaven, I don't have to do all this on clay tablets!"

"They had one advantage," he said quietly, "that your paper lacks. They lasted. They did not crumble away; the writing did not fade."

"You speak excellent English."

"No . . . not excellent. It is a language I acquired long ago, but seldom use." He gestured to the empty chair where her uncle had been sitting earlier in the day. "May I sit down?"

She was embarrassed. "Of course. Please do."

He seated himself and she typed on to the bottom of the page. As she was placing her carbons for another page he said, "I heard you asking about the old stories, the old legends. You are doing a paper on them?"

"If I can gather enough information. My uncle and I are working toward the same end from two different directions. We are interested in the earliest history of the Sino-Tibetan borderlands."

"Ah, yes. It is a place of much history. Your uncle is Dr. Bernard? The man who was studying the ruins of the temple out back?"

"Temple or fort. He is not sure."

"Temple. The fort is further back and higher up. If you would like I could show him."

"You are a Tibetan?"

He hesitated. "I have lived here many years, but I was born in Swat." She typed briskly for a few moments and he sat quietly, and then he said, "Mr. Hart looks for something?"

She paused before replying. Was he a spy? She was wary. Yet she felt drawn to the man, he was friendly . . . but so would a spy be friendly.

"He leads our expedition," she said. "I believe he is very interested in all our projects, and in China as well."

"And Mallory?"

Again she paused, "We met him only briefly."

"A very unusual man. You know that some of the Go-log believe him to be the incarnation of Kesar? The story is that when he came among them he did everything better than they. He rode their wildest horses, was an expert with all manner of weapons. You should hear the stories."

They talked quietly, and of many things. Suddenly, an idea occurred to her. "Would it be possible for you to work for us? I mean, as a guide, adviser, interpreter?"

"Of course. If Mr. Hart is interested. It is a pleasure to use English again." He watched her typing. "I was employed for a time by the British government as a cartographer."

He got to his feet, easily, gracefully. "I am called Muhsin."

He walked back toward the Inn and Renata looked after him, very puzzled. It was a little too opportune, his sudden arrival, his knowledge of English, of history . . . where was he going? Who was he? And how did he happen to appear here just at this time?

His questions had been few, and discreet, yet she was unaccountably worried.

Suddenly she was aware of Hank Carpenter. "Who was that?"

She shrugged. "A traveler. He speaks excellent English."

"How odd . . . in such a place as this."

It was exactly what she thought but somehow she was annoyed. "Well, there is an inn here."

"What was he asking you?"

Renata adjusted her carbons. "Asking? He was interested in my uncle's researches. He offered to show him the site of a ruined fort. He was very considerate and helpful."

Carpenter walked away, and after awhile Gunther Hart rode up and dismounted at his tent, then he walked over to where she was seated.

"Renata, why didn't you tell me about the other trail out of the valley?"

"Trail?" She glanced up. "Oh, that? I wasn't sure it was a trail, and then if that was the way Mallory disappeared, I did not want to mention it when Chu was still here. In any event, I am not sure there is any trail, properly speaking."

He asked about Muhsin and she explained briefly, adding a bit more than she had told Carpenter. As she did, she realized she had liked the man.

"He could be useful to us," she volunteered, and then added, almost as an after-thought, "He knows a great deal about the old history. He offered to show Uncle Ralph where the ancient fort was."

Hart turned away as Carpenter approached. Before Hank could speak, Hart said, "That man . . . Muhsin. Hire him."

"But--!" Carpenter started to protest, then stopped. "Sir? He may be a spy."

Gunther Hart merely glanced at him. "And what

do we have to fear if he is? He speaks English
and he knows the region. Hire him."

Gunther Hart walked away without even glancing
back, and Hank Carpenter stared after him.
Renata, catching his expression, was amused.

CHAPTER 14

Twice in the past few days they had seen
tracks, the tracks of one man, and he was
traveling on foot. In each case after following
the trail briefly he had come upon a flat surface
of exposed rock, and after that, simply nothing.
Mallory was tired and worried. Both were a result
of the altitude, he was sure. He had seen men
become irritable before when traveling in high
altitudes and thin air.

The pass lay just before them. He looked up at
the high saddle in the ridge with no enthusiasm.
He had never climbed mountains just to be
climbing, but always for what lay beyond. In this
case it was unknown, supposedly unexplored
country.

They camped before approaching the pass.
Lamlung Pass, some fifteen or sixteen miles to
the south, was over fifteen thousand feet. This
one was higher.

Gomba came and squatted near him. "What about
the horses?" Mallory asked.

Gomba shrugged. After awhile he said, "They
are Go-log horses, they will cross over."

They rode to the foot of the pass in the
fading afternoon and bedded their yaks where the
grass grew tall, and their horses where a watch

could be kept. A long wind blew cold off the snow peaks, and westward beyond where the Yarlung River flowed, there was another snow-crested range. Beyond that in another far-off valley was the Yang-tze-kiang, or as they called it here, the Dre Chu.

Mallory looked again at the saddle where no snow lay. They would cross over tomorrow into a land as wild, lonely and unknown as the craters of the moon.

A wild land lay before them and a wild land lay behind. In the fading light he looked again upon the hills. Brikhuti came and sat nearby.

"Is that it? Is that the pass?"

"Yes."

He was thinking of her. Scarcely six weeks ago she had been living in Europe.

"You like it, don't you?"

He looked at the pass. "Men come to places like this for places like that. There's nobody waiting over there with a cold drink, and there isn't any place a man could take a hot shower. We may be riding into a little corner of Hell, but it will be a new Hell and a place we've never seen."

"I've forgotten so much. When I talk to my brother I know I have changed; now it feels like I've stepped across some boundary into another world." She looked up at him. "What do you believe, Mallory?"

His eyes showed amusement. "If it is a god or gods you are talking about, I live with them . . . or him. There's no fit place in the world for a god these days but right where we are, up here, among the high peaks. Each meadow

is a cathedral. A man who lives high and lonely
doesn't have to talk to God . . . they understand
one another."

"And what about death?"

"It's right here . . . right at one's elbow
all the time. Anybody who thinks otherwise is a
fool. It may come one way or it may come another,
but it is never far away . . . nor is it
important.

"It's like moving picture film, you know. The
still pictures give the sensation of movement to
the characters. Life is like that, and death the
intervals between pictures."

"Then you believe as we do? In reincarnation?"

"Voltaire said something to the effect that it
would be no more surprising to be born twice than
once, that all nature was resurrection."

"Have you thought any more about going home,
Mallory? I love the United States."

"So do I . . . but you yourself have found how
difficult it is to return. As I understand it
you've been away at school most of twelve
years . . . well, I've been away ten.

"I can go back, but will I have come home? The
sights and sounds will be different than I
remembered, the people will have grown older,
settled into new patterns of living, they will
have relationships and memories that I cannot
share. I suppose after awhile one settles into
the routine again, but I am not sure I could.

"And I'd miss all this . . . the wild country.
I'd miss the unexpectedness of it, the finding of
an old trail, a ruined fort or shrine . . . the
sudden coming upon of some isolated village where

they have no idea there is a London or a New
York, and care less."

He was watching the slope of the mountain near
the pass. Something had moved up there . . . the
distance was too great to make out what it was. A
bear? Too high for a leopard . . . even a snow
leopard. Possibly a goat.

"Do you know Colorado?" she asked suddenly.
"When at first I grew very lonely I used to go
there."

"To ski at Aspen?" His tone was ironic.

"Yes, that, too. But I loved it. It was like
my own country."

By daylight they were mounting the pass.
Mallory led the way, walking ahead of his horse.
The wind was raw and cold, the trail, if such it
could be called, was narrow. In many places there
was scarcely room for a horse to move and, in
this altitude, they were having a bad time of it.

Mallory took two steps, then paused, and after
the time required for at least three steps, took
two more. His heart hammered, his head was light.
The yaks plodded along, heads down, unconcerned
by the troubles of men and horses. On the highest
passes their handlers would open a vein if they
carried too heavy a load, reducing their blood
pressure.

A few flakes of snow fell and the top of the
pass seemed even farther away. In places the
trail was almost blocked by falls of granite,
fractures had split the granite into blocks and
at the base of the cliff masses of boulders had
accumulated. Several times all the Go-log had to

come forward and help in rolling a boulder from the path. Even they were breathing hard, sucking at the thin air.

There was almost nothing in the way of vegetation as they climbed higher. The rock looked gray and cold, here and there were streaks of frozen snow, the snow which was falling had turned to tiny particles of ice that stung the exposed flesh.

The clouds thickened and the wind blew a gale down the pass. Mallory leaned into the wind. Once he slipped to his knees and staggered erect just as a lumbering yak came abreast with Brikhuti clinging to its long hair.

The yak's pace on level ground is about two and a half miles per hour; up hill and against the wind it was less than a mile per hour. The snow thickened and began to drift. Not far ahead they could see a long patch of frozen snow that extended diagonally across the pass.

The snow bank was an icy berm. Mallory stabbed at it with his wooden staff but it skidded off, making scarcely a scratch. Feeling his way through the blinding snow, he worked his way along the bank until he had almost reached the far wall of the pass. There it was lower, less than two feet deep and not over a dozen feet across.

Helping the Go-log they got the first yak started up. Its hoofs skidded, then fought for a foot-hold, and miraculously, they gripped into the ice and the yak scrambled, half-falling, over the snow bank. The others followed, each one churning the snow a little until the following horses had an easier path.

By the time they struggled to the top of the
pass the wind was blowing a gale, and the pass
itself, only a few hundred yards across, was
swept clean. With ice crystals slicing at their
cheeks, they fought their way over and started
down the far side. Twice horses fell and had to
be helped up, yet Lagskha-tsang walked steadily,
head bowed into the storm, plodding along as well
as the toughest of the Go-log.

The wind howled, lashing at them in fury, and
nothing could be heard above its howling.
Mallory, who was walking ahead, slipped and fell
to his knees. Struggling against the wind he put
his hand upon a boulder to push himself up.

His fingers gripped, felt, then he bent his
head to peer through the snow. It was a shaped
stone! Not a common boulder, but a stone shaped
by men. He got to his feet, staring into the
blinding snow.

At first he could see nothing, then during a
momentary break in the blowing curtain he saw
another tumbled block on the slide of talus
beside and above the trail.

Through the snow he glimpsed a massive
tower . . . a wall.

He caught the first yak and stopped it. The
Go-log came up beside him and he grasped the
man's arm . . . there was no way to make him hear
above the storm . . . he pointed at the wall,
then at himself and again at the wall. Then he
motioned for the Go-log to stay.

The bank was steep and icy, but he climbed
from rock to rock until he found himself at the
wall. It was massive, built of carefully cut
stones but in various shapes, all fitted neatly

together. Feeling his way along the wall, he came
to the tower. Below it the cliff fell sheer away,
how far he could not determine. Turning he worked
his way back, beyond the point at which he had
climbed, and when he had followed the wall for
sixty steps it turned sharply. Before him was a
massive gate, and inside it an impressive
courtyard. The floor of the court was paved, and
along the far side a series of stone buildings.

There was shelter here, from the wind. To go
on in this storm, along a trail steadily growing
worse, might mean the loss of both animals and
men.

He retraced his steps to the gate, then
followed a trail that slanted down to the one
upon which the caravan waited. He came down
almost abreast of one of the last animals. The
Go-log saw him through the snow and reached for
his broad-sword, then recognized him.

Catching his arm, Mallory pointed up the
trail, and the Go-log turned, leading his horse.
Those behind him followed, and Mallory struggled
along the trail against the blinding snow,
turning each man and beast back toward the
roadway to the fort.

The wind ripped at his clothing, and when he
turned to face it, drove the breath right back in
his throat. Bowing his head he pushed on, up the
steep bank to find the fort. At last they were
all within the shelter of the walls. He loosened
his collar and ear-flaps and looked around.

What he had taken for a tower was actually a
corner of a flat-roofed building, several stories
in height. The building was a typical podrang, a
fort built in a square around an open court. What

he had first seen was simply the outer wall of
the structure, which had long been abandoned and
was slowly going to ruin.

Gomba came to him, gesturing. He followed and
the Go-log led them into what must have been a
vast hall. Part of the roof had fallen in, and
snow had drifted through and frozen into ice, but
it was still more sheltered there. He noticed
some of the long dried yak chips, or argols,
indicating that others had sheltered here at some
time.

He started toward them to kindle a fire when
Brikhuti caught Mallory's arm.

He stared. Firelight flickered on a stone wall
down a corridor. Motioning to the others to stay
back, he walked that way. Two of the Go-log,
sensing a fight, were quick to follow.

It was a square room. Once there had been
wooden columns to hold up the roof; now they had
fallen, but the roof remained in place, scorning
any need for pillars. At one side of the room, in
a crude fireplace built into the floor, a fire
was burning.

There was no one there. All was silent but for
the distant sounds of men and animals, the moan
of the wind, and an occasional crackle from the
fire.

There were no packs, no men . . . only weird
shadows, dancing along the wall.

CHAPTER 15

Mallory looked at the fire, the fuel stacked
neatly nearby, and then his eyes slowly circled

the room. Nothing could be more empty. And it was
old, so very old.

"It is for you." He turned to Lagskha. "The
fire is for you."

The Incarnation stared at the flames, then
looked over at him. "Or for you, Mallory. Had you
thought of that?"

Mallory shook his head, not knowing what to
think. He dispatched two Go-log to search the
compound and the surrounding area. As hospitable
as the fire might be the mystery of it was a
potential threat and he would rest better when he
knew the answer.

They settled in. The howl of the wind was a
remote thing, wild and lonely, but outside. When
is comfort greater than when one sits within
walls and listens to the wind outside? A wind
that whines like a wild, feverish thing in a
broken voice?

"We will stay throughout the storm," Mallory
said. "I must see to the men, and the animals."

He went into the courtyard knowing the Go-log
needed no seeing to. This place disturbed him. It
was opportune, but it left him uneasy. He
wandered through the freezing rooms, many still
retaining their flat roofs, some lying open to
the wind and snow, scattered with broken rock and
ancient timbers. All were icy and still. And then
in the snow of one of them he found a track, half
a track, actually, of a large bare foot.

Brikhuti sat by the fire when he returned.
Lagskha was bundled in yak robes and asleep.

"You should rest," he advised. "It has been a
long day."

"Do you think of her?"

"Who?"

"Of the American girl."

"There is nothing of which to think. I do not know her; I'm unlikely to see her again. We have many other things to worry about."

"That is true but she was yours if you had reached out. I could see it."

He shrugged. "Renata Bernard," he commented dryly, "is a young lady of some importance in her world. She is obviously well off. In the States I am nobody, just a former soldier who worked on ranches."

"A man is what he wishes to be."

"You've lived in the States. You know how it is there. It is a world of accomplishment, of achievement. One is either doing something or has done something, and even if he has done something he must be on the verge of doing something else."

"Your country is changing. There are increases in crime, and the rioting?"

"I haven't been home in a long time. But we Americans love to exaggerate. We build up our problems enormously and then argue over how to deal with the situation. There has always been violence and turmoil . . . the Copperhead riots during the Civil War period or what happened in Europe before the Second World War . . . or in 1848. If one wants to fear there is always something to be afraid of, and there are always people aching for a chance to run, scream and tear their hair. Television and the newspapers have given them a chance to wet their pants in public, that's the only difference.

"And there's always been people ready to use that fear to their own ends. The only thing we

have to fear is over-reaction, the people, some
of them well meaning, who think that in order to
be against one thing they must join its opposite.
One doesn't have to become a fascist to fight
communism or a Communist to change
capitalism . . . in fact, it's vastly less
convincing. It's an over-reaction born of
weakness. The strong, those who don't need to be
told who they are by others, stand in the
middle."

Outside the cold wind moaned, and even as he
talked he was wondering about that fire. Was it
built for them? Or for someone else who fled on
their arrival?

"I wish whoever built this fire," he spoke
loudly, "would share it with us. The night is
cold."

Brikhuti said, "I think they have gone. I
think they ran when we came to this place."

"Whoever they are, they are welcome. We are
friends to all who would be friendly."

When Brikhuti had fallen asleep, Mallory
replenished the fire from the argols stacked
nearby, then went to the courtyard where the
animals were huddled.

It was cold and bleak. Two of the Go-log in
their conical hats, ear-flaps tied down against
the cold, sat by a small fire. Glancing at him as
he approached, they returned their attention to
the brewing tea.

Outside the open gate the snow swirled. It was
black out there, and a blizzard was blowing. At
least, they would have called it that in Montana.
He need not warn them to be alert, for a Go-log
is always alert.

Returning to the building he wandered
restlessly from room to room, most of them great,
drafty halls. Despite the ruined condition of the
building its pattern was obvious. Whatever else
it might have been it had been a monastery as
well. The outer yard where the animals rested and
the Go-log were on watch had been a court of
cells, for all about it were the tiny cubicles
where monks had lived. The room where Brikhuti
and Lagskha slept had been the refectory, or
dining hall, with a steward's room adjoining.

Alongside of it was the kitchen, and beyond
that the Hall of Assembly. Above and on a higher
level of the mountain were other rooms, perhaps
the place of residence of a higher lama, the
abbot of the monastery or whatever.

The pattern was the usual one of monasteries
in India, many had begun as monsoon-shelters for
the wandering almsmen, or bhikkhus. Although the
bhikkhus lived on donations from those who wished
to contribute, they were not classed with
ordinary beggars. Their begging was the outward
manifestation of the fact that they had given up
the things of this world, that they had become
homeless wanderers. Yet with the coming of
seasonal rains it was no longer practical to
wander. Roads became sloppy with mud, rivers
flooded the country around, and travel became
virtually impossible. It became the custom for
the wandering also to find a rain-retreat or
shelter during the monsoon. Often they built such
shelters themselves, and occasionally they were
the gift of a donor, a wealthy merchant or
prince.

Hence it became the custom when the monsoon

approached for the wanderers to congregate at
such a place for the vassa period. Soon some of
these wanderers ceased to wander and became
permanent residents and the monasteries as such
had begun. This was the way it had begun in
India, although the custom was very old, and was
ancient before the Buddha began his own
wanderings.

The first teachers from India to Tibet had
brought the pattern of the monastery with
them . . . or perhaps it had, in a measure,
preceded them. This building was built much as
many had been in India.

From the Hall of Assembly he glimpsed a narrow
stair mounting to a higher level. A moment he
hesitated. He was beginning to feel like
sleeping, and further exploration of the building
could wait. Tomorrow the blizzard might hold and
they could not continue, and the building could
be explored then. Yet the temptation of the stair
was too great.

He had a flash-light, a bit of loot from his
last successful raid on a Chinese convoy, and
another fifteen minutes without sleep would do no
harm.

Turning into the narrow opening he started up
the steps. Here and there stones had fallen from
above, and the steps were littered with
fragments. Despite the fact that two walls
protected the stair, it was bitterly cold.

He climbed, and the steps became shorter and
steeper. Emerging from the stair-well he found
himself on a roof or terrace, and across it was a
small, low-roofed house or apartment. Leaning
into the fierce wind, he struggled across to the

door, dropped a hand to the latch, and lifted it. The door opened . . . the air was warm, but the room was dark. The air smelled of smoke. Someone had been here. Had his Go-log missed this place?

He searched the room with his flash-light, but it was bare and empty. In the corner of the room was another door, a closed door. Mallory hesitated, and then with a tentative touch of his pistol-butt he crossed the floor and opened the door.

On the far wall, dimly lighted by the red glow from two charcoal braziers, was a part of a painted tapestry, a thanka, showing the tree of great masters through whom learning is transmitted. Before it, wearing a gown of reddish purple trimmed with skin of the snow leopard, sat a man in the lotus position.

"How do you do, Major Mallory? Will you sit down?"

Mallory hesitated, his eyes sweeping the room. There were several bundles of carpet nearby, nothing more. There was no one else in the room. It was warm, almost hot. The air was a thin haze of scented smoke.

"We were wondering who made the fire down below; we are grateful even if it was not for us." He seated himself on a pile of carpet. He could see the face of the other man but dimly. He appeared to be a Tibetan.

Mallory glanced at the man's feet. He was not bare-footed, but wearing red-leather boots soled with white yak hide.

"You ride a strange trail."

"Yes."

"How do you know of this track? It is upon no map."

"Your Eminence is wise . . . but there is a map. I have seen it."

The man was surprised. Mallory could sense it rather than see it. He sat very still, waiting, and listening.

How did this man come to be here? No means of transportation had been seen, and the clothing the lama wore at this moment was not fit for travel in such weather. Incense or something in the close air dulled his senses. He shook his head--he was tired . . . that must be it.

Mallory waited and his ears searched for sound. There must be others. This man could not be here alone. He remained where he was. Let this stranger play his cards, then he would do what was needed.

"I did not know of such a map. It is very old?"

"Undoubtedly."

"This track is shown . . . is there more?"

"Much more."

How old was the man? Mallory found himself unable to shape an opinion. He might be thirty, forty . . . or seventy.

"I should like to see this map."

"It is far, far from here. In a secret place." Mallory hesitated, and then said what he was not at all sure was true, but he needed help, all the help he could get. "It was in the place of Kesar."

"Ah!"

He remained quiet for a moment, and then said, "Of course. It would be so." He raised his eyes and looked directly at Mallory. "Is it true then? Are you the incarnation of Kesar?"

"I am Mallory. If I am an incarnation of anything I am unaware of it."

"The lama you have with you? He is Lagskha-tsang?"

"Yes . . . and his sister."

"You have very few men."

"More will come. We were to rejoin at the pass." Mallory paused a moment. "The way ahead? Is it open?"

"It is difficult. A man may have traveled it from time to time. I do not believe animals have crossed it in many years."

"We must cross the Yulang. Is there another crossing than that near Dzogchen Gompa?"

"I have heard of it. Does not your map show it?"

"The map was very old. If another crossing was close by it might have been the only one known at the time."

"From the crossing, where will you go?"

Mallory smiled. "Where the Lord wills. We will follow the Way."

"Ah? You do not trust me?"

"I trust my sword. It was made by a smith who knew a true edge and a thin one. As for you, Your Eminence, there has not been time to trust your temper or your interests."

"What of the Americans? What is their purpose here?"

Mallory was surprised--the Hart Expedition was days behind them. This man had good information, information that might help him in the coming days. He explained briefly, and added, "I do not

know Gunther Hart. He may have other reasons for
coming. Hart and his people are not the only ones
we left behind."

"Marshal Chu is very angry that Lagskha-tsang
escaped him. He will have men sent to the
crossing of the Dzogchen Gompa. There will be a
fight, I think."

"We shall see."

"Marshal Chu has troops at Kantse. He has men
at Paan, which we used to call Batang. There are
men waiting at Chamdo. If you go west toward
Chamdo, those forces at Paan will move north, and
those at Kantse will come up behind you. The
Marshal had planned to intercept the Incarnation,
but did not plan on you. Now, however, he has
radioed his troops and they know what to expect.
You must cross rivers, and the tracks through the
mountains are few. He has many soldiers."

"We will avoid them; if we cannot avoid them,
we will fight, but when we fight the ground will
be of our choosing." Mallory paused a moment. "I
do not think the good Marshal's men will like the
kind of country where they must go to capture
us."

"The map you spoke of? In its secret place? It
is in Go-log country?"

"Yes."

"Ah . . . well, I should like to have seen
it." He stood up. "You will need sleep. What we
can do will be done, Major Mallory, although I
fear it will be all too little. It is up to you,
and those who follow you . . . if it can be done,
you will do it."

Mallory descended the steps through the
howling wind and the blown snow. The man, lama,

whatever he was, was not an enemy, and there might be help along the way. The people of the mountains might help if they could, but he must plan without them.

Outside the wind howled with a blizzard. In Montana such storms often lasted three to four days. If this one lasted that long they might never escape.

There had once been the story of an island in the Indian Ocean peopled by enchanters who could control the winds. No ship could pass without stopping to trade, and if they attempted it they encountered adverse winds.

"I could use them," he said, half-aloud, "I could use them now. I must have a good day tomorrow, a good day for travel."

CHAPTER 16

When the morning came there was no wind. The icy peaks held still, the air silent . . . nothing moved.

It was cold . . . bitter cold. On the peaks and the high levels of the mountain there was no softness in the snow. Gray hogbacks thrust upward, their raw flanks blown clean by the wind, looking colder than the ice that lay in their crevices and shadowed places.

Lagskha-tsang was ready to travel. Brikhuti warmed her hands at the fire. The Go-log huddled over their tea, waiting. "We will go," he said, and they got up and went out to the horses and yaks.

Mallory climbed the icy stair. The lama's

rooms were empty, cold, just the rugs and the
smell of smoke. He could almost believe it had
been a dream. In the light of day the place was
in considerably worse shape than it had seemed
last night--there was dirt piled in the corners
and spider webs connecting ceiling and wall.
Where had the man gone and how had he done it
without raising an alarm? More than that, where
was there for the man to go?

From outside Mallory could see his men
readying the animals. He headed back down the
stairs.

Tibetans are born to travel, and within
minutes the caravan was strung out along the
faint track. Where they now must ride the track
lay open upon the flank of the mountain. Anyone
coming up from behind could see them from miles
away. He hoped that his rear guard hadn't been
stopped by the storm. He felt exposed, but there
was no other way.

He glanced back at the ruin, but there was no
movement around the roof-top apartments. How had
the lama come to that place? He had come, and now
he had gone . . . how? The fact that there must
be another trail disturbed him. If one man used
it, another could.

He dropped back, detailing four Go-log to hold
back and watch their trail. All morning they
followed the flank of the mountain. There were no
trees, no bushes, only the snow and the out-
croppings of granite.

They moved slowly. There could be no question
of hurry on such a slope. The mountainside grew
steeper; occasionally juniper appeared, and some
scattered brush. Once a flock of snow partridge

flew up, almost from under their feet. Even at this altitude there were insects. Wolf spiders were frequent. Mallory had seen them above nineteen thousand feet and suspected they went even higher. He did not plan to look.

Several times, riding on ahead, he studied the track with binoculars. The trail followed a slope that grew steeper as they progressed, and seemed to enter a gorge a few miles farther along. The track that lay between was only occasionally visible due to the twists and turns of the trail as it followed the mountains. The slope was now cut by water-courses or wide swaths where avalanches had swept down taking everything before them.

A rider clattered up from behind. "They come! Our people come!" he shouted.

They had entered upon a wide place before the mouth of the gorge, and Mallory gestured. "Tea," he said. And as Brikhuti joined him he said, "There may not be a place to stop once we're in that," he indicated the gorge, "and I want to hear what our friends have to tell us."

The caravan bunched around him, gathering fuel for fires. Mallory watched them, noting the argols were dry and old. A few sticks could be found, and there were several half-dead junipers on the slope to provide fuel.

Far below he could hear what must be the sound of rushing water. He listened, watching the Golog ride into the open and step down from the saddle to gather about the fires.

Marshal Chu, they reported, left the Inn immediately and moved south. Undoubtedly he was even now approaching the crossing toward which they were headed.

"And the Americans?"

"They waited a day, then followed Chu."

"Followed? Why, in God's name?"

Nobody could hazard a guess. Chu would be annoyed and suspicious when he found they had followed him. They had been let off the hook, free to go where they wished, and they chose to follow him.

His reactions would be obvious. He would have cause to wonder if they were not simply spies, or allowed to come to the Tibet area by those in the Peking government who would discredit him.

In any event, it was no business of his. They had come into this country of their own choice, and if they chose to follow Chu, that was their business. Mallory had problems sufficient for the moment.

The track now descended steeply into the black opening of the gorge, winding along the sheer face, and in some cases, simply chopped out of the cliff itself. Far below the water rushed in a torrent, and far above was the sky, a mere slit between towering black walls.

Nowhere was the trail more than four feet wide and the yaks walked the very outer edge to keep their packs from brushing the wall. Mallory remained in the lead, and he saw no tracks. If the trail had been traveled in recent years it gave no evidence of it.

Rounding a slight bend, he drew rein. The trail ahead was covered with a mass of debris: logs, heavy boulders and earth. The slide had started on the face above, and most of it

cascaded over into the gorge, but it had left
enough behind to block the trail.

Mallory swung down, very carefully, for the
edge was near. For a moment he stared at the heap
of rocks and earth with disgust. Stopping, he
picked up a rock and threw it over the rim, and
then working steadily he went at the pile.
Several of the Go-log edged along, squeezing past
their horses to get into position to help. Using
the limb of a juniper they pried a larger rock
loose and it fell, taking a few inches at the
edge of the trail with it.

For more than an hour they worked, and then
Brikhuti edged her horse past him, and slowly the
others followed. His own horse had gone on,
following that of Brikhuti, and Mallory donned
his shuba, waiting for the others to pass. Each
time one neared the trail's edge a little more
fell off until at last they were all gone, and
only he remained.

He stood alone, listening to the retreating
footsteps of the caravan. Somewhere ahead they
would wait for him, but he was not concerned with
that. The track along the wall of the cliff was
now just more than two feet wide.

Taking up the stick that he had thrown down
after prying a boulder loose, he stabbed and
pried at the remaining earth until much of it had
fallen off into the chasm. Then he threw the
stick over and started on, after the caravan. If
anyone was following they would not find it easy.
The trail could be repaired, but it would require
time and tools, and every minute gained was
important.

Already the riders had disappeared around

another bend in the trail, yet there was no
chance of their getting far ahead, and he was
content to be alone. It was utterly still. As he
looked up he could see that the sun was
declining, and the darkness would come quickly in
this deep place.

For the first time in many weeks he was alone,
and the feeling brought a sense of freedom and
freshness. The Go-log were a somber people and
not at all easy to be with. Lagskha and Brikhuti
were friendly and he enjoyed talking to them but
what he needed now was time to think.

The lama at the ruin seemed friendly, and yet
he had not made himself known to the others, and
even Mallory had discovered the man only by
exploring the building. He had seemed helpful,
and undoubtedly there were many people in Tibet
who were willing to help Lagskha escape the
Chinese. There were also sure to be a few who
would be in the pay of the Communists, and who
would do anything to assist in the capture of
either Lagskha or himself.

Despite his ten years in the area there was
much that went on of which he knew nothing. There
were old jealousies, old hatreds and rivalries,
and there were secret societies as well, men
banded together in ancient orders with purposes
of their own.

There were sects of the Red Cap monks such as
the Zek-chenpas or the Dogpas with no reason for
loyalty to Lagskha, and much reason for hating
all he stood for. Weird stories were told of them
and their secret rites, of their seeming ability
to appear or disappear at will, and their
practices that smacked of devil-worship. How much

of this was idle gossip he did not know, but they were feared by many, and in an area of which he knew nothing his way was to walk softly.

What worried him most was that someone was aware of what route they had taken, knew exactly where they were when he had hoped to vanish completely.

Overhead the light was fading. He heard no sound from the caravan. Here and there pines grew from the walls of the gorge, and gnarled juniper clung to the ragged edge of the trail. The way descended steadily, growing colder by the moment.

The track along the cliff seemed without end, winding steadily on, revealing no more than a few hundred yards at any one time. Eventually he came to a place where the trail ceased, and the builders had carried it around a great rocky shoulder by sinking timbers into the rock wall.

Mallory hesitated, looking into the blackness below, yet the caravan had gone on, so he did, walking around the face of the mountain on a platform suspended over darkness. On the far side, and some distance below, he saw a gleam of fire. They had stopped then. They had found a place.

It was just light enough to see a dozen or so yards, and the track widened and Mallory saw before him, perched precariously above the gorge, a tiny village, a mere cluster of houses, most of them in ruins. Beyond the village, there was a small meadow. On it the yaks and the horses were grazing.

Brikhuti came to meet him. "I was worried," she said, "but they were not."

He glanced at the houses. "Is anyone here?"

"I looked into some of the houses. I think
they have been deserted for a long time."

Death had come to this village, death and
something else . . . Mallory walked to the fire
and extended his hands to the flames. They turned
their heads to look, some of them, but already
they were bedding down, for they knew the day
would bring another trail.

Mallory lifted his bowl to them. "May there be
a road!" he said, and several who still drank
repeated after him, "May there be a road!"

"We will have trouble tomorrow," he said.

Brikhuti turned her dark eyes to him. How
could a woman still be beautiful after such a day
of travel? Yet she was . . . very beautiful.

"Somebody knows we are here, and that may mean
that others do too." He did not want to tell her
of the sudden feeling he had, a cold whisper of
warning.

She looked at him, then finished her tea. "You
will bring us through," she said positively.

He chuckled, without humor. "I wish I was as
sure."

"If you were sure, I would be less sure. It is
well to be afraid."

She looked around slowly. "I wonder about this
place. Why did anyone build here? Was it only a
resting place? How could these people exist?"

Gompa had come up to them. "It was a place of
the Dogpas," he said. "They lived in this
village, and before them devils lived here. Kesar
drove them out."

"He came to this place?" Brikhuti asked.

"Upon his magical horse, Kyang Go Karkar, he
rode here, where enemies waited, but his horse

smelled them out, and he destroyed them. He
turned them into great stones and rolled them
into the gorge. My father knew the words, and
often he sang the song of Kesar."

Gompa looked at Mallory. "That is why the
black spirit-shadows do not frighten us. Because
you are here."

"Do not make up stories . . ."

The Go-log shrugged. "Who else would know of
this track, Kushog, that we who live near did not
know? And of this place? For who else are the
fires lighted?"

"Fires?"

"A fire burned before we came. There was fuel.
There was tsamba."

CHAPTER 17

Nor was the fire all. Beside it, and awaiting
Mallory, untouched by the Go-log, was a large
kettle of djo, a very pleasant dish of curdled
yak's milk which had been put on the fire and
stirred briskly while boiling, then slightly
sweetened.

Mallory invited Brikhuti and Lagskha to share
it with him, only regretting it was insufficient
for all. Yet the Go-log urged him to eat,
protesting that it was his, and his alone.

The wind was cold and a light snow was
falling. The houses of the ruined village were
close by, but Mallory preferred the open air. He
could hear better, and see farther. He trusted
none of his surroundings, and had no idea whether
the food he was given was not merely bait for a

trap to be sprung farther along . . . yet the djo was no casual dish. This had been very specially prepared.

"You are favored," Lagskha remarked, smiling. "They are sure you are Kesar. There are many who believe this was the route he chose when going to attack Hor. Do you know the stories?"

"Some of them. Kesar of Ling, I believe, was the great Tibetan folk hero. He was said to have been born into the world to bring order, to suppress violence and evil, and he rode a magical horse and could perform magic, himself, although occasionally he was the victim of the magic of others. I've heard the stories sung in the tents of the Go-log in several versions."

"I have read that your scholars believe the legend dates from the seventh or eighth centuries," Lagskha said, "but some of us believe they are much, much older, and were known to the Bonpo."

When morning came the wind blew cold along the ranges, whispering where the pines grew, for now the track emerged from the gorge and wound once more along the flank of the mountain.

Mallory resumed the lead, riding on ahead, studying the trail, scanning the mountain, eyes alert for whatever might be there.

The gorge they had followed, Mallory saw, had taken them through the Kuo-Lo Shan, a range of mountains that joined the Chala Shan at right angles. Looking back, he could no longer even see the mouth of the gorge, and unless he had known it was there he would not have believed that such a pass existed.

On his left he could now look out over a vast

sweep of country: rugged mountains, canyons, all
unknown and unexplored. In the distance he could
see a river or what appeared to be a river that
was probably the She Ch'u. Closer to him there
were several gorges, each with a river that must
form the headwaters of the Ta To Ho. The Ta To Ho
eventually joined the She Ch'u, but not the
Yarlung, for a mountain range divided the two
rivers.

Mallory saw the tracks of several large bears,
and judging by the size of the tracks and the
length of the stride the animals must weigh seven
or eight hundred pounds. Once, some distance off,
he saw one eating a dead yak. He pointed, and
handed the glass to Brikhuti.

"They are very fierce," she said, after a
glance. "They have killed many hunters."

"I wouldn't doubt it," Mallory replied dryly,
"seeing the kind of guns most of them have. It
takes a good weapon to stop a bear that big."

Before them was a ridge, and Mallory slowed
his pace, approaching with caution. Slowly, he
edged his mount closer to the rim until he could
see beyond. He was looking into the valley of the
Yarlung, and beyond it another snow-topped range,
which seemed to end not far off.

Lagskha rode up beside him, pointing.
"Dzogchen Gompa is there, and the crossing is of
the Den Chu, then we cross it again, and work
north in a great loop and back south to the
crossing of the Yarlung. It is a track much used,
and the soldiers of Chu will be there."

He turned in his saddle. "The crossing is for
those traveling to or from An-ch'e-k'o-mao, but
is little traveled until the crossing of the Den

Chu, when it joins the caravan route from
Kantse."

The situation was not a happy one. In a land
of rivers and high mountains the available routes
are few, the passes known. To strike south to
another crossing would mean nearing troops
stationed at Kantse, undoubtedly in greater force
and alerted to be on the look-out for them.

The crossing must be here. A river crossing
was always dangerous, and Marshal Chu would
appreciate his advantage. A shrewd and capable
man, he would not risk his soldiers until the
situation was favorable, despite the fact that he
out-numbered them ten to one. If Chu could catch
them crossing or on the far side, he might wipe
them out.

"Mallory," Lagskha suggested, "Kesar's route
may have used another crossing."

Mallory shook his head. "I hate to gamble on
it, but from this moment on we must play it by
ear."

The descent toward the river was gradual, the
ground beneath them mostly broken up mica-schist
and slate, yet surprisingly, the route was
hidden, twisting and turning to utilize every
projection of rock, every boulder. There were
occasional junipers, and some of them left the
impression that they had been planted, scattered
along to conceal the trail they followed.

After two hours of slow descent a track broke
off from the one they followed and descended into
a hollow, a notch in the mountain with a sandy
floor and a small spring.

Near the spring was a crude circle of rocks,
blackened by fire, and near it a stack of argols

and some pieces of dead juniper. Also, piled nearby and in plain sight were a dozen sacks.

Gompa rode swiftly past, dropping to the ground near the sacks. "Barley!" he said, after a swift examination.

The Go-log went to their packs and got out copper pans and began to parch the barley for use in making tsamba. It was obvious that the people of the area were not going to let them starve. Probably they did not appear because of their fear of the Go-log, known far and wide as robbers and raiders.

Atop one of the sacks was a sheep's shoulder blade, and Gompa called Pagyar. "It is for you to read the future!" he said.

Pagyar was a noted soothsayer, a teller of fortunes, a reader of the past, present and future. The people of Kham are known to be gifted in this way, and magicians from Kham were always present at the ancient courts of the emperors of China.

When tea had been prepared and the embers pulled aside, Pagyar put the sheep's shoulder-blade in the embers, leaving it there until charred. Removing it, he studied the cracks made by the heat. The longitudinal cracks represented the way they pursued, the horizontal ones what would happen en route. The color of the bone fore-told the weather they would encounter.

Pagyar studied the cracks with care, and Mallory watched him curiously. Many times before he had seen this done, as well as divination in other forms, and he was convinced from what he had seen that the cracks actually were only something on which the soothsayer concentrated, that what he foretold came from his own intuition, clairvoyance or ESP or whatever one wished to call it.

Mallory was not a skeptic. He had witnessed too many strange things, had seen too many prophecies come true, but he knew the power such prophecies had over the minds of their followers. He suspected that Pagyar, as many of his kind, relied as much on exceptional knowledge as on what his clairvoyant powers revealed. Most such men were the confidants of hunters and travelers, they heard much, and remembered most of it. Coupled with their divination was a knowledge of trails and conditions that far exceeded that of the average traveler.

"There will be war," Pagyar said, "there will be war and blood. Men will fall, and others will flee, screaming. There will be the sound of guns and the clash of blades, yet we Go-log will win through."

He bent over the shoulder blade, the fire-light dancing on his narrow features. "There are dark shadows upon the road, shadows through which I cannot see, but there is blood again and there is mystery . . . always and forever mystery, veils of darkness are drawn across my eyes, but we will win through because Mallory leads us, and because Kesar rides beside the Incarnation.

"The white men and women will be among us again, they will come fleeing in terror from they know not what, but from what they know, also.

"In the end there will be the death of a prince, and good fortune that will come late, after much trial. Marriage vows will be spoken between a man and a maid under the shadow of fear when death is all around."

He sat on his heels and looked all around, but mostly at Mallory. "You will fight to the death," he said, "a bold fight, a strong fight."

Brikhuti looked at him, her face pale. "He did not say whether you lived or died, Mallory. Will you not ask him?"

"No. He trusts in his divination. I trust in my sword."

When they had finished their tea and tsamba they mounted again. With each minute they drew nearer to the place where they must cross, nearer to where the enemy lay, and at last they camped, ready to see what tomorrow might bring. Before they bedded down, Mallory called two of the Golog to him. "Sleep," he said. "At midnight rise and ride into the valley. See where the crossing is, and if our enemies are there. Meet me here," he drew with his finger in the dust and showed a place where the track came near the stream, "but go quietly and no fighting unless you must."

Brikhuti came over as he sat on a rock away from the fire-light, listening to their snores. "Will they be safe?"

"With any luck. They are like ghosts. Their only enemy is their bravery. Too often they would rather simply fight than choose their battles with an eye to victory."

The wind from down the ridges blew cold, it stirred the fire with tentative fingers and the flames fluttered and bent low above the coals. Mallory filled two bowls with tea. One he handed to Brikhuti.

"You were safely away from all this. Did you come back just for Lagskha?"

"My brother is a gifted man, Mallory, very gifted, and very important to Tibet and to our enduring culture. The Communists will try to destroy that culture, they will stamp out any diversity in the name of the universal man. We must be sure that what we have will not die. Lagskha needed to escape. From outside Tibet he can work, even as the Dalai Lama does, to improve the lot of his people and to prepare for a day of freedom."

"It could be a long time off."

"We will do what we must. Our roots are here, our memories are here, and the places of our religion are here. No people has the right to decide the destiny of another."

"Tibet is strategically important, Brikhuti. It sits at the peak of Asia, with all of Asia lying in a circle about it. The nations of the world have been slow to grasp that fact, but China has not.

"Tibet opens a door to India, to Pakistan, to Kashmir, to Central Asia . . . even to Iran."

They talked long into the night, and then Lagskha awoke and came to join them. He sipped his tea, then glanced up at Mallory, who stood across the fire, listening to the night. "The river crossing is dangerous, is it not?"

"Very. I am hoping there will be another, further up or down stream. If we could cross before they found us, we'd have a fighting chance."

"Could we swim?"

Mallory shrugged. "I have not seen the river

at that place, but most of these rivers run strong, the current is too swift." He thought about it. "There was an American who swam a thousand head of cattle across the Mississippi where it was a mile wide. I suppose it might be done if the water is not too swift or too cold."

Later he walked out to look down over the valley. He could hear no sound but the wind, no stirring, no warning from the night.

COMMENTS: Mentions of this novel crop up in Louis's journals and letters in 1962, 1967, and again in 1971. The subject of Communist expansion into the western regions of China proper had already figured in Dad's work; he explored it in "May There Be a Road," a short story that he wrote in 1960 (though it was not published until 2001), and touched upon it also in another short story, "Beyond the Great Snow Mountains."

By '62, Louis decided he wanted to try something bigger on the subject, and by 1967 work on this project was begun. I am not sure how far he got at that time, but the book was jump-started again in '71 when a mutual friend put him in touch with the deputy private secretary to the Dalai Lama and, through him, with the Dalai Lama himself. This was no more than a brief and superficial correspondence, but they did arrange for their Information and Publicity Office to keep Louis abreast of events in Tibet and its borderlands. They also suggested some books to help with research, though Dad was already pretty familiar with the terrain—familiar enough to mention the following in his journal:

> Have Army maps of Tibet and Sinkiang.
> Very inaccurate. The Ba Chu (a river of some
> size) [empties] into the Yellow in the area
> of which I am writing, and it is not even on
> the map. The gorge of the Ba is over a
> thousand feet deep near the Yellow. The
> place called Rircha Gompa is in the wrong
> position, much too far north, and that's the
> wrong name, anyway. Should be Rag-grya
> Gompa, or something akin to that. Many of
> the places marked on the map are mere
> campsites which the uninitiated might take
> for towns or monasteries. Several mountains
> are wrongly placed.

It is unclear how Louis knew these maps were wrong (or even if they actually are). There are stories of him traveling in China but, while my research shows that he was there, the amount of time he would have needed to journey so far west makes his having done so extremely unlikely. Probably he was comparing the maps with accounts of others or comparing the 1940s-era Army maps to older ones that he considered to be more accurate.

Soon after Dad restarted work on the book in '71, we received what he described as a "good omen." One morning, after my mother had driven my sister and me to school, she returned home to find that a white dove had flown into our garage. She left the door open for a few hours, but the bird seemed content to stay. Eventually, my mother went and got an old hamster cage. Dad held out a pencil and the bird hopped onto it and he placed the bird in the cage. When my sister and I returned from school . . . we had a new pet! We named the dove Rama and he lived with us for nearly thirty years—probably some sort of record, since he was mature when he arrived.

Little did we know the dove's incessant cooing was to plague many who called us on the telephone. I can't count the times people asked, "What in the world is that noise?" It was always kind of surprising, because we had spent so long around Rama that no one in our household really noticed it anymore.

Rama in his temporary cage.

In its early years, this story shared the title "Journey to Aksu" with my dad's other central China story, the fragments of which are published in the first volume of *Louis L'Amour's Lost Treasures*. Louis often had trouble coming up with titles, so he may simply have been recycling this one for convenience. Unless something goes terribly wrong, I can't imagine either Mallory's or Hart's group ending up in Aksu or anywhere near it. Nevertheless, there do seem to be some other similarities.

Gunther Hart may be searching for a special place, a monastery perhaps, that contains some sort of secret knowledge. Both the hidden map that Mallory has seen, and the knowledge Brikhuti and her brother may have, seem to indicate a hidden or ancient city, a place to which the Tibetans definitely do not want to lead Marshal Chu. All of this is, of course, similar to the City of the Blue Wall in "Journey to Aksu" and the repository of information for those who have "arrived," or become aware of their past lives, in "Samsara," another section of *Volume 1*.

There are a few other hints here that might link these three documents. The most amusing of them is Doctor Bernard's account of the manuscript he once read:

```
". . . twenty-five, perhaps thirty
years . . ." before. A book that was
". . . something right out of Rider-Haggard
or Pierre Benoit." And had to do with an
ancient track, a ". . . route or trail,
whatever you wish to call it, that could be
followed only by those of particular courage
or virtue, a route beset with dangers . . .
all manner of evil . . . but which led to
ancient monasteries where the old secret
knowledge was still studied by people who
came there from the ends of the earth . . .
chosen people."
```

This sounds suspiciously like Louis might have been thinking of his own, unfinished manuscript, the first version of "Journey to Aksu," which was the story of the mercenary Paul Medrac and the City of the Blue Wall.

There is also the moment when Renata runs across Muhsin, the man she thinks could help the Hart Expedition as a guide or interpreter. After she makes the offer to employ him she has second thoughts:

```
He walked back toward the Inn and Renata
looked after him, very puzzled. It was a
```

```
little too opportune, his sudden arrival,
his knowledge of English, of history . . .
where was he going? Who was he? And how did
he happen to appear here just at this time?
```

That feels a bit like the scene where Medrac hires Serat, the mysterious Ladakhi with the pockmarked face in the original "Journey to Aksu." Even more familiar is Marshal Chu, who seems to be the very same character Louis wrote about in "Aksu," just revived forty years later and with only slightly different politics!

Here are two pages of Louis's handwritten notes for the "Ben Mallory" story:

Moving on, it is interesting to watch Louis have some fun, making the character of Gunther Hart share some of the attributes of so many in the pretentious "Hollywood" culture that surrounded us in those years.

Here's a scene from Louis's notes that he modified somewhat before he put it in the final manuscript:

    Hart enters, expresses a wish to see the
    lama; Brikhuti is there, a beautiful
    attractively dressed girl. "He cannot see
    you now." Hart merely glances at her. "He
    will see me." He instructs Carpenter to tell
    the lama he is present. Carpenter is stopped
    by two powerful guards. Brikhuti tells Hart,
    "If you wish to see him, I will try to
    arrange it."
        "You know him?"
        "I am his sister."
    Tibetan assistant of Hart explains about
    lama: he is very hip; his sister has studied
    in Europe; is known at Cannes, on the Costa
    Brava, on the ski slopes.
        She also knows Hart, is not impressed.
    Marty Wells, later, is playing a folk
    song on his harmonica when the lama enters.
    He is young, attractive, very interested.
    Hart enters, is offended that the lama who
    would not see him is now talking to a member
    of the expedition. The lama tells him he
    would be happy to see him later . . . if
    there is time.
        Hart tells the lama he is Gunther Hart,
    but the lama knows nothing of him. Brikhuti
    smiles.

And then a last note about Hart:

    Realization of inadequacy and his
    resentment creates desire to destroy those

who exposed him, not only to others but to
himself.

Louis also played around with having Lagskha, the
young lama, act as literary critic. He experimented in his
notes with the following paragraphs:

So many of your literary magazines amaze
me. They view the world with so much
immediacy . . . none seem to have any
perspective. They are obviously written by
intelligent people, but they wail, one and
all, about the end of civilization without
seeming to realize that what we have now is
much what we have always had . . . the only
difference is that more people care, give to
charity, protect the environment and support
the rights of others . . . what could be
better than that?

I miss the stories of character. I find
no Shakespeare, Dickens, Balzac or
Dostoevsky anymore. No one interprets
character anymore, not from their own
experience. All have seized on the misguided
Mr. Freud, who seems quite a bright man,
really, but so obsessed with his own
problems that his spectacles became fogged.

Your best writing that I have seen comes
from journalists. They see much more clearly
than novelists. The novelists no longer are
story-tellers, they are [so] obsessed with
being considered "important" that they
become bogged down in causes that are so

temporary that a later generation will not
be able to comprehend what all the
excitement was about. They have forgotten
that the story is man himself not the
passing fads of politics.

It seems very likely that these lines were opinions Dad
considered placing in Lagskha's mouth. They were just
notes, but the last one is sort of ironic in that Louis was
writing what was, at least for him, a political book. I also
want to be cautious, however, because I believe it is a mistake for readers to assume that they know the difference
between the voice of an author and the voice of a character.
Dad tended to jot stuff like this down and, occasionally, he'd
even talk like this in an interview. But he almost never expressed himself privately in the manner of these experi-
mental quotes. I guess that raises the additional question of
the difference between an author's personal and professional voice!

At one time I considered expanding this story fragment
into a complete novel but eventually decided to put off that
decision. Though Louis wrote many chapters, and there
may be indications of what he intended to do hiding in
"Journey to Aksu," "Samsara," and his short story "Beyond
the Great Snow Mountains," I am still considering whether
or not to proceed. It is quite likely that even he didn't consciously know where he was going to take the story next.
However, that was always the situation that excited him the
most.

———————————————

THE DEATH OF PETER TALON

The Beginning of a Western Novel

CHAPTER 1

When I glanced back over our trail there was blood on the snow, blood from ice-cuts on our horses' hoofs.

The snow was a foot to two feet deep and a few days back it had warmed enough to melt the surface, then frozen again into an icy crust. Often when our horses' hoofs broke through that ice cut like a knife.

We had been nine hours in the saddle, riding in the bitter cold. The horses were struggling now and Charlie's gelding had gone down once. We were hard put to get him back on his feet.

"We got to get under cover." Charlie's voice was muffled by the bandanna tied over his nose and mouth.

"This here's a trail of some sort," Burt said. "I seen a wagon track back yonder where the snow had blowed off."

Luckier than the others, I had a wool muffler tied across my face, knitted for me by a girl whose name was Mary. I never expected to see her

again but she'd left kindly thoughts in my mind.
That muffler was a god-send and I'd have given
plenty to be putting my feet under her table.

I squinted through the slowly falling snow at
the bulk of the mountain ahead, and the way the
trees climbed its side. I'd never been to this
part of the country before, so why should it seem
familiar?

Like that big old oak tree where we'd camped
last night? And the spring where I'd dipped up
water.

"Fence," Charlie pointed.

Sure enough, there was the corner of a split-
rail fence just off the road; the fence running
alongside the road as if to hold back the trees.

"Thank God!" Burt said. "There'll be a house
and a fire!"

We needed it. We just weren't going much
further. The cold was intense, night was coming
on and our horses were played out. Three days
we'd been riding now with mighty little rest.

The trees ended at the edge of a small meadow
covered with snow. Up the road a ways we could
see a gate, and back against more trees was the
house. There was a barn and a corral with a big
stack of hay alongside. No smoke came from the
chimney.

"It will be shelter," Charlie said. "There's
got to be a fireplace or a stove."

"Let's hope there's wood, too," Burt said. "I
ain't in no mood."

The gate was closed and Charlie leaned from
the saddle to slide back the bar. Glancing up at
the sign arching above the gate, it took me a
moment to read it: The Burning Lamp.

Burt, he stared at it, too. "Now what the Hell does that mean? Anyway, I'd rather it was a burning fire in the stove."

Me, I didn't say anything. I took another look then pulled my chin back behind my coat collar. Something about that sign made me feel all funny inside, and that was foolishness. <u>The Burning Lamp</u>, what did it mean, anyway?

No hoof marks or those of sled-runners. No smoke from the chimney. We waited while Charlie closed the gate. No ranching man ever leaves a gate open that he finds closed, and habit was stronger than the cold.

We rode up to the house. Snow all over everything. Heavy on the roof, on the porch. Snow blown against the shutters leaving white lines like bars.

"Hello, the house!" I yelled.

Wind blew a whiff of snow off the eaves, and a dry branch scraped against a roof-corner. One of the horses stamped impatiently. Burt turned his mount and walked him toward the barn.

Stepping down from the saddle, so stiff I could only fumble at the front door. It was locked. The porch and the steps creaked when I left them to walk around to the side of the house.

"We'll have to break in," Charlie suggested.

"Let's try the back door first," I said. Cold or no it went against the grain for me to break into anybody's house. Although Western folks usually expected people to stop by. All they wanted in return was to leave things as they were found.

There was a stack of wood, as much as two

cords of it, stacked alongside the house, and in
the shadows of the covered back porch I saw an
axe, and a cross-cut saw.

Stepping into the cold stillness of that back
porch, I tried the door.

Locked.

On a hunch I looked up along the door frame
and saw a key hanging from a peg. Not a nail, but
a peg. Well, a lot of folks used pegs. Nails were
scarce.

Unlocking the door, I pushed it open. It was a
small kitchen, oil-cloth on the floor, a big old
kitchen range and some pots here and there. The
wood-box was filled. There were a few dishes on
the shelves.

Charlie went back for the horses and I stepped
into the next room.

There was a pot-bellied stove, another full
wood-box, and some pitch-pine slivers laid out
ready to start a fire. Standing in the icy
stillness of that empty room, I stared at those
slivers of pine. I said, "I'll bet the fire's
laid, too."

Opening the stove, I peered in. There it was,
some crumpled bark, some small twigs, slivers of
pitch-pine and heavier wood. Squatting before the
stove I struck a match. It flared up and I leaned
in, touching the match to a thin, curled edge of
bark. It caught, crept along the edge, showing a
tiny blue flame, then it gathered strength and
reached hungrily for the twigs. I closed the
stove door and stood up.

No sound. Only icy stillness. An empty house
can be the coldest place in the world. Slowly, I
let my eyes take in the room.

Two doors opened into other rooms or closets.
The floor was well-made, the planks tightly
fitted. No rugs on the floor but there had been
rugs, for I saw a dark stain, straight along one
edge as though something had spilled partly on
the rug, partly off its edge.

I shivered. What was it about this place?

The room was dim with only a little light
filtering through the shutters. On a small table
there was a coal-oil lamp, half-filled with oil.
I crossed the room, struck a match and lifted the
lamp chimney to touch the match to the wick. Then
I replaced the lamp chimney and blew out the
match. Adding fuel to the fire which was blazing
up, I crossed to the nearest door.

A bed-room, bed built against the wall. A
home-made bed with leather straps for springs. No
mattress now. Pegs on the walls for hanging
clothing, one picture I could not make out in the
darkness. Leaving the door open to warm the room
in case somebody decided to sleep there, I went
to the other room.

The second room was smaller, but there were
two beds, pegs on the walls here, too, and an old
trunk between the beds. When I turned around I
noticed there was a bar for the door, a bar on
the inside.

"Odd," I said aloud.

The stamping of feet on the porch brought me
back to the living-room. "Took care of your
horse," Charlie said. "Took the gear off and
rubbed him down a mite. There's plenty of hay and
whoever built that barn, built it tight and
strong." He glanced around. "Same as this house."

They walked to the stove, peeling off their

gloves to extend their opened fingers to the
heat. "Man! That surely feels good! Didn't take
you long to get a fire goin'!"

"It was already laid."

Burt glanced around at me. "Grave out yonder."
He gestured toward the woods near the barn. "Seen
it when I was gettin' hay."

Burt was a big, quiet man, a top-hand on any
outfit, and older than Charlie and me. Burt was
out of Arkansas by way of Texas, and he'd been up
the trail to Kansas a time or two. Easy-going
man, but no nonsense about him, either.

"Good place," he said, looking around. "Makes
a body wonder why they left it."

"Trouble in the family," I said. Indicating
the second door I said, "Whoever slept in there
had a bar across the door. Ain't likely a man
would want to keep anybody out, so it must have
been a woman."

"Pretty bad if she had to use a bar," Burt
said. He was opening his pack. "Seen a skillet
out there, and I'm goin' to fry up some bacon."
He glanced around at me. "Any of that bread
left?"

"Most of one loaf, all of another. And I've
coffee. We'll make out."

Burt left the room and we heard him moving
around outside. When he returned he had a bucket
of snow which he placed beside the stove to melt.
"Pump's froze," he explained.

Uneasily, I looked around. There was something
about this place--"Be glad when we can get back
on the trail," I said.

Burt glanced at me. "Have you looked outside?
We'll be lucky if we can move out for days. She's

comin' down pretty good out there. Anyway, it's snug and tight in here and it ain't likely we'll find anywhere else."

"Our horses are done in. A few miles further and we'd have been afoot. We were shot with luck when we come up to this place."

From the wood-box I added sticks to the fire. The room was warming up.

"I'll bring in some more wood," I said, and went to the door. Burt was rinsing out the frying pan with melted snow-water.

Outside the snow was falling faster, and so thick I could no longer see the gate. Gathering an armful of wood from the pile I brought it inside, then followed it with two more.

Charlie was squatting near the stove when I came in. He was a thin, tall man with a drooping yellow mustache from which the ice was melting.

"I'd have lost my horse," he commented.

"Burt's right," I admitted. "We should hole up here a couple of days."

Charlie and me met up when we were punching cows on the Slash Seven. He'd been there just a few days when I hired on and we made a team of it. He was a good man with a rope and he tied fast. Me, I was a dally man, myself. Just take a turn around the old horn when I latch onto something.

For a few months there we rode some serious country together, gathering strays out of the canyons and working the rough string. When you said rough string on the Seven you meant it. Some of those horses were rounded up out on the mesa

from wild stock and they'd been rode mighty
little. I was a fair hand but Charlie was better.
Burt was the best rider of us three but he wasn't
hunting any bad ones. "You kids can have them,"
he said. "I cut my teeth on wild mustangs and
they've jounced me around enough."

We'd been riding together, Charlie and me, for
eight or nine months when we met Burt.

Burt was down in a buffalo wallow with a dead
horse, and he was smoking it out with a bunch of
Arapahos. He'd been burned by a couple of rifle
shots and he was down to his last four
cartridges.

When we showed up we taken the fun out of it
for the Indians and they taken off waving their
hands and slapping their behinds at us.

Burt stood up and says, "You boys come along
at the right time. I'd just a few beans left in
the mill." That was when he showed us the four
cartridges he had left.

"You nailed one of them," Charlie said.

"That was right off. I never did get a good
shot at anything after." He glanced down at his
horse. "I surely do hate to lose my outfit. I've
set astride of that old saddle across some rough
country."

"You can ride with me," Charlie said. "My
horse can carry double. Copper will take your
gear."

It was forty miles to town, a settlement
gathered around a box-car that doubled for a
railroad station, general store and saloon. There
were some loading-pens and four or five dry
farmers, bucking the odds and the dust storms.

At the bar where he taken us to buy a drink,

this gent looked over at us and said, "I'm Burt Hoogan."

Charlie, he just nods, so I say, "They call me Copper, because of my hair."

My hair wasn't red, just about the color of dusty copper. My folks said I taken after a woman who married into the family. She was my great-grandmother or something of the kind.

Charlie never said what his other name was and nobody asked him.

"Glad you boys come along," Burt said. "I was fixing to get almighty lonesome, and them Injuns wasn't much comp'ny."

After that the three of us rode together and when the Seven let us go for the winter we hit the trail together.

Burt was slicing bacon into the pan when I came in with the last armful of wood. He glanced at me. "That grave I seen . . ." he said, "I went over and taken a look. Eleven years old. That was all. Name of Peter Talon."

Well--

Burt, he looked at me again, mighty sharp. "What's wrong? Copper? What's the matter?"

"That kid . . . Peter Talon . . . I think he was my brother."

CHAPTER 2

They stared at me, and then Burt said, "You mean you know this place? You _lived_ here?"

"I never saw it before. I've never even been

in this part of the country. If this is the place
I heard about I think it is my pa built this
cabin, with ma helping. The Talons were mostly
builders, and he took after them."

"What happened to your ma?"

"Last I heard she was in Kansas, and Petey was
with her, but they were headed west.

"She an' pa had been out west and they'd built
a cabin, but when she was fixin' to have me they
went back east where she could have care. Pa, he
left her there and guided a wagon train west and
he did some more work on this place, fencing it,
and the like. He put in a crop, bought some cows,
and then he came back east to be with ma.

"After I was born pa was building a bridge and
so he stayed by. Then he got another job working
on a fort the Army was building, and then as a
teamster with the Army. That took him right where
this place was. So he stayed on awhile, fixing
things up and building the barn. Then he came
back.

"We moved from Tennessee to Missouri. Petey
was born after a bit, and all they did was talk
about their place out west. It was like a dream
to them. Pa taken sick and died. He caught
pneumonia. He was all strong and happy like, then
he was down in bed and then he was gone. I don't
recall the years. Pa left ma with a little money
and she taken care of us, but she was scared.

"You know how those days were. Missouri was
wild. There was a lot of bad blood over the War,
and occasional shootings. There was several men
wanted to marry ma, but she shied away from them.
Then this one man came around and he sort of
warned the others off. He was a strapping big

man, handsome, and better dressed than most. Ma thought he was like pa, but he surely wasn't.

"Once they were married he began to ask questions about the place out west and about grandpa. I used to hear them talking, and I knew ma couldn't make head or tail of it, and he would get mad. He thought she was hiding something from him when she just flat didn't know what he was after.

"I knew, and one time when he was down to the saloon, I told her. It was that ol' treasure story. Pa told it to me like he told me a lot of other stories, and he didn't think there was anything to it, and it wasn't grandpa at all, but much further back than that.

"Even before they were married my step-father had been curious about a medallion my mother wore. It was gold and it had funny markings on it. Pa said it was an heirloom from his family and wanted my mother to have it.

"Maybe Pa had never told her the story, thinking it fanciful, but I was a little boy and him hard put to come up with fresh stories for me, he told it to me.

"An ancestor of his, away back, had been a pirate. Not in Jamaica and those islands like you hear, but off in India somewhere. I don't know much about that over there so all the names and places were strange to me, but I recall they had wonderful sounds.

"Pa talked of places like Madagascar, Coromandel, Zanzibar, Borneo and such-like. Anyway, this ancestor of his was the one who first took the name Talon, took it because he'd had one arm cut off and a claw to replace the hand. An old devil by all accounts.

"He'd raided and marauded and captured ships here and there and finally sailed back with four big ships, heading across the Pacific. By the time they came to the shores of America, and that was some time in the 1600s, they were in bad shape.

"They had to abandon one vessel, and as they were all heavy loaded, they buried that treasure. Millions, they said.

"They were attacked by Indians but got safely off after losing a few men. Further south they had a fight with a Spanish ship and it crippled another one of theirs, so they buried what they had from it and what they'd taken from the Spanish ship.

"They sailed around the horn with just two ships left. They were taken with scurvy and some died, and some were lost in storms so when they finally came into harbor on the coast of Canada, a place called the Gaspe, later, they were short-handed.

"That first Talon, he chose to stay right where he was, and some stayed with him. Some stayed, some went. Those who went were given shares of treasure but of course, they wanted more. At the end they sailed off, then came back to seize the rest, but the old man was waiting for them. There was a mad fight there on the shore and some men died and some lived. That time when they sailed off their ship exploded. Blew right up, and some do say the old Talon rigged it so.

"Anyway, some carried the story that a Talon

knows where there's treasure, hidden somewhere in the West. Where there was one story there's now a dozen, all different, and treasures hid in places no Talon ever was, but folks will believe what they wish to believe."

"What about the loot buried on the West Coast? From that first ship?" Charlie asked.

"She's still there, wherever that is. So far as I know the Old Man told nobody. Maybe he went back and got it. He had ships there for awhile, and he did what he said and gave land to those who stayed with him.

"Anyway, that heirloom ma wore, that was supposed to be a gold piece from the treasure, handed down in the family. This man who married ma, he heard the name Talon, and he'd heard the story before. Talon had been set on going west, had a place out there, somebody said. Somehow he got it in his mind that where the cabin was, that was where the treasure was.

"She didn't even know what he was talking about until I told her, then she told him it was all nonsense. He couldn't accept that. To believe that he had to admit he was a damn fool.

"He'd talked mighty big about all he was going to have, and now he had nothing. Instead he was spending what he had taking care of us. Only he took what ma had, too, and when I went to work, he took what I earned, little as it was. He drank more and more and he beat us more and more. He couldn't give up on the story but I don't know if he believed it anymore, either.

"He got me to one side and tried to get out of me what I knew. I told him the only treasure I heard of was buried afar off, at sea. He whipped

me for that. If I hadn't run off, he'd of killed
me. Now I'm wondering what happened to Petey."

"And to her," Burt said, "to your ma."

The idea chilled me. "I've got to find out," I
said. "I've got to find out what happened."

"There's that trunk," Charlie suggested.

"There's another place, too," I said. "There's
our secret place back in Missouri where Petey and
me used to hide. Ma knew of it, and she left
notes there for me, time to time, warning me when
he was drinking and such, so's I could stay
clear. She used to leave grub for me."

"Your pa ever look for that treasure?" Burt
asked.

"I asked him that, and he says, 'Look where?
Two places in maybe three thousand miles of
coast? I wouldn't even know where to begin, nor
would anybody else. The whole story may be a pack
of lies. I don't know. It's just a good story,
that's all. If there's any proof it's true or not
it's right back there on the Gaspe, where the Old
Man lived . . . and died.'"

Burt fried some bacon and made coffee. "Beats
me why they'd leave such a snug, warm cabin," he
said. "Your pa was a sure enough builder. Look at
how those corners are fitted. Ain't a chink
nowhere, and the window sashes fit. I tell you a
body doesn't often see work like this."

"Ma loved this place," I said. "I can't figure
why she'd leave."

"Maybe after her other boy died there was no
reason to stay."

We sat up to the table and made do with what
we had and when I was washing up after I turned
to them and said, "Boys, I've got to quit you. I

know we figured on going out to the Nevada country but I've just got to find out what happened to ma."

Charlie lay back on the bunk where he'd spread his blankets. "You just do that. Burt an' me, we ain't in no hurry, and she's mighty cold in the saddle."

"Nevada will look a whole lot better in the spring," Burt agreed. "If we lay in some grub there's no better place to last out the winter. A snug cabin, good stove, and plenty of fuel."

Charlie slept in the main room and Burt took over one bed-room and I slept in the room which had the bar on the door. That, I figured, might have been ma's room. She must have slept here with Petey in the other bed.

First, I lit the coil-oil lamp and then I rustled around for some paper. All I could find there at first was a couple of old envelopes.

With a stub of pencil I sat down and looked at the back of those envelopes. Some folks think well in one way, some in another. I like to get something on paper where I can look at it, study it and add a thought here and there. Tracing in the dust with a twig or scratching on a piece of bark is nigh as good.

This was pa's place out west. That was why that oak tree where we camped had seemed familiar. He had told me of camping there. Ma had come here with Petey and that man . . . my stepfather. Petey had died here. Ma was gone.

That man . . . Frank. Somehow I even hated to say his name. Frank had expected to find something and he had found nothing. So what would he do?

He wouldn't believe it. He couldn't believe
it. He had his dream, too, of easy money,
somebody else's money. People hunting treasure
are mighty unreasonable people as a rule. You can
prove to them there isn't any gold and never was
any, and they simply won't accept it. I'd seen
that before.

He would think there was something. He would
think ma knew and just wasn't going to tell him.

COMMENTS: Like the first fragment in this collection,
The Bastard of Brignogan, this piece contains a good deal of
information on the progenitor of the Talons. Not all of the
material in these fragments is completely consistent; if you
read carefully you can see Louis trying out slightly different versions of the Talon backstory to see which one he
likes best. More about the family can be found in *The Ferguson Rifle, Rivers West,* and even a bit in the Sackett novel *To
the Far Blue Mountains.*

While there are quite a few coincidences in Louis's fiction, this character accidentally winding up in his own family home is a whopper! I've never been quite sure why
coincidence plays such a big role, but, though I'm fairly
critical of my father's work, I'm left with the feeling that it
wasn't laziness. The concept of synchronicity or connect-
edness between people was such a powerful force in Dad's
imagination that he devoted his first novel, *No Traveller Returns,* to that very theme.

We should also remember that the world was a smaller
and more compact place during his formative years. The
population was less than half of what it is today, and with

class and race barriers being what they were, connections between people who were very much alike may have been significantly more common. Dad transcended more of those barriers than many of his time, working as a laborer alongside people of all races from all parts of the world, and then living as a celebrity under conditions where people sought him out to remind him of their connection to his life. It all leads me to wonder if there may have been fewer degrees of separation between the people of his era than we tend to think.

This story was created late in Dad's career (1986 or so), and in his journal he revealed that he got the idea from a picture on a postcard. Wanting it to develop differently from other stories, he had chosen to "start it earlier in the story to get the full effect of the men lost in the snow storm and finding the cabin." This refers to him not starting at some high-stakes moment, which was his usual modus operandi. His notes included the following brief description of the story, which will give you some clues as to how a slightly different version of it evolved:

> A cowboy, drifting with two buddies, and broke, comes to a ranch gate with a sign over it THE BURNING LAMP. It gives him a twinge . . . long ago his Ma had said she'd keep a lamp burning in the window for him. He rides into the gate and they come up to a deserted ranch-house, an empty barn. They go in and he finds things that tell him this is, indeed, the place where his mother and sister had once lived. With his little brother, too. And another girl, taken in by them when her folks were killed.
>
> They warm themselves in the cabin and he putters about finding a fragment here and

one there, he remembers the last letter he
got, worn almost away in his pocket and the
trouble facing them.

He had run away at his mother's urging
when his stepfather threatened to kill him.
His sister had added a note to the last
letter telling him of her "secret place," a
hollow in the old tree where she kept her
diary. He starts to ride away in the
morning, then on a chance, turns back to the
tree and finds her diary and the last, sad
days. Under the trees he finds his brother's
grave.

He begins a lonely trail and at the end
when the conflict comes to a head his two
old trail partners join him in the shoot
out. They just couldn't see him face it
alone. Build into this all the charm of an
old folk song, even the rhyming words, a
line here and there until the song is ended.

_____

THE JADE EATERS

A Treatment for a Motion Picture

COMMENTS: Of all the movie treatments in the Lost Treasures project, this is the only one that actually made it into the development process that might have led to its becoming a feature film. Dad kept careful files of his contracts, and *The Jade Eaters* appears here with the permission of (and special thanks to) Universal Studios.

As many feature film projects tend to do, *The Jade Eaters* dragged on interminably. A producer optioned the raw idea, some notes describing the narrative were set down in this treatment, but then the time came for another option payment to be made to Louis. The producer, typically, begged poverty, and Dad allowed him to keep trying to sell the project for free for a while. Amazingly, he eventually succeeded: Universal purchased the concept, and, in the best of circumstances, that would have been the start of a process where the story was discussed and perfected and a screenwriter was hired. However, for one reason or another, the project was abandoned. The number of stories that disappear into the black hole of studio "development" is astounding . . . some time ago the odds against a project's ever being completed were rather generously considered to be around 30 to 1.

The majority of correspondence about this project is dated 1956, and, having compared several sets of records, I believe the treatment reprinted here is actually an early draft. What was delivered to the studio may well have been a later and possibly more sophisticated version.

You will notice that character names are capitalized the first time they appear. That is a convention in the film business intended to allow a quick assessment of how many actors are needed and how to schedule them. The other stylistic aspect of a film treatment is that it is supposed to be written in the present tense. As a writer of traditional prose, Louis had a difficult time with this when he would write a treatment, and so, along with a few other corrections, I have converted this entire document into past tense . . . the way Dad would have been most comfortable telling this story.

It is important to remember that a treatment is really just a testing ground for ideas, an attempt to interest a buyer, and a point of departure for the continued development of the story concept. Even in this early phase it is interesting to see Dad playing around with ideas much more esoteric or even occult than those usually found in his published stories. As with some of the other Lost Treasures material, there are aspects of the narrative suggesting that James Hilton's *Lost Horizon* and possibly the work of Talbot Mundy were of greater influence on him than his writing in the Western genre would suggest.

Unlike many of the other stories in this collection, this manuscript is missing its first page rather than its ending. Page two begins in the midst of describing the protagonist, BEN STROUD, and his wife . . .

. . . RUTH, the daughter of a client, and had
two years of married life before leaving for
Korea.

His background fitted him perfectly for what
he became: one of the war's most successful
combat patrol leaders. Twice recommended for
decorations he never received, he had finally
been cut off with his company, and had brought
them out with the loss of but one man after a
harrowing retreat.

Awaiting him was news that Ruth had been lost
in a plane crash over southern Mexico. She had
been visiting her sister in Jamaica, and had
started back with friends in a private plane,
planning a stop in Mexico City. Caught in a
storm, the aircraft disappeared over that
unknown, unexplored area of Mexico where the
three states of Oaxaca, Chiapas and Veracruz come
together.

Search planes had flown over the area and,
when not socked in with clouds, the few glimpses
showed only an unbroken jungle into which no
known man had ever penetrated. An expedition
starting in on the ground had come to an area
where nothing lived. No bird, snake, animal or
insect. The expedition doubled back, finding
nothing, and in a hurry to get out.

Ben Stroud could not accept the idea that his
wife was dead. Once before, in their first year
of marriage, they had gone hunting and she had
fallen over a cliff into a tree. Below her lay
two hundred feet of sheer rock, and the slightest

move might have caused her to fall. Later, after he had found and rescued her, she told him, "I wasn't worried, Ben. I knew you'd find me and get me out."

Discharged from the service he had gone at once to Mexico, and when he had spent his savings in flights over the jungle and mountains, he turned to free-lance photography to make a living and continue his search.

Twice he was able to get into the area on the ground. He found tapir, wild boar, jaguar, deer, and other life, but no people. Yet there were rumors, queer stories of people who had lived unmolested in the forest since before the time of the Maya, of a people who retreated there to escape conquering tribes and had never emerged nor come in any contact with civilization. There were rumors of strange creatures, half-man, half-animal, and myths that the water-filled caves were the portals to Hell.

Stroud believed none of it, but he did know that people are strangely resilient creatures with a great capacity for survival. He knew that Ruth had both hunted and fished from the time she was a small girl, and she was more than ordinarily practical and intelligent. If she had emerged alive and unhurt from the crash, she would have at least a fifty-fifty chance of survival.

Everybody advised him to let go. There was no chance that anyone had survived. The area was trackless jungle, drenched by torrential rains, haunted by fever. And then he met ERIK PLATTNER.

He disliked Plattner from the beginning, but Plattner had money and a willingness to go into the jungle. He was a commercial explorer searching for medicinal herbs and rare orchids, all the while keeping an eye out to find gold, diamonds, or an ancient ruin filled with priceless antiquities, of which he was a good judge.

Plattner introduced him to DR. TITUS SHAW, half-Mexican, half-American, and a distinguished archaeologist who divided his time between the United States and Mexico. Dr. Shaw had theories about the Lost Jade Mines of Mexico. Strange theories.

They had formed an expedition, each with their own agenda for exploration yet all looking for something in the same intractable wilderness. The last to join them was JANINE, Titus Shaw's daughter. After setting up a base of operations in the village of Chimalapa and stockpiling supplies, Ben made the run back to civilization to pick Janine Shaw up at the muddy, seldom used airfield.

It was immediately obvious why Erik Plattner was willing to have her along. She was young, attractive, and seemingly not put off by the mud, heat, and mosquitos. Gathering her bags, Ben had loaded the jeep and started back to Chimalapa.

Tooling the jeep over the muddy, deeply rutted road, Ben Stroud remembered what Plattner asked him on the first day.

"Ever hear of the Indian jade mines?"

"I know they carved jade down there, and that's all I know about it."

"Much of it was of high quality, fabulously

beautiful and extremely rare. The Conquistadores
could never find where it came from, nor has
anybody else."

"Well, maybe someone will know something. We
can always ask around."

"Unless they were afraid to talk . . . unless
somebody has reason to keep them from it."

"You sound like you know something about it,"
Stroud suggested.

"The Doc's heard some strange rumors and
I . . . well, the Chinese believed jade
contributed to health, they even believed that
ground up and mixed into a drink it would enable
a person to live forever."

"Sounds like a lot of malarkey."

"Who knows? We live in an age of miracles, and
we are using a drug now called rauwolfia, and we
refer to it as a miracle drug, yet it has been
known and used in India for 2,500 years."

"So?"

"So how many other things did the ancients
know that we've forgotten? What of the tens of
thousands of books, many of them on medicine and
science, that were destroyed in the library at
Alexandria in Egypt? And the libraries right here
in Mexico destroyed by Bishop Landa?

"Who knows but what the Chinese were right?
They were a thousand years ahead of us with
vaccination for small pox, and even so simple a
thing as the wheel-barrow they had for a thousand
years before Westerners did."

"But that jade business doesn't make sense. It
sounds like a quick way to get kidney stones,"
Stroud laughed. "I mean, if a man lived beyond a
hundred years, everybody would know it."

"Not if he did not want it known. Suppose only a limited supply of jade was available and those who knew wanted it all for themselves?" Plattner had ended the conversation abruptly.

"Anyway, don't mention jade to anyone, d'you hear?"

The jeep pushed its blunt nose up a small slope and straightened out onto the longest stretch of road they would travel all day. Far ahead of them an old peon stumbled along in the night and the mud. Thunder rumbled in the far-off mountains and there were flashes of lightning.

"Look!" Janine touched his arm. "That old man fell down!"

"Some old Indio with a skin full," Stroud suggested.

"I don't think so. I believe he's hurt or sick."

The old man had gotten to his feet, but managed only a few steps before he fell again, and as the jeep drew abreast of him he struggled to rise.

Ben Stroud brought the jeep to a halt and studied the jungle with suspicion. Such a trick had been used by bandits in the States and might be used here. He reached inside his shirt which he wore with a button unfastened and eased the Smith & Wesson .44 magnum into a better position. Then he got out.

Again he swept the jungle with hard, probing eyes before taking the old man by the arm and helping him up. He was amazed at the fragility of the man. Lifting him as he would a child, Stroud

put him on the baggage in the back of the jeep.
As he put the old man down the aged eyes
flickered open. "Gracias," he whispered.
"Gracias."

"Chimalapa?" Stroud inquired.

"No." In an area where few people spoke
Spanish, but mostly Zapotec or Quiche, this old
man suddenly spoke English. "The Rancho
Encantada."

"Never heard of it. Anyway, we're only goig
as far as Chimalapa."

"It is before Chimalapa. It is four . . .
perhaps five miles. At the Place of Nawales."

"Nawales?" The name was unknown to Stroud. He
picked up his map-board from the front seat.
"Show me?"

The old man placed a fingernail upon a spot on
the map not far ahead of them. Obviously, he was
no stranger to maps. "There! Will you take me
there?"

Stroud stared . . . the fingernail that
indicated the spot was manicured! Neatly tapered,
perfectly polished, and with a straight white
scar across the brown finger below the nail.

He lifted his eyes to Janine's and she was
staring at him. She had seen it too. He lowered
the curtain and walked around the jeep and
slipped into the driver's seat. "Bad road ahead,"
he commented, then added, "No telling what we're
getting into."

"Encantada," she mused. "It is a beautiful
name. It means enchanted . . . or haunted."

"I've been over this road several times, and I
didn't notice any turn off."

Thunder grumbled in the far-off peaks. If it

rained again before they reached Chimalapa the road would be impassable and they would be bogged down for the night. Yet he could not put a sick old man out on the road in weather like this. Wherever he was going they must take him . . . and, wherever that was, there might be shelter.

He could hear the old man's heavy breathing, but whether he was asleep, unconscious or merely breathing badly he did not know. He had taken the old man's pulse after placing him in the back of the jeep. It had been frighteningly weak.

He glimpsed the opening suddenly. Narrow, scarcely more than a game trail, he saw a faint, almost obliterated track running deep into the jungle. The trail was so narrow leaves brushed both sides of the jeep. He twisted and touched the old man's shoulder. "Is this the place?"

Struggling, breathing in short, hard gasps, the old man sat up, blinking his aged eyes like an owl in a sand storm.

"Si!" he gasped. Then from his pocket he drew an iron key all of seven inches long. "Here."

They coasted down a small incline, splashed through a pool that was hub deep, and then struggled up the slippery slope beyond. For a mile farther they twisted, doubled and turned along the trail until suddenly mounting a rise they found themselves stopped by a massive iron gate with a huge, old fashioned lock. The key opened it easily and after closing the gate they drove on.

The road was smoother now, and suddenly striking a place where water had washed away the sand or earth, Stroud saw the track was paved,

with a width of seven feet and the pavement of
stone blocks, perfectly fitted.

"Father should see this," Janine whispered.
"He believes the civilization they call Olmec
originated near here."

"I've seen some of the carved stones they left
behind. Strange things, just big heads with no
body."

"You're interested in archaeology?"

"All I want is to find my wife and get out of
here."

"How long since she was lost?"

He said nothing for a moment, peering ahead
through the rain, which was beginning again. Then
he said, "Three years."

He knew she believed him a fool. How could he
hope to find her alive after so long?

They emerged from the jungle into a ranch
yard. Before them was a long low building with
boarded up windows, a barn, pole corrals, but no
sign of life.

Pulling the jeep up close to the over-hang of
the porch, he got out and banged on the door. The
sound reverberated emptily within. He waited and
tried again, pounding with his fist. Just as he
was turning away he heard a vague sound from
within, and then the door was unlatched. A big
Indian in a serape and wide hat stared out at
him. Briefly, he explained.

The Indian carried his lantern to the jeep and
held it up as Stroud drew back the curtain.
Instantly, the Indian handed the lantern to
Stroud and lifted the old man gently in his arms,
then taking the lantern went inside and closed

the door after him. They were left alone in
silence and the falling rain.

It was impossible to go on. He knew the road
before them too well, and he also knew there was
no other shelter, anywhere. They were going to
remain here if they had to sleep in the barn.
Returning to the door he pounded and pounded, but
there was no response, no movement or sound
within.

He walked back to the car and got the key the
old man had given him. From the looks of the lock
on the door it would work here as well.

When the door was open his flashlight showed
him a very large and very empty room that showed
no evidence of occupancy for many years. Three
doors opened off this room and behind the first
he found two carefully made beds, one of them in
a small alcove out of sight of the first. This
room was neat, clean, and seemed to have been
used more recently than the outer room could have
been.

Behind the next door was just a bare, empty
space containing nothing but dust and cobwebs.
The third door opened into a large area that
might have once been a kitchen. There was no
furniture, not even a bench, but on the coals of
a dying fire was a large, blackened coffee pot.
He hefted it--there was coffee.

On the floor near it was a spot where water
had dripped from clothing . . . or something.

Where a man had waited, perhaps? Waited for
the old man to come home? Waited for a peon who
manicured his fingernails?

He had opened three interior doors and there
were no more. Where, then, were the two men? They

might have gone through the back and outside
again but there was nothing visible in that
direction but dense forest.

Janine glanced at him, "Ben, it gives me the
shivers. It's . . . it's like they were ghosts."

"Maybe they were, but if this coffee is any
good we're going to have some. I'll get our stuff
out of the jeep."

He moved their gear into the bedroom, and then
they returned to the fireplace with two cups. The
coffee was scalding hot, black and strong.

"We're staying here?" Her eyes searched his.

"Unless you're afraid to sleep in the same
room as me."

"I'm not afraid," she replied coolly.

He tried a sip of the coffee. "You probably
think I'm crazy to go hunting for Ruth after so
long a time."

"You must have been very happy with her."

"I don't know. I used to think I was. Now, I
don't know. Ruth was a great pal, but she . . .
well, she wasn't very affectionate."

"But you're looking for her."

"I just keep thinking she's back there waiting
for me to come and get her."

"She must have great confidence in you."

"Maybe . . . I guess so." He got up. "We'd
better get some sleep." He glanced at her. "Are
you nervous about staying here?"

She got up with him. "I carry insurance," she
said coolly, and drew a compact .32 automatic.

He grinned at her. "It looks like a good
policy."

He removed his boots, jacket and shirt, then
stretched out on the bed with his pistol under

his jacket and close to his hand. After a moment
he got up and taking his duffel bag placed it on
the floor just inside the door where anyone
entering would be likely to trip over it. Then he
went back to bed.

He awakened suddenly, his hand gripping the
Smith & Wesson. The door was opening . . .

How long he had been asleep he did not know,
but the light in the room seemed faintly gray.

He watched the widening crack of the door but
was not worried. He knew what that .44 magnum
could do. There was a muttered exclamation as
someone stumbled against the duffel bag.

In the darkness Stroud could see it was a man
and he carried a tray. The gun muzzle, still
concealed by the jacket, covered every move as
the man approached the bedside and placed the
tray on the table. Then the figure retired softly
and drew the door shut after him. Stroud sat up.

"What was that?" Janine asked from her bed.

"Breakfast," he said, seeing a coffee pot, two
cups, some small cakes and fruit on the tray.
"Come and get it before the genie takes it away."

He turned on his flashlight and found a candle
on the tray, and some matches. He lit the candle.

She joined him and they ate a quick, silent
breakfast. "I'd like to see that man we picked
up," Janine said. "I wonder how he is?"

"We should get out of here. I fear somebody is
trying to speed the parting guests."

The house seemed as deserted when they left as
when they had entered it and the mystery only
deepened.

———

They were nearing Chimalapa before Janine
spoke of their experience.

"Ben, that was very strange but I don't think
we should let Erik know we spent a night in the
same room."

He had been thinking the same thing. He wanted
no complications on this trip. As far as he was
concerned there was only one thing he
wanted . . . get into the jungle, find the plane,
find Ruth if he could, and get out. And he wanted
no trouble with Erik Plattner, who, he was sure,
was a man it would be easy to have trouble with.

"I'll tell dad," she said, "but I'd rather
nothing more was said of it."

"All right." He swung the jeep into the narrow
street and scattered chickens in every direction,
then braked to a halt before the cantina.

Plattner and Shaw emerged at once. "Get caught
by the storm?"

"We were lucky enough to get through at all.
When do we leave?"

"We don't . . . not for awhile anyway. We've
lost our guide."

The guide had disappeared. Chimalapa was a
very small village but the ALCALDE could not help
them. He offered one suggestion . . . why not
give it all up? There was nothing back in that
jungle, anyway. Nothing at all. Ben Stroud,
hanging back and allowing the others to do the
talking, got the idea that the alcalde knew all
about the missing guide.

Stroud didn't think that the guide sounded
like much of a loss and when the argument died

down he said so. Nobody, according to the alcalde, knew anything about the jungle, anyway. Stroud felt himself to be as good with a map as anyone the Army ever taught, Plattner was familiar with the wilderness and Dr. Shaw had done his bit of exploration. They had their supplies and permits and were as ready as they were ever going to get. Given the situation, Stroud told them, he was ready to proceed without a guide.

The alcalde vehemently protested, arguing that their well-being is his responsibility. But none of the Americans had trusted him from the start and so they made their plans to depart the next day.

Erik spent a good deal of time with Janine. To Stroud their relationship appeared to be more than casual and yet they were not truly a couple either. He made sure to carefully avoid them. Whatever the situation, it was none of his business.

They met in the cantina to eat, and as they sat over the remains of their meal Ben noticed an OLD INDIAN who stood nearby, seemingly very drunk, yet the old man was obviously listening. During the course of the conversation Ben stated that all he wanted to do was find his wife, and those words seemed to attract the attention of the Indian.

Titus Shaw told them of an old legend to the effect that South America's fabled Andes highway, built long before the days of the Aztecs, had actually originated somewhere in the north, near here, at the Place of Nawales. Janine shot Ben a startled glance and Erik, though quick to see it, said nothing.

Nawales, Shaw explained, means "wise old ones," but exactly what this "Place of the Nawales" was he did not know unless it referred to some temple where priests had once stayed.

After more than a year in Mexico, Ben's command of the Zapotec tongue had become more than sufficient for ordinary purposes. Leaving the others to talk he wandered over to the bar and bought the old Indian a drink. The man was a Zapotec, once a chicle hunter, and Stroud's comment about searching for his wife caught his attention. "I never knew what an angel my first wife was until I remarried!" the man said.

Then he leaned close to Ben's ear and whispered that even he, a poor Indio, knew something that might help. Beyond the village called Potrero there was a deep cut, marked by a huge cypress tree. If one was to go down that cut he would come to an ancient road, paved in stone, that would take him far back into the jungle. It was the ancient route to the mountains.

Ben walked to the door, looking out into the night. From the shadows he heard the sound of a scuffle and a cry for help. He stepped down into the street. TWO MEN were struggling with the old Indian. He leaped into the fight, and knocking a man down, was struck himself. By the time he managed to get to his feet the two men had run off and the old man was dead . . . knifed.

The townspeople were suspicious, but Plattner told them that he was watching Stroud when he heard the cry, and saw Stroud rush out to save the old Zapotec only after the attack had begun.

Another man from the cantina eventually agreed; this was what he saw also. As he said this a boy of fourteen slid into the room and stood against the wall, listening carefully.

Ben had the strange feeling the locals were less interested in finding out what happened than what he might have seen. Who, then, were the killers? And had the man been killed because of the information he had given to Stroud? Or was it because of something more that he might have said?

Stroud discussed these points with Janine and the others. As he did so, he noticed the boy hanging around in the background. His attitude was seemingly dejected yet he was focused intently on Stroud and his party. Excusing himself, Stroud strolled across the street letting the boy follow. When they were together under the trees, the boy introduced himself and explained.

His name was MIGUEL. The old man was his grandfather. He had no other family, and Stroud had gone to help the old man. So now that the old man was dead, if Stroud would have him, he, Miguel, would be their guide, saying he knew where the old road was, as his grandfather had shown it to him.

Despite the protests of the alcalde, they decided to leave, taking the muddy road toward Potrero. If they could find the track of which Miguel and his grandfather had told them then they would be on what could be called the North American stretch of the Andes road and might be able to drive far back into the jungle.

Twelve miles out, and several hours later, they were forced to camp because of the bad road conditions. They were directed to their camp site by a rider they met beside the trail, a man obviously of some education, wearing neatly pressed clothing, and riding a fine-looking horse. The man introduced himself as SEÑOR DE MORLA, and explained that he happened to live at a nearby hacienda. He then asked if they would join both him and some of his neighbors for dinner. There were, he said, few visitors and so company was always welcome.

Plattner's group agreed with little discussion, the prospect of learning more about the country from the people who lived there enough to get their promise, and De Morla rode away.

Plattner looked after him curiously. "Nice looking man. How old would you say he was?"

Stroud was suspicious, and said so. Shaw was skeptical and Janine amused. Only Plattner was silent. Stroud and Janine walked back to where the rider had been standing as they came up the road. From the tracks it was obvious the horseman had been on the spot for quite awhile, for the horse had shifted his feet many times. In other words, they had been intercepted . . . but why?

"Too much coincidence," Stroud told them. "I think somebody doesn't want us to go back in there, not at all."

"You could be right," Plattner suggested. "If I knew where there was a jade mine, I don't think I'd tell anybody, myself."

———

The hacienda was an ancient but well kept
place; its fortress like lines had been softened
by gardens and many flowers. Stroud noticed that
several large trucks were parked in the mud to
one side of the house. He wondered if someone was
in the process of moving in . . . or out. Three
of the trucks were heavily loaded ore carriers,
yet there were no indications of any sort of
industry or agriculture nearby.

Their host met them at the door in a white
dinner jacket, and the woman with him was very
attractive but . . . strange. Her features were
young but her eyes were old as the ages.

"Welcome. It's a bit of a going away party but
we are glad you could join us."

Ben Stroud followed the others inside, and
they were offered drinks. The house was
beautiful, comfortable, and well decorated. Shaw
gasped. He crossed the room to stare at a vase,
frankly astounded. It was, he explained, a museum
piece.

De Morla smiled. "Naturally, being on the
ground, we have opportunities others do not. I
could show you more but we are in the process
of--um, moving north for the season."

Later, Shaw whispered to Stroud and Plattner
that there was at least a million dollars in
antique pottery and stone carvings within the
room and the bar adjoining.

There were a dozen people present, several of
them having strongly marked Indian features. Only
one of them might be called young. She was
introduced to Ben as ELVIRA DE LEON, the daughter
of a man who owned another hacienda not far off,
DON JUAN VELASQUEZ DE LEON.

Her father was a tall man of commanding
physique and a neatly trimmed Van Dyke beard.
Elvira carried herself beautifully, and had fair
skin and dark hair. Their name rang a responsive
chord in Ben's mind though he could not remember
why.

De Morla drew Dr. Shaw away from a hallway
lined with cartons and suitcases. "Are you the
Dr. Shaw, the archaeologist? It is fortunate you
have come at this time. We have just located a
ruin just north of here that has never been
examined by anyone. Would you like to be the
first, Doctor?"

Dr. Titus Shaw was a short, stocky man of
great enthusiasms, boundless energy and perpetual
good humor. He was also a man utterly without
suspicions, devoted to his work, and without
interest in financial gain other than that
necessary for the continuation of his research.

Throughout the evening there was a casual but
nonetheless persistent effort to convince Stroud,
Plattner and Shaw that going south into the
jungle would be a waste of their time. They were
told there is nothing to the south, and there
never had been. Yet there were many unexplored
ruins close by.

Leaving the conversation to the others, Stroud
strolled around, looking at the art objects, some
of them fantastically carved, and eventually he
wandered out onto the terrace.

He found Elvira De Leon there, alone, and for
the first time he saw that suspended from her
throat was a jade pendant. Intricately carved, it
was a tiny figure in a wreath of strange
characters. Stroud froze, flat-footed with shock,

his eyes riveted on the pendant. As he recovered his composure her lips twitched into an amused smile, obviously mistaking his interest in the pendant for interest in her obvious physical attributes.

She was a beautiful woman but there was another reason for his shock. The last time he saw that pendant was when he put it in a box in Japan and mailed it to his wife, Ruth. In fact there was a companion piece which had been made into the setting for a ring which was even now in his pocket.

Stroud's mind worked swiftly as he talked. Ruth must have survived the crash . . . or at least, the plane had been found and the pendant recovered from the wreckage. So why was the finding of the crashed plane not reported? And did it not also mean that somebody had been back into the jungle?

Somebody obviously did not want that jungle examined. The killing of the old man in Chimalapa and this party were examples of the lengths to which they were prepared to go.

This beautifully appointed home, miles from anywhere, was more than it seemed. The gracious smiling people about him seemed to be suddenly filled with menace. Instinct warned Stroud that an outright question about where the pendant came from might cause trouble, and he was prepared to wait.

"The girl with you . . . she is beautiful."

"Janine?" He shrugged. "I suppose she is."

"Strange . . . that one should be so preoccupied as to ignore a beautiful girl. It is not flattering, Mr. Stroud."

"I'm not the flattering sort of guy," he said, "but that's a beautiful stone you have there."

She lifted the pendant and glanced at it. "Yes, our people do lovely work . . . it is very old, I think."

She changed the subject. "The tall blond man? What does he do?"

He explained about Plattner, then commented, "Do you travel very much? I'd think you'd like Paris, Rome, perhaps the Far East . . . but you probably know all those places."

"I have not been away for a very long time. Now, it seems that I shall have a chance . . . to leave home after a long time, it is a challenge."

"I'm sure you will enjoy it; there are so many places for us to see . . . you know, before we die."

Her expression changed and her face seemed to stiffen. For a moment she looked almost gray, old. "Do not talk of death." Then she tried to smile, "You know, you never think about it, then suddenly . . ."

"I hope that doesn't mean anyone you know is ill?"

"No, no. We are well, um . . . provided for."

Feeling that her answer was somewhat odd, Stroud walked to the edge of the terrace and leaned on the balustrade. Possibly her choice of words was just that English was not her principal language.

The jungle was no more than a hundred feet away. A solid mass of foliage, just beyond the lawn. In the shadow of the trees he could see the faint outlines of an ancient stone wall. He had seen that wall as they arrived; it completely surrounded the place and, old as it was, must still form a protective barrier.

"I am puzzled," Elvira leaned on the balustrade beside him, "as to why you wish to go into the jungle. It is a frightful place . . . like another world. If you go in you may never return."

"Don't let it worry you," he said quietly. "If we go in, we'll come out."

He glanced back into the room where Shaw was in animated conversation with several men, and Erik Plattner was talking to Janine and an older woman. He was conscious of his own rumpled whites, which looked sad beside the smartness of Erik's dinner jacket.

He felt a hand on his sleeve. "Mr. Stroud, you must not go. We are the closest thing that you could call civilization for many miles. Within a day or two most of us will be gone and there will be no one to help your expedition. I fear if you go into the jungle only disaster can come of it, disaster, destruction and death."

"It can't be that bad," he said. "Men have been going to difficult terrain the world over and, most of the time, they have come back."

She was impatient. "You are an attractive man, Mr. Stroud, but you are also a fool."

He reached out, lifted the jade pendant and turned it in his fingers. "Beautiful," he said, "really beautiful."

On the back, etched into the gold, was the Chinese character tao . . . the way, the path.

He remembered the man who had given him that jade. It had been for bringing his child out of a battle ravaged town in Korea, and he remembered

the old Chinese who had set it for him. Now here
it was in Mexico, half way across the world.

She looked at him coldly. "You are familiar,
Mr. Stroud. I do not like that."

His smile was equally cold. "You've convinced
me of one thing," he said. "I'll find what I'm
looking for."

Turning away, he walked back into the living
room. Plattner left the people to whom he was
talking and crossed the room to him. "Ben," he
whispered, "we've walked into something."

Stroud waited, listening.

Plattner lowered his voice. "Shaw was right.
Look around the room--there's easily over a
million dollars worth of artifacts here!" He
paused. "Do you know what this means?"

"You tell me."

"It means they've found something, a ruined
city, a cave or tomb or a dozen of them,
something no archaeologist knows anything about.
If we could make a find like that we could become
rich, all of us."

"We'd have to get whatever it was out of the
country. Mexico won't allow antiquities to be
taken out, and I don't blame them."

"You leave that to me."

"If we found this site, and there was anything
left for the taking, do you suppose they would
just let us walk in and help ourselves?"

Plattner smiled. "Ben, why do you think I
wanted you along? Because of your beauty? I
wanted you because you were a trained,
intelligent, fighting man."

"How do you know that?"

"I checked your background." He nodded at a

gold mask on the wall with garnets for eyes. "Look at that, the finest example of Zapotec gold work I have ever seen."

He lowered his voice again. "Ben, there's something they don't want us to find, and you know something else? We're going to find it."

"Erik," he said quietly, "you're right about them not wanting us back there in that jungle. They don't want anybody back there, including searching parties. They found the plane, Erik. Elvira De Leon is wearing a pendant I gave Ruth."

Erik shot him a swift glance. "You're sure?"

Ben Stroud took the ring from his pocket. "They were twins, made by some artist during the T'ang dynasty."

"I'll be damned!"

"What about Shaw? How far will he go?"

"To find a ruined city nobody ever saw? To find artifacts like these? To be the first scientist on the ground in such a place? Believe me, Ben, Shaw would do anything short of murder, and he's a good man."

The dinner was excellent, conversation light, casual and amusing until at the end, over coffee, De Morla suggested Dr. Shaw investigate the temple they had found, "older than Monte Alban. It is to the north. I could mark it on a map."

Thoughtfully, they drove back to their camp. Miguel, their guide, was nowhere to be found. Stroud faced around sharply, concerned and ready to act. "Doc, I think we should break camp now, right now."

"And fail to examine a temple older than Monte

Alban?" He shook his head. "It would be criminal!"

"If we don't move now, and fast," Stroud said, "I don't think we'll get out of here at all!"

Shaw shook his head, and they argued. Stroud was impatient, and worried. Miguel's grandfather had been killed in Chimalapa, and the discovery of Ruth's plane seemed to have been covered up. There was no telling what was going on or how far these people would go. Some or all of them had seemed to be moving or leaving but he couldn't be concerned about that; several seemed to be important individuals and they had a number of trucks full of possessions; they couldn't easily disappear.

First, he must find the crash site. If he found that and got out safely, he would have an argument for the authorities, enough to ask for an investigation. Then he could smoke out De Morla and De Leon if he had to. But first he needed proof.

Shaw had been impressed by his new friends and would hear no argument against them. It was ridiculous. They were wealthy people. What reason could they have for keeping a scientific expedition out of the jungle?

Stroud walked out of the tent into the night, and after a minute, Janine followed. "What's the matter, Ben? You're behaving very oddly, you know."

"Something's bugging me. Something's all wrong around here and I'm trying to put my finger on it."

He explained about the pendant. Janine had noticed it and recognized the ring as the twin of the pendant.

"She's either dead," Stroud concluded, "or a prisoner."

"That's absurd . . . isn't it?"

"Erik has some ideas that make a sort of logic . . . he believes they have something to conceal. I think so too. Even though they seem to be leaving there is something they want to hide. I think the further we get away from here, and the faster we leave, the safer we'll be and the closer we'll get to whatever it is."

"I agree, senõr. We must go now!"

They turned swiftly to see Miguel standing behind them. There was blood on his head and face, and his white trousers were covered with swamp mud.

"They shot at me," he explained, "with a gun that made no sound. They could not find me in the swamp, but for a long time I was lost."

After they left Miguel had been prowling about, worried about his new friends, and curious about this hacienda of which he had heard much. There was a place near the swamp where a gate had been standing open. He had approached from that angle, and had been shot at. He fell, hit his head, and ran away. But before that, he had found there was a branch canyon behind the house with a well travelled road leading into the mountains. It was also a very old road, but in better shape than the one he knew of.

Shaw was adamant, wanting to stay for a few days, but both Erik Plattner and Stroud insisted on pulling out before their hosts could turn violent. Stroud got out a rifle and loaded it. Swiftly they bundled together most of their possessions, and leaving the pyramidal tent where

it was along with some of the bulkier baggage,
they took off.

Stroud and Miguel rode in the first jeep. In
places the road was rough, and at all times it
held to its width of seven feet, but they sped
along through the night with the canyon slowly
narrowing. At daybreak they pulled off to the
side of the road and in the first gray light of
dawn, they made breakfast.

Stroud kept a restless watch on the road. It
was doubtful that the people from the hacienda
realized their party was gone, yet it would not
be long, and they must make time while they
could. How far had they come? Was it forty miles?

He felt like he had when on patrol. There was
real danger here, he was sure of it. The place
where they had stopped was silent and eerie.
Prowling about, he walked among some boulders and
suddenly found himself standing at the edge of a
tiny and long-abandoned graveyard.

There were a dozen graves without markers,
perhaps more, but there were at least six with
stones carrying inscriptions. Curiously, he
walked over to the nearest grave and squatted to
read the inscription.

He looked, then looked again to make sure he
had seen aright.

Xcumane
1497-1911

It was absurd, on the face of it. If those
dates were correct then the man Xcumane had died
when he was more than four hundred years old!

He checked the stone beyond it, a stone that

had tipped sidewise and was half-covered with earth. He studied the date and name.

Francisco de Torres
1457-1890

It was ridiculous, but there it was again. He checked three other stones and then got to his feet. "Dr. Shaw!" he called. "Will you come here, please?"

Shaw came through the boulders followed by Erik and Janine. "What is it?" Shaw asked as he approached.

Stroud indicated the dates. "You give me an answer."

According to the stone markers not one of these people, if the dates were to be believed, had lived less than three hundred years.

"It's some sort of a joke!" Janine protested. "It's ridiculous!"

Dr. Shaw was silent. He studied the stones and the patina of years that smoothed their sides. He walked thoughtfully around the graveyard. He did not smile.

Erik Plattner walked close to Stroud. His voice was excited. "Ben! This is it! Remember what we heard about the jade? That people who drank powdered jade might live forever? Well, they are apparently doing it!"

Silently, they walked back to the jeep and loaded their few belongings. Without a word said by anyone, they started off again.

He had thought it ridiculous, and yet . . . was it? What was ridiculous, and what was not? Was it not ridiculous to cut open a man's heart

to save him? To see a picture on television taken
hundreds of miles away?

And what of the stories in the Bible of men
living hundreds of years? Were they merely fable?
Mistakes, exaggerations, or differences in
counting time?

Suppose those people back there had
antiquities because they had always had them, or
because they knew where all the lost cities were
because they had known of them before they became
lost?

When he had been speaking to Elvira, he had
asked what was important to her, and she had
replied, "To live, and to go on living."

Wouldn't someone who had lived a very long
time in good health want to protect their life at
all costs? Those who are safe and secure tend to
become more and more fearful, while people who
live in tough conditions and with their lives in
jeopardy are more ready to risk everything. He
had seen it over and over in Korea.

Dr. Shaw spoke suddenly. "I have seen no
sickness since we left Chimalapa."

"You haven't seen many people," Janine
objected.

"I was not thinking only of people, but even
plants. I have seen no disease . . . the air is
fresh from the sea, drawn inland up this long
canyon from the coast. It is high, for we must be
almost a mile above sea level."

Stroud saw a trail of smoke above the trees.
He swung the jeep over and lifted a hand. Erik
stopped behind him and Miguel, who had been
riding with Erik since the last stop, walked
forward.

"There's a fire," Stroud said. "Wait, I'll have a look."

He returned with the information that three men with rifles stood guard at a cross-roads a hundred yards farther along. Through the glass they looked like tough, competent men, and were obviously Indians. Beyond them the valley widened out and there were cultivated fields; as near as he could make out there was coffee, cacao, yams and some citrus fruit. There were men at work in the fields.

"We've come sixty miles," Shaw said thoughtfully, "and this is supposed to be wild country."

"There's an old road off to the right," Stroud suggested, "and with luck we might cut around through the jungle without being seen."

"Any sign of buildings?"

"Yes . . . there's a ruin in the distance--it looks like a very large one."

Successfully they skirted the guards and got to the old road. It showed no signs of recent travel, and they sped on.

Ruth might be ahead somewhere. Suppose she was alive?

The mountains loomed above them now. From time to time, climbing some knoll to look around, they could see miles of cultivated fields behind them. And the ruined city, which they approached by a roundabout route, was drawing nearer.

At one of their stops, Janine came close to Ben Stroud. "I'm scared," she said frankly. "I'm

scared and yet somehow it's all so amazing I
can't believe it is happening. I just can't."

"I want a look at that ruin," Plattner said.
"Do you know of anything like that around here,
Doctor?"

"Nothing . . . we've come upon something
unknown to the world outside."

"We'd better take it easy," Stroud advised.
"From now on we're heading into trouble."

"Or it may be nothing at all," Shaw said
uneasily. "We may be building danger when none
exists."

They pushed on, more slowly now, with frequent
stops. Miguel was wide eyed with curiosity and
apprehension, and Janine sat quietly beside Ben,
saying nothing. At each stop the second jeep drew
up alongside the first, so they could talk.

The road dipped down and they drove through a
small village to the outskirts of the ruined
city. There were chickens, pigs . . . but there
were few people around.

"They seem frightened," Shaw said. "Probably
they haven't seen any strangers in years."

"I don't think they know we are strangers,"
Plattner said. "I think they have a reason to
fear people in vehicles."

The road dipped into some brush and climbed a
low hill to the edge of the ruined city. Beside a
tumbled wall they looked out upon the broad
expanse of a plaza. Ben got out of the jeep and
mopped his brow. Upon both sides of the valley
towering ranges lifted into the low-hanging
clouds, and beyond the city with its massive

ruined buildings, its pyramids and columns, the valley cut back still deeper into the mountains.

Plattner climbed a wall to look around and Dr. Shaw disappeared behind a building, studying the inscriptions. Miguel and Janine stayed close to Stroud.

There was no sound, and the very silence was disturbing. They walked out into the great plaza and looked toward the village. Suddenly there was a call from Plattner and he came down the wall, running, scrambling, finally jumping to the ground.

"Two vehicles are coming in from the west down a mountain trail, and another group from the north. I think they are hunting for us."

Stroud shouted for Dr. Shaw but he was preoccupied and merely waved a hand. They piled into the jeeps and swung by, getting him into the jeep with Plattner. Stroud led the way toward the upper end of the ruin, racing the jeeps across the plaza and dodging from sight. It took several minutes before they could find the road again, and then it was only a dim trail. Stroud braked around a narrow bend and saw before him another ruin, and beside it a jeep with four riflemen and De Morla.

De Morla advanced to meet them, pistol in hand. "I am sorry," he said coolly. "You could have gone north and found many ruins. You have chosen the wrong direction."

"What seems to be the trouble?" Plattner was walking calmly up the road, his vehicle stashed somewhere in the shattered walls and foliage behind them. "Are we trespassing?"

"Unfortunately, yes. And we must take you back. Now!"

"This is ridiculous, senor!" Shaw protested. "I have a permit from the government for archaeological exploration. It covers this area."

De Morla shrugged. "Unfortunately we do not recognize this or any other government of Mexico." His smile was not pleasant. "We manage our own affairs. In fact, we do not recognize any government at all."

"Nor the laws of humanity."

De Morla turned his eyes on Stroud. "What was that?"

"You don't report plane crashes," Stroud said, "but you do rob the victims."

"Rob? What kind of talk is that? We rob no one. Why should we? We have the wealth of ages at our fingers. Nonsense!"

"The jade pendant Elvira De Leon is wearing belonged to my wife."

De Morla was obviously surprised. "You are a fool. Such a thing could not be."

"I identified it by the character <u>tao</u> placed on the back of the setting. It was put there in my presence."

"So?"

"Where is my wife? Where is Ruth Stroud?"

De Morla turned sharply away. "Bind them," he said, "and bring them in. We must return to the <u>hacienda</u>. We have a day, no longer."

Ben Stroud was ten feet from the edge of the jungle and when the guard was between himself and the rifles of the others he turned nonchalantly toward him. The rifle covered him, held waist high, but moving swiftly he grasped the muzzle from underneath with his right hand, and stepping in, grasped the action with his left and ripped the rifle from the guard's hands, then hit him on the jaw with a smashing butt stroke. Reversing the weapon, Stroud shot at the next guard and then lunged into the brush.

The entire action had taken no more than a split second. He hit the brush, dropped to a crouch and ran at right angles. Bullets cut leaves where he had entered the jungle, then swung to follow the sound of his movement. He came to a game trail and stopped, holding low and waiting for the shooting to cease. Then he went on, but silently. He ran along the narrow trail, vaulted a ruined wall, and crawled in among some rocks.

Behind him there were shouts, then a piercing whistle. Stroud lay still, panting.

He could hear the searchers, but his hiding place was secure. A huge slab of rock was above him and the hole into which he had crawled was small.

Ben Stroud waited. He kept telling himself they would not kill the others until they had him, for as long as the others were still alive they could always talk or bribe their way out of this.

The shadows were growing long; it had been some time since there had been any movement at all, and then he heard a faint rattle of gravel and something moved below him. Something moved down there, very quietly, something that could be a man . . . or a jaguar.

Whatever it was stopped and stood still some distance away. He crept close to the opening and

looked down. For an instant he did not believe
what he saw, and then the head turned . . .
"Miguel!" he whispered.

The boy turned and looked up the slight rise
to the ruins of the building where Ben Stroud was
hiding among the rocks. Then the boy scrambled up
the slope. "I look for you," he gasped. "I get
away, too!"

In a few minutes he had explained. The others
had been taken to the temple, which was also
something of a fort. And in the morning there
would be more men and they would make a careful,
painstaking search. The men from the hacienda
were very frightened of something that was about
to happen. They wanted to be far away but they
also needed to remove any potential
witnesses . . . the question was, witnesses to
what?

Scrambling out of his hole, Stroud came down
the slope. His wrinkled whites looked ever more
shabby now, but he felt good. He had the rifle
and there were still four shells in it, and he
had the Smith & Wesson with a full box of
ammunition.

He led the way into the jungle. They were
higher now, and once away from the ruins and
secondary growth, they came into a forest that
was almost without brush, just huge trees. They
walked on and in the distance a great wall could
be seen. Overgrown with vines and brush, its
ancient stones closed off the upper end of the
valley. Finally they paused near a stream.

"You know the people down there?" Stroud
asked, gesturing back toward the ruined city and
the fields.

"I do not know them. I think no man knows them. My grandfather, he says they were evil . . . they are men who never die, but evil, not like the good ones?"

"Good ones?"

"The Nawale." Miguel pointed up the canyon. "They live in the forest beyond the wall, and they are good men. My father has seen them, and once when he was bitten by a snake, they cared for him. They do not like Senor De Morla and those Indios with him."

They started on with the first gray light. The boy's story gave him some hope. Ben Stroud had an idea of what he could do, but first he would need help. If the Nawale would help him, then something might be possible.

They walked into an open area. Stroud caught a movement from the corner of his eye and wheeled, raising the rifle. Before them a tall man with dark hair was standing. He wore a white robe with braid around a square cut collar.

Miguel tugged Stroud's sleeve. "The Nawale!" he whispered. Stroud lowered his rifle and walked forward to greet the old man. He spoke in the few words of Quiche Maya he had picked up, but to his surprise, the old man replied in English.

"You have found trouble?"

Ben Stroud's explanation was brief and to the point, and the old man listened attentively.

"I cannot help you," he said finally. "We do not participate in the violence of others, but your friends are in more serious danger than you suppose."

The old man explained then that a rebellion was planned by the workmen from the fields and the jade mine. De Morla and his associates had enslaved many of the local Indians, and even some of the Nawale who had not yet fled to the forests. These workers also drank the powdered jade and within a generation the older ones were reliant upon it to keep their youth and strength, for if it was not administered regularly, the aging process returned with devastating results.

Addicted to this drug they were trapped, doing the work so that a small community of Spaniards and aristocratic Indians could live in comfort and wealth. But now there was little of the jade left and De Morla and De Leon had kept it a secret just how much or little they had stockpiled over the years as the miners searched for a new deposit. The time period between treatments with the jade had been stretched to the maximum and the day was coming when they would simply cease giving their workers the needed dose.

"Are all those people going to die?"

"Yes." The Nawale nodded. "And De Morla is foolish, for it is not the jade that has kept us alive these many years, but a quality in the jade . . . a substance that is veined through it. It actually takes very little to prolong life. They have trapped themselves here for centuries and are now convinced that they are doomed."

Suddenly, they heard the baying of hounds. But at their eagerness to go the Nawale was only amused. He took something from his leather purse and scattered it upon the ground. "This will stop them," he said.

"Is it a magic powder, Nawale?" Miguel asked eagerly.

"It is a magic powder that once changed the world's history," the Nawale said, smiling. "It is pepper . . . red pepper."

He took them to a place near a gate in the great wall that shut off the valley. Beyond that, he explained, was their home. There was no friendship between them and those below, who were late comers.

"Late comers?"

"We of the Nawale came long ago, when Kukulcan came, and we have preferred to live here. Once we occupied much of the land you have crossed, but when the Spanish and their allies, who were northern Indians, came we retreated into these mountains.

"You have met De Morla. He was one of them. Juan Velasquez De Leon was another. Both were listed as missing by Cortez and were believed killed, but both took Indian wives and preferred to remain here, where there need be no death."

"Suppose they follow us?"

"They will come no further. They will be angry, but they will come no further."

"How is it that you speak English?"

The Nawale explained that from time to time men from their valleys went out into the world, on pilgrimages, or to find books or supplies they needed. There were men among them who spoke many languages. They went out, but they always returned; sometimes, but rarely, they communicated with scientists or physicians.

Stroud waited in the shadow of the wall, but the pursuers evidently lost the trail for the dogs failed them and the sounds of pursuit died out. The morning wore on, and he became increasingly worried. Despite himself he kept thinking about Janine.

He asked the Nawale about the plane crash, and discovered that only one had survived . . . a woman, a young woman. She had been found and taken away to the settlements below. "But she tried to escape and was killed," the Nawale explained.

"Who killed her?"

"It was De Leon . . . who was the Conquistador. When he first came he was one of the best, but endless life does not always make one a better man. He is corrupt, Mr. Stroud. Long life has corrupted him."

Ben Stroud grew restless and finally he got up. The Nawale glanced at him. "Yes, it is time. They have gone back, the searchers have, and they will not come again. But you must hurry if you would save your friends.

"You will find them," the Nawale continued, "in the temple. Approach it from the rear and there is a way through the ruins. But you must hurry; they distribute the jade at sundown and when it is discovered there is no more there will be a rebellion. The Conquistadores will need to flee and they will allow no one who could identify them in the wider world to live."

Ben Stroud picked up his rifle and started down the hill. He did not wonder at what the Nawale knew, nor did he doubt any of what he had heard. Perhaps it was nonsense, perhaps it was

not, but what he wanted to do was to get back and
get his people out of there . . . fast.

Crouched among the ruins at the edge of the
huge plaza they looked toward the temple. Beyond
it there were scattered groups of the workers who
shouted to those in the temple that it was time,
time for the jade that kept them young and
strong. Tools and a few weapons were brandished
and several of the hacienda's jeeps had been
overturned; one was burning.

Then De Leon appeared on the steps and yelled
back. Stroud could not distinguish the words but
Miguel told him that De Leon was telling them
they must wait, and they were shouting that they
could not wait, that it must be now. Suddenly the
knots of men grouped together and began to push
toward the front of the building. De Leon lifted
a pistol and fired downward. A man fell, but the
rest rushed and as several others fired at the
guards De Leon ducked back under cover.

Circling behind the building Stroud found the
door he'd been told of. The thick wood was shaped
and bleached to look like stone, and the two of
them entered. There was a short, walled passage,
and then a room.

Only one man was on guard and he whirled in
surprise at their approach. Stroud was in no mood
to stop--he smashed into the man, knocking him
down, then covered him with the rifle. Gleefully,
Miguel grabbed the guard's rifle and rudely
jerked the bandolier from the man's shoulder. To
their angry demands he could only gesture toward
the interior of the building. Stroud shoved the

man outside and advised him to run for it. He
barred the door behind him.

From in front of the building there were
shouts and yells. The people were attacking.
There was a rattle of gunfire. Ben Stroud lifted
a curtain and peered into an inner room. There,
against the wall, stood Janine, her face stiff
with fear. She looked at him, then glanced
quickly away so others would not be drawn to him
by her gaze.

Dr. Shaw was on the floor and there was blood
on his head, dried blood, from a blow some time
back. Erik Plattner was there and he was talking.

At first Stroud could hear nothing, and then
he caught the words.

". . . you've lost unless you listen to me.
You can keep them out, keep them out until they
die out there. But what of you, De Morla? You
intended to be long gone by now. What of De
Leon?"

"I have a jeep hidden away. I can take you to
it. I can save you. But I want the contents of
the room back there at the hacienda. I want
everything that's in it."

Stroud shifted his position. He could see no
one but Janine and Shaw because the others were
near the door, and he could not take a chance on
stepping in the room to face them for they would
have the advantage of position . . . and if they
fired at him Janine and her father would be
beyond him, in the direct line of fire.

De Morla growled, "I won't kill you if you
tell me where it is and give me the keys. If you
are lucky they won't kill you either."

"Trust a dying angry mob? Forget it. Without a vehicle you'll never get away!"

"I do not trust you. Once away from here your group will not keep our secret." Turning, De Morla raised his voice and called out, "De Leon! Get ready--we are going to attempt an escape! We don't have much time!"

"Just take me," Plattner argued. "You can make me one of you. I am just one man--give me the jade like you did for them." He gestured to the mob outside. "You know you can trust me if I need the jade!"

Janine was staring at Plattner, shocked.

De Morla hesitated.

Stroud gripped the rifle in both hands, ready to take a chance. From the front of the building there was another out-burst of rifle fire, and the sounds of a struggle.

"They might get in." Plattner was calm. "And even if they don't, they can hold you here. They may die, but you will die also. I am your only hope."

De Morla suddenly agreed, then added, "But the others must stay." At that, Plattner merely shrugged. He started for the door and De Morla turned his pistol on Shaw.

"Hold it!" Stroud stepped into the room, his rifle high.

"We are going out the back," Stroud said, "and you two are coming with us." Stroud jerked the barrel toward Plattner and De Morla. "At least as far as the door."

Plattner hesitated. "Ben," he said, "we can walk out of here. We can make a deal."

"I only want to walk out of here," Ben replied shortly.

Janine helped her father to his feet. Stroud demanded to know where De Leon was. The firing out front had stopped, and there was no sound. Neither De Morla or Plattner would reply.

Stroud began to back down the passage, his rifle on Plattner and De Morla. He directed Janine and her father to go first but to keep to one side of the passage and out of the line of fire.

"You go out there," De Morla snapped, "and they will kill us all."

Stroud refused to listen. He had seen the jeep parked just off the road, and he knew what he was going to do. There was nothing here for him. Ruth was dead and De Morla knew of it, but it was De Leon that he really wanted, and wanted badly. With any luck having De Morla hostage would allow him to get close to the other Spaniard.

"Stroud," Plattner said, "I've made a deal. Everything in that room back there, everything, and all of it for us. And the secret of the jade."

"There is no secret," Stroud replied, "except the something that even he," indicating De Morla, "does not know. It's not the jade. There's another substance, found within it. When refined it actually takes very little of it to have the same effect."

De Morla was pale. "What do you mean?"

"I talked with the Nawale. They know. It's never been necessary to mine jade in such volume."

De Morla's lips worked. "You're wrong. You must be wrong!"

"Neither one of you is going to get what you want but maybe we can get out of this situation with no more bloodshed. So, shut up and get moving!"

They left the building by the wooden door and Stroud started for the jeep, forcing them to follow. Shaw reached it and was helped in, managing to start it. If they were to escape now it must be quickly. If they didn't get away the angry mob was apt to tear their oppressors apart and any strangers along with them.

He did not know exactly how long a man could live after the time came for the drink, but from the way these people were behaving he suspected it was not long. He was sure now that the man they had picked up on the road to Chimalapa had been such a man, one of those who had been searching for other deposits or a Nawale returning home after his supply of the purified substance ran low.

Stroud crouched on the tailgate of the jeep, rifle in one hand, the other clenched around one of the canvas covered ribs. "Take it easy until you're in sight of them," he warned, "then gun it."

As the jeep rounded the front of the temple the workers started forward in a ragged line. There was a shot from De Leon's defenders and a man fell. That was followed by sporadic firing from the crowd. Stroud glanced toward the fighting and in that instant Erik Plattner swung a back hand blow that knocked the rifle from his

hand. The jeep lurched and his grip was torn
loose and he fell.

Bullets smashed into the pavement beside him
and the jeep was tearing away. Janine, who had
grabbed wildly at him, had fallen also. Coming to
his feet, Ben Stroud caught the girl and,
running, they reached the shelter of the temple
wall again. They hugged it closely as bullets
raked past them. The gunfire had not been from
the mob, but from the temple top.

Running, they ducked back into the door from
which they had come only a short time before. It
was but temporary shelter, yet any move to leave
it might expose them to fire from the top where
De Leon and some of the guards were waiting.

From inside the temple there were running
feet. Flattened against the wall, Stroud shucked
the Smith & Wesson. A guard came into sight and
he fired. The heavy slug hit the man and knocked
him back onto the steps from above, the
concussion of the big pistol loud in the narrow
passage.

Then there was a noise of a door scraping open
from the passage behind them. Stroud started to
turn, but was stopped by a cold feminine voice.
"Drop the pistol or I will shoot you both."

It was Elvira.

He dropped the pistol.

De Leon came running down the steps with two
men at his heels and a sword raised to strike.

"Now!" Janine said, and shot Elvira with her
hidden .32 automatic.

The woman fell, with a low, moaning cry of
horror, and De Leon lunged. Ben Stroud turned on
the ball of his foot and knocked the blade aside

with his left forearm. The man reversed and cut viciously and as Stroud backed into Janine, he tripped, and the two of them went down. One of De Leon's guards grabbed the arm of the Spaniard and pulled him out the door and toward the plaza.

Stroud scooped up his fallen gun and followed Janine from the passage. They headed for the ball court across the plaza. The jeep wheeled into sight with Erik Plattner and De Morla. It jerked to a stop near De Leon and there were a few hurried words as De Leon piled into the jeep.

Ben Stroud paused on the rubble strewn slope of the court, taking cover and gasping for breath. Janine, still clutching the .32, held his arm.

"You all right?" he asked.

"Yes."

They were looking for a better place to hide when the jeep ground to a halt below them. Some of the workmen who had scaled the temple walls were shooting down at it. Their bullets caught one of De Morla's guards and he fell . . . but then, without any of the men in the jeep returning fire, one of the marksmen collapsed, another went to his aid, but then it seemed as if neither could arise.

"We have to go. Now! Get back in the truck and drive!" De Morla ordered.

But Erik turned and ripped the pistol from De Morla's hand. Flipping the gun around he shot the other guard in the back of the head. He then turned the pistol on De Leon.

"Hand it over!"

He surrendered his weapon. "Just help us get back to the hacienda!" De Leon begged. "You can

have what you want but we must get back to have
our potion. If we do not our fate will be the
same as these peons."

Erik came out from his cover behind the jeep.
Stroud's gun was thrust into his waistband but
his hand was hooked in his belt and he turned
slowly.

Stroud hesitated, catching his breath. "If I
shoot," he said to Janine, "run."

"Without you?"

"I'll be right behind you."

Plattner walked to the side of the court.
"Ben," he said, "why don't you join us? You know
too much; you have to be in this thing or out of
it, and there's nothing waiting for you on the
outside.

"You can run this end of things if you want.
We can get this stuff out of the country and in
the States it will make us rich. They've got a
stash of the jade back at the hacienda. If you're
right we'll be rich enough to figure out exactly
what it is that creates the longevity. What d'you
say?"

"Where's Shaw?"

"We dumped him back yonder."

"Alive?"

"Sure . . . we just didn't want him around for
awhile. Later, we can use him. He knows how to
dig, and how to preserve what we find."

"I want no part of it. I'm clearing out."

"That is not an alternative. This is your last
chance!"

"You're going to work with them?"

Plattner smiled. "I'm where the money is, Ben,
you know that." He grinned and while Stroud

didn't doubt that he had just heard the pitch
Plattner had given De Morla and the others, he
knew that in his case it was just window
dressing--the man was going to kill him no matter
what he said.

Ben Stroud saw the movement of Plattner's
shoulder that brought the gun up and he yelled,
"Run!"

The gun had fairly jumped from Stroud's
waistband. He fired from waist level, knocking
Plattner back against the jeep. De Morla twisted,
whining like a sick dog and tearing at Plattner's
coat and Stroud realized he was trying to get the
keys to the jeep from the dead man's pocket.

De Leon struggled to get out of the vehicle
and then tumbled headlong to the stone.

Juan Velasquez De Leon, the man who had been
one of the trusted captains of Cortez, got to his
feet and started toward them. Then he seemed to
stagger and he stopped, peering up at Ben Stroud
as if staring into the sun.

Stroud paused, gun up, but holding his fire.
All sound had ceased.

De Leon advanced another step and then seemed
to crumble as his knees gave way and he fell. De
Leon tried to rise, then lay back.

Gun ready, Ben Stroud descended several steps,
then froze. The face of De Leon was that of a
wizened, dried up old man . . . or a mummy.

Ben Stroud looked beyond him to the still
twitching body of De Morla; the face up-turned to
the last rays of the sun was monkey-like with
age. The clothing sagged about the shrunken
figure.

There was no more shooting, no sound from the

crowd of mine workers, nothing. He turned and
started up the steps toward Janine.

"What is it?" she asked. "What's happened?"

"Let's go find your father," he said. "There's
no more to do here."

They descended the steps. In the distance, far
back of the plaza they could see Dr. Shaw picking
his way through a maze of bodies. His clothing
was rumpled and dirty, and his face and head were
bloody, but he was all right.

"Mr. Stroud?"

They turned . . . it was the Nawale. Though
exhausted, head ringing from gunfire and
emotionally spent, Stroud noticed his hands. The
carefully groomed nails, the scar on his finger.

"Do you still have the key I gave you?"

It took him a moment to remember. Their night
in the mysterious house seemed such a long time
ago.

"Yes."

"It works on the gate in the wall also. Come
if you wish, Mr. Stroud. We would welcome you
among the Nawale."

He turned and started off.

"Throw it away," Janine said, "it frightens
me."

He paused, key in hand, ready to toss it into
the ruins. The Nawale was far off now. Ben Stroud
weighed the key in his hands, glanced at it,
smiled, and slipped it into his inside coat
pocket.

THE END.

THE FREEZE

The Beginning of a Science Fiction Story

There, now . . . a fire going. A few dead
branches from the lower part of that tree, some
bark from the under side of the big log . . .
drag that dead-fall closer. It's going to be a
cold night.

Nothing looks so good as a fire when a man is
cold, or when he is hungry . . . or alone. Stirs
memories, too . . . takes a man back . . .

Cold . . . and rain. Setting in for a
miserable night. I'd better lace the branches
tighter, pile on some more evergreen boughs. I'm
not feeling too good . . . not so young as I used
to be.

How many fires? How many lonely fires? And
each one I have built with careful hands, with
tender hands. Fire is a precious gift, a sacred
thing . . . the first step Man made in his march
upward from the beast.

The shadows play, the wind touches the fire
and it ducks its points of flame and gives a
gusty sigh . . . a stick falls and the sparks fly
up . . . I add another stick and another . . .
now let it blow and let it rain, I have my fire.

Black are the columns of the trees . . . black
are the masses above where the wind plays tiny
violins among the pine needles . . . and off
there a bare tree chafes its branches
together . . . a cold sound, a lost sound.

How many miles did I make today, I wonder?
Miles have lost their meaning, of course. If I
could find a car . . . but there would be small
chance of that. In a city I could find many
things lost, useful things to me.

I feel the cold more now, even though it is
growing less. This year the ice melts a little at
noon. It is a sign, but a small one. I think the
dust is going away and someday we will have the
sun again.

The sun . . . how long since I clearly saw the
sun? It was the day I started to return, coming
down the river. It was about ten degrees below
zero that morning, but bright and cold . . . and
then it happened.

We should have known, all of us. It had
happened before and there was nothing to prevent
it happening again. We had the evidence . . .
mammoths or bison had been found frozen and
completely preserved, even with green grass in
their stomachs. The last time it had happened, a
chap from Columbia University had established the
time by carbon-dating . . . 28,000 years ago.

A sudden deep freeze, everything alive frozen
in their tracks. Killed . . . dead . . . wiped
out, just like that.

What had caused it? Nobody speculated very
much. The theories of cataclysms were out of
fashion right then, and scientists, creatures of
fashion as are we all, carefully avoided any

facts that seemed to controvert their pet
theories.

A mammoth with green grass in his
stomach . . . obviously frozen very quickly . . .
a perfectly preserved ancient bison . . . the
last was in Alaska, the former in Siberia. But
there were a few vague theories about
interstellar dust clouds shutting off the heat of
the sun . . . and it happened again, in April
1954.

More fuel . . . the appetite of a fire is
amazing . . . the tongues of flame lick the chill
from the dead branches. More fuel here now than
there was twenty years ago. Two or three days
more and I should reach the site of Palm Springs.
What would they think at that once desert resort
to see it now? All the northern Mojave and most
of the old Colorado deserts have been sprouting
pine forests for the last several years.

Snow falling . . . the rain is changing to
snow. It is May if my calculations are right. It
was seven years ago this May that I saw my last
human being . . . it was a woman, she was dying.
Dying when I found her.

Starvation . . . cold . . . exhaustion, and
loneliness. She had nothing. Had seen no living
human being in four years, she said.

It had come so suddenly there was no chance to
prepare. Somewhere some scientist may have
recorded the temperature. My own thermometer
showed minus 30 Fahrenheit before it went out of
whack. The temperature might have fallen to 60
below zero. Possibly colder . . . my advantage
was simple. I was coming back from a year in the
Arctic, taking the route up the Mackenzie River,

and I had plenty of warm clothing and was
conditioned to great cold.

At a trappers cabin I holed up, and the snow
buried it except where I kept an opening. It
snowed for more than a month, but the winds blew,
and sometimes I could get out for more fuel.
There was food, so I stuck it out. It was more
than a month before I appreciated what must have
happened.

After awhile the food got short so I loaded
the rest on a hand-sled I found near the cabin,
loaded up a little dry fuel, and struck south. By
that time I was ready for the cold. My body had
adjusted itself to a degree. I was always cold,
but I survived.

Three Indians were living at the trading post.
They let me have a few more supplies, and I
continued on. But after that one city . . . after
that I learned to avoid them.

The cold had struck at the end of winter and
fuel supplies had been low. A rail strike, for
reasons I never understood, meant food supplies
were depleted also. There was open war in the
city, bitter fighting over food, and ransacking
and looting of houses and stores. Thousands had
died in the first awful weeks of cold, many of
them trapped in apartments that, without
electricity, were their only shelter.

It had been a warm spring in the States. The
cold had struck with daytime temperatures in
Minnesota, the Dakotas and Maine cascading
downward from the middle 70s to below zero within
a month.

The human body is amazingly tough, and

amazingly adjustable to change . . . only it requires time, and there was no time.

Twenty-four, that's what I was, just twenty-four years old, with all my future before me, before my whole generation. But it was neither my education nor my training that saved me, it was my hobby . . . Hunting, tracking, living off the country. I knew how to survive.

Got to move, getting stiff. That's the penalty of growing old . . . and I'm old now, although in good shape from activity and out-door living. Got to get more fuel before I settle down, and some snow to melt for water.

One thing about cold . . . it preserves. My advantage was that I was away from cities, that I knew what to eat, and where to find it, and that I avoided civilization and the chaos it created.

It is probable that thirty percent of the world's population died within two months of that April.

Others died within subsequent days, and then still others in the struggle for existence and in fighting over food, clothing and fuel. Here and there small groups organized and worked together for mutual benefit. These groups made out best of all, some to finally die, but often to survive on down the years.

COMMENTS: This is likely Louis's earliest attempt at writing science fiction. Though later in life he would occasionally buy a sci-fi novel, most of it was foisted upon him by me. I was an avid reader of the genre, and, while he liked it too, Dad was never entirely at ease with the idea of creating his own SF stories. He preferred to have more of a foundation in reality. He was, however, continually fascinated by the possibilities and by the "frontier" aspects of the genre. Because of a connection facilitated by a friend of mine, composer Fred Paroutaud, Dad eventually joined Dr. Thomas Paine, head of NASA during Apollo, when he formed the National Commission on Space. It was an incredible opportunity for my father to discuss a good deal of the science without the fiction.

While the cause of the sudden cooling of the earth in this story seems to be an interstellar dust cloud, the mid-1950s was a time when a new ice age was considered a real possibility. Fears of global cooling—caused by space dust, the humidity from a warming trend creating more snow and glaciation, increased volcanic activity, or nuclear war—lasted through the 1980s.

In this case the direct inspiration seems to be the mystery of the "Berezovka Mammoth," which had been discovered in Siberia around the turn of the century. The Berezovka Mammoth was found with grass in its teeth and mouth, suggesting that it had died and been frozen fairly suddenly. Dad mentioned this connection, and his ongoing interest in it, in the following journal entry from October of 1986:

```
   People wonder how I write so much. I
wonder why I write so little. People suggest
stories when my brain is loaded with
stories . . . and [I] would be telling them
by the roadside if not with a
typewriter . . . my study is filled with
fragments of stories. I have just read one,
a few pages written long ago of a man who
```

survived a terrible disaster to the earth, something like when the mammoths were frozen, some with grass undigested in their stomachs. This man was in the far north and survived, stayed away from cities. Good story there, may never find time to write it.

It's interesting to see Louis make a stab at a postapocalyptic tale. With its emphasis on man-against-nature survival, if he had ever found time to return to it, "The Freeze" might have been right up his alley.

Being from North Dakota, Louis was more familiar than he wanted to be with cold weather. For a short time he trained soldiers in winter survival and tested newly developed gear in Michigan's Upper Peninsula.

BEN MILO

The Beginning of a Crime Story

When Ben Milo returned to his cabin he put on the coffee pot. That was pure habit, of course, the ingrained pattern of years. Then he stood in the middle of the room and tried to think it out.

He had seen the car come bounding and plunging over the desert as if driven by a madman. Certainly, nobody who knew this country would drive like that, or even venture onto his old trail in anything without four-wheel drive. It was a burro trail, not a highway.

A few years back he would have waited cynically for them to come, wiry, able, confident. But his mind worked a little slower now and arthritis had stiffened the hands that had once handled a gun with deadly speed. Ben Milo had been born to hard country and rough living; however, that was eighty-six years ago.

Ben had been an outlaw for too many of those years but his lawless deeds lay buried in the graves of his generation. If anyone suspected him now it was that young highway patrolman, Jim Garrity, who was always asking questions about the old days.

Ben Milo liked Garrity. He was a salty youngster, fit to have walked with the old breed. They had worked together a time or two . . . like when that Prescott youngster was lost over east. Ben's eyes were not much for reading print, but he could still read sign. They trailed that youngster nine miles over the badlands before they found him.

Three times since then Garrity had called on Ben to lend a hand and each time they had found what they went after. Old . . . yes, Ben Milo was old, but he could still walk twenty miles in any kind of weather and over almost any kind of country.

When he first saw the car he had stopped to watch. It was shining and new, but when it hit the wash below his place it stopped as he knew it would. By direct travel, up and over the hillside, the wash was only ten minutes from his shack, but by the trail it was a good hour of walking around the rocky backbone of a mountain that thrust up boldly from the desert.

He knew that wash, and nothing short of a tractor was likely to get them out of it. He had stood listening to the roar of the motor and the spinning of tires in loose sand, heard the swearing as they hurled blame back and forth, and then they came up out of the wash pushing the girl ahead of them.

There were three of them, boys or young men, and they wore city clothes and one of them was carrying a suitcase. Another one carried some kind of a weapon, too short for a rifle, but obviously heavy. Might be one of those tommy-guns

he'd seen at the picture show. They were packing
no grub and not one of them had a canteen.

Ben backed off the ridge and returned to his
cabin. When he had the coffee pot on, he gathered
his canteens and water sacks and hid them away.
Had it not been for the girl he would have gone
back up in the rocks and waited them out, and Ben
was an Indian when it came to waiting.

That girl . . . she was in real trouble, and
in Ben's day even an outlaw would go out of his
way to help a woman. It looked like she might be
a hostage. Certainly, that outfit was on the
dodge. That suitcase now, it might be filled with
loot.

He must be careful. The last thing he wanted
was a shooting. Folks asked too many questions
these days, and they pried into a man's past. It
was best to let the dead past remain dead.

Ben was a hard old man whose life had been
lived among hard, fiercely independent men. The
law was often too far away to call, even if a man
had been of a mind to. A man fought his own
battles back then; most of the time he didn't
have a choice.

His baptism of fire . . . at least familiarity
with it . . . came one evening when he was a
youngster playing in the street back at old Fort
Sumner . . . that was in '81. He had seen Sheriff
Garrett come up the street with his deputies,
John Poe and Tip McKinney, and stop at Pete
Maxwell's place. The deputies sat down on the
steps and Pat walked back to the room where
Maxwell lay in bed sick.

A few minutes later he saw Billy come out of
Deluvina Maxwell's adobe, and he heard her say,

"There's a side of beef hung up on Maxwell's porch. You cut yourself a steak and I'll fry it for you."

Ben had seen Billy start for Maxwell's place and he called after him, but Billy had just waved a hand . . . and a minute or two later there were two gun shots. One of them had killed Billy, the other they found years later, embedded in the bottom of a wash stand. Garrett had fired and thrown himself to the floor. His second shot missed by nine feet.

Only a few of the old breed lived on. Wyatt died in '29, George Coe, Jeff Milton, Chris Madsen and Dee Harkey in the 1940s. The old ones were like that. They lived on hard work, beef and beans and if you didn't shoot them they'd live forever.

That outfit coming up the trail. They weren't going anywhere, they just thought they were. Why didn't they learn about the country before high-tailing it off into the desert that away? They must have spotted this trail and turned off into it to hide . . . or to cut across country to the other highway. They had ridden into a death trap, but the trouble was it could mean death for Ben Milo and for that girl, too.

He could see them come up the slope to the bench where the old mine was located. The cabin where he lived, a ramshackle sheet-metal shed and the gallows-frame over the shaft were all that remained except for a few foundations. Nobody had tried working the mine since 1905. Long after it was abandoned, Old Ben moved in, filed on several claims, and did the assessment work.

The tall one had his shirt out of his pants

and he carried that tommy-gun. He was tall, but
thin. The second one was thick-set and the third
a gangling youngster of sixteen or so. The oldest
could be no more than nineteen.

The girl? Well, say seventeen . . . and mighty
pretty.

She took a quick look around when they reached
the bench, and he would have gambled it was not
the first such lay-out she had seen.

Ben Milo stepped into the door. "Howdy, folks!
Glad to see you! Coffee's on!"

The gun muzzle lifted and the stocky one
started his hand toward his waist-band. So he had
a gun, too.

"Coffee? On a day like this? You got a beer?"

"No ice." Ben's eyes went to the girl. The
utter despair in her eyes had changed to hope. A
body would think he was four men, the way she
looked at him. What could he do? What chance did
he have? "No electricity," he added.

"No telephone?" The tall one seemed to be the
boss-man. His eyes swept the area. "You've got a
radio? TV?"

"Nothin' like that away out here." Ben's eyes
surveyed them mildly but shrewdly. "Like I said,
no electricity."

The tall one gestured with the gun. "Stand
aside, Old Man. Buzzer, you go inside and have a
look-see."

Ben Milo moved aside, careful to make no
sudden moves. The tall one with the tommy-gun had
a shoulder-holster beneath his shirt. It was open
far enough to make grasping the gun a simple
thing.

Buzzer went up the steps and into the house. A moment later he appeared. "Nobody here."

"There's coffee," Ben suggested mildly.

"What else have you got? To eat, I mean?"

"Beans . . . I live mostly on beans and rice. Time to time I make myself a batch of sourdough bread."

Buzzer stood aside as they entered. "Crumby lookin' shack. On'y two rooms. This'n and the bedroom behind the blanket."

Ben Milo walked to the cupboard and took down cups and saucers, then poured the coffee. He had just enough cups to go around. They needn't have said it was crumby . . . as desert shacks went, it was mighty neat. He always liked things kept in order. Took after his ma, that way.

"How far to the highway?"

"Quite a piece. I never go that way myself. I usually go up to Blythe." He paused momentarily. "Or east."

"East?"

"To the river . . . the Colorado."

It was a critical moment. Old Ben Milo wanted to get them off his hands and east would be the way if they would take the bait, but it was a slim chance. He had been reading men too long to doubt the sort of man this tall one was . . . he would kill quickly, heedlessly, almost without thinking. Killing would be his first solution to almost any problem.

The one called Buzzer now . . . he was the tough one. A bad one he might be, but there was a deep toughness of fiber built into him. He would take a lot of punishment, a lot of killing.

The kid . . . there was a weak link. The kid had stumbled into more than he bargained for.

The easiest way out was the way they had come, and there was small chance of their making it out alive by any other way. But they were running from something and going back was probably not an option.

"What's on the river?" Buzzer asked.

"A few fishermen, maybe. They camp along the river sometimes, launch their boats off the banks. Otherwise, there would be nothing. Just Yuma . . . and Mexico." The idea was planted now. He could not raise it again without causing suspicion.

"Fix us something to eat." The tall one slouched into a chair. He glanced at the girl. "You help him."

She came over to Ben obediently and he showed her where the plates were. They were gray enamel dishes, the simplest kind of eating ware a man could buy. There was a big pot of beans, some rice, the remains of a loaf of sourdough. There was also a comb of honey he'd robbed from the bees in the wash over east.

With a queer certainty Ben Milo knew he was not going to get out of this alive. They would want no witnesses left behind to say where they had gone.

They did not yet realize the situation they were in . . . maybe the girl did. Young as she was, she had a knowing way around a desert cabin and around a mine. He had watched her, and there was a certain air of familiarity in her way of doing things.

He considered the possibility of a shoot out. He could have a try at it. His guns were cached and if he could lay a hand to one of them he might nail at least two of them before they got him. Coolly, he judged his chances and knew they were good. He was a dead shot . . . a little slower than of old, but once he lifted a gun he hit what he aimed at.

Only that tommy-gun would spray lead all over the cabin. He didn't trust a gun like that and he didn't trust the man who held it. If something happened at the wrong moment the girl was almost sure to catch some. Reluctantly, he yielded before the realities. Without the girl he might have tried it.

The tall one sat down astride a chair with the tommy-gun across his lap, his arms on the back of the chair. He turned his blue eyes to Ben Milo. "You live here all the time, Old Man?"

"Thirty years."

"Thirty years? You must be nuts." He turned to Buzzer. "You hear that? He's lived in this god-forsaken desert for thirty years!"

"It ain't so bad," Ben said quietly.

This one thought he was tough, and would be likely to try to prove it somehow. The other one . . . Buzzer . . . he was the toughest of the lot. His eyes shifted to the third one . . . he didn't belong. He shouldn't be here at all.

The cool, tough ones a body could figure out. You could study on them and come up with an answer, but the hotheaded, rattle-brained types were dangerous to themselves and everybody else.

COMMENTS: Looking at Louis's life, there's a good deal of familiar territory covered in these few pages. The mining claim the old man lives on is similar to several Dad worked in his youth, though, as far as I know, none were so far south. I believe he set this story somewhere southwest of Blythe for reasons relating to the plot, so that his criminal characters can be tempted by the idea of getting to Mexico via the Colorado River. The story of the death of Billy the Kid is also something out of Louis's past. He worked for Deluvina Maxwell one summer in the 1920s and heard her, as well as others who had actually been there, tell the story of Billy and Pat Garrett.

Though I have labeled this a "crime story" it is really a Western, contemporary to the time, probably the 1950s, when Louis wrote it. A twentieth-century Western, it contains classic Western genre elements, like commenting on the passing of the frontier era and on the conflict between generations. In this case the commonly used twitchy kid-with-a-Colt type character has been replaced by a juvenile delinquent with a sub-machine gun.

California, a distance of over a hundred miles,
when the owner failed to pick him up.

IN THE MEASURE OF TIME

A Complete Adventure Story

Black was the sea and dark were the skies
above, low clouds bulged with rain unspilled.
Morgan looked at the sky and at the sea and knew
in his heart he was frightened.

He was alone on the wide Pacific and the skies
turning to storm. He watched the mountainous
waves and tried to recall the lore picked up in
many ports or read in books. His tiny craft was
tossed along like a scrap of paper before the
gale. He, a merchant seaman from the great iron
ships, was a man used to oil or coal, not a
handful of wind caught in a few yards of fabric.

Then, from the sea there was a quavering cry,
and he saw a raft, and clinging to it, something
that might have been a man. His only hope for
life was to hold his course, hold his bow into
the storm . . . a thin and lonely chance.

Yet out there was a human being and it was not
in him, who needed hope, to deny it to another.
He looked upon the black water and was shaken by
fear, but he let the boat lose way until near the
raft.

It was a dark skinned old man with the look of

the islands, a rack of bones that held a child.
Morgan saw a great sea rise, and then the raft
lifted and he took from the scrawny arms the
child, and reaching for the man, caught a frail
wrist.

He clung to the hand and the old man's eyes
looked into Morgan's . . . and then the sea
lifted the man and Morgan drew him aboard.

He shared with them his water, and he held to
the tiller until muscles ached and his body
yearned for death, but he fought the sea and a
day came when haggard and beaten he lay across
the rail and the ocean around them was still.

As if to win where the sea had lost, the sun
came out, and the fresh water dwindled. The man
raved against god and challenged the elements to
destroy him . . . and then a fresh wind came and
he lay in the boat's bottom and the naked brown
child looked upon him with ancient eyes.

And one day the boat came to a still lagoon
where palms leaned over a beach, and the old man
lifted the child and said to Morgan, "Come. Come
with me."

Somehow he found strength and followed through
a wood to an ancient square where grass grew
among the stones and vast temples opened their
halls to the sky. And the old man took leaves and
ground them to powder and filling a pipe, said,
"Smoke this," and Morgan did.

He smoked and darkness fell, though it was
mid-day, and he was no longer at the temple but
running, and in his hands he held a rifle, and
was pursued by Asian soldiers in rough uniforms.

Suddenly in a hollow of ground was an ancient
temple, something incredibly old, beyond the

count of years, and in the temple was an idol,
like no other he had seen, but he ran behind it
and pressed a flat stone, and the stone moved,
opening a space, and suddenly he was drawing a
girl into the space with him and the opening
closed and they clung together in darkness.

Morgan was a tall young man with humor in his
eyes, and he told the story and people smiled at
the delirium and mariners said there were no such
islands, not upon the sea where he had been.

"Though," a geographer said, "there are
legends. A Portuguese sighted them in 1533, and
they were seen by a whaler in 1840, but no, not
in reality were there such islands. The seas were
thoroughly mapped."

"The native," they asked, "what did he say?"

"Only that the child was the last of his race,
the son and grandson of a thousand generations of
priests."

In the passing of years Morgan read of lost
continents and Easter Island with its heads of
long-lobed ears, of the gigantic helmeted heads
of stone found in Central America with features
blunt and powerful, of the strange city of Nan
Madol in the Carolines and roads that came out of
the sea on Malden Island, and a fallen monolith
on Vanua Levu, covered with hieroglyphics. But he
found no clue to the island of the ancient man
and the child with the eyes old beyond their
time.

———

The Red conquest of China caught him
unprepared. His friends helped him along country
roads to a tattered fragment of an army, valiant
fighters who did not flee to Formosa but remained
to fight. On the Mekong River they found refuge
and gained strength. Skillful at war, Morgan
joined them.

Returning from a raid he found a girl in the
door of his quarters, smiling. "Are you the
American? I'm Lori King."

A theatrical unit playing for French troops in
Indo-China had flown in to do a show for the tiny
Chinese force. She was a tall girl and blonde,
and they were much together. The plane of the
unit was damaged, and departure delayed.

"You'll return soon," he said. "I'm sure
they'll get it fixed."

"And you?" she asked.

"I have no one to go back to," he said.

Her head was near his shoulder. "I'd like you
to come back," she said, and meant it.

"I'd want you with me then," he said, "and it
would not be easy. I've never made much money."

"I'd be with you."

The Mekong rustled along the bank, chuckling
with age-old humor. Beyond the river there were
temples, their history forgotten, their beginning
beyond time. "I'd like to see them," she told
him, watching moonlight on the walls.

"There's a patrol to the villages tomorrow,
just going for food. Come with us."

The morning was bright and there was laughter
in the trees. Morgan walked to the village with

Lori, and they talked with the women there, and
looked into the round faces of the children. At
the edge of the village the people said, "Do not
go . . . they are strange temples . . . the
ancient ones have left their spirits there."

Then men were coming toward them on the double
and a mortar bomb exploded, and suddenly the
village was a flaming nightmare of exploding
shells and death.

Troops wearing the Red Star burst into the
upper end of the village, and there was sporadic
firing. Then he and Lori slid down a muddy
hillside into a canyon and were running . . .
running . . . running . . .

Their breath came in gasps, torn by fear they
climbed among the ruins. Behind them was a shout,
then a shot, another. Before them in a grove was
a temple. Its roof had fallen and great stones
lay upon the floor. There were high walls and
deep shadows, stones that dripped with jungle,
and a floor deep in the death of centuries.

"They are coming, Jack!" Lori whispered. "Oh,
Jack, I--"

And he looked into her eyes and saw there all
the love, all the promise, all in this world that
any man could ask.

"Come on," he said.

One man with thirty rounds . . . against fifty
men?

They ran through an ancient door, behind them
a shout, then Morgan stopped and his face was
white and he stared around him. He knew this
place . . . he knew . . . There came to him then
an odor, pungent, intangible, drifting.

"Lori!" He grabbed her hand. "We're safe!"

Astonished, she looked at him, but he caught her hand and went through the door to the inner room where stood an idol, incredibly ancient but he did not stop to look but ran behind it and pulled aside the vines.

"We're safe, darling," he said, and pressed hard upon a flat stone. It moved under his hand . . .

COMMENTS: Strange, yes? Digging deep in my memory I believe I heard something about this piece. Louis once told me of a very short story that he banged out in the middle of the night in response to a dream. In the morning it wasn't a tenth as brilliant as he had thought when he was writing or dreaming or whatever state he was in when he created it. I'm sure we've all had moments like that.

I include this story here because, as has been obvious, one of the interesting aspects of *Louis L'Amour's Lost Treasures* is the amount of mysticism that shows up in Louis's unfinished or unpublished work. This story has a dreamlike quality and may well have been written in what was nearly a trance state. The rapid yet oddly smooth shifts in time and place and the reoccurring use of words like "and" and "then" make the narrative seem very much like a dream. Louis very rarely wrote when he was tired—he was much more of an early morning sort of guy. It is also interesting to note that this may be the only case in his career where he has a principal character using something like a hallucinogenic drug.

There are a couple more interesting points; Louis includes this line:

```
and followed through a wood to an ancient
square where grass grew among the stones and
vast temples opened their halls to the sky.
```

This sounds a good deal like the same place he described in *Jeremy Loccard in Louis L'Amour's Lost Treasures: Volume 1,* a place in the East Indies that Dad might have read about or even visited. In the notes following *The Bastard of Brignogan* in this collection, Louis, again talking about a character traveling in the Indonesian/Malaysian area, writes:

```
. . . Finds Neolithic settlements . . .
```

I'm guessing it's the same mysterious spot he's either imagining or referring to.

The other issue is Dad's interest, which we've seen in a number of stories, in the Chinese interior and in the Communist revolution in that country in 1949. He was certainly fascinated by China and the role that it would play in the future of our world. Some of that may have stemmed from his own travels in Asia many years before, as well as from the experiences of his brother Parker, who briefly served with the American diplomatic mission to China toward the end of WWII.

When I first read this story I was tempted to joke, "What was Dad smokin'?" But I really think it was fatigue and the vague edge of some not quite articulated or resolved idea that spurred this odd little story into existence.

THE PAPAGO KID

The Beginning of a Western Novel

CHAPTER I

A sudden rush of rain-drops did quick finger-taps on my hat, living up to the promise of the bulging clouds that hung low above the desert. Reaching around, I pulled the draw-strings holding my slicker and shook it out.

The first rush of rain went off across the desert, stirring dust as it fell. Shrugging into the slicker brought an end, for the moment, to the rain. A last few reluctant drops falling, amused by my struggles.

Well, I was ready. If it was going to rain, let it come.

Along the horizon mountains lay like a heap of rusty scrap-iron and the nearby desert was salmon-pink dotted with sage-brush gray and the shabby green of greasewood. Under the low sky the wide valley before me lay empty and still. Hugh had certainly known what he was talking about when he told me I'd meet nobody on this route . . . he knew I wanted to avoid travelers.

The only spot of real green anywhere in sight

was the sharp, strong color of pines showing from
a notch in the rust-red mountains, and that was
the place I'd come from Texas to find.

This was where I could hole up and rest until
Hugh Taylor sent word for me. It was something
great to have a friend like Hugh to give you a
hand when the going was rough. When I returned
from Mexico to find myself a fugitive from
justice, he had been very quick to offer help.

It was like Hugh Taylor to know of such a
place as this. He had taken off from home when
only a youngster, riding far and wide upon the
land and he seemed to have connections
everywhere.

The drops came again, and then a rushing
downpour that made me turn up my collar and tug
down on my hat. This looked to be settling in for
a hard, long rain.

Rowdy, my big black gelding, was beginning to
feel the rough going of the past few weeks. It
was the first time I had seen the big horse even
close to weariness, but it was no wonder. We had
come out of Dimmit County, Texas to the Apache
country of Arizona, and the way had been long and
hard.

The trail puzzled me. It was rough, but many
Western trails were, and it was too good a path
not to be better known or traveled. In three days
of riding I had seen nobody, not a person, not a
ranch, not a mine shack. Most trails led to
towns, to where people were, but not this one.

The camps were good, and they were spaced
right for a hard riding man. At every camp there
was grass, water and fuel. At every camp there
were signs of occasional use, horse droppings and

the ashes of fires, often places where small
herds had been held.

There were no tracks of wagons on any of it,
and no recent travel. The trail held to low
ground, winding among buttes, up dry washes, an
easy route on the whole, and a hidden one.

Several times I pulled up to study the lay-out
of the country. It was not the first time I had
ridden such trails, nor probably the last. Most
of them were made by Indians who did not want to
be seen, and were traveling only from water-hole
to water-hole.

The red rocks of the mountains began to take
on form and line, to shape themselves from the
stuff of distance. Here and there were the raw
cancers of washes that ate into the face of the
plain, and the deeper scars of canyons. Here or
there lines of gray or green climbed along
creases in the rock, evidence of underlying water
or of gathering places for run-off from the
higher peaks.

The trail curved north, skirting mountains
toward the waiting pines. "Ride right to the Tin-
Cup Ranch," Hugh Taylor had said, "and ask for
Bill Keys. He'll be in charge, and he'll take
care of you until this blows over. I am sure we
can get this straightened out, and you'll be free
to come home."

Suddenly the mountains seemed to crack wide
open on my left, and the trail went gently up a
slope into the pines and along the side of the
canyon. Blue gentians carpeted both sides of the
trail and crept almost up to the trees in a mass
of sky blue. The trail was faint here, rarely

used, but two riders had gone ahead of me not long ago, headed right into Tin-Cup Canyon.

It was a time to be careful. This was the kind of country frequented by outlaws, and even honest ranchers were suspicious of strange riders coming in out of wild country. Nothing in my years had bred carelessness in me, so I drew up in the deepest shadow and waited, listening.

And then I heard a shot.

It rapped out, a sharp, bitter sound, ugly in its finality.

A single shot, then silence.

My rifle rode right ahead of my right leg. I was doing no roping on this trip so I carried that rifle where I could draw it almost as fast as a six-shooter. It slid into my hand, and I waited.

Rowdy knew what a shot meant as well as I did, and he stepped forward, light and easy, ears up, nostrils wide. So it was that we first looked down into the little hollow that was the Tin-Cup, a stone barn, a stone house and two pole corrals adjoining. Near them were two riderless horses.

Then I saw them. The air was clear and they were not more than two hundred yards away. There were three men, but one was sprawled on the ground near another horse.

The man standing over the body turned it with his boot toe and I heard him swear. Then he yelled at the other man, who waited under the porch. "No, it ain't him!"

And then they both saw me.

Panic must have hit them at the same instant. One made a break for his horse, the other for his

gun. Honest men do not start shooting when a
stranger rides up and my rifle was ready.

The nearest man fired. I was not worried as
the action must have been sheer impulse and he
was much too far away for accuracy with a pistol.

He sprang for his horse and I waited until he
was down in the saddle. He lurched like he was
hit and I saw his six-gun fall into the rocks,
and then both of them were getting out of there.
Holding my fire, I let them go.

Rowdy was not gun-shy. With me in the saddle
he had no cause to be for we had been through a
lot down Sonora way. That had been part of my
life that even Hugh knew nothing about, and to
him I was just a quiet kid he had seen grow up on
our uncle's ranch, the XY.

We had always been friendly, but Hugh was not
a man with whom one became close. He was
handsome, fine looking in every sense, and he
carried himself well, but he did not confide in
me and did not invite confidence. Older than I,
he had been a fine horseman, a good hand with
cattle, and good enough with a gun for most
purposes. Often when he wanted to ride off to
town to see some girl or other I had done his
work as well as my own, but never minded. I
admired him, and he knew it.

Occasionally, he brought me presents. A fine
new hat, a pair of boots, and another time some
Mexican spurs. Whenever I tried to thank him or
pay him he just brushed me off saying, "Oh,
forget it, kid! You've done a thing or two for
me."

With the two riders gone I rode up to the man
on the ground and swinging down, felt his pulse.

He seemed to be dead, all right, and I had
guessed as much before I got down from the
saddle. No man with a hole in him of that size
was going very much farther.

Two holes . . .

The first shot was a little high, and there
had been some interval between shots for the
blood around the first wound had coagulated.

A horse's hoof clicked on stone, and I turned
to face them. My rifle was in my hands but you
don't try anything fancy when you're facing four
men at that range.

"What did you kill him for?" The speaker was a
squat, broad-chested man with a square red face
and hard blue eyes. He looked as tough as a long
winter in the mountains, and at least two of the
riders with him looked just as mean.

"Don't jump your fences, stranger. I didn't
shoot this man, and I don't even know who he is.
When I rode into The Cup two men were standing
here, and one of them right over him. They took a
shot at me and then high-tailed it out of here."

"We heard shootin'," the square-faced man
said. "He's dead an' you're here."

My eyes went over them, sizing them up. Nobody
needed to burn any brands on this hide for me.
Here I was on the dodge from one killing, which I
had not done, and now I'd run into another.
Nobody had seen the other riders but me, so a lot
depended now on who and what these men were.

My quick glance at them told me only one of
the four would be inclined to believe me. He was
a nice-looking young fellow with brown eyes and
dark hair. He looked smart and he looked honest,
although a man can be fooled on both counts.

That square-built man who had started the
talking seemed to be the man in charge, if there
was one. "Who are you," he demanded, "and what
brings you here?"

Something in the way he asked that question
decided me that I had better be careful. I was
downwind of an idea that had not quite come home
to me. The last thing I intended to tell them was
that I was Wat Bell.

"They call me Papago Kid," I said. "I'm from
down Sonora way.

"As for what brought me here, it was this
black horse and a lot of trails strung together.
I've been a lot of places before this, and when I
decided to ride out, nobody stopped me."

He didn't like that. This was a man who liked
riding rough-shod over things. His lips kind of
thinned down and the look in his eyes was not a
pleasant one, but suddenly I wasn't feeling
worried anymore; I should have been. A man ought
to think of himself in a spot like that, but
something about trouble makes me light-hearted.

This man believed he was tough. He wore a gun
and he was prepared to use it, and I was a
stranger and fair game. Yet when I told him my
name a funny thing happened to his eyes and I had
the feeling he had expected to hear another name.
The idea was there and ready for branding, and it
slowed him down a little.

The truth of the matter was that in Dimmit
County, Texas, I was Wat Bell, and in Sonora I
was the Papago Kid. The first name I'd been born
to, and the second had been sort of tacked on me
during some scuffles down yonder.

The young man interrupted. "Lynch, let's get

in out of the rain. I liked Tom Ludlow too much
to see his body lying there like that. We can
just as well talk over coffee, anyway."

Lynch had no liking for me and was itching for
trouble, but he shrugged, and turned to the
others. "You two pick up Tom's body and carry it
to the stable. Better put the horses up, then
come on in." He paused a moment, then added,
"Don't leave anything undone, Bill."

When I heard the name a suspicion stirred, but
I did not look up or give any sign that the name
meant anything. Of course, Bill was a not
uncommon name. Still--

My question was answered almost at once when
one of the men took the dead man by the
shoulders. "Grab his feet, Keys."

Lynch led the way to the stone house, and I
followed with my horse. There was no talk in the
stable, and I gave them no chance to have a look
at my outfit. Taking my horse into the stall I
put down some hay for him and then taking my
rifle and saddle-bags I followed them into the
house.

Lynch had removed his slicker and I got a
shock. He wore a badge.

"The coffee was your idea, Dolliver," Lynch
said. "You want to make it?"

Dolliver agreed, glancing at me. He had
noticed my reaction to the badge and was
obviously curious. He turned to the shelves and
began taking things down like he knew the place,
and in the meantime I was doing some fast
thinking. It was time to scout my trail and
figure out what kind of situation I had gotten
into.

Hugh Taylor had told me to ride to the Tin-Cup and ask for Bill Keys. Yet when I arrived there was a dead man who wasn't Bill Keys but who was apparently the owner of the ranch. Keys appeared to be riding for the sheriff, for what reason I had no idea.

The cabin was neat as an old maid's boudoir and the smell of coffee that soon filled the room gave it a warm, cozy feeling. The fireplace was huge, the copper utensils all bright and well-polished.

Dolliver was quick and sure in his movements, but he was missing nothing, either. Taking off my slicker I hung it over a chair within easy reach of my hand. I had not unsaddled, nor had any of the others. Obviously they were going on, and what I would do remained a question.

Lynch had dropped astride a chair and started to build a smoke, but when I took off my slicker his fingers stopped dead still for a moment. I was wearing two guns . . . not a common thing, one being expensive enough, and something about me disturbed him. It was not the guns, and he was not afraid. It was the fact that I was wearing them that seemed to bother him, not what I might do with them.

"You call yourself Papago Kid?" Lynch's question was sharp.

My eyes held his. Lynch and I were not going to be friends. For some reason he was distinctly irritated, and with me. I had the feeling he had expected to find somebody here, and that I did not fit the picture of the man for whom he looked.

"I've been called that, sheriff," I said
easily. "I'm not a Papago, but they are a good
people and the name's an honor. I got called that
because I rode through their country a couple of
times."

"You say you saw the two men who shot Ludlow?
Did you get a good look at them?"

"I saw them, but they were too far away. One
of them ran for his horse, but the other one
grabbed for his gun. Naturally, with a dead man
on the ground and a man about to take a shot at
me I didn't waste any time looking him over."

"How many shots did you hear?"

"One."

Dolliver turned around from the coffee. "I
heard three."

"That's right," I agreed. "One shot apparently
killed the old man. Then one of these men shot at
me and I shot back. As you saw, the old man was
shot twice. The way it looks to me is he was shot
elsewhere, then they trailed him back to his own
ranch and shot him again."

"What gives you that idea?" Lynch demanded.

"If you noticed, sheriff, the rain had not
washed out the old man's tracks. They came from
the corral. Even from where I stood I could see
he'd fallen down twice before he was finally
killed."

It was obvious that the sheriff had seen
nothing of the kind, but he studied me carefully.
I was doing my own thinking. The reason the
sheriff had not seen those tracks was because all
his attention was centered on me. Now that was
natural enough, considering that I was there with

the dead man, and was a stranger. Still, he should have looked around. He should have noticed.

Dolliver, whose attitude I liked, brought coffee to the table, and cups. He was a clean-cut youngster and no fool. I had a hunch that had he not been present I might have been in a lot more trouble than I was.

It struck me as faintly curious that Sheriff Lynch was making no effort to pursue the possible killers nor even to see in which direction the tracks led. Did he already know?

The thought was unbidden, but once in my mind it would not leave. His actions worried me. It was as if he had decided who was guilty or who he intended to prove guilty and that he had no further intention of investigating.

This was strange country to me, and I knew no one here. The man I had been told to find, and who was supposed to give me a place to hide out, was now standing with his back to the fireplace and his attitude was not friendly.

Nobody needed to tell me that I was in serious trouble. Nor had I any desire to shoot my way out of a situation such as this even had it been practical. I had committed no crime, although I was wanted for one, as Hugh Taylor had warned me. I did not wish to break any laws or get in any deeper. Every sense I had warned me to move carefully.

I tasted my coffee and it warmed the chill from me. Dolliver filled his own cup and sat down. I had an idea he knew I was in trouble and intended to stay close.

"You ever been in this country before?" Lynch asked.

"Never. When I left California I crossed into Arizona near Yuma. Then I headed off down into Mexico. I worked there for a spell, then decided to drift."

"How'd you find this place? It ain't the easiest spot to find." He stared at me suspiciously, but I put on my most innocent face.

"Did you ever cross the desert right behind here? The only spot of green you can see is right in the notch back there, so I headed for it. I figured where things were that green there'd be water, and more than likely people who could set me on the trail to a town."

That was obvious enough even to him, but he was not satisfied.

"You come from California? You sound like a Texan to me."

"Hell," I said carelessly, "it's no wonder! That outfit I rode for in Mexico all talked like that. Fact is, out in El Monte where I come from half the people who settled the place were from Texas."

That was plausible, too, but he still was not ready to accept it or me. He spooned sugar into his cup and stirred it around, then drank with the spoon still in his cup.

"What's the problem, sheriff?" I asked. "Is this a posse?"

"We're huntin' a Texas outlaw name of Wat Bell," he said, grudgingly. "We got word he was headed west so we're cuttin' all trails."

"Bad weather for riding," I sympathized. "Is

this Bell a bad hombre? Will it take four of you?"

Dolliver chuckled. "I am not one of them," he said. "I have a small ranch right over the mountain from here. I joined these boys back in the pines to see who was shooting who. My ranch is the Tumbling T."

COMMENTS: In the introduction to this volume I mentioned that Dad took us on an extended trip around England and Ireland in the late 1960s. Rural Ireland was a different place in those days; Gaelic was still occasionally spoken, to the exclusion of English in a few places, and electricity, telephones, and central heating were rare in many of the towns and farms at which we stopped. While our hotel in Dublin was pretty fancy in an Old World sort of way, it still had blackout curtains on the windows from the time of World War II.

Somewhere in our travels, we came to the ruins of a huge old stone house. The story I remember was that, hundreds of years ago, it had been sort of a local execution chamber. If you wanted someone killed off, and had enough clout, the man who owned the house would issue an invitation . . . and visitors never returned. There was also a version in which the invitation was given to the wrong person—or perhaps it was given by the intended recipient to a friend or family member—leading to the death of the wrong man. It was a long time ago and my memory is not what I'd like it to be. Regardless, Dad loved the possibilities associated with such a setup.

I get the feeling that the Tin-Cup Ranch in this tale is that same sort of place and a similar situation is being played out. For that reason and based on the style of the writing, I would set the era of this fragment to sometime in the 1970s.

Dad and my sister, Angelique, in one of
the ruined manor houses we visited in Ireland.

KRAK DES CHEVALIERS

A Treatment for an Adventure Story

In Alexandria, to a meeting place for drifters from all the world comes BARAMUS, a man of the Levantine coast, of no particular nationality or origin, a go-between, a procurer, an occasional thief and occasional murderer. He comes looking for a group of men to do the impossible, to enter an impregnable fortress and extract an old man and his granddaughter and then escape with them to the coast.

Alexandria in the 12th century appeared to be a dying port. Yet it was still one of the most cosmopolitan cities in the world. Always more Greek than Egyptian, it had become a staging area for mercenary soldiers awaiting a war, merchant seamen between voyages to the East or Europe, adventurers and soldiers of fortune from all quarters of the world.

It was a period of change and excitement. The Crusades, which had offered employment and quick wealth to fighting men, were tapering off; the Mongols of Genghis Khan were settling down in Russia or retreating to Asia; for the Vikings the great days of raiding were coming to an end.

Here, in this place, were men from Bristol, Dieppe and Cadiz, from Venice, Constantinople, the Malabar coast and Madagascar, men with no present loyalties, and with no interests beyond gold, women and wine.

Observing the room, Baramus spots three whom circumstance had washed up in this backwater of the world: KEVIN O'MORE, Irish chieftain, swordsman, fighter who fled his own country to escape the English conquest; SIR WALTER DE MALEBISSE (pronounced Malbis), a Crusader knight who had given up vast estates in England to go to the Holy Land; and ERIC THE GOLDEN, a Viking, his ship destroyed in a storm, his crew lost at sea. YAKUT ALI, a noted warrior from the castles of the Assassins in the Elburz mountains of Persia, sits nearby. At his table sits BATU KHAN, a Mongol . . . lately they were enemies, now friends.

Suddenly there is a crash of an over-turned chair. Nine men, swordsmen all, are approaching one who stands alone, facing them feet apart, waiting. This one is MINAMOTO TAKANORI, a samurai.

O'More starts to rise. "One man alone? I'll help him."

From the adjoining table Batu Khan puts up an arresting hand. "Wait," he advises, "and learn."

The nine rush. There is a terrible moment of flashing swords and death, and the nine are destroyed. (This feat, portrayed by Toshiro Mifune in THE LEGEND OF MUSASHI with 12 men, is both spectacular and believable.) O'More invites Takanori for a drink, and the group are approached by Baramus.

He makes an intriguing proposition: For 25,000 gold pieces they are asked to enter a castle no army has ever captured, and get out with the girl and her grandfather.

To aid them they also recruit CHAWAMBI, an African warrior of the Watuta, a war-like tribe, and ZALIM SINGH, a Rajput warrior from India.

Baramus takes them to a house on the sea shore where they meet PHILLIP ARCADIUS. It is he who wishes the girl and her grandfather free of the castle.

As they make their way up the trail to the house ANTONIUS, Phillip's nephew, asks, "Will they succeed?"

"If anyone can, these men will."

"And how many will survive?"

A shrug. "One or two . . . perhaps three."

"It will be much money for those who live."

Arcadius glances at him, amused. "You are very naive, Antonius."

"You mean--?"

"After all, as you say, it is a lot of money, and only two or three will be left . . . perhaps they will be wounded. So why waste money on such as these?"

"But--?"

"Leave such matters to me, Antonius. In time, you will learn."

Baramus enters: "These are the men."

Arcadius studies them. He is cool, composed, worldly. He is a man who has come up from the

gutters of Constantinople and Alexandria to
wealth and power, and is eager for more of both.

"25,000 pieces of gold," he suggests, "it is a
great sum. All the greater because some of you
will die."

"And those who return?" O'More says. "They
will be paid by you?"

"You are afraid I will not pay?" Arcadius
smiles.

"Oh, no!" O'More replies cheerfully. "The sum
will be placed in the hands of the Banco Giro, of
Venice. They will pay."

There is no pleasure in the eyes of Arcadius.
"What do you, a savage from a wild northern isle,
know of the Banco Giro?"

"Enough to know their future depends on their
faith. If they do not pay the word will go round
the world, and they will no more be trusted. As
for the savages of a wild northern isle, why, we
had poets and sages when your ancestors were
dabbling in the shallows for shell-fish."

"You say that to a Greek?"

"You call yourself a Greek, but would a Greek
call you a Greek?"

"I do not think I like you, Irishman."

"Does it matter? Do you woo my affections or
my sword?"

Arcadius brushes it aside. "No matter. Now
what will you need?"

"A boat . . . not large, not new, with but one
sail. Food for thirty days, spare weapons, much
rope. I shall make a list."

"Do that. And for now?"

"Thirty gold pieces to drink your health . . .
and ours."

"Very well. And you leave . . . when?"

O'More shrugs. "Have the boat tomorrow night by the ruins near Cape Lochlas. We will take it when we have need of it." When they are gone, Antonius says, "The Banco Giro? You did not think of that, Uncle?"

Irritated, Arcadius shrugs it aside. "No matter. I know the Banco Giro . . . and they know me."

Baramus is to guide them to their destination. He is to supply them with the plan of the castle, the great KRAK of the CHEVALIERS, perhaps the strongest castle ever built. There will be four men to sail the boat, and to guard it while the fighting men are ashore.

En route they are attacked by pirates, the pirates are defeated, and aboard their ship a girl prisoner is found. She sees Baramus, although he does not see her, and she is frightened, begging not to be seen by him. They hide her below.

That night, anchored in a cove awaiting a SECRET AGENT who will apprise them of conditions within the castle, O'More and Sir Walter see somebody from the ship encounter somebody from the shore. It is too dark to identify, and they whisper. O'More suspects betrayal.

Sure at least that it is not Chawambi, O'More gets him to track the men. Two men upon horseback, who ride away, but not toward the Castle.

Who are they? What does the midnight meeting portend?

Yakut and Batu capture an OLD MAN with a

donkey. Holding him, they disguise themselves and enter the village at the foot of the mountain where the castle is.

A SOLDIER from the castle reports them. He has recognized Yakut as an Assassin. "I saw him once. He was from Alamut, a protégé of the Old Man of the Mountain."

Suspicion is aroused--someone from within may have been carrying out information regarding their captives. Only three have been out of the castle. Under torture the Secret Agent talks. He is the creature of Baramus and Arcadius, but they believe he lies because there are so few men.

Girl and her grandfather questioned. They know nothing. They wish to pray . . . can they enter the chapel at night? Well, why not? They are given permission.

A reconnaissance reports no ships off shore, only one small trading vessel. Since no force of any consequence seems to be nearby, the commander does little more than to increase the guard at the gates in the outer wall.

The Grandfather trusts Arcadius; the girl, GABRIELLE, does not. They have been informed they are to be rescued. What the Grandfather does not realize is that the danger is greater to them from Arcadius than from their captors.

The Krak of the Chevaliers was considered by T. E. Lawrence of Arabia and many others to be the most formidable castle ever built. It was constructed toward the end of the castle-building era, and summed up the best defensive knowledge of the time. It is massive beyond belief, with towering walls and guarded approaches. The entrance from the main gate is narrow and covered with openings above so that an enemy can be attacked while in the passage, if they should get so far.

Kevin O'More leads the attack. They scale the hill, and surmount the massive outer walls by a method, never used in film, to be told in the story. A highly exciting method, and very effective.

Once inside they send three of their men to capture the other postern gate near the main gate by which they will retreat.

Eric, Zalim Singh and Batu Khan have this mission.

Thus far there has been no alarm. They have moved with speed and skill, yet they must now get to the upper ward of the castle and to the chapel where, if plans have gone well, Gabrielle and her grandfather will be waiting.

One by one they cross the lower ward and attain the wall near an inner gate. Chawambi disappears in the night. GORDON, Sir Walter's squire, moves closer. O'More saunters up to the gate and is challenged; making believe he is drunk he tries to push on in and there is a clash of swords, and instantly the others are behind him. In the close confines of the entrance the fighting is brief but intense, and then they enter the upper ward and move silently to the chapel.

Then Gordon turns and runs from them into the center of the ward. Puzzled, they turn to face him. Suddenly he blows a shrill whistle. "You fools!" he shouts at them. "I have tricked you all! All! Every one of you will die!"

He whistles again, and suddenly many men appear, armed and ready.

They retreat into the chapel, only to be attacked by GUARDS who await them there, and then they see across the room the old man and the girl and Chawambi is there. He has dropped in through a window in time to prevent the guards from taking them away. There is a bloody fight in which each do heroic deeds, and then the chapel door is forced shut and barred.

Chawambi leads them through the window to the wall and along the wall to the main gate where their friends are fighting fiercely to hold the gate. They have horses. Gabrielle and her grandfather are swiftly mounted. Batu Khan dies fighting. "Go!" Zalim shouts. "I will hold the gate!"

"And I!" Eric joins him.

On horseback they flee down the stone-paved ramp which lies in a sharp V shape. At the point they turn and start toward the main gate, fired at with arrows from loopholes, or sudden attacks from concealed posterns. Directly before them a portcullis drops and they are cut off. O'More quickly reverses and charges back up the covered ramp, but Sir Walter is a couple of jumps ahead of him. At the gate toward which they are headed two armed guards leap out to stop them. Sir Walter's sword cuts them both down, but he takes a bad blow in the process. Charging the gate, they fight their way through and ride for the shore where the boat is to be waiting. Within moments a group of horsemen are in pursuit.

En route to the coast, Yakut is shot from his horse by an arrow. O'More rides back to pick him

up, but he is dying and waves him away. He tries
one more shot with his bow, then dies as O'More
rides away.

There is a tremendous fight on the lonely
beach with the boat lying off shore in which
O'More, Sir Walter and Takanori fight off the
encircling enemy with swinging swords, while
Chawambi uses arrows to pick off enemy archers.

Meanwhile Gabrielle and her grandfather are
smuggled aboard the boat by Baramus and his men.

Instantly, the sail goes up and the boat pulls
away, leaving them on the beach, faced by their
enemies.

The four prepare to defend themselves to the
death, but now their enemies, seeing the girl and
her grandfather escaping, ride away. They have no
wish to go against such fighters when there is
nothing more to be gained.

Dejected, abandoned, the four mount their
horses and start back along the shore. Then,
O'More remembers the mysterious meeting in the
cove, and a remark he had over-heard at the last.
Now that remark returns to memory: ". . . and
afterward? Here?" And the reply, "Here."

Instantly, the four bring their horses to a
gallop. If there is to be a meeting at the
cove . . . if there is even a chance . . . they
might make it first and be there waiting.

Antonius is at the cove with two men. The two
men with him are his own fighting men, and he
tells them, "The old man and Baramus . . . kill
them. We need them no longer. If Gordon is with
them, kill him also."

The sail appears, a smoke signal goes up, and the boat comes in. Baramus comes ashore with the old man and the girl.

Antonius walks toward him, hand out-stretched. As he clasps the man's hand, the two slaves move in and kill Baramus.

The four riders arrive, O'More catches a hand of the girl as her grandfather is killed by Antonius, then as Sir Walter is fighting with one of the huge slaves, Antonius plunges a knife into his back, and is killed himself by Takanori.

Sir Walter is buried up the shore and the three remaining men, O'More, Takanori and Chawambi, take the boat.

"To Alexandria?" asks Takanori.

"Venice," O'More says.

In Venice, Gabrielle goes with O'More, Takanori, and Chawambi to the Banco Giro.

The banker is there, and with him, Phillip Arcadius.

The money is paid. Arcadius shrugs. "It was a gamble. One wins, one loses . . . I lost."

"Antonius, also."

"Ah, yes. Do you know he planned to kill me, too? But I suspected as much, and planned to kill him." He shrugs. "And with the old man gone, the secret of the treasure is lost. Now nobody will find it. It is lost forever."

Outside in the street the four stand together, and Gabrielle says, "With this we can get a larger boat."

"Larger?"

"For the treasure, darling. I know where it is!"

THE END

COMMENTS: I suspect this was written in the mid-1960s, because I have a vague memory of some discussion about it between Dad and British film producer Euan Lloyd. It certainly has the sort of "high concept" pitchability necessary in Hollywood: "The Magnificent 7 vs. the World's Greatest Castle." And, of course, there are a variety of great casting and action opportunities. I can remember sitting in my father's lap and him leafing through a book containing many color photographs and architectural details of the castle. I'm guessing that was just a few days before he took a break from whatever he was working on and pounded this treatment out, a process that took only a few hours. It's a fun beginning, but to get it to the point where it would have been truly producible there are still a lot of loose ends to be wrapped up and a lot of fleshing out to be done.

What role was the girl, taken on after the pirate raid, supposed to have played? Why did the squire, Gordon, suddenly betray our heroes to the men in the castle? Who are the mysterious (though possibly known to history) residents of the Krak des Chevaliers who are holding the old man and Gabrielle prisoner? And, seriously, why intentionally kill the old guy who knows where the treasure is? I have to assume that was just a mistake. These and more questions would have needed to be answered before Louis tried to sell this to Euan Lloyd or anyone else.

The group of misfits and mercenaries would also have needed some time and adventures (like the pirate raid) in which to bond. Their gallant, in some cases suicidal, defense of one another during the attack on the castle would be meaningless without their road to friendship being fraught with conflict and tests of one sort or another.

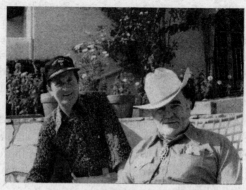

Euan and my father showing off
their new hats in the early 1980s.

The Krak des Chevaliers is a real crusader castle in
Syria, though prior to the nineteenth century it was actually called Krak de l'Ospital after the order of the Knights
Hospitallers, who were its longtime residents and who,
over a period of many years, dramatically improved the
original Kurdish fortifications on the site.

The unnamed secret weapon our band uses in the attack,
the special way over the outer walls that Louis alludes to
but is keeping to himself, is almost certainly the use of a
large lizard, like a monitor lizard. He had used this same
gag (filmmaker slang for a stunt) in the short story "The
Hills of Homicide" to allow a murderer to scale a cliff:

```
    . . . the smaller monitor lizards are
from India, running four to five feet in
length . . . It is those lizards that the
thieves use to gain access to locked houses.
    A rope is tied around the lizard's body,
and he climbs the wall, steered by jerks on
the rope from below. When he gets over a
```

parapet, in a crevice, or over a sill, the
thief jerks hard on the rope and the lizard
braces himself to prevent being pulled over,
and they are very strong in the legs. Then
the thief goes up the wall, hand over hand,
walking right up with his feet on the wall.

It is my guess that our Rajput knight, Zalim Singh,
might have brought this trick to the group's attention as
they planned their attack. One can only imagine the fun you
could have with our heroes trying to locate, capture, or
steal such a lizard!

There are a couple of details mentioned in connection to
this story that I find particularly interesting. Sir Walter De
Malebisse might have been intended to be a fictional relative of my mother's. Hugh de Malebisse, an actual relative,
came to England with William the Conqueror and several
generations later there really was a Walter and he did go on
a pilgrimage to the Holy Land.

In some of the notes associated with this draft Louis
uses the following description of the spot where the men
first meet in Alexandria:

In an alleyway near the Gate of the Moon,
within a minute or so from the Canopic
Street, was a leather-worker's stall. There
were saddles made, bridles, whips, and all
manner of leather goods, and at the back of
the stall and on the left as you faced it,
was a rack of already made bridles hanging
from a point near the ceiling. They hung
close together and in great numbers,
effectually concealing a door to a passage
that led to the back of the building.

The leather-worker seemed always to be
there, an ancient man with a face that might
have been made from his own goods, yet
wrinkled and seamed with age, wisdom, and
evil. Attending him were his two sons, huge,
irritable men, and his daughter.

To those who knew the old man or who
seemed to be of the right sort, a son would
step aside and let the visitor pass by . . .
if no one watched or seemed interested . . .
going through the curtain of bridles and
into the hidden passage.

And within might be found all
nationalities from the shores of Norman
England to those of China, from Madagascar
to India and Sumatra.

For this was the resort of men of the sea
and of the wars, here they might free
themselves of their burdens of wealth . . .
if any . . . or find employment.

Footsteps echoed along the passage, and a
great oaken door studded with iron opened,
and the newcomer passed through to an odor
of roasting meat, incense, and sweaty
humans. Another door, the odors stronger,
and then a room filled with tables, benches
and the sound of music drowned by the murmur
of voices.

This idea of the leather worker's stall and the screen of
bridles being a cover for a haven for mercenaries appears in
other places in Dad's notes about his own life and in reference to other stories he might write about North Africa.
Sometimes the location is one city, sometimes another, but
the description of the entrance remains basically the same.

I'm guessing that it reflects something he read or was told, since, as far as I can tell, the only time Louis had access to North Africa was during the short time a ship he was serving on transited the Suez Canal. He may have had some time ashore in Egypt, but not very much.

There are two oft-used L'Amour themes present in this treatment. The first is the idea of a payoff that would be divided among all those that survived. Thus the fewer who survived, the greater the reward. That concept is echoed in other places in this book and in Louis's previously published works.

The second is that of finding a treasure. Treasure shows up many times in Dad's work, and I have always found that fact sort of interesting. Louis was a very hard worker and had no problem paying his dues. He was not a gambler, and certainly one of the subjects I discuss in this book deals with how cautiously he approached his career. It's my guess that the sort of windfall symbolized by a treasure is the highly material (and male) version of "and they lived happily ever after." It may be a holdover from the poverty of his younger days and his dream of being able to afford some leisure time in which to perfect his craft.

Additionally, treasure is not only a staple of the adventure fiction of earlier generations, an era when access to great riches was denied to average men and women through vagaries of class and education; it may also reflect a time when Dad was searching for an audience of paying customers. To him, fame and the remuneration that could come with it may have seemed like the "bestowed by God" or "good luck" aspects of finding a treasure. And for a writer, a treasure, a fortune of valuable items once owned by man but now lost, implies a story . . . and a good story is a real treasure!

IBN BATUTA

A Proposal for a Nonfiction Book

COMMENTS: In early 1960, Louis tried to promote a series of nonfiction books based on the lives of the great scholar travelers of the Middle Ages and Renaissance. Included were to be Hsuan-tsang, who lived from around 602 to 664; Ludovico di Varthema, 1470 to 1517; Jean-Baptiste Tavernier, 1604 to 1689; Nicolao Manucci, 1638 to 1717—and Abu Abd al-Lah Muhammad ibn Abd al-Lah l-Lawati t-Tangi ibn Batutah . . . or, for those of an informal bent: Ibn Batuta, 1304 to 1368.

Batuta claimed one of the most extensive travel itineraries in history, a series of journeys and adventures that boggles the mind. His travels are considerably better chronicled today than in 1960, although some historians doubt Batuta actually traveled to all the places he described. Regardless, the Moorish adventurer's tale definitely struck a chord with Louis, who found in Ibn Batuta both a kindred spirit and an inspiration.

THE WORLD OF IBN BATUTA
A Proposal for a Nonfiction Book

A proposed nonfiction book based on the
journeys of the great Moorish traveler of the
14th century. His world is the world of the
Arabian Nights, of mystery, adventure, romance,
caravans, the diamonds of Golconda; the Vale of
Kashmir, of betel and hashish, of myrrh and
frankincense, of harems and beautiful slave
girls, of strange empires, singing sands, of the
Golden Horde, the Mongol khans, of Samarkand,
Tashkent, Delhi, Bukhara, Baghdad and Damascus;
of scimitar and Greek fire, of pirate galleys and
the sciences of the East.

Born of Berber parentage at Tangier on
February 25, 1304, into a family with a tradition
of judicial service as qadis, he received the
usual education of his class before setting out,
at the age of twenty-one, on his pilgrimage to
Mecca. It was his intention not only to fulfill
the duty of his faith by making this pilgrimage,
but to prepare himself for future judicial
offices by broadening his education through
contact and study with the great scholars of the
East. It is likely, from his care in listing the
scholars and saints he encountered on this first
trip and the diplomas conferred on him at
Damascus, that this may have been his primary
object in making the journey.

Gifted with a mind eager for learning, a quick
eye for detail, and a consuming interest in
everything he saw, by the time Batuta reached
Egypt he was already obsessed with travel. He
reached Mecca by the way of Syria on this first
pilgrimage, and then explored the classic lands
of Islamic culture. He proceeded by a complicated
route through Iraq and southwest Persia to
Baghdad, thence to Tabriz, and northern
Mesopotamia before returning via Baghdad to
Mecca.

Although young, he was already a person of
consequence, and living in an age and area where
scholars were greatly honored and respected, he
attracted great attention wherever he went. He
was interested in the personalities and histories
of the countries and sultans along the way, yet
at the same time contrived to benefit from their
generosity.

Nearly everywhere he stopped he was given
purses filled with gold, Arab horses, slaves or
silk robes. And everywhere he was lavishly
entertained by the amir, bey, sultan, shah or
whoever happened to be ruler. All wanted to talk
with him, many wished to acquire his services. An
astute young man of inquiring mind, Batuta
studied as he traveled and talked with the best
minds everywhere. He was a good judge of
personality, and had amusing and sometimes
caustic remarks to make about the various people
whom he encountered.

He then devoted several years (more than two,
and probably almost three) at Mecca preparing his
great plan of travel. During this period he went
down both shores of the Red Sea, visited Yemen,

experienced monsoon rain for the first time, and sailed from Aden to the trading ports of Africa, then back along the southern shores of Arabia to Oman and the Persian Gulf. During these travels he heard many tales of far places that aroused his desire for further adventure.

It must be remembered in this connection that while many European authorities claimed the monsoon winds that carried ships from the coast of Africa (region of Zanzibar) to India were discovered by Hippalus in approximately 45 A.D., ships sailed by Arabs had been making this voyage for a very long period of time. In the period from say 30 B.C. on through to about 90 A.D. up to 120 ships a season were sailing from Myus Hormus on the Red Sea coast of Egypt to India.

Actually, one of the rarely mentioned but contributing causes of the decline of the Roman Empire was an adverse trade balance with India.

Another pilgrimage to Mecca was made in 1332 or about there, and he planned a trip to India and to the court of Muhammad bin Tughluq, who was noted for his generosity to scholars, but destiny intervened and he traveled through Egypt again, and through Syria to the land of the Turks. He became the basic authority for the history of the region during this period at the beginning of the Ottoman venture.

He then crossed from Sinope to the Crimea and visited the territory of the Khan of the Golden Horde, then the ancient capital of Bulgaria, and Constantinople in the retinue of the Khan's third wife, a Greek princess who was returning to visit her family.

There is more than a possibility, which I intend to develop, that the relations between this Greek princess and the young Islamic scholar were something more than platonic.

After travel in Russia, Batuta returned in the winter to Sarai, the capital of the Golden Horde, and then started for India overland through Khiva, Bukhara, Samarkand and Balkh, then by a difficult route through Afghanistan and Khurasan, to reach the Indus on September 12, 1333 with an imposing array of attendants.

Batuta, it might be said, was very adept at securing gifts from the various kings he encountered. Most of these were freely given, but where this was not so, Batuta had his own methods, many of them devious, for getting what he needed to continue his travels. Like Varthema, who came later, he seemed interested only in traveling and learning, and there was little interest in wealth for its own sake.

Batuta spent some time in India which made a deep impression, but there was a court intrigue in which he barely escaped with his life, although he was later restored to favor and entrusted by Sultan Mohammed with a mission to China. Before this he held the job of Malikite grand qadi in Delhi for some time. It was during this period that he became the victim of the intrigues mentioned above. Batuta, it seems, was a stern judge, and his ideas of morals were rather more severe than those in some of the areas where he served. He was envoy to China in 1342 . . . a trip he was long in carrying out due to a series of adventures and delays.

He made an adventurous trip through central India and down the Malabar coast. He spent 18 months in the Maldive Islands (off the coast of India) as qadi, but left for Ceylon. He went along the coasts of Coromandel and Malabar, again to the Maldives, and then resumed his trip to China.

While waiting for the sailing season he took trips to Bengal and Assam, then went by ship to Sumatra, traveling from there to China by junk, and on to Peking. He returned to Malabar by way of Sumatra in 1347, through the Persian Gulf to Baghdad, then Syria (while the Black Death was ravaging that area) and again to Mecca via Egypt.

He sailed from Alexandria to Tunis, and in a Catalan ship via Sardinia to Tenes in Algeria, overland to Fez. Later he crossed the strait to visit Andalusia where the kingdom of Granada still flourished. Returning to Morocco he crossed the Sahara to the empire of the Mandingos, and is one of the few authorities on the great African empires which existed in the region of the Niger during the Middle Ages.

Returning to Fez, at the behest of the Sultan, he dictated his memoirs. He probably ended his days as a qadi. His travels covered the period from 1325 to 1354.

As exciting as is the material in Batuta's original work, the one translation that is in any respect adequate has been written by a scholar for scholars and is replete with footnotes, many unimportant and unnecessary village names, which

are fine for the historian but of no importance
to the casual reader. Much in the way of context
has been left out that could be included.

What I propose is to write an entertaining,
exciting, and substantial book based on the
travels of Ibn Batuta. It will be a thorough
study, yet written for the layman who wishes to
be entertained while he is learning. In his own
account Batuta is inclined to pass over a
shipwreck in a couple of paragraphs and a court
intrigue in scarcely more, and he devotes little
time to his affairs with women. The outlines are
there, so without digressing or throwing the book
out of proportion, I expect to enlarge upon these
stories to add to the color and entertainment
value. As a man of that world Batuta saw little
reason to discuss what conditions elsewhere were
like or how his times fit into the greater
historical picture; that too will be placed in
context.

My knowledge of the area and the period are
quite complete. I have traveled in person over
some of the same routes, have studied the
histories, religious beliefs and sciences of the
countries he visited, and know something of the
personalities with whom he came in contact.

The travels of Ibn Batuta are, I believe, one
of the greatest experiences a reader can have,
for it opens a world largely closed to Western
readers. From frequent lectures I have discovered
there exists an enormous market for such a book,
and a vast curiosity about the subject matter.
Above all, it opens a relatively new field of
interest to the general reader. Alexander,

Charlemagne and Tamerlane have been done. The
story of Marco Polo, a mere commuter by
comparison to Batuta, is known. Above all, this
is an intelligent viewpoint from behind the
scenes . . . this is a Muslim commenting on the
Muslim world, a participant telling the story of
what he has done and seen. Too many of our
scholars are purely European scholars, unaware
that there is any scholarship other than their
own, or any viewpoint different from the one they
hold.

What I hope to write is an exciting, colorful
and highly informative book for laymen, one in
which a scholar will find few faults.

GOALS:

1. To cover the travels of Ibn Batuta as
   described in his books.
2. To provide added background on those
   places he visited, conditions at the
   time, circumstances of travel beyond what
   he himself tells, and further background
   on people he mentions.
3. To locate towns and places according to
   their modern names. All this without
   footnotes.
4. To provide further background on customs,
   education, medical practices, some of the
   things he missed.
5. To place all these things in relation to
   what was happening in Europe at the time
   so the reader is fully aware of the
   period of which he is reading.

COMMENTS: This proposal has been pieced together from several different documents. The original was sent off to Henry Holt and Company, one of the oldest hardcover publishers in the United States. Initially, Louis pitched them the idea of doing one nonfiction and one fiction title a year . . . a proposal that they balked at immediately, claiming, "That increment may be too frequent for us, or any other publisher, to handle profitably."

They were, however, willing to look at his Ibn Batuta book proposal. Unfortunately, their response, while probably appropriate considering Louis had, so far, only written fiction, was somewhat less than what he was looking for . . .

> We have read the outline for IBN BATUTA with great care and interest . . . The material you sent is indeed an informative description of Ibn Batuta's life and does serve to support your points about the exotic adventures and historical importance of the subject . . . [I]t does not really show how you will handle that material in the book . . . Nevertheless, we are nervous about how we could sell this book without a sample of the book treatment itself.

I suspect Dad was looking for the credibility a substantial work of nonfiction would give him, but the real issue was whether he could afford to take the time to write such a work. Serious research would be required, not the sort he put into a Western but work that was specifically sourced and carefully documented in the text. That would have created additional expense and a clerical challenge the likes of which he had never undertaken. Perhaps it was all for the best that he did not find support for this project . . . all for the best because my father also had another idea brewing: a work of fiction, the story of another young man, another wanderer in the medieval and Islamic world . . .

By December of 1960 Louis had finished *The Walking Drum.* Whether the life of Ibn Batuta inspired the adventures of my father's fictional hero, Mathurin Kerbouchard, or was simply a research source is unclear. However, there are many resemblances, including planned but unwritten sequels that followed a path similar to Batuta's to both India and China.

Over the next six years Dad sent *The Walking Drum* to Bantam, Doubleday, St. Martin's Press and, no doubt, Holt and a few others. He rewrote it based on notes he had received. He retitled it *May There Be a Road,* hoping that would help. Nothing worked. No one was the least bit ready to allow a writer of paperback Westerns to try his hand at a swashbuckling historical adventure novel, any more than they were ready to let him publish the history of a fourteenth-century Moroccan traveler.

By 1984, however, the world was a different place.

———————————

SHANTY

Two Beginnings to a Western Novel

CHAPTER I

So I gave my heart to a bend in the road, and off I went, a'yondering.

There was nothing behind me but trouble, and nothing before me but dreams, but there was sunlight on the hills that morning, and stories I'd heard of the Western lands to color the thoughts in my head.

There was a yearning in me, too, a kind of uneasy yearning back to a ghost-memory land, for I'd been born in the West and lived there a time.

Of that I remembered little, just vague drifting things in my mind of a night time, memories of long grass blowing in the wind, of icy peaks against the sky, and the hoarse bark of rifle guns.

Yet the wide sky gave me a call, and the prairie left me something to dream on, so I saddled my old roan and pointed her nose into the West.

Sometimes there had been worrying voices in the night time, voices I knew belonged to my

father and mother, but the things they said were
not clear, nor had I any memory of the conditions
that might have caused such anger.

Two days later I fetched up to a creek bank
where a man was cutting cedar posts. My belly
lining was chafing my spine from hunger, so I
hired out for a dollar a day and found, to cut
posts.

It was hard work, and John Burdick was a
driving boss, one who worked less after I came
up, but spent his time yammering at me. Being a
fair hand with an axe and a cross-cut saw, I did
my work, and well. But when a week had passed and
I'd smoothed some wrinkles out of my belly, I
told him he could pay me off.

He was a big shouldered man with a lot of
mustache and a hard, free way about him. He'd
also a liking for the bottle and some notion of
himself as a fist fighter. "You got nothing
coming," he said, "you et enough for three men."

"It was a dollar a day and found," I said,
knowing as I said it this was no time for
arguing, nor would I get any place.

"If you work two weeks longer I'll give you
ten dollars," he said.

"Seven dollars," I said, "and you pay me now."

He grinned at me. "Kid," he said, "I got a lot
of wood cut for nothing. Now you beat it, before
I give you a hiding."

So I walked up to him and hit him.

"Mister," I said, "I earned seven honest
dollars. You going to pay me?"

He got up off the ground and made as if to
wipe the blood from his mouth, and then he came
at me. So I fetched him a clout alongside the

ribs, and when he swung a wide right at me I went
in and belted him with another right in the
belly. He went down to his knees and stayed
there, and I said to him, "Mister, I got seven
dollars coming."

He gave it to me.

So I caught up that roan and crossed the
river, going on into the woods. Come night fall,
I stopped by a cabin and hollered at the house.

The man who came to the door had him a
shotgun.

"I was riding by," I said, "and figured I
might work out a bait of grub."

He looked me over, and then he nodded. "All
right, get down and come in, but if you're one of
that Ryerson outfit the best you'll get is a dose
of lead."

"Only Ryerson I ever knew was a steamboat
captain on the Ohio," I told him.

When I put up the roan in his barn and went
inside I found he had him a neat little cabin,
right well made, and a pleasant faced woman with
two youngsters. He had a plowed field outside the
barn yard and a few chickens. A body could tell
by the way the house was made that this man was a
workman, a first-rate carpenter or millwright.

"Name of Sturgis," he said, "Henry Sturgis. We
settled here five, six months ago. Sorry to meet
you like that, but there are toughs around. They
stole two cows from me last night. You forget
about working--I do all the work to be done
around here. The wife and I are just pleased for
the company."

She put on a cloth and fixed the table up
some, and time to time she glanced at me, pleased

like. Women folks set store by company, and this
was a lonely place, with woods all around and
dark except where they'd cleared land.

"Thank you, ma'am," I said, "you cook a might
fine meal. I'll often remember this in the
Western lands."

"We came from Pennsylvania," she said, "and
started west. Where are your folks?"

Me, I looked up at her. "Ma'am, I've no folks,
anywhere. They were killed when I was a boy,
maybe six, seven years old. Truth to tell, ma'am,
I must have been younger. I don't rightly know my
own name, nor how old I am, nor where my folks
came from."

She was some cut up at that, and we set around
the table until real late . . . why, it was after
nine o'clock before we went to bed. They gave me
a place to sleep in the hay-mow, with blankets
and all.

Setting out there in the hay, a'looking out
the door, I got to thinking how many homes I'd
been in, and none of them my own. Seemed like
everybody but me had a place to go to, come night
time.

They were fine folks. Mrs. Sturgis, she told
me come day-light I could have breakfast with
them and they would fix me a packet of grub to
take along, which was kindly.

Setting there thinking, like that, I heard a
noise outside. It was a whisper of a noise only,
but next thing I knew there was a man standing in
the doorway.

"New horse in here," I heard him whisper.
"Where'd he git the horse?"

Me, I just set there. Struck me a mite funny,
that man going to take my roan. That roan being
one of the most miserable animals a man could
find in a year of looking. Born with a sore
tooth, I guess, but that roan didn't like anybody
at all. Except maybe me. Animals take me
friendly, and I sort of make up to them . . .
nothing ever belonged to me before, except that
roan.

Meantime I felt around. I didn't move, because
that floor would creak and those men were armed.
That hay would rustle, too. Moreover, I was
afraid if a disputation started up Mr. Sturgis
would come high-tailing it out to help me, and
maybe he would get hurt.

Since I was old enough to hold up my hands I
been fighting my own battles, and I don't know
how to do much of anything else that matters.
Except how to do a lot of hard work.

There were three, four of them, and I set
there a'waiting for that man to go to the roan's
stall. He stepped forward and that roan kicked
out and knocked that man sprawling across the
barn.

"Why, that--!"

Another man stepped in and I saw him draw back
his rifle to swing on the mare with the rifle
butt, and I took off from that loft edge and
piled him up alongside the kicked man. He hit the
deck in a heap, and I drew back my fist and
slugged him, then I wrenched that rifle from him
and shot at the man in the doorway.

Here is another, more personal, version:

CHAPTER I

Somewhere my love lies sleeping behind the
lights of a far-off town.

So I gave my heart to a bend in the road, and
off I went, a'yondering.

Each rise in the road was a challenge, each
bend in the road a lure, each light a beckoning
finger that drew me onward.

How many times had I looked upon house lights
with longing? How many times had I stopped upon
the road to look into the window of a home,
watching a father reading a newspaper by lamp-
light, his wife sewing, his children doing their
school-work? To all of this I was a stranger, for
I had known no such home, nothing but a haunting
memory that flickered, a tiny flame, in the back-
shadows of my mind.

My home had been a campfire, and there is
nothing like a campfire for dreaming. A lonely
man can find in a campfire those things for which
he is forever longing, and no crystal ball will
ever read the heart of a man with half the
campfire's truth.

There was nothing behind me but trouble, and
nothing before me but dreams, but there was
sunlight on the hills that morning, and the
stories I'd heard of the Western lands to color
the thoughts of my head. And I had memories, too,
for it was from the West I'd come. There was a
yearning in me, a yearning to go back to those
ghost-memory lands before the time I'd lived with
the Sioux.

Of that I remembered little, just drifting

will o' wisps of thought that slipped from the background of the mind during darkness or when busy with something else, memories of long grass blowing in the wind, of icy peaks against the sky and the hoarse bark of rifle guns.

These, and something more . . . the sound of a woman's voice singing, of a man's quiet tones, of strong arms that carried me and soft arms that loved me. There were other times, worrying voices in the night, voices I knew belonged to my mother and father. I remember fears of troubles I was all too young to grasp.

Until now mine had been a sorry life by all standards but my own. Growing up any way at all, working since first I could remember, learning to trust few of those whom I met, for a boy without family can expect little enough in this world.

Always there had been within me a feeling of destiny waiting in the West. I suppose all young men feel destiny awaiting them somewhere, but this went beyond that, and always there seemed something awaiting me just over the horizon, something connected with those intangible memories.

Each time I looked upon a town strange to me, I looked upon it with hope.

The wide sky gave me a call, and the prairie gave me something to dream on, so I shouldered my pack and pointed my nose to the westward.

My age was an uncertain thing, and of my rightful name I knew nothing, but it was likely that I was scarce eighteen when I started to the west again.

Yet, how old is a man? Is he to be measured by years or by accomplishment, by energy or despair, by strength or hopelessness? When does a man cease to be young and begin to be old?

For surely, all men do not age at the same rate. Of one hundred men of the same years, some will be forty, some eighteen, some already seventy. With some the age is physical, with most, it is of the mind; some men are born old, and some are forever young.

He who lives an even, uneventful life, who knows few women, marries young, works long at the same tasks, troubled by little, eating the same food . . . is he seventy then, or is he ten in the years of experience?

He who knows strange, far places, customs varied with each port, the tastes of exotic foods, the lips of lush, foreign women, the mysteries of the jungle, of dark, narrow streets, the beat of surf on an icy shore, the sounds of a ship's bells tolling the half hours, the bow-wash about the hull . . . is he who has known hunger, despair, hatred, fury, the agony of thirst and hatred and the glories of love, is he of the same age as that other, although their years are alike?

No man can cut himself adrift from the life he has lived, or the things he has felt, the food he has eaten, the people he has known. For these are stored in the memory, each to become a part of the man, each to have its place in the color of his future actions, each a part of what he has become and is becoming.

Of the memories that come to me in the night all are wiped out by that last, terrible night of fire, gun smoke and hoarse yells, ending in darkness, quiet and a boy alone.

There had been before that a long time of wagon-riding, and I can hear today the rocking, rumbling roll of wagon wheels, loaded heavily. For the longest time before that there had been nothing but prairie and sky.

The gentle hands of my mother I remember, and the quiet voice of my father . . . but I recall a time when his tones had a deadly sound, too. And sometimes I seem to hear both their voices speaking in a different tongue, a strange, musical sound that I loved to hear.

The morning after the massacre I do remember.

Sunlight sparkled upon the water when I awakened, the water of a small creek that chuckled amiably among the rocks.

For a long time I lay still, smelling the smoke from across the creek and knowing what it was, yet afraid to cross the stream, to see what fire and nightmare had left.

Three Indians found me.

They were big men, as tall as my father had been, and strong. They spoke to me but I had none of their words and so one of them gave me a strip of jerked beef on which to chew, and that I understood well enough. He took me up on his horse and patted my shoulder.

And then for several years I was an Indian.

How old was I when they found me? Was I five or six or seven?

More likely five, although it might have been even younger. Months passed in which I learned what Indian boys learned, and with them. Months when I hunted and fished and played at war with Indian children.

They were Sioux, and I was with them for four

years, sometimes in Montana, sometimes Canada, more often in Wyoming, but it was in Canada they took me at last to a Hudson Bay post. The white man there asked my name but I had nothing to tell him, for all had been wiped clear by that night of terror and death.

The Sioux remained long in the vicinity of the post and I was much with them. Often I went into the woods with Man-Who-Walks-With Birds, a medicine man who had taken a liking to me. More than any other he taught me how to live with the woods, the plains, and the mountains.

The factor at the Hudson Bay post was a friendly, bearded man who occasionally sat down to talk to me, and once when I said a word which my father had often used, he was curious about it.

Did I know any more such words? I remembered a few . . . I believe he hoped to find a name among them, but there was none.

There were books in the library at the post, for many of the trappers were great readers and they traded books as they did all things. In one of them he showed me the first map I had ever seen, and he showed me on the map where the post was, and where the Sioux told him the wagon train had been massacred.

Often I would take that book from its shelf and look at it, and the map seemed strange to me because there were no woods and streams, nor did it show wagons or fear. But I did not forget the map.

One day they took me away. They carried me off to the east and left me at a home for other children without families.

Until then I had been among friendly people,
but when they first allowed me to walk in the
yard with other children a boy walked up to me
and struck me. He struck me hard in the mouth and
laughed at me.

Suddenly out of the mystery that was my past I
heard my father's voice, speaking to someone in
that tone which had frightened me. "Come around
here again, and I'll kill you."

The boy hit me again, and laughed again, and
within me burst something white-hot and I struck
out at him.

Four years in the woods I had run and played
with Indian boys, wrestling with them, fighting
with them. Now I sprang at this boy and hurled
him hard to the ground and when he got up I
battered him down again with my fists, so filled
with anger that I was frightened of myself.

The headmaster of the school came at me, but I
ducked away from him and backed to the wall,
frightened at this strange place where I found
myself.

The yard was square and stone-walled and
floored with coarse gravel, and other children
stood around, staring at me, and the boy who had
struck me got up slowly from the ground, his
mouth bleeding.

The headmaster reached for me, and then the
boy I struck opened the gate to go to the pump to
wash away the blood and I ducked under the
headmaster's arm and ran past the pump and into
the woods. The headmaster and some others came
after me but they were not men who knew the
woods. Hiding quickly, I let them search all

around and waited until darkness came to move off.

For more than a week I walked, living from the woods as I had been taught. When I walked it was on the roads, but when I slept it was in the forest. I knew how to make fire and three times I caught fish, and the other times I lived from roots or the inner bark of trees.

One day I came out upon a sandy shore where the wind was cold in the morning and where the sea was. The sea rustled upon the sand and my feet made crunching noises as I walked along the shore toward a dory where a man was mending nets. Beside him there was a fire, and food cooking.

For several minutes I watched him, smelling the cooking food and feeling my stomach growl with hunger. At first I think he did not see me and when he did he said nothing for some time, but at last he said, without looking up, "How are you, boy? Hungry?"

His accent was familiar, but I knew not why. He took the pipe from his mouth and looked at me. He had shrewd, friendly eyes and an easy way about him. He shifted the net upon his knee. "The net is old," he said, "and my fingers are clumsy. How are you, boy, at mending nets?"

"I never mended one," I said. "I never even saw one before . . . not like that."

"It is time for eating. Will you join me?"

Some faint memory stirred with me. "Thank you, sir," I said, and he looked up at me, surprised and pleased.

"Well, now. There's a thing. A boy who speaks like a gentleman. It is an accomplishment, boy, and don't you ever lose it. There is nothing," he added, "like proper speech and manners for impressing people, and they are a gracious thing."

He was a slender man, but wiry and strong, with graying hair and tiny laugh wrinkles at the corners of his eyes. He had hot coffee with many slices of bacon and some baked bread, and it tasted very good.

"You look to have traveled some," he said. "Have you run away from somewhere?"

At this time I had not learned caution in dealing with people, so I told him I had been a week in the woods.

He looked at me with some doubt, but when I responded to his questions by explaining how I had lived his doubt turned to respect. "Think of that, now. I doubt if I could do as well. Perhaps at sea. Where did you learn the like of that?"

"I was four years among the Sioux."

So after a bit of bacon and the warming of hot coffee in my stomach I told him of my few years and the home to which I'd been sent and the fight I had.

"You hit him then? Good lad. You'll find his type all too often in this world, and it's little else they understand but blows.

"Well, I should send you back, but I am something of a rebel myself, and if you'd like I shall make a fisherman of you. For the time being."

He gestured at the sand dunes about us. "This is a place I often camp. My home . . . if it can be called that, is off shore on Monhegan Island." He glanced at me. "I'm Welsh, you know. David Penderyn's my name."

The red crept up my neck. I could feel the
hot, shaming flush of it climbing up my face.
"I've no name," I said, "I've no name to call
myself."

"Ah?" He added fuel to the fire. "A name can
be an important thing for a man, and you'd best
pick one out. For a convenience . . . until you
find your own."

The Sioux had given me a name . . .
Haokah . . . it was no rightful name. At the home
to which I'd been sent they had told me they
would find a name for me, but they'd not had
time. They didn't even have a name for the
records there now, unless they invented one after
I left. More likely they were pleased to be free
of me . . . who wants a boy without a name?

Why could I not remember? Why I had lost that,
too, I did not know. Yet lost it I had. Since
then I'd said over all the names of which I could
think, and so had the Hudson Bay factor, trying
to help me, but none of them had a familiar
sound.

"There's no need to hurry," Penderyn added
quietly. "We'll camp here tonight, and tomorrow
we will go to the island. I live alone
there . . . in a little shanty I found myself."

"Call me that, then," I said, "since you found
me, too. Or I found you."

"Call you what?"

"Shanty. It's as good a name as any."

We fished the next day, and made it back to
the island after dark. The shanty in which he
lived had three rooms. There was a kitchen, a
bed-room, and a large living room filled with
drawings, books, and all manner of odds and ends

in which he was interested. He had a collection
of arrowheads, another of shells, and some odd
bits from old wrecks found along the shores of
Maine and the off-shore islands.

"Cabot came here in 1497," he commented,
indicating some odds and ends of old iron, most
of which I could not identify. "He was exploring
the coast looking for a way to the East, but I
think there had been others here before him. I've
found old campfires along the coast that
certainly were not made by Indians. Basque,
Breton or Norman fishermen, probably, and there
are some ruins over across the island."

He pointed out a cot along the wall. "You will
sleep there," he said. That was the beginning of
it.

We fished off the Grand Banks, and sometimes
we traded for furs along the Brunswick coast, and
I learned how to handle a boat under oars or
sail, to mend nets and to fish.

Sometimes we would stay at the cabin for days
while he puttered around with his drawing . . .
mostly drawings of old wreckage, of ships or
boats or trees . . . sometimes of waves.

"A rebel I was, and a rebel I have remained,"
he said,"although they trained me for a barrister
in England. It was not the life I wanted, and the
girl they wished me to marry was not the one I
wanted, so I walked away from it all, married a
girl I loved and we came here to fish and paint.
Marie died, and the boy too." He glanced at me.
"He could have been your age, and I hope he'd
have been the man you are."

He walked across the room, listening to the
wind. "Storm blowing up," he commented, "and

until you've seen a storm off these islands . . .
a real storm . . . you will have seen nothing."

My hands grew strong with the hauling of nets,
and my shoulders with the cutting of wood for the
house, but he had started me learning from the
books he had at hand, and from the tales he told
me at odd moments throughout the day, or in the
evening hours.

"You should go to school," he told me, "but
the best school is in these books and others you
will come upon. Let them lead you one to another,
for all any school can give you is the barest
outline of an education, then you must fill in
the spaces yourself.

"Nor will acquiring information make you wise.
Wisdom comes when you begin to draw conclusions
from what you have learned or observed."

He was Welsh, as I have said, and in him there
was a strong mystic vein. He was half a poet, I
think, and half a seer, but a quietly practical
man always with a gift for fishing and feeling
for sea and wind beyond that of common men.

"Don't believe too much, boy. When you believe
too much you must also disbelieve too much."

He told me that one day, the thought coming
from nowhere. Nowhere, that is, but the recesses
of his own mind.

He knew poetry, and loved it, and it was he
who first brought The Iliad and The Odyssey to my
mind, and read them aloud in the long hours of
the evening. Yet he was not a well man.

Each time now that we went for the fishing, it
seemed that drawing the nets took longer, the

pull for shore was slower, and more and more I
began to take the weight of it upon my shoulders.

When I first came to him upon that windy shore
of Maine, I was ten . . . perhaps eleven years
old. Four years went by, and they were good years
for me, and for him, I think, for he had been
lonelier than he realized.

Toward the end there was a kind of haste in
him, a realization, I think, that he had not long
to live. During those last months he tried to
teach me everything he knew, and once far out at
sea he stopped, his face gray from hauling the
heavy net, and he said, "Knowledge was meant to
be passed on, boy. Do you always remember that.
Sometimes I feel . . . there was a German who
wrote lines that went something like this . . .
'I am like a bee that hath gathered too much
honey, I need hands reaching out for it.'"

That was the last time we went far out from
shore. When we reached the cove at last, I was
hauling the oars alone, but strong enough to do
it, for I was fourteen by then.

It was that night he sat up suddenly and spoke
across the room to me. "Boy, if anything happens
to me, go to Henry Trefethren. He will see that I
am buried beside my wife. He has been told about
you, and will sell what is left and give it to
you.

"Also, there is a black box in the trunk. Open
it with the key that's around my neck and mail
the letter that's written and sealed. Keep the
rest of the contents of the box for yourself, but
keep them close to you."

Two weeks later when I returned from the
fishing, he was dead. The letter was mailed that

night, addressed to some place in England or
Wales with a long, complicated address. Otherwise
there was little in the box except two hundred
dollars in gold pieces and three letters
addressed to me.

In the first of the letters there was a will,
leaving everything in my name . . . or the name
we had decided on.

In the second letter addressed to me, he said
this:

The years you have spent with me have been
the happiest since losing my family, and I
have felt as if you were my own son. During
this time I have listened to the inflections
in your voice, noticed a few words you have
used from time to time, and your own
behavior as well as the rare odds and ends
you remember of your own parents.

I believe I can safely say your family
were of Welsh, Cornish, Irish or Breton
extraction; that they were people of good
background and of some education. I believe
they were better off than most families
going west in the 1850's.

There may have been a reason for their
going west other than the desire for land or
gold. I do not believe your wagon train was
massacred by Indians. I believe your father,
or perhaps your mother, had an enemy they
feared and that it was this enemy who
followed and attacked the wagon train.

Knowing you are curious about your
family, I offer these comments for what they
are worth.

The enclosed letters to you are to be delivered to Mr. Jefferson Hodge, in Boston.
Mr. Hodge is my attorney, and on your
eighteenth and twenty-fifth birthdays these
letters will be returned to you.

                        My best wishes.

When I had delivered the letters to Mr. Hodge,
I went down into the street and stood there
alone.

I was fourteen years old and after buying
clothing and my passage to Boston I had but
sixty-three dollars remaining, and no place to go
until I chose such a place.

The three years to come were to be three of
the hardest and most brutal of my life.

COMMENTS: The first of these Boy-With-No-Name
drafts, though relatively straightforward, doesn't get very
far, nor is it anything but a typical Louis L'Amour beginning. I believe it was written several years prior to the second attempt.

But the second fragment is much more interesting. The
first several pages wander around a bit. I get the feeling
that Dad might have been waxing a bit rhapsodic about his
own life, exploring some exaggerated or fantasy version of
it as a possible background for this particular character.
However, this might have indicated that, at the time this
was written, Louis was thinking about putting together
some sort of autobiographical or semi-autobiographical

project. That could explain why he chose to lift the first few lines of this story to use as the lyrical introduction to his very personal short story collection, *Yondering*.

Around 1960 Louis mentions coming up with an idea for a novel using that title. He states in his journal:

> Decided to do a novel called <u>Yondering</u>. A western in hard-back, and will try to write it in May.

I doubt that either of the two attempts you have just read dates that early, but I do believe it was this story he was considering. The reference to it being "in hard-back" also suggests Dad was going to try to up his game a bit, to make it a more significant, potentially personal, piece.

In the *The Bastard of Brignogan* section that starts this collection, I note that in the 1970s we went on a long trip through eastern Canada. Dad's family lived on both sides of the border and he wanted to explore the territory of his ancestors in order to use it in future stories.

I suspect we took our eastern Canadian trip between the writing of these two versions and that something about connecting with his mysterious Canadian roots inspired Dad to revisit this story. This personal connection might also have brought him back to that wonderful first sentence when he started gathering the material for the short story collection he eventually titled *Yondering*.

Both *Yondering* and Louis's "memoir," *Education of a Wandering Man,* are fascinating projects, because they were examples of Louis's compromising with himself over writing an autobiography. He wanted to do it. Other people— his fans, his publisher, and his family—also wanted him to do it. But there was something (perhaps a number of somethings) keeping him from it. He often claimed he would write an autobiography only as fiction, thus not making it a true autobiography at all. Whatever the tension was that both pressed him forward and held him back, it helped create two wonderful books that we might not otherwise have.

————————————

KRAG MORAN

The Beginning of a Boxing Story

When the bell sounded Krag Moran went out
fast. Gomez was coming right in because that was
the way Gomez fought, the only way he knew how to
fight. He was a short, thick-muscled bruiser with
a square jaw and a flat face. And he could
punch . . .

Moran saw the left start and went inside with
a belting right to the heart that landed solidly.
Even as the punch connected Moran was rolling to
miss the right aimed for his head, and he was
hooking his left to the ribs. Then he completed
the combination with a right hook to the ear that
shook Gomez and slid away.

Gomez looked at him, looked into his eyes,
startled. Moran ignored the expression, feinted
to bring Gomez on in, then stiffened the left
into a blow that smashed his lips into his teeth.
Moran's right crossed and connected hard to the
cheekbone and Gomez staggered, momentarily off-
balance.

Moran did not follow it up. Gomez was at his
most dangerous in wild slugging matches and Krag

Moran was not a gambling man. He moved around, looking Gomez over.

The Mexican had been hurt, and another fighter would have been cautious. Gomez was not because it was not his way. There was a growing welt on his cheekbone where the right had landed.

Moran jabbed lightly, three times to the face. Two of the jabs were to the eye above the welt. Gomez circled and tried to work Moran into a corner, so Moran went along with the game. Gomez rushed and Moran side-stepped so swiftly that Gomez unloosed a punch at an empty corner, then furious at the laughter of the crowd, he whirled. His turn was sudden, violent, and complete. He met a right hand that struck like a bat hitting a line drive. He turned over at the count of eight, but that was all.

Gillerman had his money on the desk. "You can hit," he said, "you can really punch. Want a fight next month?"

Krag Moran shook his head. "I won't be in Panama next month," he said, and he walked outside.

A thick-set man was standing on the street smoking a long cigar. "Let's eat," he said, lifting his eyes to Moran.

"What do you want?" Moran's voice was rough.

"To make a fast buck. How about you?"

"Where do we eat?"

"Feliciano's suit you?"

"If you pay for it."

"Sure," the man said, unsmiling, "I pay for it."

When they had ordered the man lit his cigar again. He was shaved too clean and smelling too strongly of lotion. He had thick, moist lips and wet, slightly protruding eyes. He was a man, Krag was sure, who was strictly on the make for a buck, who could not be trusted with anything out of eye range.

Krag Moran was twenty-eight but looked younger. He was an inch over six feet and weighed one-eighty. His hair was rusty-brown, his eyes slate-gray, his cheekbones high and his jaw strong. He had no marks of the ring. He wore a rumpled linen sport coat, a blue shirt and gray slacks.

"I'm Zavatarri. You got fifty bucks for tonight. I can get you a grand for the same job."

Zavatarri took a clipping from his pocket and put it beside Moran's plate. It was a magazine picture of a fighter. It was Johnny Coleman, the light-heavyweight champion of the world. "Who does he look like?" Zavatarri asked. Then he pointed at Moran with his middle finger. "He looks like you. You could be his brother."

"So what does that get me?"

"Dough . . . big dough and fast dough. There's a town called Tangabar. A month ago it was a dozen mud huts and a boat landing. They found a mountain of iron there, then oil. Today there's fifteen thousand tough men in that town, all loaded with money they have nowhere to spend."

When the waiter put their food down Moran started on the steak. Let the man talk--this much was his.

"They've got a fighter there. He looks good, he hits good, he talks a good fight and they like him . . . and he couldn't go five rounds with you."

"So?"

"So we drop into town by plane. You're Johnny Coleman on vacation but not backward about picking up a fast buck. They make an offer, we fight this guy, we collect, we lam."

"You're nuts. They sign this fight, Coleman reads it in the papers, then we're in trouble."

Zavatarri shook his head. "Look. How many times you seen in the paper where a champ signs but doesn't fight? How many times does some jerk promoter say he's signed the champ when he never even saw him. Publicity, that's all. That's what they'll think this is."

Moran cut into his steak. It was a thick steak, a juicy steak. It was the first steak he had seen in three months. It was his first good meal in two weeks.

"You look good in there," Zavatarri said through a mouthful. "You can move around. You box like Coleman. You can hit, all right. You ain't as good as Coleman, but who is?" He waved his fork. "Far as that goes in a place like Tangabar I can hold up any news release until we're out of town." He rubbed his fingers. "Tell them you're tryin' to make a buck without your manager, who takes you for everything."

Tangabar was two double rows of sheet metal on frame buildings. Only the hotel had two stories. The town had fourteen gambling houses, twenty saloons, five restaurants and a half dozen greasy spoon joints. It had fifty shacks with women sitting in the doorways.

It was a town where they had a fighter named Monk Burman. He weighed two hundred pounds even and his name was not Burman, but Krag Moran did not know that . . . or care. It was a town where a lot of guys had a lot of money that said their fighter could take Johnny Coleman.

Krag Moran moved into a thin-walled hotel room and from his suitcase he took three pairs of dirty socks which he washed in the basin. He took out an extra pair of slacks, his boxing gear and a dirty shirt. The dirty shirt was wrapped around a .380 Colt automatic with three extra clips, all loaded.

He put the clips in his pocket, the automatic behind his waist-band under his shirt and went down into the street. It was a tough town full of tough men. Men who weren't going to like it if they got gypped.

Women followed him with their eyes as he walked along the street and men took a second look at his shoulders. He bought a clean shirt for twice what it was worth.

Zavatarri was sitting on his bed when he got back to the room. Moran's suitcase was facing opposite from the way he had left it.

"We're in, kid. Took just that long. Night after tomorrow. Publicity's no trick here. All they do is mention it in a couple of saloons. Anyway, there's nothing else for them to do but drink, gamble and go after women. They can do that any time."

"What do I get?"

"You get a grand, like I said."

Krag Moran rolled up his sleeves and ran water into the basin. His forearms were brown and powerful, his hands thick and square across the knuckles. He looked at Zavatarri in the mirror. "Get yourself another boy. There'll be four, five thousand men there. Maybe twice that many. You're dealing for Coleman now. You asked for fifty percent, at least."

Zavatarri didn't like it. He didn't like it even a little. His eyes got mean and he took his cigar from his mouth. "You cheap bum! You got fifty bucks for Gomez. You didn't have a quarter when you got in there with him. Why, you lousy--!"

Moran took him by the collar and lifted him. He held him like that until his face started to turn purple and his eyes bulged. Zavatarri struggled uselessly. "Don't call me a bum." Moran's voice was flat, conversational. "I don't like it." He dropped Zavatarri on the bed. "Sure," he said, "I didn't have any money. But you didn't have a fighter that looked like Johnny Coleman, either."

He lathered his face and put a blade in his safety razor. He looked at Zavatarri's mottled face in the mirror. "We split fifty-fifty."

Zavatarri started to complain but Moran was watching him in the mirror. After a minute he shrugged and said, "All right, all right."

Zavatarri sucked on his cigar. "You think you can lick this guy? We could make a buck bettin'."

"I can lick him."

"This guy's big. He's rugged."

"If he was any good he wouldn't be here."

"You're good."

Moran chuckled without humor. "Not good. Just good enough. I've had 'em on with the good ones, though." He looked at Zavatarri. "Anyway, I'm not a fighter. I'm just a guy who can fight who needs a buck."

When he was cleaning his razor he said, "You bet the way you like. I'm bettin' my end on me."

When Zavatarri was gone Krag took off his shirt and bathed his body. He took the .380 and cleared the shell from the chamber. Then he put the gun in his suitcase.

There was a saloon and gambling place called the Queen's Bar. Krag walked to the bar and ordered rum and looked around. He had a good memory for faces but he knew none of these.

There was a girl dealing blackjack. She had a still, expressionless face and large, beautiful gray eyes. She dealt very fast, never flickering an eyelid, and she said nothing at all to anyone. She looked up and saw Krag Moran watching her.

He sat without drinking, just keeping the rum in front of him. She did not look curious. She did not look anything. She just turned back to her game. She played fast, straight, and while he was watching, she made money for the house.

The bartender came up to him. "You Johnny Coleman? Heard you were in town."

"Who's the babe dealing twenty-one?"

"Mag Kelly. She's all right."

After awhile he drank his rum, got off the stool and went to the door. He glanced back and saw Mag Kelly watching him. He lifted a hand, then went out. She had not smiled, had not answered his wave.

He went up to the hotel and stretched out on

the bed with a two-bit Western. He read until he was sleepy, then undressed and got into bed. At three a.m. he awakened and the town was still alive. He heard Zavatarri stirring around, heard a low woman's laugh. He went back to sleep.

At daybreak he rolled out and dressed, putting on a sweater. He was always in shape . . . he walked fast, avoiding the mud flat and taking the road down the coast. He trotted a hundred yards, walked fifty, sprinted fifty. When he had covered a couple of miles and felt good, he shadow-boxed a little, then stripped off his clothes and went into the sea.

It was a warm, milky sea. He swam for only a few minutes and then came in. He stretched out on a rock until his body was dry, then he dressed. While he was dressing he saw a house standing alone down the coast among some rocks. He was slipping on his shoes when he heard a step and turned. It was Mag Kelly.

Her hair was down to her shoulders this morning and she looked younger and softer. "You shouldn't swim in there," she warned, "there's sharks."

"I didn't see any."

"A boy was killed, just last week." She turned to go. "I didn't know who you were. I just wanted to warn whoever it was."

"What's the rush?"

She stopped and turned. "I'm getting breakfast." She started to go on, then stopped. "Have you eaten?"

He got up and hung his sweater around his shoulders, looping the arms in front. "Thanks," he said, "I don't mind if I do."

There was an old man sitting on the step with a shotgun. He looked up at Krag Moran and then at Mag Kelly. "This one all right?"

"This morning."

They went inside and Krag watched her. "What did that mean?" he asked abruptly.

"That's Hongkong. He takes me to work. He brings me home. I don't like to be bothered."

"Always with the shotgun?"

"In town it's a pistol."

Krag Moran had seen old men like that before. He had looked into the old man's eyes. He had a feeling the old man would kill him without a qualm.

Over breakfast they talked of books, of the town, of the sea. Then she said, "You're in trouble. Burman is good."

"So?"

"So you're not Johnny Coleman. So maybe even Johnny Coleman couldn't beat Burman. And his name isn't Burman. And some place, some time, he was very, very good."

"What makes you think I'm not Coleman?"

"You're not. I've seen him close enough to know you're not him; maybe a little in build. But you've got better shoulders."

"You haven't mentioned it?"

"Of course not. That's your cup of tea. But I'm not coming to the fight. I don't want to see what happens to you."

She was younger than he had believed, and her father had owned a plantation but had lost it when she was in her twenties. He had died when she was twenty-five. "Since then Hongkong's been with me. I take care of him, and he takes care of me."

"He looks like he could."

"He can."

She walked to the door with him and pointed out the path. He thought she lingered a little, and he knew he did not want to go. Finally, he did. When he looked back, she looked after him and waved.

Zavatarri came to his room. He looked worried and sat down on the bed. "Where you been?" His voice was impatient.

Moran stretched out on the bed and looked up at the ceiling. It was made of one by six boards with small spaces between. There was a peaked roof over that. Moran yawned, "I took a walk," he said, "a work-out."

Zavatarri was obviously relieved. He lit a cigar and smoked, talking at random. He kept coming back to the fight. "This guy is good," he said. "You sure you can take him?"

"You can always hedge your bets," Moran said quietly, "but remember: lay off my dough."

Later he went down to a restaurant for lunch and saw a half dozen rough-looking men sitting around. One of them said something, and the others laughed. One was a big man with a thick stomach and a beefy red face. "I could myself," he said. "He don't look so tough."

"Even his manager doesn't think so." The speaker was a little man with a crooked face. "He's bettin' on Burman."

When Moran finished eating he started out and

the red-faced man said, "Better take a good look,
he'll not be the same again."

Moran was behind him and he reached over and
clapped a hand over the man's face and jerked
back. The chair and man went over backward and
Moran stood waiting, his stand indolent but
ready. The red-faced man started to lunge up,
then thought the better of it.

Moran looked around. "Any time," he said, and
walked out.

He had a bad feeling about the town. The
stinking mud flat, the thrown together buildings,
the riff-raff . . . none of these was the matter.
The place just did not feel right. He went back
to the hotel and got his gun. He checked and it
was all right. He lay down on the bed and looked
up at the cracks. A lizard came through one of
them and angled down the wall. He threw a paper
wad at it and it scuttled indignantly away.

It was very hot . . . there was no breeze. He
wanted to swim but the sharks gave him something
to think about. He got up from the bed finally,
and slipped into his coat and walked outside. He
could hear the sound of hammers from the open
space beyond the town. They were throwing up a
ring there. There was a natural bowl where
spectators could sit around on the ground to
watch.

He walked that way but stopped some distance
off. He saw Zavatarri talking to Pete Salmi, who
was promoting the fight. He went back to town and
very thoughtfully looked around. Monk Burman had
followers all right, and most of the betting was
on him. He sat down on the steps of a saloon and
waited, watching the road down the coast. In a

little while he saw them coming, Mag Kelly and
the old man, Hongkong. She glanced at him but
said nothing until he spoke, getting to his feet.
"I want a man in my corner," he said, "an honest
man."

She nodded, "All right . . ." She walked on
inside.

He was sitting on his bed in the hotel when
there was a knock at the door. The man who came
in was thin and tall with lack-lustre eyes and a
cadaverous face. He wore a shirt outside his
slacks and he looked at Moran.

Then he closed the door and said, "You ain't
Coleman."

"Coleman draws more money than I would."

"To fight this guy you'll wish you were
Coleman."

"Who is he?"

The man shrugged. "Looks familiar, but I don't
know him." He held out a thin hand. "I'm Tilho.
Worked behind a few fighters."

"Seen him go?"

"Uh-huh. He's got it all. So much he shouldn't
be here. There's got to be something back of him
that ain't good. But that won't help you."

"How do they like it here?"

"Rough. Above the belt anything goes."

"All right with me." Moran sat up. "I'll give
you fifty bucks. If I win, a hundred bucks and
ten percent of my bets."

"You must figure you're bidding."

"Maybe," Krag said. "And they could go

stronger than I can. But I figure you're on the level."

Tilho got up. "You better." He started to the door, then stopped. "You better think about leavin', too. If you win," he said, "there'll be some who won't like it. You better also think about collectin'."

"Yeah," Moran agreed. "Thanks."

He had been thinking about both of those things. He had been thinking about them a lot. He did not like the feel of this town, and he had been in a lot of tough towns. He knew the tough streets in the tough towns. He knew Malay Street in Singapore, Blood Alley in Shanghai, Grant Road in Bombay and District Six in Cape Town. But he didn't like the feel of this place.

Zavatarri and Salmi were betting on Burman. They were betting heavy, and part of what Zavatarri was betting was from his part of the purse. "It better only be his part," Moran said, and went into the saloon where Mag was dealing.

After awhile she closed the game and came over for a drink. They sat there without talking until he said, "You like that place of yours?"

"Not much."

"How about this?" He glanced around.

"Not at all."

"All right." He turned on his stool. "Mag," he said, "I like you."

"I like you, too," she said softly.

There were not four or five thousand at the ringside, there were twice that many. Everybody

was there who could walk. This was probably the
only different bit of entertainment they would
see all year.

Krag Moran went down to the ring and alongside
the ropes. He took off his coat and folded it
carefully. He made sure which way the pocket
opened. He took off his shirt and folded it, then
his slacks. He wore his old blue trunks under the
slacks. He folded the slacks. The Colt .380 was
in his coat pocket.

He got into the ring. He moved around lightly,
getting the feel of the canvas. When the crowd
roared he knew why, and when he felt the jar of
the ring he knew his opponent was climbing in.
The referee called them for instructions and Krag
looked out from under his brows.

Kid Morowitz . . .

A tough Polack who came up from the wrong side
of the tracks, from the small clubs to a title
contender in two years. For three years he
whipped everybody in the light-heavy class until
he outgrew it. He had whipped the old champion
twice in over the weight matches, and he had
fought to a draw with Johnny Coleman.

He was sneering, powerful . . . thirty pounds
heavier than Moran and he grinned when they came
face to face. "You? Coleman?" He chuckled. "This
here's gonna be good."

Kid Morowitz, now Monk Burman. He was wanted
on a murder charge . . . a waterfront killing. He
had vanished after that, just dropped from sight.
But here he was.

Tilho took the towel from Moran's shoulders.
"That's Morowitz," Moran said, "the Kid himself."

"Yeah," Tilho said, "you take your time out there."

Tilho had not seemed surprised . . . Moran saw Mag Kelly in a ringside seat, old Hongkong beside her. Mag looked up and smiled. It was a sad smile.

The bell rang . . .

Krag Moran went out, taking his time. Burman tried a left and was short. Krag feinted but Burman ignored it. Moran feinted again and was surprised when Burman came all the way in. Burman's jab jarred on his forehead and a solid right clipped his chin. Moran felt the wicked jar of the blow clear to his heels. He worked around Burman, boxing carefully. The big mug could hit.

Burman came in, jabbed twice to the head, crossed a right that missed and took a smashing left to the ribs. Moran went inside, hooking short and hard to the body, then clinched. Burman was a bear in a clinch but Moran liked it rough. He always had. He pushed the bigger man, treading on his instep and trying to twist him. Burman broke away and stopped Moran's rush with a left to the head. The left came again and Moran went under it with a right to the heart, left to the ribs and a right to the ear. He broke away, and as Burman started in, stopped him in his tracks with a jarring jab that split Burman's lip and drew first blood. The bell rang and he walked back to his corner.

"All right," Tilho said, "you're moving."

"You know this guy."

Tilho looked down at Moran, touching the sweat from his face with a towel. "Yeah, I know him."

Moran walked right on in when the bell

sounded. He slipped a left jab and crossed a
right over the left. They went in close and
suddenly he was winging them in with both hands.
The attack surprised Burman. Toe-to-toe they
slammed it out for ten fast seconds and then
Moran broke ground suddenly and when Burman came
in, Moran nailed him with a right uppercut that
set him on his toes.

Burman was shaken. His eyes grew ugly and he
rushed Moran into the ropes where Moran side-
stepped fast trying the same stunt he had pulled
on Gomez. Burman turned swiftly, dropping at the
knees as he turned. Moran's blow missed and he
took a wicked punch into the belly. He backed up,
gasping, and Burman moved in, hitting him on the
chin with both hands. Moran fell and hit the
canvas, rolling over.

Moran took a count of six, then came up.
Burman moved in, tried a left which Moran pulled
away from, then Burman shot his right and Moran
slipped it, smashing his own right to the head.
Burman backed away, surprised.

"How d'you like it, Kid?" Moran said.

He felt Burman stiffen and he shoved him away
and in the instant of surprise, stabbed a hard
left to the puffed lips. Burman tried to clinch
again, and Moran said, "You dirty killer! I'm
takin' you back!" And he fell away to his left as
he spoke, one hand on Burman's shoulder, and then
he whipped a jolting right to Burman's chin.

Burman caught it turning and it shook him to
his heels. Moran hit him with one fist and then
the other and Burman went down. Moran backed off,
waited, and when Burman got

COMMENTS: Stylistically, I suspect that this slightly Hemingwayesque story is from the immediate postwar period, though there is no mention of WWII itself. However, it also has some crossover with a tale from Louis's life prior to WWII, a story about him getting into a boxing match with a very large, very tough guy in a Borneo oil camp. There is little evidence that proves the Borneo tale is true, but this story fragment has a few similarities to the various versions I have heard of it.

Dad was briefly in Panama in the 1920s, just long enough to soak up some of the atmosphere. I love the moment where the character "stretched out on the bed with a two-bit Western." I have always wondered if Dad had any inkling that he would be the guy writing those 25-cent Westerns within a few short years.

Louis emerging from a workout at
a mining camp locker room.

STAN DUVAL

The Beginning of a Crime Story

The big man walked to the empty stool beside
him. He probably weighed twenty pounds more than
two hundred, and his face was splotchy red.

Stan cupped his hand around the Bourbon and
soda. He could feel the big man staring at him in
the mirror. He was in no mood for trouble but he
could sense something building up in the man.

The big man ordered a drink and the bartender
put it on the bar in front of him, standing with
his hands on the edge of the bar, waiting for the
man to pay. The red faced man took a thick wad of
bills from his pocket, tossed one of them on the
bar without looking at it and stuffed the rest
back in his pants.

There was a girl down the bar who was on the
make. She was sitting with another woman who
looked like the girl would twenty years from now.
Probably her mother. He smiled to himself. The
girl looked like a chippie off the old block.

He avoided her eyes. In avoiding her eyes, he
caught the sardonic expression of the big man
beside him. There was something in those eyes
that made anger rise within him. He started to

speak, then took a drink of liquor and tried to forget about it. He was a stranger in town and about to start looking for work. Getting arrested in a bar would be a poor way to start.

"You're wasting time," the big man said suddenly. He had spoken without lifting his head. Neither did he turn. "If I were you, I'd light out."

"What do you mean?"

The big man was turning his glass in his fingers, and suddenly, Stan was afraid. This man was not trying to start trouble, that was his imagination. There was something else going on.

Lifting his glass to his lips the big man spoke softly. "Well, she's lying back there dead. There's sure to be somebody dropping by at some point. Then the cops will be looking for you."

"Are you nuts?" Stan stared at the big man in the mirror. He had a wide neck. His hands were thick fingered and heavy. He was a bruiser. In a brawl he would be hard to handle.

"Me? You're the one that's nuts. If I'd killed my wife I wouldn't be sitting here!"

Killed his wife?

Stan felt a chill of apprehension go over him, and his hands shut down hard on the bar. He glimpsed his face in the mirror and he looked pale.

Then it hit him. The man was insane. Stark mad. Stan forced a smile and shrugged. "I wouldn't either," he said, "but then I haven't killed anybody."

"You don't have to kid me," the big man said, "I ain't a bull. But the cops won't figure it that way. If I were you, I'd blow out of here, but _fast_!"

Stan was puzzled and angry. Who was this guy? Who did he think he was talking to? "Listen, chum," Stan said, "I don't know what your angle is, or who you're trying to kid, but I don't have a wife, never had a wife, and I wouldn't have killed her if I did!"

The man hunched his big shoulders and leaned his elbows on the bar. He was one of the most powerful men Stan had ever seen. "Isn't your name Duval?" the big man asked. "Henry Stanley Duval? Weren't you in Klamath Falls for awhile?"

Stan felt the tightness go out of him. He felt at that moment much as he did before a close shot at a tiger. The cold sense of awareness, the instant of waiting before the big head shoved through the bushes, the knowledge that one shot would be all he might get. His muscles and his mind relaxed and he felt wariness creeping over him with a faint, remote chill.

He spoke, and his voice was quiet, very calm. "Yes, my name is Duval. I have been in Klamath Falls. I am a man who has been many places. But I am not married, I never have been, and I know no one in this town."

"Nobody but her, and she's dead. You better blow, bud. I ain't a squealer. Nobody else knows so far."

"But _you_ know," Stan suggested. "How do you know? Maybe you killed this woman you say is my wife?"

"Me?" The big man chuckled. "I liked Madge. She was a good kid, only maybe she had too many friends. But don't get any ideas. I got an alibi. I got a honey of an alibi. How's yours?"

Alibi? He didn't have the shadow of an alibi. An hour before he had come into town with a man in a Buick sedan. The man's name was Gardiner. He had dropped Stan off at the bar and told him he would meet him there in an hour or so and they would have dinner together.

Madge?

The name struck fire in his brain. Madge? Klamath Falls? He took a swallow of liquor, then said without turning his head, "This supposed wife of mine. What was she like?"

"Hell, you should know. A honey of a blonde. Tall, willowy babe, with a little scar on her ear lobe.

"Don't get me wrong," the big man was saying, "I don't blame you. You guys come back from overseas and find your wives playing around. Hell, I wouldn't blame you."

Stan wasn't listening. Madge. That would be Madge McClean, but his wife? Why, he had known her for no more than a week. They had dinner, he recalled. She was a dancer and singer, and pretty good . . . well, pretty good for Portland.

She had been going up Morrison Street tucking some things in her bag. As she passed him she dropped her coin purse. He had to follow her two blocks and through two traffic signals before he could catch her to return it.

They had talked a little, had a drink together, and then dinner.

It was one of those cases of two lonely people, mutually attracted. He had some business in Klamath Falls, and by that time they were

liking each other quite a bit. She knew who he
was, had read all three of his travel books, and
he liked her. They had decided to make it a
twosome.

They had registered at a hotel there . . . it
hit him right in the wind . . . as man and wife.

Stan Duval took another drink and stared at
the big man's reflection. "I don't get it," he
said, and his voice was suddenly hoarse. "What's
your angle?"

The big man shoved back off the stool. "Hey,"
he said, "I'm just a friendly guy. Always doin'
things for people! My name's Fin Campo, if you
want to know. I just hate to see a good guy in a
bad spot. And brother you're in one!"

Campo turned and went out. Stan sat there,
staring at his drink. It didn't make sense, none
of it did. He hadn't seen Madge McClean in four
years . . . almost five. Before he went into the
Army. Nor had he heard from her in all that time.

The whole thing was insane. He was married to
no one, and had never been married. How had Campo
found him in that bar? Who was Fin Campo? And
what, he wondered suddenly, had become of
Gardiner?

If there was anything to this he was going to
need Gardiner. Gardiner could prove when he got
to Los Angeles, where he had been until he walked
into the bar.

Stan got up suddenly. The telephone directory
gave Madge McClean's address as 2203 Parkington
Row and the map in back showed it to be close by,
a stiff twenty minute walk . . . shorter if he
could get a ride.

"Listen," he said to the bartender, "if a

small man with a broken nose comes in here asking
for Duval, tell him I'll be back in about an
hour."

He walked out into the street, his mind
suddenly made up. No matter what happened, he
must know. He saw a cab and flagged it down.
"Twenty Two O Three Parkington Row," he said, and
sat back in the seat, staring ahead of him.

It didn't make sense no matter how you looked
at it. He had returned from overseas two months
before. He had gone through the war, and then
because of his experience they had asked him to
stay on. Having made some good friends, he
volunteered to remain one more year.

When he got back he was tired of everything.
He wanted some time to adjust himself, to relax,
think, and make plans for the future. Before the
war he had been an explorer, hunter, and
professional wanderer who wrote books of his
travels and lectured.

A friend in New York had a car he wanted to
sell so Stan bought it and started west. He was
in no hurry. He had stopped many times, wrote a
little, camped out here and there. In San Diego
he sold the car, and while trying to make up his
mind on the next move, dropped into a bar.

That was where he met Gardiner. They were
sitting side by side, and started talking. When
Stan mentioned his name, Gardiner was immediately
interested. They had talked and Gardiner had told
him he knew just the man he should see in Los
Angeles, somebody who wanted some jungle films
made. The plan was to head north by the end of
the week; it had seemed like an opportunity to
restart his life.

———

The cab rolled up in front of the door and he got out. All the lights were on in the house and a police car stood at the curb.

"Looks like the joint's been raided!" the cabbie said.

He paid the man off and started up the walk. Four men were standing in the front room, looking at the body of a girl.

Stan stared down at her. Her golden and beautiful hair lay around her head like a halo, a halo stained at the top with blood. There was a widening pool of it on the carpet and floor.

They looked up when he entered. There was a tall, very lean man with sandy hair and a sad face. "Who are you?" he asked.

"My name is Stanley Duval."

"Duval?" The sandy haired man smiled. "You're her husband, then?"

"No," he said. "I'm not."

"I'm Lieutenant Haynes," the officer said. "Let's get this straight. You say you aren't her husband? She's listed as Mrs. Stanley Duval?"

"There's a mistake somewhere. Her name is not Duval, and I am not married to anyone and never have been."

A plain clothes man with a beefy face and small mustache smiled cynically. "I suppose next thing you'll be saying you didn't know her!"

"Oh, no," Stan said. "I knew her all right. I met her about five years ago in Oregon, but her name was McClean, not Duval. We saw a good deal of each other for about a week, and I haven't seen her since."

Haynes shook out a smoke, then handed the pack around. He studied the girl thoughtfully. "You say you haven't seen her in all that time? Then how do you account for this?"

In his hands he held a letter, which he showed to Stan. It was addressed to Stan Duval, General Delivery, San Diego. It was a letter he had picked up at the post office the day before. He controlled the urge to check the pocket in which he had placed the letter . . . that would be the action of a guilty man.

Fear came to him then, a cold fear that crept up his legs and left him standing in an icy chill. "I don't account for it," he said, "I can't account for it. You found that . . . here?"

Haynes was looking at him through the cigarette smoke. "Yeah. Right over there by the divan."

"You say," the other plain clothes man said, "you weren't married to her. Here's a rental receipt made out to Mrs. Stanley Duval. She's been paying rent under that name for two months."

"How did you know this address if you haven't seen her in five years?" Haynes was speaking in a conversational tone, quiet, almost lazy. "How'd you happen to come here tonight?"

"Why, there was a man in a bar gave it to me. A fellow named Campo. He said a woman with my name was murdered here."

"My God! I've heard some yarns in my time. How'd this guy know you?"

"I don't know." Stan's mouth was dry and he felt empty in the pit of his stomach. "He just came in and sat down beside me and started talking, said this girl was murdered and that I'd better get out of town."

"In spite of this letter you say you haven't seen this girl in five years?"

"That's right. I just got in town tonight. Came up from San Diego."

"How'd you come? Plane or train?"

"Neither. I rode up with an acquaintance. A fellow I met in San Diego."

"Oh, where's this guy now?"

"I don't know. He was coming back to meet me in the bar where I met Campo. But after I talked with Campo I thought I'd run out here and try to find out what this was all about. He may be there now. His name was Gardiner."

"In other words," Haynes said, "you've no alibi for the time of the murder?"

"No," Duval said, "I've no alibi. I'd no idea I was going to need one. This girl," he added, "was just an acquaintance. She was okay, a pretty nice kid, but except for one week I never knew anything about her."

"That," Haynes said, "is the thinnest yarn I ever heard. You understand," he glanced up at Duval, "I'm not saying it isn't true, but without doubt it is the worst yarn I ever heard anybody tell. You say you haven't seen her in five years, but there's a letter of yours on the floor. A letter that from the date must have been dropped here tonight or yesterday.

"You say you got her address from a guy in a bar who told you she was murdered. Hell, man, we hadn't been here over three minutes when you got here. How could anybody know? We found the body."

"Maybe this guy Campo killed her."

Haynes rubbed his chin. "Duval, you don't know what you're saying. I haven't a doubt you met Campo in a bar. He spends a lot of time in bars. But him telling you anything like this . . . it's just plain goofy."

"You know him?"

"He's a special investigator for the District Attorney. Not much goes on in town that he doesn't know. I might add that he's got enough political pull to make it felt anywhere."

Haynes looked around at the other plain clothes man. "Potter, see what's wrong with the medical examiner. He should be here by now!"

"The car's just pulling up, Lieutenant. He'll be right in."

Two men walked through the open door. One of them had a black bag. He knelt over the body, and Haynes leaned over to watch. The policemen were craning their necks and Potter had stepped into the next room.

It was a moment, a fleeting instant that might never come again. Stan Duval turned and walked quietly from the room.

His heart was jumping and his mouth was dry. When he got to the door he stepped out on the porch, then off onto the lawn, and walking across it, leaped the hedge into the next yard. He was going through the gate into the alley when he heard a yell from the house.

He started running. He was frightened now, frightened as he never had been. Running on his toes, he made the end of the alley, his heart pounding. A siren started somewhere behind him, and he walked across the street, forcing himself to walk, then sprinted another block.

Stan came out on the street. Ahead of him and on the corner was a drug store, and beyond it, as he turned the corner, was a neighborhood theatre. It was a large theatre, and several people were buying tickets. Coolly, forcing himself to be calm, he stepped into line.

The siren was whining behind him, and he could hear it turning a corner, then stop. They would be flashing their spotlight down the alleys. He got his ticket and walked into the theatre.

He had no more than a few minutes at best, and no plan of action. They might not think of the theatre; it would seem a trap. Maybe it was. He went into the men's room and glanced at himself in the mirror. His face looked white. Turning, he walked out. The usherette had stepped inside the curtains to watch the picture; the lobby was empty. Directly opposite him was a huge Chinese vase, over six feet high. There was one on either side of the lobby.

Stan started for one, and then he saw the girl. She was watching him, but when their eyes met, she looked away. Her figure was trim, neat and her eyes beautiful. She walked toward the curtains.

There was an overstuffed chair near the vase. Putting one foot on the back, he caught the top and pulling himself up, dropped lightly inside. Then, his heart pounding, he sat down.

His heart was throbbing painfully and he was perspiring profusely. Sitting still, scarcely daring to breathe, he waited. It was late. Within an hour and a half the theatre would close. He would be safe. He would have a long night before him to plan.

Then he heard the voice. It was so soft he scarcely heard it, but it was unmistakable. "Why did you get in there?"

A woman. It must have been the girl who had been watching him. "I'm powdering my nose," she whispered then. "Even if anyone sees me they won't guess about you. Why did you get in there?"

It sounded silly, but he whispered back, "I'm hiding." He hesitated. Oh, well. She knew he was here. "From the police," he said.

"That siren was for you? I saw you buying a ticket. What did you do?"

"They think I killed my wife. I'm not even married. I got away."

There was silence, and he could almost hear the girl thinking. Who was she? Why hadn't she reported him at once?

"Better stay here all night," she said.

He heard her moving away, and he could hear voices from the outer foyer, from the snack bar. Footsteps approached again, and he could hear her humming. Then her voice. "Catch."

Stan glanced up. Two candy bars came over the top. He caught them deftly, then heard her moving away.

He put the candy in his pocket, suddenly aware that he was hungry. Next time he ran away from the police, he told himself, he would wait until after dinner.

Time dragged slowly. The bottom of the vase was just large enough for him to sit with his knees against his chest. There was no room to stretch his legs, and he dare not stand up for fear someone would hear him.

The girl puzzled him. Why her interest?

His flight had been instinctive. Considering the plight he was in it had seemed the only obvious course. Haynes could not be blamed. His story was absurd. It was absurd, and it was the truth, all of it.

What _was_ it all about? Thinking back over it, he began to realize that his involvement had not been due to accident nor to a coincidence.

A lot of things began to click into place. The letter was the key to it all. He had received that letter in San Diego. He had put it in his pocket to be answered the next day. Then he met Gardiner, and decided to take a chance on the jungle film deal. In any event, he had planned on going to L.A.

The last he had seen of the letter was when he put it in his pocket. Had his coat been off since? No. Therefore, if the letter left him, and it had, it had to be taken from his pocket while the coat was on him. That necessitated opportunity. Who had the opportunity?

Gardiner. Stan remembered then that he had fallen asleep several times on the trip north from San Diego. But that meant that Gardiner was involved.

Well, why not? Campo had come into the bar while Duval waited for Gardiner. Could Gardiner have sent Campo there? How else could Campo have known?

But what was behind it? _Why?_

Why had Madge been killed? Why was she using his name? Who had killed her?

He remembered how struck Gardiner had been when he heard his name. Stan had merely believed

he was another man who had read his books; now it
seemed to mean something else. Somehow, or some
way Gardiner had known something about him, or
about Madge. Perhaps Gardiner was the murderer.
Possibly he had been planning the crime even
then, when suddenly a scapegoat was offered in
the person of Stanley Duval!

A coincidence, but it still didn't make sense.
He was satisfied with his solution of his own
involvement. Gardiner could have lifted the
letter from his pocket, got in touch with Campo,
who was somehow involved, and arranged the whole
setup.

The show was ending and he could hear people
leaving. Somebody tossed a gum wrapper into the
vase. Bit by bit people drifted out of the show,
and he could hear their comments on the picture.

"I thought he was simply _wonderful_! Don't you
like his _voice_, though? It just _does_ something to
you!"

Then another voice, close beside the vase.
"Listen, Ruth, it's early yet. Let's go up to my
place for awhile?"

"George, I've told you that I'll never--
besides, Andy's home."

They drifted out, and silence settled. Then he
heard a rattle of brooms. "Let's get it over
with," somebody said, "I want to get home. My
kid's sick."

"Yeah? What's the trouble?"

"I don't know, the Doc says . . ." The voice
dwindled.

They moved away and Stan let himself relax. He
waited, his legs asleep. Finally, he heard them

leave. By the luminous dial of his wrist watch he waited a half hour longer. Then he got to his feet, straightening his cramped legs. He chafed them, rubbing the circulation back into action. Then he reached up and catching the top of the vase, pulled himself up.

Waiting an instant for correct balance, he dropped to the chair, and then the floor.

All was dark and still. Through the doors he could see the street. A police car stood by the corner. The drug store was still open. No, it was closing. The reflected light snapped out, and then he heard voices. Two policemen got into their car, but they just sat there and did not go away.

Stan sat down in the chair and took out a bar of candy. He couldn't remember ever being so hungry before.

Under the wrapper was a white card with a name--Judith Baird Kegley Apts. On the back was the note.

If before 8 a.m. or after 5:30 p.m. come.

He ate the candy thoughtfully. Why the devil was she helping him? Or willing to help? Who was she?

Undoubtedly the police would be patrolling the area. The prowl car in front of the theatre was an example. They had lost him near here, and they would be watching closely. In any event, he would find a better place to hide. The vase was too dangerous.

Going down the side aisle he walked through the vast and empty theatre. All was pitch dark

here, the light from outside killed by the thick,
velvet curtains.

Striking matches, he found his way backstage.
There was a small backstage office, probably used
now by the janitor. In the office, he prowled,
striking many matches, but putting the stubs in
his pocket. In one drawer he found a flashlight.

If he left the theatre now, and he was sure he
could leave through one of the exits used for
fire or emergencies, he would be on the streets
in a section of town where anybody might be
questioned . . . after all there had been a
murder nearby.

His best chance was to wait until morning, and
to mingle with people on their way to work. Money
was no handicap. He had nearly three hundred
dollars in his pockets. That should be sufficient
for any immediate purposes.

Stan got up and, using the flashlight
sparingly, he made a careful reconnaissance of
the theatre. The door of the manager's office was
unlocked, and he stepped inside and looked
around. Seeing a knob in a panel, he turned it
and found another door. It was a small closet
with a wash basin and mirror, and . . . an
electric razor!

When he had the plan of the theatre clearly in
mind he chose a loge seat and sat down, leaning
back, and went to sleep. He was not worried about
sleeping too late. He had always been able to
awaken when he wished.

Yet it was after six when he opened his eyes
again. He got to his feet and for five minutes by
the watch, listened for any sound. Assured that
no one had yet entered the theatre, he went to

the manager's office, shaved, washed and combed his hair.

Replacing the flashlight he went to a ground floor exit and pushed down on the handle. It opened easily, and holding it open a crack, he studied the situation. The exit opened on an alley. Opposite the theatre was a market. A truck was backed up, unloading boxes and crates. It was a new truck, still bright and without dust.

When the driver had a load in his arms and turned toward the market, Stan Duval opened the door and stepped out. He walked over to the truck and was standing there, admiring it, when the driver came out of the market.

Stan grinned at him. "That's a slick looking rig you've got there!"

"Yeah," the driver was in his twenties, "she sure is. Better'n the one I been driving."

"You in the service?"

"Sure was. Infantry. How about you?"

"Tank Destroyers. It was just about as bad."

"Yeah." The fellow wiped the sweat from his brow. "What you doing now?" he asked, looking curiously at Stan's tailored suit.

"Thinking about buying me a couple of trucks. That's why I was looking."

The driver glanced at the remaining cases. "Stick around until I get those last cases off and I'll drive you where you're going. You can see for yourself how she is."

"I'd like that! Okay, I'll wait."

The driver came out and they got in. Stan commented on the cushions. "Pretty nice, all right," the boy said. "Softer than those G.I. trucks!"

He swung the truck around and slowed at the alley entrance, then seeing the way clear, pulled out. A prowl car was standing at the corner, facing them. Stan looked straight ahead, making conversation.

"Which way you headed?"

"Going down to Spring," he said, "Seventh and Spring or anywhere close to it."

When he got there, the kid dropped him off. "Thanks!" he called, then he walked over to a newsboy and bought two papers. He started up the street. "I hope," he told himself softly, "they don't have a picture!"

Stopping in a small café he sat at the counter and opened the papers. They had a picture, all right. He should have known they would. After all, before the war he had been a sort of minor celebrity.

It was not a good picture. It was undoubtedly the worst ever made of him. A newspaper photographer had snapped the photo when he was returning from Guatemala and recovering from a hard bout of malaria.

He ordered coffee and a sandwich, and then looked at the headline. It was a jolt.

EXPLORER FLEES MURDER SCENE

Henry Stanley Duval, noted explorer and author of three books on his adventures, is the object of a statewide search today. Duval is wanted for questioning in regard to the murder of a woman alleged to be his wife.

COMMENTS: Here we have a fragment of a crime story written for the postwar pulp magazines. It's a classic concept, a regular in noir fiction: a man caught between two unforgiving forces—a criminal conspiracy and the relentless and impersonal process of law enforcement. He must escape the law and confront the criminals to clear his name.

Below are some of Louis's notes. These were created prior to the story fragment above in an attempt to work out the plot. Typical of a healthy writing process, Louis's manuscript did not stick exactly to the plan. In my opinion, the critical juncture in any story comes when what you are writing begins to diverge from what you intended. Those differences can, of course, stop a story in its tracks (as, perhaps, it did with this one), but it can also be where the magic happens. It's where the elements of the story take on a life of their own and lead the author through the process.

Later in his career, Louis learned to forgo the planning to a great extent and dwell more and more in that magic creative zone. Though *Louis L'Amour's Lost Treasures Volumes 1* and *2* document the times he did not immediately succeed, the Lost Treasures materials that we have added as "Bonus Feature" postscripts to many of Louis's completed and long-reprinted novels are testament to the fact that he was able to pull off that combination of skill and minor miracle more often than just about anyone.

CAST OF CHARACTERS:

Stan Duval--ex soldier and explorer.
Judy Baird--secretary to Pres. of Culloden
    Airlines.

Madge McClean--casual girlfriend of Duval.
Cord Becker--multimillionaire inventor and
    manufacturer.
Gardiner--racketeer and crook.
Fin Campo--spec. inv. for D.A. and in pay of
    Becker.
Donna Gregg--show girl friend of Madge.
Sam Gaynor--inventor, murdered before story
    begins.

Stan Duval returns from overseas. He is
tired, and wants to relax. Also, he just
wants to get around the country a little.

He goes west to San Diego and . . . one
night comes into a club and [meets] Gardiner
[who] tells him about heading to L.A. He
himself is going to Reno . . . would Duval
like to ride to L.A. with him? Duval would.
The journey up is leisurely. Twice Gardiner
turns off the road to look at pieces of
property.

They arrive in L.A. at night and Gardiner
lets him off near a bar. He is there when a
big man who calls himself Fin Campo tells
him he had better leave town as the police
will be wanting him for murdering his wife.

He has no wife. The man mentioned her
name, Madge Darnal [also referred to as
Madge McClean], and he places her as a girl
he once knew and liked, and once spent a
night with in a hotel, registered as man and
wife.

He has not seen the girl in five years.
He goes to the address Campo gives him, and
finds the police making an investigation. He

denies being married to Madge, denies killing her, denies ever having been in the house before.

The detective shows him a letter, addressed to him, with a date only two days earlier. They had found it on the floor.

Also, a neighbor woman declares she has seen him coming and going, declares she heard a conversation in which his wife said "Oh no, Stan, wouldn't . . . !" And "But, Stan!"

Madge has been killed by a blow on the head with a water pitcher. She has been dead for about an hour. No fingerprints are on the pitcher except those of Madge.

Several men had been seen coming and going to the apartment.

-- Stan finds himself faced with these facts!
- He has no alibi.
- The letter and the testimony of the woman next door place him at the scene of the crime at the right time.
- The letter proves to the police he is a liar.
- The motive: jealousy.
- The girl had been passing herself off as Mrs. Stan Duval.
- Records prove they were registered that way at a hotel in 1941.
- He says he was given the address by Campo.
- Campo when found denies it.

- No Gardiner can be found in Reno or
  elsewhere.
- Record of a marriage is found in
  Stentora, Arizona.

While the police are occupied, he walks
out. He escapes after quite a chase,
registers in a small hotel, and tries to
figure something out.

- Why should Madge be killed?
- Why involve him?
- How about the marriage?

It becomes obvious that he is the victim of an
elaborate and carefully worked out plot.

- Yet why was Madge using his name?
- How did the letter get to her floor?

Obviously, Gardiner must be involved. How
else could the letter have gotten there? A
letter that was in his pocket when he left
San Diego. How could Campo have known where
to find him? Yet why? What was behind it
all?

Madge, he discovers, was one of three
nieces of Bernard Thornton, millionaire
impostor. There is also a nephew. He also
learns that Madge had been blind for three
years.

Elsie, one of the nieces, had been killed
in an auto wreck a year previously.

Another niece is married to Roderick Howard, owner of a large Funeral Home.

The key to the problem lies in a conversation Madge Darnal had with Stan on the weekend in Klamath Falls.

It was a chance remark, a remark that returns to him and enables him to find the solution to the crime.

Stan discovers that Madge had drastically changed her way of living in the past two years, living in seclusion and moving often.

He decides she was afraid of something. Yet, of what? The origin of the fear seems to begin with his meeting with her. Could it have been something he said? Something she learned while with him?

He wonders: why does one kill? What are the motives for murder? He decides: for wealth, for love, for protection.

He believes he can eliminate love as there is no evidence of it.

Therefore the killer must have killed for wealth or for protection.

Madge had no wealth. She was an heiress to no fortune.

Therefore, the killer must have killed for protection.

Protection from what?

Madge was making no effort to harm anyone. She herself seemed in fear.

Hence, the killer must have been afraid of something she <u>knew</u>.

What did Madge know?

The answer would lie in Madge Darnal's past life.

He had met her in Portland. She had seemed willing and anxious to leave Portland. Therefore the answer might lie in Portland.

What had she been doing there?

He remembered her saying something about being a bridesmaid at a wedding.

Had the killer committed a previous crime? One that would warrant murder to prevent its being known?

That would seem to imply two possibilities. Either the previous crime had also been murder or the killer now held such a position that his previous crime being known would cause disgrace and ruin him.

That held that either the crime had been murder, or the position held was a good one.

The solution lies in the past life of Madge Darnal. He has little time and few resources. Perhaps the solution lay in his own subconscious.

He and Madge had talked. What had they talked about? In intimate moments women talk of many things close to them. They had been together for days. He remembered her eagerness to leave Portland. He recalled one occasion when she showed fright while they were in Klamath Falls. What was that occasion?

. . . He must dig out every memory, write all he could think of on paper and try to reconstruct those past hours. Where had they gone? What had they done?

He remembered then her reluctance to

leave him. How she had clung to him at the last moment. Love, or fear?

She knew something, became aware about the time he met her that her knowledge was dangerous, and stayed with him for protection.

Then he remembers a girl she knew. A girl who had once worked in a show with her. The girl's home was in Whittier. He finds she is working in a night club.

She tells him that Madge often spoke of him with affection. That he apparently was the one man in her life. That she had loved him. He discovers Madge had moved frequently, had used other names, finally his name.

Had Madge ever expressed fear of anyone or anything?

No, but she had seemed frightened. She hated to stay alone. She often moved. She patronized various stores in different parts of town. She watched closely for any mention of Stan's name, wanting to find him again.

Had they [the women] been together in San Francisco? Yes. Why had they left? A sudden notion of Madge's. They had been at the Top o' the Mark, came down in the elevator, and she bought a paper. Something in the paper seemed to disturb her.

What day? She didn't know. What paper? She didn't recall. On an inside page? Yes. The month? August. The week, perhaps the first week of August.

He delves into the papers, searching for a clue. He finds one. He returns to Madge's

friend to ask more questions. She is dead.
She has been murdered.

What next?

He will be murdered.

He has no clue.

Something in the papers? What?

What could suddenly make her wish to
leave town? All had been well. Only one of
two things, probably: that the police had
started investigating something in which she
was implicated, or someone had come to town
of whom she was frightened.

If it was mentioned in the papers, it
meant the man was of some importance.

He has a feeling the police are closing
in on him now. All right. He must find and
lead them to the real criminal. He must
force him to act, force him to fear, force
him to disclose himself. The . . . murder
was evidence that he was becoming
desperate . . .

Suddenly, Stan realizes something. The
killer would no longer want him captured!

The killer would want him free! He would
be afraid of what Stan might have learned.
Therefore there was a chance that he might
aid Stan to escape and therefore disclose
himself!

Yet, that meant Stan must put himself in
the killer's hands!

When on their trip they had stopped all
night with a friend in his home near Ashland
[Oregon]. When they entered, Madge had two
bags, and when she left, but one!

He must contact his friend. Find out if that bag still existed. He starts north. Discovers he is being followed. Tries to lose his pursuer, and fails. He recalls a small hamburger place, and stops there to eat. A car pulls up and two men come in. One is Fin Campo, the other Gardiner. One sits on each side of him.

When he finishes eating, they try to take him out with them. He refuses to go. Succeeds in throwing Gardiner, then slugs it out with Campo. He rushes out, a third man fires at him but he escapes.

He gets to his friend, finds the bag, and learns that Madge had mailed a package [to the friend] only a week before! The package is addressed on the inside, to him. It is a diary . . .

In the diary he finds a report of Madge dating a man. A man named Cord Becker.

<u>Cord Becker!</u> The inventor, the manufacturer! He reads on.

They had played cards one night with a man named Sam Gaynor. He and Becker had talked for a long time, and later she had met Gaynor on the street, and he had seemed worried, had asked her many questions about Becker, his honesty, how long she had known him.

Then there had been a boating accident and Gaynor had drowned.

Shortly thereafter, Becker patented some new process and began building a fortune based on that process.

She had unwittingly mentioned to him that
she had a long talk with Gaynor, his
[Becker's] manner had seemed very
strange . . . he had pried into her
conversation, finding out enough to become
suspicious. Then putting two and two
together, he had decided she knew more than
she told. Then she had become frightened,
and left.

Stan, through a private detective friend,
digs into Becker's and Gaynor's past. He
discovers that Gaynor had been working on
these processes for a long time, that he had
come to Portland to secure capital. There
was no record of previous experimentation on
Becker's part.

Stan goes to the former district attorney
in Portland. He talks to him of Becker and
arouses his interest.

He explains he is wanted, does not tell
his name, begins the discussion of the case.

You can tell from the scattered nature of these notes that
Louis was putting every idea forward that might help him
work out the mystery and therefore the plot. At some point
Dad began a less bewildering outline:

Duval is deliberately involved in a plot
to cover the murder of Madge McClean, a girl
who had once used his name. In struggling to
clear himself, he escapes from the police,
enlists the aid of Judy Baird, and begins
investigating Madge's background. He
discovers she knew of an invention by one

Sam Gaynor. That Gaynor had been murdered
and Becker patented the discovery.

Donna Gregg is also murdered to prevent
her talking. Duval recovers bag and diary,
but is slugged and the bag taken away. He
retains the diary.

Gardiner, in San Diego, encounters Duval
and calls Campo who directs him to bring
Duval to L.A. The crime has been decided
upon, and with Duval in L.A. the time has
come. Not only can they rid themselves of
Madge, but have a made to order suspect!

Duval meets Judy in the theatre.

Unfortunately, my father never went further with this
second set of notes, which might have given us a simpler
overview of his concept for the story. You can see, however,
that it was becoming more streamlined and easier to tell . . .
all part of the process of working through the details.

Within this story fragment there are a number of slight
references to places and events in Louis's earlier life. Dad
had lived in Portland, Oregon, for a couple of years and in
Klamath Falls before that. While there he visited Ashland
on a number of occasions.

Dad served in the Tank Destroyers stateside until the
combination of his age (too old, at thirty-four, to begin
combat duty) and his unit's deployment forced a reassign-
ment to the Transportation Corps. While in the Transportation Corps and managing cargoes for the Army in the
Bay Area, Dad was billeted at the Mark Hopkins Hotel . . .
where there is a penthouse restaurant and cocktail lounge
by the name of Top of the Mark.

During his getaway, Stan talks to a young truck driver
who is a war vet, and they commiserate about how hard-
riding G.I. trucks were. Louis had ended up as a lieutenant

in a Quartermaster Truck Company delivering tank and aviation fuel all over France, Holland, and Germany. Most of the time he was lucky enough to have a jeep and driver, but he knew all too well the fatigue driving a heavy-duty truck could cause.

LOWIE

The Beginning of a Western Story

The tunnel belched and their candles went out
and in the darkness there was a smell of dust.

A heavy, cushiony sigh went through the
mountain and with it a sound like a fat man
sinking into a deep leather chair, only vastly
greater.

Sand trickled . . . somewhere pebbles rattled
briefly, and then the sounds dwindled and died.
Nobody stirred, their minds suspended in
blackness, transfixed by the awfulness of what
had happened, beyond the need of words, knowing
the mountain had trapped them.

In the same instant of realization and shock
came the knowledge that it was probable they
would never, could never escape. They were beyond
help except what they could give themselves.
Nobody, anywhere, knew where they were. Very
likely nobody cared. They were sealed here, to
die of suffocation, unless they could make their
own escape, find their own way out. Inexperienced
as one or two of them were, they knew the fall
had been great, that it had been no minor
cave-in, easily dug through and shored up.

"Anybody hurt?" Lowie asked. In the stillness that followed the collapse of the drift the sound of his voice was flatly casual, conversational.

There was no reply until Dud said quietly, "And nobody even knows we're here."

"Scared?" Skinner's voice held a faint uncertain sneer.

"If he's scared I wouldn't know," Lowie said, "but I am."

They had been wary of this, knowing their danger. Never before had all four entered the drift at one time. Working two to the shift had the advantage of keeping Dud and Skinner apart, but it also meant there were always two men outside to start rescue operations in case anything happened. Yet this morning they had all entered to discuss a change of direction to trying to cut into the vein of the old Spanish working, a tunnel that entered the mountain from the south. As if the mountain had waited for just this moment, the hanging wall had caved and they were sealed in, trapped.

"You all right, Charlie?" Lowie asked.

"Uh-huh. Has anybody got any water?"

"I filled the olla," Lowie said, "and my canteen is with me."

The nearest white man was sixty miles away and knew nothing of their presence here. They were in Apache country, the location of their claim a carefully guarded secret. If they escaped it must be by their own efforts.

Skinner shifted his feet. "Maybe we're wrong. Maybe it only caved a few feet. Maybe only eight or ten. It wouldn't take us long to cut through that."

"Sounded like the whole mountain came down," Charlie said, "but the drift is holding here, so it's not that bad."

"That was bad ground," Dud said. "There was twenty feet of tunnel we had to shore up with plank an' timber, remember? That was all loose ground, above there. But when we used that timbering I thought we had it whipped."

"Nobody ever whips a mountain," Charlie said. "Those Spanish couldn't whip it. We found some outside, an' you can bet some were trapped inside."

It was Lowie who brought them here. He heard a rumor of the old Spanish mine from a friendly Indian. He had traced the rumors, searched out the old Spanish trail on several careful forays into Apache country, and he had found proof of the mine's existence.

Lowie was twenty-two but had lived his life in the West, while Dud and Skinner were in their late twenties and Charlie was forty or more. They had pooled their efforts and come on in, taking a risk, for Cochise was on the warpath and all this country was covered from time to time with Indians. Yet the canyon was lonely and their camp carefully concealed. Only twice had they seen Indians, and none close by.

"No use to sit here and die," Dud said, "I'm starting to work."

"Go ahead." Charlie struck a light to the candle which had gone out when the air belched. "I'll spell you."

"It's going to be tough with that loose ground caving all the time," Lowie said, "but might as well get started. I'm going up to the face."

"What's up there?" Skinner wanted to know.

"Maybe nothing. But I've a hunch we're not far from the spot the Spanish were working, the one with the open drift. If we could cut to it, we might have an easy way out."

Dud moved to the muckpile, shovel in hand. He looked at it, then stooped, the candle throwing a colossal shadow of him on the rock wall.

Dud was a big man, wide of face and of shoulder. Impatient of restraint, he had a flaring temper and a quick fist. Skinner, whom he had chosen for enemy, was slim, saturnine and bitter. The two had begun snarling at each other on the first day of travel. Skinner had the reputation of having killed two men, and Dud was known to be quarrelsome. Not the men to be chosen for such a trip, but there was little possibility of choice. Men who would venture into Apache country were few, and quarrelsome as the two might be, they were equally fearless, and had proved hard workers.

The ore had been rich. The few samples they collected carefully from the old Spanish working had proved that, yet that drift was a death-trap to be avoided. Hence they started their own attempt to penetrate to the vein, and had almost reached it when trapped. Yet they had already gathered some gold. The creek had shown some placer gold, and they had each taken a turn at the pan, with some luck. If they had to abandon the larger prospect, they would at least have a stake.

Dud bent his back and began to move dirt. Taking his time not to foul the air with dust, he worked steadily. Yet each time he moved his shovel, the sand-like soil slid down to fill the space. Lowie scowled at the sand and then turned away and with his own candle walked to the face of the drift.

He was a tall young man with broad shoulders and a lean body. At six feet two inches he weighed only one hundred and sixty, but hours and days and months of using a single-jack and drill had packed beef into his shoulders. He tapped the wall and it gave off with a flat, hard, unrewarding sound. He tried the side walls and the hanging wall with the same result.

Thinking, it seemed to him that the old Spanish tunnel had come this way, and their own drift had trended a bit south. Hence, the two might be separated by only a few feet. Yet it was all guess-work, and they might work their hearts out only to find it useless--and the short time they had left was regulated by the supply of air.

He thought again of that sliding sand. It was peculiar, here in the heart of a mountain, to find loose sand. By rights the pressure should have packed it to sandstone by now. Unless there was no pressure, and that meant an open space above. Yet, supposing such an open space existed, how much sand was there? It might be more than enough to fill their drift before they could break through. Yet it was a chance.

Would they ever see sunlight again? Or drink cold water? Hear the birds singing? Lowie got restlessly to his feet and walked back to the others. Skinner was working now, and he was working steadily, carefully. His shirt was off and sweat and dust coated his body. There was fine dust in the air. Lowie extinguished his

candle and watched, studying the hanging wall of
the drift.

Slowly and steadily they worked. An hour
passed, then two. A third followed. Still the
fine muck sifted down, and they had made
progress, but not enough. One candle burned.
Lowie himself worked. Dud lay on the floor, face
down, breathing carefully. Skinner leaned back
against the wall. Sweat trickled down his body.
The heat was stifling.

Charlie got up slowly. "I'll take it, boy."

Lowie leaned on his shovel. "She's rough,
Charlie."

The older man's face was drawn. "We gained six
feet," he said. "But it ain't enough."

"How much longer we got?"

Charlie shrugged. "Not long. Air's mighty bad.
Dud's about all in."

"Look at this stuff," Lowie said, "it isn't
sand and it ain't just rock. It's finer than
dust."

Charlie took a pinch of it in his fingers. He
felt of it, he sniffed it. "Smells a mite musty
like. Funny sort o' stuff to find in here."

Lowie grabbed Charlie's wrist. "Charlie! It's
guano!"

"Guano? What's that?"

"Bat manure! And bats live in caves! There's a
cave above us somewhere!"

Charlie looked up. The edge of the hanging
wall was visible. At first what they had dug out
was broken rock and muck with a few ends of the
splintered hand-hewn planks used for shoring, but
this dust had been sifting down through that
hole, filling up all the crevices.

"How long you reckon they lived in that cave? An' how many of them?"

"Maybe millions of them," Lowie said, "maybe for thousands of years."

The impact of his words registered slowly. The guano could be many feet thick, there might be more than enough to fill all this space and more before they could break through into the cave above. Yet it offered a possible solution. If they could not get out through their own tunnel, they might make it into the cave above, and if there was a way out for the bats, they might enlarge a way out for themselves . . . or find one ready made.

Dud got slowly to his feet. He swayed drunkenly. "Ready for me?" he whispered hoarsely.

Lowie shook his head. "Stay close to the floor. Only move back. Take Skinner with you."

Dud stumbled away, and Charlie leaned against the wall, staring at Lowie. The candle flame seemed to have grown smaller; breathing was an effort now. The air was hot and stale. It was stifling in the narrow drift. "What you goin' to do?" Charlie asked.

Lowie shrugged. "Got to figger," he said. He mopped his face with his hands. "We must sort've be on the edge of that cave," he said. "Don't appear that guano would weigh heavy enough to make that break. I reckon it was forward o' the cave. If we had any plank we could shore up that hole an' maybe dig out."

"We got no plank," Charlie said, "we've got nothing."

Lowie's head was throbbing. He sat down,

heaviness in his muscles. He stared at the
sifting dust, thick over and between the rocks.
It was enough to break a man's heart.

Skinner got to his feet. His eyes were sunken
and he moved like a man walking in his sleep. But
he got hold of a shovel and moved up to the pile.

Looking at Skinner, Lowie knew how he must
look. Like he felt. There wasn't much time now.
He felt sleepy, and his head ached. He got up.
Skinner was working steadily, like an automaton,
and surprisingly, he was forging ahead. He
cleared as much in a few minutes as they had in
more than an hour. Charlie found some slabs that
had fallen, and built a wall to hold back the
sliding muck.

Skinner continued to work, and then suddenly
he slid forward on his face. They dragged him
back and splashed water on his face. "Leave him
lay," Lowie said, "air's better down there."

He picked up the shovel and went to work, yet
he had moved not more than three shovels full
when Charlie yelled.

Instinctively, he half sprang, half fell
backward. With a gasping rush, the sifting, bone-
dry guano shot down, carrying a few chunks of
rock. It hit the space cleared and filled it,
then piled up. A few final grains sifted down;
the trickle stopped.

They stared dully. All their work for nothing.
They were trapped. They would never get out. They
would die here. Dud was far away at the face but
they could hear him gasping slowly, straining for
breath. Lowie lifted his eyes and suddenly, he
stopped, his gaze riveted on a black hole.

COMMENTS: Louis started this story twice, so he had something in mind; it wasn't just an experiment to see what would turn up. People regularly write to me, asking questions about Louis's real-life experiences in the West. I'm sure most would like to hear that he spent some time as a cowboy, and I hate to disappoint them, but that just wasn't the case. Louis had plenty of typically Western jobs, but they were more of the farming and mining sort than punching cows. He spent a lot of time underground and thus you get stories like this one, "Dead End Drift" in the collection *Yondering*, "Under the Hanging Wall" in *Beyond the Great Snow Mountains*, and novels like *The Comstock Lode*, *The High Graders*, and several others.

Louis and his father, L. C. Lamoore, on the steps of the Katherine Mine bunkhouse, Arizona.

SOUTH OF PANAMA

A Treatment for an Adventure Story

LARKIN FURY had been on lookout during most of the night, but he found that daylight brought no beauty to the shores of Sotavento Bay. Behind the rocky shoreline the rugged hills lifted in a bleak and tawny mass unrelieved by any growth of tree or bush.

Through the morning mist the Caribe moved ghost-like upon the dark water, feeling its way up the channel toward the dock. Details at last began to arrange themselves. Two rocky islands, white with guano and seabirds, appeared briefly to starboard, then vanished into the mist.

At the head of the cove buildings took shape, and a long dock pointed an inquiring finger toward the incoming yacht. Along the dock was a narrow tramway ending in an ore chute. Close beside it stood the gaunt and rusting skeleton of a giant crane. Shoreward, its gray bulk dwarfed by the magnitude of the mountain behind it, was the smelter. No smoke issued from the tall chimneys.

Closer to the dock and lining a street facing the water and a second street at right angles to it were a scattering of weather-beaten, nondescript buildings. A low-roofed store, a long warehouse, and a cantina, among others. Behind them along the mountainside, a scattering of huts and houses, most of them mere shacks.

It was nothing or less than nothing, an outpost of civilization at the foot of the cordillera, a place seemingly forgotten, and located upon one of the most bleak and lonely coasts in the world. From the deserts of Chile came nitrates, from the mountains copper and sulfur, and the rest of the coast offered nothing but heat, mighty winds, and the sudden chill blasts from off the Humboldt Current, a river in the sea carrying cold water north from the Antarctic. Along this coast men live only to work. There is nothing to attract them but the mining. The climate is severe, the landscape bleak and unpromising.

The town they approached was over a half mile up the channel from the lonely sea, and seemed cut off from all that was real, familiar or normal. Even the barren sea with its threats of a coming storm were preferable to this loneliness.

Larkin Fury had thought of nothing for days but to get home and get ashore. The situation aboard the Caribe had gone from bad to worse, an ill-assorted group of people subjected to all the strain of the close confines of a yacht on a long voyage, and now that strain had reached the breaking point.

At a movement beside him Fury turns to find that WENDY FORREST has come up from below. There is no one else on deck although they are visible

from the wheelhouse where there is a sailor at
the wheel.

Wendy is a slender, graceful girl in a linen
dress. She is poised, lovely and exciting, all of
which Fury knows only too well. She is also
reported to be the fiancée of BLAIR MURDOCK, who
owns the Caribe . . . and who is Fury's employer.

Larkin Fury had returned from the Korean war,
was discharged, and shortly after was offered a
job by Murdock as a bodyguard. At first this
seemed unnecessary, but Fury soon discovered
Murdock was a man who made enemies, and his need
for a bodyguard was very real. Fury is a tall,
rugged-looking young man of nearly thirty with
considerable experience getting around in the
rough places of the world.

Now he turns to Wendy. "You shouldn't have
come here."

"I couldn't sleep." She looks around. "What is
this place? A ghost town?"

"On the chart it is Sotavento Bay. Last night
the starb'rd engine broke down and we're going to
put in for repairs. There should be some help,
and a machine shop."

To proceed up the coast in the face of the
impending storm would have been foolhardy at
best, yet Larkin Fury would have preferred it. He
wanted nothing so much as to be ashore in the
States.

The voyage had begun on a golf course.
Murdock, Fury, DAVE BRACELIN, and KEN FARRELL had
been playing. No one of them was well known to
the others. They were simply a group of men who
had made up a foursome after reaching the
clubhouse. Murdock had drafted Fury to make the

fourth man; he had been working for Murdock only a few days, scarcely enough to know his employer.

As the game developed Murdock commented on the trip down the coast he was planning and the difficulty in finding a navigator for his yacht. Bracelin replied that he held a master's ticket and had commanded a Navy supply ship during the war. Farrell, a mining engineer by profession, had been a navigator aboard bombers during World War II. Murdock already knew Fury had once been something of an amateur sailor. All were free at the time. Bracelin was looking around for some investments and Ken Farrell, a lean, pleasant man, was between assignments.

Both Bracelin and Farrell were married so it was decided to bring their WIVES along, and Murdock would invite his "fiancée" and another girl.

The Caribe was a beautifully appointed diesel-powered craft of eighty feet over-all, and carried a cook, steward, waiter and four seamen, two of whom worked on deck and two below. Their work was supplemented by the guests themselves, who took turns standing wheel-watches. The plan had been to cruise south along the coast of Chile and Peru, fishing the Humboldt Current.

Blair Murdock was a short, heavy-set man who proved to be extremely arrogant. Given to a master-of-all-he-surveys attitude, he was determined to have all his acquaintances in some way beholden to him. He has helped Wendy out of difficulties and Larkin Fury is employed by him. The others are indebted as his guests. This attitude, not obvious until the voyage was well along, made conditions aboard increasingly difficult.

Animosity eventually developed. Bracelin, an able man when sober, rarely was. His wife was neurotic, lonely, and envious of Wendy's youth and beauty. The Farrells were tactful and considerate. They developed a liking for Fury and for Wendy. GAIL MATTESON, the other girl, was an athletic, attractive brunette with a quick tongue, often edged with acid, but a capable, interesting person. Youth and their natural attractions drew Wendy and Larkin closer together as the voyage continued.

Until the return trip had begun all had been fairly amicable. Ashore in Valparaiso, Larkin Fury had met Wendy and they lunched together, returning to the yacht, laughing and talking. Murdock had seen them come aboard and had become angry. This Ken Farrell observed, and he warned Fury.

"Watch yourself, Lark. He's an ugly customer."

Realizing for the first time that Murdock was jealous, Fury began to avoid Wendy. He was not afraid of Murdock, but the small space aboard the Caribe was no place for trouble. It was better, and certainly more polite, to avoid friction.

More and more the task of handling the Caribe had fallen upon the shoulders of Farrell and Fury. Murdock made no pretense of doing anything beyond taking the wheel occasionally, and Bracelin was drunk or nearly so most of the time.

The trouble that had been impending finally broke the surface as the yacht was proceeding up the channel at Sotavento Bay. Wendy explained her situation to Fury. She was not, she insisted,

engaged to Murdock. He had proposed and she had
agreed to give an answer when the voyage was
completed. He had been friendly and helpful when
she had fallen ill, and she owed him money. He
had suggested that be forgotten and that she come
along on the trip to recuperate. When they
returned would be time enough to discuss
repayment . . . or marriage.

Murdock had dated her several times. She had
found him good company and genial. It had taken
the close confines of life aboard the Caribe to
convince her that living with him would be
impossible. She has avoided bringing the matter
to an issue, wanting no hard feelings while
aboard the yacht. Like Fury she is eager for the
trip to be ended. What had started as a glorious
and exciting vacation was ending in a deadening
feeling of futility and animosity.

Murdock arrives on deck while they talk and
this leads to angry words. Agnes Bracelin adds a
catty remark of her own to an already tense
situation.

Further trouble is stopped by Ken Farrell with
the comment that there's trouble enough without
fighting among themselves. They can see no
evidence of life ashore, although two very dirty
fishing boats are moored at the end of the dock.
Not even a stray dog is visible.

"Deserted," Bracelin comments, looking ashore.

"No," Farrell says, "look."

A MAN in dirty whites and a battered straw hat
has appeared from between two buildings. He does
not move forward, but merely stands watching
them. Another appears beside him, and then still
another, until there are at least a DOZEN. They

show no evidence that they wish to be friendly.
In response to shouts, they make no reply, but
merely stand, staring.

Blair Murdock goes to the dock and starts
toward them, muttering irritably. His short,
thick-set figure shows both arrogance and anger
as he strides forward. "Hey, you!" His voice is
harsh. "Who's in charge here?" There is no
response, no movement, no indication that he has
been heard.

"We'd better go with him," Farrell suggests,
"he's apt to get us all in trouble."

Their footsteps echo hollowly on the ancient
wooden dock. There is nothing in the faces of the
men to reassure them. Most of them seem sullen
and menacing. Only one or two have a more
positive attitude, but these are afraid to speak
or step forward.

It is obvious to both Farrell and to Fury that
something is drastically wrong, that they have
unwittingly stepped into a situation loaded with
danger. Furthermore, nothing in Murdock's
attitude is likely to alleviate the situation.

The men on the shore look toward the graceful
white lines of the yacht. On the deck are four
women, young, attractive women. There is greed in
the eyes of some of the men, greed and hunger.

Glancing beyond the group, Fury can see
nothing but solitude and emptiness. Obviously,
the mines have been abandoned and the town is all
but deserted. But why have these few stayed on
here? And what is wrong? Fury speaks to them in
Spanish and one man finally replies. A tall man
of gaunt face and thin body.

The mines have, as they had surmised, recently

closed down. The rich vein of copper that had
been worked there has been lost . . . first the
smelter closed down, then after some futile
attempts to find the lost vein, the mine closed
down. The machine shop is closed and the
machinists and mechanics are gone. No one is in
charge here now.

To his question as to why they have remained,
the man hesitates, then replies this has always
been his home, the grave of his father is here,
and that of his mother. His wife is here, and his
son. Where else will he go? What will he do?

As to the others, some are like him. Some, he
admits, have remained behind for other reasons.
Some, he adds, are "the men of Arango."

Arango, it seems, is a local bandido, a rider
of the hills, and a most dangerous man. With the
closing of the mine this place has occasionally
become his hideout.

At this there are some angry remarks from some
of the rougher men in the group. Fury does not
like the way these men look toward the yacht, and
he is impressed anew with their helplessness.
What, he wonders, is to prevent an attack upon
the boat, a looting?

Farrell is professionally interested. He
wishes to examine the mine. He is, he tells the
tall man, whose name is PIETRO, a mining
engineer. If the vein did not play out, but was
broken off, he might be able to locate the lost
vein. He is an expert in this sort of thing and
has been employed by many of the largest mining
corporations to uncover lost ore bodies.

Fury suggests they might find tools in the
machine shop, but his comment provokes immediate

reaction. Several of the men come forward
threateningly. They are not to go near the
machine shop. It would be dangerous in the
extreme to persist at present. Fury can see this.

Murdock interrupts and declares they must have
tools and spare parts. This is not exactly a wise
comment, and from the exchanges between some in
the group, Fury can see that there are those who
would like to keep them from leaving.

They return to the Caribe to debate the
problem. The few good men of the crowd disappear
and only the gentuzas (riff raff) remain. They
crowd to the edge of the dock and look at the
yacht and at the women. Gail Matteson, a tall,
shapely brunette, is wearing shorts and a halter.
Wendy is dressed in the same way. Bracelin comes
on deck carrying a bottle and a glass. This
excites further muttering among the group on the
shore.

Only when rain begins do they leave. Looking
out a few minutes later, Larkin Fury sees the
dock deserted, likewise the town. During the
first hours of darkness, Pietro slips aboard and
tells them they must go, that word will be taken
to Arango. The men know the yacht is helpless and
they will seize it. Murdock scoffs and refuses to
be impressed. Bracelin is drinking and seems
unaware of any trouble. The crew are working
about the yacht, but obviously do not like the
situation.

To try to escape in the face of the storm is
extremely dangerous, and Murdock refuses to allow
them to drop down into the channel. As he says,
the men ashore have boats and could attack
anyway, if they wished. He is not afraid, and

implies Fury and Farrell are building up fears
from nothing.

Larkin Fury determines to have a look at the
machine shop. If they can get the necessary
articles to make the repairs, and the tools they
need, it is possible they might complete the work
in a few hours. In the darkness and the rain he
lowers a dinghy and gets into it. At the last
minute, over his objections, he is accompanied by
Wendy.

A driving rain is raking the harbor waters.
They go up the shore to the smelter, a great,
gloomy building, creaking and groaning in the
wind.

They open a window and make their way through
the machinery to the mechanic's shop.
Occasionally they believe they hear unnatural
noises, only to pause and find nothing. They go
into the machine shop and searching about, find
tools, and some lengths of pipe. Suddenly, Wendy
catches Larkin's arm and points. He looks up, and
there hanging from a rafter is the body of a man!

This, then, has been the reason for the fear
and threatening atmosphere in the village. This
is the reason why they were not wanted near the
smelter. Realizing that if they are caught here
they might be killed, they start to move out, and
get back into the main building. Suddenly, they
hear muttered conversation, and in a lightning
flash, glimpse three men. Then one lights a
cigarette, and in the flare of the match they see
a dark, mustached face under a wide hat. He is a
fat, sloppy, dirty man . . . but one look is all
they need to know that he is also a dangerous
man.

Carefully, they ease their way out of the
smelter and return to their boat. They make their
way back to the yacht and climb aboard.

Bracelin, who has been on lookout, is drunk
and has passed out. Fury finds several of the
gentuzas are aboard. One is raiding the bar,
another is stuffing himself with the night-lunch
put out for the watch. At the point of a pistol
Fury drives them from the yacht, but they get
away with several bottles and the knowledge that
the yacht is ripe for the plucking, stored with
quantities of food and wine.

Murdock had slept through it all. Gail
Matteson has succeeded in escaping to her cabin,
and although a man tried the door, he did not
attempt to break it down.

Despite the seriousness of the situation
Murdock will not be impressed. Part of it is
obviously that he is contemptuous of the
Chilenos, part of it that he wishes to show Wendy
how unafraid he is. He scoffs at their story of
the murdered man . . . they saw a sack or a
shadow. Nothing to it.

Day breaks with great storm clouds at sea and
white caps on the water. The crew falls to work
to attempt repairs. This is all kept secret for
the knowledge that the yacht is being repaired
might precipitate trouble.

Ruth Farrell comes to Fury. Her husband has
gone ashore with Pietro before daybreak to have a
look at the mine. He believes something may be
done, and Pietro has told him that only fear of
the policia would prevent trouble. If the mine

was to be reopened and the <u>policia</u> were coming back, the worst of them would take to the hills with Arango and there would be no danger.

Pietro has told Farrell and his wife of the dead man. He was the smelter boss, hated by some of the men who favor Arango. They had tortured him, believing he was taking away a large amount of gold. It had turned out to be very little, but some of them believe there is more hidden around the smelter. They say that along with the copper the mine produced some gold, and this man had kept it hidden for himself.

Fury slips ashore and talks with Pietro's son. The boy tells him there are good men in the village, and a half dozen women, but that the <u>gentuzas</u> outnumber the good men, and are dangerous. Yet they will begin nothing by themselves. They fear Arango.

Fury tells the boy that he believes Arango is already in the village, and described the man he has seen in the smelter. The boy agrees he must be back and looking for the gold. Some of the good men, the boy tells him, are being swayed by the <u>gentuzas</u>. They are horrified that the smelter boss was tortured and killed but they are hungry, for food is short, and they are being told there is much food on the yacht.

The mine, the boy tells him, was a rich mine. It was the life of the village, of the people. Here they wished to stay, and they had remained, hoping without cause that the mine would live again. Farrell, the boy says, has told his father there is hope. That he had seen a formation like this, that an earthquake might have faulted the ground . . . and there are many quakes here.

Fury returns to the <u>Caribe</u> and is fortunate to get back aboard for now a dozen tough-looking men have gathered on the edge of the dock near the gangway. Sounds of the work going on below have been heard.

Fury warns them away and they laugh. They are doing nothing, but who is to stop them no matter what they do? And if the yacht disappears, who will know it was not lost at sea? Suddenly the crowd opens and Arango comes through.

He wears sandals and has a bulging waistline, and a straggly black mustache. He starts to come aboard and Fury orders him back. He smiles what is meant to be an ingratiating smile and tries to convince Fury that he wishes to help. He indicates several men whom, he says, are mechanics. They will make repairs. When this fails his manner shifts alarmingly. He becomes furious. He gestures. He threatens. There is a moment of tenseness when it might come to shooting, but Arango is covered at close range by Fury's pistol and he backs off . . . then shrugs, laughs, and implies he was only having "fun," that he means no trouble. He starts away, then suddenly he turns and spits on the deck, anger and vindictiveness alive in his expression.

The crew are working desperately on the engine and believe it will soon be ready to go. It is late in the day but Farrell is still ashore. Larkin Fury decides to go after him, for when the time comes to move, they must move fast. When Fury prepares to leave, his pistol is missing. Murdock offers his own. Wendy wishes to go along, but Larkin will not have it and Murdock offers objections also. Larkin goes ashore.

Later, Wendy overhears Murdock telling one of
Arango's men that Fury is ashore, and the men
leave at once. Wishing to go ashore, and warn
Fury, Wendy is forcibly restrained by Murdock.
Hurrying below, she attempts to awaken Bracelin
and tell him. That fails, and leaving Gail to
work on him, Wendy goes below to where the crew
are working on the engine. They refuse to believe
that Murdock has deliberately sent the men after
Fury. And anyway, unless the diesel is repaired
they may all get caught.

The steward will not go ashore. He is afraid.
The waiter is warned by Murdock that if he leaves
without orders from him, he had better not
return.

Ashore, Larkin Fury moves among the abandoned
buildings. He is aware that Arango would like to
catch him ashore where he could be murdered with
impunity. Arango is no fool, and whatever he does
he wishes to have as few witnesses as possible.
It is one thing to know a man is a thief and a
murderer, it is quite another to prove it.

Soon Fury realizes he is being stalked, yet he
evades his pursuers in the darkness while working
his way through the village toward the mine.
Somehow they have learned he is ashore. He can
tell that much. Leaving the buildings he works
his way over the rocky mountainside toward the
mine.

Gentuzas are waiting there, too, waiting for
Farrell, who is inside the mine. Fury starts a
small rockslide to divert attention, then runs
for the mine, but is seen just as he enters. They

rush him, he tries to fire, the gun clicks . . .
he realizes that Murdock has sent him ashore with
an empty gun.

Fury escapes into the mine and sees lights
bobbing toward him. It is Pietro and Farrell.
They have drilled a round of holes and spit the
fuses. At his warning, they duck into a cross-
cut. Their lights are hastily put out, there are
running footsteps and lights that bob by the
cross-cut, then a shout as the runners smell the
burning fuses. Footsteps rush in the other
direction. There is a roar and then silence.

Farrell returns to see what has happened at
the face of the drift. Farrell is sure that work
in the mine was ended on the verge of
rediscovering the old vein. Fury is shown by
Pietro another way out of the mine, an old
working used now only as an air shaft.

Back in the abandoned streets, Fury runs
across a sentry. He disarms the man and keeps the
gun. At the edge of the dock he finds the yacht
gone . . . then through the drifting fog he sees
her out upon the water. Murdock has at last moved
away from the dock.

In the distance Fury sees men climbing aboard
through the rail from a fishing boat. He hears a
shout of laughter from the boat, and a woman's
scream. He rushes down to where he had moored the
dinghy in which he came ashore to avoid the crowd
at the gangway. He pushes off and fog closes
around him. He listens. Yells and cheers from the
boat draw him on. He comes alongside and crawls
aboard.

There is loud laughter from the after deck--
they have already found the liquor cabinet. They

have formed a rough circle and in the midst is
Murdock. His shirt is torn to ribbons, he is
battered and bleeding. Each time he attempts to
escape the circle of his tormentors, he is hurled
back or struck.

Slipping aboard, Fury finds Bracelin in the
chart room. He has been beaten unconscious. Gail
Matteson and Ruth Farrell are there also, working
desperately over him. His wife has shut herself
in her cabin and the crew are locked below.
Bracelin is coming out of it; shaken, he tells
Fury, "I'll be all right. Just give me a few
minutes." Fury leaves Bracelin, telling him to
release the crew and arm them . . . any way at
all.

Bracelin starts for the crew. Fury hears Wendy
scream and he goes down the ladder. Suddenly he
is face to face with Arango, who has Wendy by the
wrist. Murdock lies against the rail in a bloody
heap. Arango stares at the gun in Fury's hand,
then at Fury.

Arango smiles, he insists they are friends,
his boys are just having "fun"--they want no
trouble. He starts edging closer, talking softly.
Fury orders him to stop, to release Wendy.
Arango's smile fades into a snarl.

Bracelin appears behind Fury with the released
crew. They all have clubs and heavy spanners, and
are ready and anxious for action. But they are
outnumbered three to one and several of Arango's
men have pistols and rifles.

Fury orders Arango to release Wendy and get
off the boat. Arango suggests that if they let
him keep Wendy, he will go. After all, they have
a boat, they have money, they can get many women.

After all, he leers at Wendy, she is "thin" and
"not too much." They will not miss her. Fury
lifts his pistol and Arango jerks the girl in
front of him.

Arango backs toward the rail, keeping the girl
close.

Suddenly, they are hailed from the water. It
is Pietro and Farrell in the other fishing boat.
The blasting in the mine has exposed the
vein . . . the mine will be working again!

This penetrates the consciousness of the few
good men who have been swayed by desire for food
and liquor. They draw back. A few of the
gentuzas, the more cautious or cowardly ones,
also hesitate. The police will come back, Pietro
shouts--and they all know their police are not to
be trifled with.

One by one they slink toward the fishing boat.
Seeing himself deserted by all but a handful,
Arango is suddenly vicious. He swings Wendy to
arm's length and hurls a knife. The action is
sudden, but Fury has never taken his eyes from
Arango. As the bandit hurls the knife, he fires.
The knife misses by a hair, but Fury does not.

Arango goes down and the remaining gentuzas
rush. There is a few minutes of pitched battle,
and then from below comes a full-throated
throbbing. One of the men has remained below to
put the last bit of work on the broken down
diesel.

As suddenly, the fight is over. The battered
gentuzas clamber over the rail after the better
men, and one leg over the rail, his shoulder and
hand dripping blood, Arango looks back at Wendy.

"Oh, well," he shrugs, "she probably wouldn't
know how to roast a goat, anyway!"

COMMENTS: It is likely but not certain that this was the
first draft of a motion picture treatment. It definitely has
the feel of an early '50s, low-budget adventure film similar
to Louis's *East of Sumatra*.

Though I've removed a good deal of excessive and re-
dundant description and rejiggered the odd paragraph
structure in this manuscript to make it more readable, those
issues tell me that Louis stopped and started this piece
fairly often. I get the feeling he was frustrated with it or
having second thoughts about bothering with it at all. As
usual he was uncomfortable with the present tense require-
ment for treatments. Often it was only in his final polish
that he got this problem squared away.

In the hard days between the decline of the fiction magazines and his breakthrough into paperback originals, Louis
was often tempted to sell ideas directly to the film industry.
In the end it was probably no easier than mailing away a
manuscript to a publisher or agent and hoping for the best,
but at least he could meet the people who were doing the
buying one-on-one, and it was an additional market. Unfortunately, it is very common for people around Hollywood to
tell writers that they know—that they are absolutely
sure—that some star or some studio wants to make a particular sort of picture. If only a treatment could be produced or a pitch developed on the double, the idea could
immediately be sold and everyone involved would be on
their way to greater fame and fortune.

I've been there myself and ninety-nine percent of the time it's a delusion, a figment of the Tinseltown dreamer's imagination and the writer's desperate hope. Writers in Hollywood end up with stacks of these unused and often half-baked ideas; they burn them to stay warm on winter nights. Although Louis sold a fair number of treatments over the years, I fear he also fell victim to "producer's dream syndrome" more than a few times.

'STREETS OF LAREDO'
A Paramount Picture in Technicolor

It is amusing to read the description of the stereotypical bandito Arango, because I know just who Louis had in mind: the man who had almost single-handedly immortalized that unfortunate caricature in Hollywood culture, Alfonso Bedoya. Louis and Al were good friends, and I have a feeling that Dad may have pulled him out of many a fight in many a bar. I suspect Dad was trying to make the type so unmistakable that, if it was ever produced, Al would be first in line for the part.

Bedoya was a veteran character actor who made hundreds of films in Mexico and is best remembered for his delivery of the classic line "We don't need no badges! I don't have to show you any stinkin' badges!" in *The Treasure of the Sierra Madre*. From what I understand, Al was a *serious* badass. Louis didn't allow a lot of people like that into his life lightly, so I've got to assume they were quite good friends.

Louis was fascinated by the Chilean coast. This story seems to be set in the north, but the southern stretches appear in a number of other stories. He had extensive charts, "Sailing Directions" guidebooks, and various traveler's accounts of the southern areas from several different time periods. "Sailing Directions," or pilot books, contain specific information for ships approaching various ports, including descriptions of the coastline and threats to navigation like reefs, sand bars, or sunken vessels. I suspect that the early description of the location of this story, and thus a good deal of the plot, was directly inspired by an old entry in one book of sailing directions or another.

THE ROCK MAN

Notes for a Television Series

DAN BYRON is a mining engineer &
geologist, a cultured, sophisticated man of
the world.

BORN to wealth, his family lost all they
had in a bank failure, and Byron worked his
way through school with a series of jobs,
and through college as a karate instructor
and Shift-Boss in a hard-rock mine.

HIS FATHER had been a diplomat, a stern
but capable man; his mother an actress on
the stage, an accomplished, intelligent
woman. Many doors are opened to Byron
because of his parents and who they were.

HE STUDIED the martial arts in Japan and
Korea as a boy when his father was connected
to the U.S. Embassy. His first teacher was
his father's chauffeur, the sole survivor of
a school of karate from western China,
almost unknown in Japan or Okinawa.

BYRON studied at Cal Tech and moved from
there to further practical experience in his
field in Australia, South Africa, Mexico,

Guatemala, Brazil, Iran and the western
United States.

HE is now a consulting geologist and
mining engineer with a background
supplemented by extensive reading and
travel. He works with the latest technology,
makes surveys by plane with a magnetometer
and other such equipment, or on the ground.
He will also have occasion to make minute
examinations of aerial photos . . . on which
many things aside from minerals may appear.
He will occasionally be consulted by the FBI
or the CIA where his knowledge is needed.

HIS WIFE of many years was lost when her
plane crashed during a hi-jacking. So far as
he is aware she is dead, but not legally
dead.

HIS DAUGHTER, now in college, often went
into the desert and mountains with him; she
is skilled at getting around on her own and
takes no nonsense from anybody. She has a
good sense of humor, is critical of and
often amused by her father's occasional girl
friends, and when she disapproves, often
makes mild fun of them for her father's
benefit. They are in the best sense of the
word, comrades. She is the one person he can
talk to, for since the death of his wife he
is a lonely man, immersed in his work.

INCLINED to be easy-going, Byron is a man
who knows his own skills, knows he is tough
and is under no pressure to demonstrate it.
He will often yield a minor point to avoid
trouble, but once moved to action he is a
veritable engine of destruction. His

physical encounters are apt to be brief, sudden, climactic.

HE SERVED in the Korean War, saw a good bit of action, and knows how to handle himself in any kind of trouble.

HE likes women, not only sexually but as people, mixes easily in any kind of company, and being a single man to whose name there is a hint of tragedy, and a lonely man as well, he is especially attractive to women, many of whom believe they can make him forget his wife.

THE MYSTERY of his wife's disappearance will be held over for future stories: In a foreign city he sees a man in a crowd that he recognizes as having been on the plane. He tries to follow, loses the man in a labyrinth of streets.

END, perhaps, with man or other man denying other survivors. First, however, it is essential to see Byron in action as the geologist, on the ground, in the American West or British Columbia working as he will.

Nothing to do with above, but what of a man who steals a steamboat loaded with gold on a Western river? Disguises the boat and heads upstream at the season's end? He gets a dancehall girl to put on a fantastic show, tips off the crew and passengers so they all rush ashore on a dark, rainy night. He casts off, with two or three men to help, and takes the boat upstream knowing the stream will soon freeze over. He has received word a chinook is blowing and moves out quickly

in the night. When they return the boat is
gone . . . vanished. Everyone assumes the
boat has gone adrift and floated downstream.
Perhaps the boat is frozen in? [The crew is]
All bored. He feels the Chinook start, or--?

After that digression Louis goes back to his notes on
The Rock Man:

A geologist-mining engineer of
international reputation who in the course
of his work becomes involved in plots,
crimes, investigations of all sorts. He is
on a first name basis with premiers and
national figures of many kinds and because
of his knowledge is frequently called in for
aid or consultation.
   In these days when minerals, rare earths,
etc. are in great demand so are the services
of those who can find them.

Open with a sequence in which attempts
are made to kill him, he has no idea why. An
attempt to run him down with a car; a shot
taken at him with a silencer; then a man
approaches him for information; he wants the
information before it can be given to the
party who is paying for it. He is
threatened.

Office in Century City; a ranch in
Colorado; his meetings can take place in
resort hotels, country clubs, luxury homes
or remote cabins. He has a secretary and a
right-hand man.

Interesting locales--bizarre characters--
suspense--international importance--

Use the dead man from the Suez Canal bit
from Lucas; analysis of dust or sand; in
certain areas only such dust can be found;
they find a body in the desert but the man
was drowned . . . in salt water. His body
flown out and left in the desert. He tracks
to the plane that brought the body. Hence
man was killed on or near salt water. Draw
heavily on police books.

The first story must show him in action,
working as a geologist. Perhaps the secret
missile base in the Colorado Mts.? He
discovers clue to oil or mineral from
ancient missiles.

COMMENTS: In the mid-1970s Louis put together these
notes for a possible TV series. A well-known, but aging,
actor of the time had come to Dad to see if he could create
a show for him to star in . . . Dad came up with this idea and
pitched it to the actor and his agent, but ultimately no deal
was made. Louis wrote the following description of one of
the meetings in his journal, saying that the star was enthusiastic:

. . . his agent less so. Agent believes
networks will not even know what a geologist
is . . . I disagree. I have more respect for

the people out there than the agent does. As
for the Networks, that may be another
question. In any event all that needed to be
said was said in a few minutes and the rest
was rehashing of the same topic to no point.
[The star] called afterwards and wanted to
keep up my interest. I really don't care as
I've too many books to write . . . I haven't
time for much else.

Century City is a complex of office towers that went up
on what had once been part of the 20th Century Fox back
lot. Local legend has it that the spectacular amount of
money lavished on the Elizabeth Taylor–Richard Burton
version of *Cleopatra* (which exceeded the film's original $2
million budget by over $40 million) caused the studio to
sell off its back lot for an amount that was not much more
than the film's final cost. Regardless, from the late 1960s
into the 2000s it was the prime corporate real estate in Los
Angeles.

I assume the comment about "ancient missiles" is some
sort of a mistake, though I'm not really sure what Louis
was trying to say.

I love the digression about the steamboat story right in
the middle of the material on "The Rock Man." Although
the structure of the *Louis L'Amour's Lost Treasures* volumes
doesn't give us many opportunities to appreciate it, when
Louis was working, one idea frequently fed directly into
another. For better or for worse, many of the ideas we see
here are the results of, or the victims of, multitasking.

BORDEN CHANTRY II

The First Ten Chapters of a Western Novel

CHAPTER 1

No man knew where the wind began nor how its
shadows moved through the sun-silvered grass.

Borden Chantry sometimes thought such things
but told no one, not even his wife. She was a
good woman, one of the very best, but without
poetry and she would have been made uneasy if he
expressed such thoughts.

He took the roan diagonally up the slope of
the long hill and from the crest could look four
directions into infinity.

Only the grass where the wind played shadow-
games, only occasional out-croppings of bare
black rock, the broken bones of old lava flows
breaking through the earthly flesh. He sat still
in the saddle, listening to the wind, feeling it,
sensing something upon it. A distant cloud of
antelope floated across the plains.

This was not a place for a man but for the
wild horses who ran, manes and tails streaming or
the occasional buffalo, very rare now,
remembering their distant thunder upon the earth.

These moments he loved, alone upon the plains that ran on for endless days of riding to the east, south and north. Only to the west, over beyond the horizon, did the plains come to an end against the vast eastern wall of the Rockies, the Sangre de Cristos here, but a part of the Rockies none the less.

A little more than two years ago he had been a rancher, with wide acres of land and over three thousand head of white face and long horn cattle. The land was still his but the cattle were gone, some caught in an unexpected five-day blizzard, others sold at a loss to pay his debts. To make a living he had become town marshal.

This, where he now sat in his saddle under the wind, this was where he belonged. Here he was at home. Here he knew what to do. In the town where he lived he was uneasy, restless for the hills, uncomfortable even among those who respected him and had asked for his services.

He frowned, watching a distant buzzard against the sky. Something was wrong in his town, something he should know about but did not. He was a sensitive man, and he felt an uneasiness that should not be there. He shook his head, irritated with himself. He was becoming a fool, imagining things that were not there.

He glanced again at the buzzard. Buzzards. There was more than one. A dead critter, no doubt.

The sooner he could save enough to re-stock his ranch, the better. He had saved money, then bought cattle with it just before the freeze-up. He reined his horse sharply around, turning away

from the thought that never in his life-time
could he save enough money to start over.

In the days when he began ranching it had been
easier. Many cattle ran unbranded on the range
and he had found strays in the valley of the
Purgatoire that had been there for years.

It was different now. All cattle were branded,
all the land claimed by someone, and even though
he still owned land, starting over would be
difficult. He had gone to Hyatt Johnson, the
banker in town, but Hyatt hedged. Nobody wanted
to loan money on land, there was too much of it.

He was riding toward the buzzards, still some
distance away. His eyes cast for the tracks of
horses. Nothing fresh. He would have been
surprised had he seen any for this was empty
country. Nobody came here except to hunt for
strays at round-up time when they brought
everything in. And last night's rain would have
wiped out signs of recent movement.

He saw tracks of unshod horses. That would be
the wild bunch who roamed his own range. There
were a dozen to sixteen in the bunch led by a
gray stallion with black tail and mane. They knew
each other, he and that stallion.

Five years ago he had come upon him suddenly
in the Mesa de Mayo country. The stallion had
stopped, facing him, nostrils flared, ready to
fight or run.

"Go on!" he said tolerantly. "Get out of here
before I put a rope on you!"

With an angry snort the stallion had turned
and herded his mares back up the canyon.

Now he drew up and let his horse suck water

from a shallow pool caught in a hollow of a rock they were passing.

He glanced again at the buzzards. He was closer now, and there were four or five of them. Something was dead down there, or something about to die. Whatever it was must be down in Sheep Canyon, in its lower reaches where it started to flatten out.

When he topped the next rise he could see it, something resembling a heap of discarded clothing, but he knew it was a man.

. . . Or had been. Death had been here and the man was gone; only the shell remained.

Nothing had been at it yet. The buzzard is a wary bird, and from long experience they know some creatures die very hard, indeed, and some will fight until the last breath.

Borden Chantry sat in his saddle and studied the situation. The worst thing he could do would be to charge down there and mess up any tracks that had been left.

The body lay sprawled on bare sand among patches of grass and clumps of brush. He had been a short, stout man wearing a store-bought suit and a town man's shoes, incongruous in this wild and lonely place. A carpet-bag lay open beside the body. Somebody had gone through it and through the dead man's pockets.

There was no horse, nor were there tracks of one. Borden Chantry had been walking his roan closer and now he drew up again to study the body and the position in which it lay.

A glance told him most of what he needed to know. The body had been lying there all night because there had been a brief shower, a hard-driven pelting shower that indented the well packed sand. It had left the clothing damp and muddy where it touched the ground.

Shot through the head. He could see the bullet-hole clearly enough. Borden Chantry dismounted and squatted beside the body. The pockets had been gone through, yet had they taken everything?

How did the man come to be here, of all places? It was only a short distance from Borden's now empty ranch-house, a short distance, he reflected, by Western standards, but several miles, actually.

This was an area where no one came, not even he himself and nobody lived closer. A year might pass with no more than one or two riders even passing within several miles of this area. So how did this man, a stranger, come to be here?

Where was he coming from? And where was he going?

Back there was an area known locally as the Black Hills, and all that was wild country except for the stage station.

Had the man left the stage? If so, why? Was somebody pursuing him?

Beside the body was a stick, lying loose on the sand. That stick did not belong where it lay, and it was too short for the man to have used it as a cane or a staff to assist his walking. A stick lying among sage-brush or cacti acquires a fine silting of dust and the sand beneath it acquires an indentation where the stick has been lying. None of this was present, and yet one end of the stick had sand in among the slivers of the broken end.

Half-concealed by the body was a hole in the sand into which the end of the stick might have fitted.

"Well, I'll be damned!" he said aloud. "I'll be double-damned!"

He looked again at the position of the body and the way the stick was lying.

"Somebody," he said aloud, "brought the body here, propped it up in a sitting position with that stick and then shot into the head."

Now, why in the devil--! He sighted from the body's position toward the bank of the arroyo, some sixty yards away. Leaving his horse ground-hitched, he walked toward the bank, climbed it, and looked around. It needed several minutes before he found anything, and it wasn't much. Somebody had knelt on the ground, leaving a very slight knee-print and a somewhat deeper toe-print.

It was here a man had kneeled to take his shot into the body that lay below. Why anybody would go to such trouble he could not guess, but that was for tomorrow, today he was concerned only with this.

He looked around for something to use in measuring, but no stick was available and the yucca leaves were not long enough. Taking off his belt he measured the distance from the knee-print to the toe-print, then marked the edge of his belt and put it back in place.

This was none of his business as he was only the town marshal whose jurisdiction ended with the town limits. He would have to inform the sheriff or the Deputy United States Marshal.

Returning to the body he studied it again.

Whatever he could learn might help his fellow officer, and in any event any crime in the area might sooner or later come to rest in town, his town.

Squatting on his heels beside the dead man, Borden looked him over with care. Not a very clean man, certainly. The under-side of his coat sleeve was polished as from rubbing on a desk or bench. The cuffs of his pants were somewhat frayed. The shirt was dirty at the collar and cuffs, unchanged for several days. The hands showed no familiar calluses but the nails were dirty and there was something dark, ink perhaps, on the fingers.

The pockets had been searched but he found a couple of small coins, unlikely in a Western man's pockets as nothing was used smaller than a two-bit piece. Either this man was from the East or he had recently been East.

Several times he had stopped his examination to look around, and was becoming increasingly uneasy. The killer was probably miles away but he could not be sure. Borden's roan was waiting patiently, not twenty yards away, yet suddenly he began wishing he had his rifle in his hands. He doubted if the killer was anywhere around but he had the uneasy feeling of a man who is watched.

Gathering brush he piled it over the body to keep the buzzards away. It would worry them for awhile and before they became confident he would have a wagon here to pick it up.

Mounting, he rode away at a rapid canter, his eyes alert for any movement or anything like a clue. He rode on to his own abandoned ranch-house, coming down from the north into the small

valley with its big old cottonwoods and the
shabby little cabin standing in their shade.

The corrals were empty; the open-faced barn
that had offered shelter to his saddle-stock
during good weather and the stronger, tightly
built barn for winter storms remained as he had
left them.

He walked his horse down the slope and looked
at the cabin. He did not want to go in. Too many
memories there. He had built that cabin with his
own hands, and he had brought his bride here with
some small pride, yet he remembered how she had
looked when he carried her over the threshold and
put her down.

"This? This is it?"

He would never forget her tone. Of course, she
could not be expected to know how he felt about
it, or how other such places were. She was an
Eastern girl and evidently had expected more. Yet
she had been a good wife, and was a fine person.
He wished he could have had more, and but for
that turn of bad weather he would have been a
rich man by now, able to afford what he wanted,
what she wanted.

He did not know what she had envisioned when
he spoke of his ranch. Evidently it had not been
this. He loved the place: the cabin, its cold
spring, the rustling cottonwood leaves, the small
vegetable garden he had planned so carefully. He
sensed her disappointment yet he believed she had
come to love the place.

Borden glanced around a little, walking his
horse from place to place, then he took the trail
for town. He would have to get a telegram off to
the U.S. Marshal.

His thoughts returned to the body. He did not
know but he was sure the man had already been
dead when shot in the head. For one thing there
was no blood. The air was crisp and cool, really
cold at night, so there would be little change in
the body.

Brought from some distance away, deliberately
shot, then left. In such a place it might have
lain there two or three years unfound, so why the
bullet? Insurance, he suspected. Somebody wanted
an obvious cause of death in the event the body
was found.

Why not just leave the dead body? If found,
the killer must have decided, there must be an
obvious cause of death so investigation would go
no further.

That implied there was something more to be
found; it also implied the killer had something
to be worried about, something he did not want
investigated. It also implied that whoever
disposed of the body knew the country, knew this
was an empty area, that Borden Chantry no longer
worked his ranch, that even a round-up in the
area was unlikely. That implied somebody with
local knowledge.

When he left his ranch behind he let the roan
choose his own pace and settled down in the
saddle to do some thinking.

Where had the dead man come from? What was he
doing in this country, obviously a city man?
Where had he been killed? And why? And by whom?

Somebody with local knowledge, and that meant
somebody who knew him, somebody who might wonder
where he had been riding today. Somebody with

something to hide who was willing to kill to keep it hidden.

This was ranching country with a railroad that ran right across the state. His town was only a whistle-stop. It was cattle country, and sheep country as well. What could the dead man have wanted here, of all places?

And he had not been around town or Borden would have seen him. Borden swore softly, with amused exasperation. When he went to wire the U.S. Marshal, Harold, the telegrapher, would take the message. And what Harold Cuff knew, the whole town would soon know.

Nevertheless, he rode his horse up to the window overlooking the tracks. "Wire to the Deputy U.S. Marshal, Harold. To Thurston Jones . . ."

"No need to waste your money, Bord. Thursty's in town. He's up at the cafe, lookin' for you."

"Thanks." He turned his horse.

Sometimes it helped to know Harold Cuff.

CHAPTER 2

Borden Chantry rode up to the cafe and swung down, tying his horse at the hitching-rail. Automatically his eyes took in the street. Big Injun was sitting in his chair outside the jail. Borden gestured to him, and the Indian got up and walked slowly down the boardwalk to him.

"You'll need the buckboard, Injun," he said, then explained where the body lay. "Cover it with a tarp and get it over to the old barn where Doc can have a look." He paused. "And Injun? Take a

look around. You might see something I missed."
He explained about the stick and the kneel marks
he had found.

When Big Injun had gone he went inside.
Thursty was seated at Borden's usual table. He
stood up and extended a hand. "Good to see you,
Bord. Wish you were still sheriff around here."

Chantry sat down. He wished he was, too. The
additional money had helped for the two years he
had been in office, but he was no politician,
knew nothing about campaigning, and he had lost
by a few votes to Nathan Johnson, Hyatt's
brother.

"Breaks of the game," Chantry replied. "He
knew how to run for office, and I stood on my
record. It wasn't enough."

Ed brought coffee to the table. "You wanna
eat?" he asked.

"Bess will have supper waiting, so I'll just
have the coffee and maybe a doughnut."

"I have to take a run out to Frisco," Thursty
began. "Be gone a couple of weeks. I'm to testify
in a court case out yonder, and I need somebody
to stand by for me. I talked to the marshal and
he suggested you." The other man's smile was
hidden by his cup. "I was about to ask for you,
anyway."

"What's going on?"

Thursty sipped his coffee and looked out the
window at the gathering darkness. "Nothing that
needs to worry you," he spoke carefully, "except
for Turren Downer."

Borden Chantry accepted the coffee and
doughnuts Ed brought to the table, then glanced
out the window.

"What about Turren Downer? Isn't he in prison?"

"Was. He isn't now. He's out and around."

"Do you think he'll come back here?"

"He's already here. Somebody saw him over at Trinidad a few days ago. He got some time off for good behavior and there's a story he saved a guard's life when some rocks caved on him, but Turren's a tough man and where Turren is, there's always trouble."

Borden Chantry knew all about Downer. He'd been a top hand on several outfits, then started running with a bad crowd. Borden had heard that was partly because he had a thing for Zaretta Clyde.

Zaretta Clyde? Borden frowned, disturbed by the thought of her, living so close yet out of his jurisdiction. She had made no trouble but from time to time there were rumbles of suspicion and gossip.

Zaretta lived well on a small ranch, running a few cattle and quite a few horses. The trouble was that she lived too well for the outfit she had. Of course, she might have money.

He did not even know what she looked like although she had been spoken of as a handsome woman.

"I'll stand in for you, Thursty, but don't be gone too long. I may give up the job and take the family back east."

"You? You're a Western man. This is your country."

"I know it, but Bess came from the East and she's wanting to go back. She figures I'll do well there."

Thurston Jones shook his head. He glanced at Borden. "You're Western, Bord, as Western as any man could be. You'd die back there."

"Tell that to Bess. She wants Tom to get a proper education and go on to college. She may be right, though. The country is changing."

Chantry changed the subject. In as few words as possible he explained about the body he had found, that he had sent Big Injun to bring it in, and the puzzling aspects of the discovery. "Doesn't make sense," he summed it up, "a man like that in such a place. It's a cinch whoever dumped the body did not expect it to be found right off. The bullet was a precaution."

"Precaution against what?" Thurston wondered. "Why did they want an obvious cause of death?"

Borden Chantry was silent, thinking. After a moment he said what had been in his mind from the beginning. "I'm going to have Doc do an autopsy. There's something funny about this. I think they did all they could to keep anybody from guessing who he was or where he was killed.

"First, they hoped the body would not be found until it was torn up by animals or wasted away, but they did not trust to that. Just in case they wanted an obvious cause of death that could be readily accepted.

"This one is for you. I'm a rancher, not a detective."

"You did pretty well on the Lang Adams thing."

"Just common sense, that was all, and cow country savvy. This is different."

He finished his coffee. "Bess will be worried. I'm going home."

"Bord? I'll be gone for two weeks. Look into

this and give me a report, then if you want me to take over I'll do it."

"Well . . ." He hesitated, but had to admit the hesitation was not honest. He did want to investigate. Puzzles bothered him, and leaving the body close to his own ranch, that almost made it his problem. "All right, but hurry back. Meanwhile I'll see what I can scare up."

Tom and Bess were at the table when he came in. Bess got up and went to the stove. "How are things at school?" he asked his son.

"All right, I guess, but Ol' Lady Graham is sure piling on the home-work."

"Old Lady? She's no old lady, Tom. She's young and almighty pretty."

"You noticed that, did you?" Bess said.

"I sure did, Bess." He smiled at her. "But I saw you first."

He paused. "I came by the ranch. Those wildflowers came up where you scattered the seed, a whole mess of them."

"Pa? Can I ride out there with you someday? I miss the place."

"One of these days. We've a little trouble out there right now." He explained about the body.

Bess brought his food to the table and sat down opposite him. "I wish you had another job. I live for the day when we'll be away from here."

"There's crimes back east, too, Bess."

"But you won't have anything to do with it." Or with anything else, probably, he told himself. What would he do for a living? What could he do? He had spent a lot of horse-back time just thinking, in the saddle. Or over a cup of coffee at the restaurant. He would have to come up with some kind of a plan, something he could do. They wouldn't have much money because he wouldn't sell the land for what Hyatt would give him for it, and he was sure that was just what Hyatt was waiting for. Sooner or later he expected Borden to get into a jam and come to him for money.

The night was cool and he added some sticks to the fire. Bess was knitting and Tom was at the table with a book open and writing on a tablet. He had never had much schooling himself and whenever Tom wasn't around and his books were, Borden liked to dip into them and read a little. Someday, if there was time . . .

"Thursty's going out to California," he volunteered. "Got to testify in a case. I'll be taking over for him for two weeks."

"You'll be investigating that murder?" Bess asked.

"Sort of. Nathan Johnson will be on it, too."

He did not like Nathan Johnson nor did Nathan like him. It went beyond the election, and was, Borden realized, a matter of personality. Nathan had been county clerk before he ran for sheriff, and had visions of running for the state legislature. He would not be Borden's choice for any office. Yet, the man had a way of making himself liked and he could get the votes. Better than I could, Borden reflected. Give the man his due. He knows his business. And his business was politics, it was not solving or preventing crimes.

Soon everybody in town would know about the body. Some must have overheard him talking to

Thursty Jones, others would see the dead man when Injun brought him in. The talk might stir up a clue. After all, there was no other town within miles.

It also might warn the killer that his crime had been discovered sooner than expected.

Borden Chantry considered that and warned himself to walk carefully. So far the killer had been quite sure of himself. No doubt he still was, but there was always a point when fear came, and the instinct of a frightened killer was to kill again.

He did not fear for himself, but suppose, just suppose the killer tried to retaliate against his family? He glanced quickly at Bess and then at Tom. Maybe Bess was right. Maybe he should get out of this business.

Yet the discovery of the body and the talk about it might help. His experience, limited though it was, inclined him to believe that if a criminal is pushed he makes mistakes. And all criminals, he believed, were optimists. They had to believe they could get away with it, they had to believe everything would go right for them. The trouble was somebody was always noticing, and the criminal could never be sure he had not been seen or that he had not, inadvertently, left some clue.

Borden Chantry knew little about the detection of crimes, but of one thing he was sure. The greatest ally the law had was the mind of the criminal itself. In a larger city it might not work so well, but he knew what it could do, for better or worse, in a small town.

What he must find out was who the dead man had been, and how he came to be where he was.

The first thing was to find out how he got to this part of the country. He had to have come on the steam cars or from the south by stage. Obviously, he was no horseman.

Of course, he might have been driven in by somebody, by buckboard or wagon. The killer, perhaps?

Tomorrow he would begin inquiries. If he had arrived with somebody or been met by somebody someone would have seen it. People liked to talk. They liked to know, to be able to tell others what they had seen. It gave them a sense of importance. Of course, they might be afraid. Those who knew might be frightened by the killing.

He would talk to Cuff. The dispatcher rarely missed noticing who got on or off the train. After all, he sat behind his telegraph key looking out the window at the tracks where the trains stopped.

Then he would talk to the livery stable to see if anybody had hired a rig. A difficulty was that he had no time limits. He did not know when the man arrived, yet wearing those clothes he had not been here long.

Priscilla, at the post office, might know something.

In fact, she always did. She was uncommonly nosy, but on the other hand, she was not inclined to gossip and rarely spoke of what she knew.

If the killer was in town or even in the country close by he would soon know what Borden was doing. He would be able to observe every step of Chantry's progress, and would know when Chantry was getting close and take the necessary steps to prevent discovery. In the morning he must see Nathan Johnson. By that time the body should have been brought in. He would have to get Doc Terwilliger on the job, too.

"I had a letter from Ethel," Bess said. "She says the Dornbecker farm will be for sale. Old Charlie died and the boys are working in Boston now. I remember it well, when I was a child. They had such a lot of maple trees and we used to go over for the sugaring."

"How big a place?"

"Eighty acres. There's a small orchard, mixed fruit trees, just for their own use, and a big barn. The kind you always wanted out at the ranch.

"Ethel said they would sell it on time, to the right person."

Borden shifted in his chair. He had enough of being in debt, of fighting the weather for crops. At least he knew what he was doing out here, and back there he would have it all to learn. Still, it sounded like a good place.

"Did she give you any idea what they were asking?"

"She said she'd find out."

Ethel was Bess's sister, a nice woman. He knew how they missed each other.

He got up and reached for his hat. "I've got to make my rounds," he said. "Don't wait up for me, Bess."

"Borden? Be careful. Please?"

Outside he moved away from the door and stood

listening to the night. Caution was as natural to
him as breathing.

The piano was going in Time Reardon's Corral
Saloon, and he heard somebody ride down the
street, heading out of town.

He supposed it must be hard on Bess. When a
man was keeping the peace his wife never knew
when he walked out of the door whether he would
come back, or not. Yet things had been quiet in
town, and the jail was empty. Nothing for Big
Injun to do but keep the place swept out.

Kim Baca, his former deputy, now had a small
horse-breeding ranch just out of town. Well, that
was one thing he had done, if nothing else. He
had turned Kim from a horse-thief headed for a
hanging into a good deputy and a man on whom he
could depend.

He did not go out through the gate in the low
picket fence. Instead he walked under the
cottonwood tree and stepped over the fence,
keeping himself in the dark until he reached the
street alongside the cafe.

Three horses were tied at the Corral's
hitching-rail and a buckboard with a sorrel team.
He knew the horses. They were M-Bar-W stock,
cowboys returning from a small drive over to
Trinidad. The buckboard was one he had not seen
before, but it was old.

He crossed the street to the saloon.

CHAPTER 3

Time Reardon was tending his own bar. He
nodded briefly to Chantry. There was mutual

respect between them, not friendship, but each understood the other very well indeed.

The three M-Bar-W cowboys were at the bar, and a stranger sat at the nearby table. He was a square shouldered man in a gray suit coat and matching vest. His ears were tight against his head and his eyes busy. In front of him was a stein of beer. He wore a handle-bar mustache and his face showed signs of the sun.

"How are you, Bord?" Reardon asked. "Everything quiet?"

"Yes, and I hope it stays that way."

Time mopped the bar, then he said, "Hear you found some work for Nathan."

"For me, too."

Reardon looked up. "You? Here in town?"

"Thurston Jones has gone to Frisco. He asked me to handle whatever came up so Nathan and I will be working together."

"Does Nathan know about this?" Was Reardon disturbed, or was it his imagination?

"Not yet. I thought I might find him in here."

"He hasn't been in." Reardon leaned his forearms on the bar. "This body you found? Local man?"

"Stranger. City man."

The M-Bar-W cowhands were listening. All three were known to Chantry as they had ridden on round-ups together when he was still a cattleman. "In Sheep Canyon?" The cowhand's name was Hayes. "How the Hell did he get away out there?"

"Not by himself, he didn't," Hinge, another of the cowboys said.

"Murder?" Reardon asked.

"He'd been shot in the head. My guess would be

a rifle, fired from fifty, sixty yards off.
That's just a guess."

These men, if interested, could be a help.
They rode the range south of where the body had
been found, and they were friends. Borden Chantry
was one of their own kind. When you ride an empty
land you notice things another might ignore. You
see the tracks of a strange horse or glimpse a
rider in the distance, you are curious. It was a
country where not too many were moving around and
those who were knew each other, and understood
what the other was doing and why he was where he
was. Anything or anyone who did not fit into that
pattern was reason for curiosity.

Nathan Johnson came in. He was a few inches
shorter than Borden Chantry, and had grown a
little fat sitting behind a desk.

"How are you, Borden? Hear you found some work
for me?"

"For me, too, Nathan. Thursty asked me to
stand in for him. He's gone out to Frisco to
testify in a case."

"Glad to have you aboard." Despite the fact
that they had run against each other for office
there was no obvious animosity. But so far there
had been no need for cooperation, and their paths
had gone off in opposite directions. "I'll be
glad to have any information you can give me. I'd
like to get this closed up fast."

Borden Chantry lifted one boot and rested it
on the brass rail. "That may be tough," he said
quietly. "This isn't any ordinary killing."

Two men had come into the saloon and seated
themselves at a table near the door. From the
corner of his eyes he saw that one was a

stranger, the other a man whom he knew slightly as a small rancher in the southern part of the country.

Nathan turned to face him. "Now what does that mean?" He was suddenly interested, and Borden could understand why. A big case now might mean much in the future, if as many believed, Nathan aspired to higher office.

"It is not a simple murder," he said quietly. "The man himself, the obvious attempt to prevent his body being found until nature had destroyed it, and other aspects. It makes a man wonder, Nathan, just who would go to all that trouble, and why. If it was simply a robbery his body would have been left where it was robbed."

He stepped away from the bar. "I'm having Doc take a look at the body. After that we should know more."

He walked to the door, glancing at the newcomers as he went out. Their eyes were averted and they did not glance his way, which seemed unusual. One's eyes almost automatically observe movement when close by, but neither looked up, either so engrossed in conversation they were not aware of his passing or deliberately avoiding his eyes.

Two horses had been added to those at the rail. Both wore the Double O brand. He knew the brand belonged to the man inside. What was his name? Mitchell? Hitchell? Something of the sort.

Borden Chantry walked along the street to the bank, then crossed the street to the front of the Express Office, where he checked the door. He waited there in the darkness under the over-hang, his eyes studying the street, alert for movement.

He was expecting no trouble, but he was thinking as well.

Who was the man with Hitchell? And that other man? With the somewhat sun-burned face? He was not from around here and was also not used to exposure to the sun, or at least not lately.

The marshal of a small town had to know who strangers were and what their business might be. Usually he understood at once, but these were not stock buyers, nor were they prospectors. This was not mining country yet there were always a few optimists.

His thoughts returned to Bess and the East. He might try farming but he had done nothing like that since he was a boy when he had helped his father, before they came west. He knew next to nothing about raising crops, or even what crops might grow back where Bess wanted to live. He would have to look into that.

Was he actually thinking of it? Seriously? He took off his hat and ran his fingers through his hair, watching the street. He had to think of it. Bess was serious, it was clearly what she wanted. He hitched his gun into an easier position and checked to see if the thong was off the hammer. He only kept it in place when he was riding, and here in town, where he might need it quickly, he kept his gun free.

A light was on in the office when he stepped in. Kim Baca was playing solitaire on the desk, using their battered cards.

"All quiet?" Kim asked.

"Hitchell's in town. Know anything about him?"

"Small outfit, runs about three hundred head, I think. Neat little place, neat house, backed up against some low hills. He doesn't come this way very much. Usually rides into La Junta or Trinidad."

"You seem to have him pegged?"

Baca shrugged. "A man can't make a living with three hundred head, not with prices the way they are. It's mostly young stuff, of course, and likely he's building up a herd."

"Does he own a buckboard?"

Baca shrugged. "Not that I know of, but it could be. He's got a nice barn, well-built, strong. In fact, he's got the best barn I've seen around this country."

Except for the saloons and the cafe it was a nine o'clock town. By that time everybody was in their own home, concerned with their families and preparing for bed or tomorrow. He saw the three riders from the M-Bar-W come out and mount up and he walked out on the street where he could be seen.

As they rode abreast of him he said, "Hayes?"

They pulled up and he walked over to them. "You boys get around out there. If you see any strange tracks, I'd like to know."

"Anything in pa'tic'lar?"

"Maybe a buckboard or a wagon, but just anything at all."

"All right, Bord." Hayes lifted a hand. "See you around."

He strolled on down to Alvarez's cafe and stepped in. There were a half dozen Mexicans in the place and a couple of Anglo punchers whom he knew. He nodded, went to his usual booth.

Alvarez came over with two cups of coffee and sat down opposite him. The population of the town

was almost a third Spanish-speaking and Alvarez
was something of a leader in the community. He
had two sons and a daughter attending school and
his sister was a teacher.

"Al? Is everything all right with your people?
No problems?"

"Nothing, Bord. All is quiet." The Mexican
sipped his coffee, then put the cup down
carefully. "But it is not among our people for
you to look." He paused. "You are my friend." He
drank his coffee, then looked over his cup into
Borden Chantry's eyes. "Be careful. Be very, very
careful."

Borden Chantry knew better than to ask
questions. When Alvarez knew something, if he
knew something, he would tell him. They talked
idly of range conditions, of horses, and their
families. Borden finished his coffee and got up
to leave. Alvarez rose also and said quietly, "We
have a new sheriff now. It is better that he
handle those things not of the town."

"Gracias, amigo." Borden Chantry lifted a
hand. "I think I shall go home now."

When he looked back, Alvarez was still in the
doorway, watching him go. Puzzled, Borden stopped
in the shadows and looked around again. There was
nothing, yet the Mexican had been trying to warn
him, suggesting he confine himself to the town,
and he could do just that. Thursty would not
expect him to solve any crimes, just to keep the
lid on until he returned.

Yet he had an uneasy feeling that he was
missing something important. Crime in a community
is like a cancer--it grows, eating away at the
underside of a town until there is total

corruption. It is all too easy to tolerate an evil if it avoids the public eye, and something was wrong here.

He had small experience with crime. He was no detective, and had come into law enforcement by the back door, so to speak. True, he had been asked to take the job, and without it his family might have gone hungry. Well, maybe that was stretching it a bit, but he had needed a job, and desperately.

Until he had taken the job as town marshal he had known the towns-people only casually. He bought supplies at the general store, picked up mail at the post office, ate occasionally in the cafe. Sometimes he dropped in at one of the saloons for a drink, although he wasn't much inclined that way. He and his wife attended church here in town and, eventually, Tom had gone to school here.

Since he had become marshal the town had taken on a new look. These were people he had to protect. He had solved the murder of Joe Sackett and he had, with Tyrel Sackett's help, frustrated the attempted bank robbery by the outlaws Monson and Clatt. If he was going to go back east he had to leave the town clean, so whatever was happening, he had to know.

Bess was sitting by the fire when he came in. She was reading Quentin Durward, by Sir Walter Scott. "You should read this, Borden, you'd like it."

He filled his cup and sat down at the table.

"Bess, what do you know about Zaretta Clyde? I mean, what are people saying?"

"What can they say? Nobody knows anything about her. She's been here more than a year and hasn't been in town three times, although they do say she has visitors."

"Visitors?"

"Men, mostly, some of them city men. They don't come to town, either. They get off the train at a place near her ranch and are met there. She meets them sometimes with a buckboard, and sometimes it is that foreman of hers, Clint Meyers."

He chuckled, shaking his head. "You ladies don't miss much."

Bess shrugged. "It's mostly Priscilla. There at the post office she hears about everything that's said, and Clint Meyers gets his mail there. He writes to some woman in Denver. She used to be at Cheyenne Wells, according to Pris, but moved to Denver a few months ago. Pris knows it's the same woman. She recognized the handwriting."

"And Zaretta?"

"Mr. Meyers picks up her mail, most of it business, judging by the printing on the envelopes. Pris thinks she has investments."

Borden Chantry sat long over his coffee, thinking. All to no purpose, for he came up with nothing. Zaretta Clyde was the only new person in the area of whom he could think, and those men in Reardon's place, but there were always travelers coming through. He would have to check with Elsie Carter at the hotel.

Morning dawned bright and clear. He sat by the

window of his home and watched the train pull in. No passengers left the train and only a couple of packing cases were unloaded. "Bess? I'll be around town all day." He paused. "If you talk to Pris--"

"Why don't you talk to her? You know she thinks the sun rises and sets in you. Really, she does."

"Doesn't act it. She's scolding me most of the time for letting things happen over which I've no control."

"That's Pris. But she still thinks you're the best and she would tell you things she would never tell us."

His house stood on a narrow lane that ran along behind the stores and shops on Main Street, directly behind the cafe.

On the other side of the house and some hundred yards off was the railroad, and from his kitchen window he could watch passengers dismount from the train.

Kim Baca was at the desk when he entered the office.

"All quiet," he said. "Doc says he wants to talk. He'll be at the cafe." Baca paused. "Said you an' your corpse kept him up half the night."

"You talked to Big Injun since he got back?"

Baca jerked a thumb toward the jail cells behind him.

"He's back there, sleepin'. He was up most of the night, drivin' down an' back."

Doc Terwilliger was alone in the cafe but for Ed, and Doc was dozing over a cold cup of coffee. Borden dropped into a chair opposite him. The

doctor was a small man in a worn gray suit, a
white collar and red tie.

He opened his eyes when Borden sat down. "Took
you long enough," he grumbled, "for a man who
wants everything done right now."

"Have you seen the body?"

"Seen it? Inside and out! White man, about
forty-five years old, advanced case of
tuberculosis and a bad heart along with it. And
you were right. He was shot after he was already
dead, been dead for several hours, I'd guess."

Ed brought two cups and a pot of coffee,
carrying the cold cup away.

"How did he die?"

Doc poured some coffee into his saucer and
blew gently to cool it. He looked over the saucer
into Borden's eyes. "You ain't going to believe
this, Bord. You ain't going to believe it at
all."

"Well?"

"He was drowned. He was held face-down in some
shallow water by somebody with a mighty strong
grip."

CHAPTER 4

The coffee tasted good. He took another sip
and put his cup down carefully.

Drowned.

A dead man found on the plains of eastern
Colorado, miles from water, and death by
drowning.

"Got any idea what kind of water he drowned
in?"

Doc Terwilliger chuckled. "Now I just knew
you'd ask that question! An' not many would think
of it. Matter of fact, that was almighty obvious.
He was drowned in alkali water. Lungs, nostrils
and throat had that white stuff. He swallowed a
good bit of it in gasping for breath."

"Shallow water, then. Face pushed down into it
and held there." Borden Chantry turned toward
Terwilliger. "Have you told anybody about this,
Doc?"

"Only you. Nobody else was around but that
little McCoy boy. You know, the youngster who
lives alone."

"Billy won't talk. He's mighty cagey. Just the
same, I'll have a word with him."

Doc nodded. "I like that boy, Bord. And I
think he's got a good feeling for medicine. He
should get a chance to go to school."

"Narrows it down, Doc. This narrows it down."
He glanced at Terwilliger. "Why would someone
move a body in the first place? Simply because it
was too close to home, or to something they
didn't want seen. No doubt they hoped it would be
torn up by animals or would simply fall apart
before anybody saw it. Nine times out of ten that
would be exactly what would happen."

"Only you happened along?"

"The buzzards found him first. And you know
any Western man knows buzzards mean something
dead. Whoever left the body wasn't thinking of
that."

Borden Chantry looked at him. "You'd think of
it, wouldn't you? Billy McCoy would think of it,
too, and Time Reardon or Ed here, they'd think of
it."

"What are you gettin' at?" Doc asked.

"Whoever left that body wasn't thinking of buzzards, and that, too, might narrow the field."

He pushed back from the table. "What about his clothes?"

"Big Injun took them. Said you'd want to see them."

"Good!" Chantry got up. "Doc, there are a lot of curious people around. The cause of death was a bullet wound, wasn't it?"

Doc shrugged. "Of course! Anybody could see that. Right in the middle of his forehead." He smiled. "Got to get over to see Elsie's aunt. She's ailin'."

Borden chuckled. "Is she ailin', or does she just want the good doctor to hold her hand?"

"You got enough to worry about without bothering about sick women. That's my department. Besides that, she's right handsome when you get down to it."

The sun was bright when he walked into the street. He paused there, looking around. Ed had followed him from the cafe and was sweeping off the walk. Far up the street Judge Alex McKinney was talking to Priscilla in front of the bank.

There was nothing much to the town when you came right down to it, but he'd miss the place. He would miss the people, too.

Billy was loitering nearby, tossing small rocks at a circle marked in the dust. He was pretty good. Nearly every rock was landing in the center.

"Billy? I wouldn't talk about being in the stable with Doc when he did that autopsy."

"No, sir. I won't." He tossed another rock. "Mr. Chantry, I'd be careful if I were you. Somebody's been staked out near your house."

"What's that?"

"Yes, sir. Last two nights. Maybe it's not anybody watchin' you, maybe he's watchin' the railroad, but he's been behind that stack of ties yonder alongside the tracks."

The stack of railroad ties were alongside the tracks and just opposite the house. A boy like Billy was a canny youngster. His father had been a good friend and Borden Chantry had brought justice to his murderer.

"Thanks, Billy. You're a top hand in any man's outfit. You be careful, now."

He paused. "There's something wrong around town, Billy, something very wrong, like when your father was killed."

"I think they're scared, sir. Why else would they be watching you? Maybe it's like before."

"How do you mean?"

"Like Lang Adams, sir. He killed all those people because he was scared, and there was no reason for it. I think these folks are scared."

"Good thinking, Billy, but you stay out of it, you hear? I've got enough to do without looking out for you, too."

"Yes, sir. But if I see anything--?"

"I'll listen. You know that, I'll always listen, just like your dad would have. You have any problems, you come to me, or if I'm not around, to Bess."

He walked back to the office, hung his hat on

the rack and sat down. The dead man had drowned, and in alkali water, shallow water.

He had been drowned and then taken miles away, probably by night, and his body dumped in a remote place. He had then been shot.

What did this imply? Just as he had decided, somebody did not want the body found where he had been killed. Somebody did not want the cause of death known. The pattern of thinking was not Western, although he could not rely upon that.

A body would attract buzzards, which any Western man would know. However, the buzzards might not be noticed as the area was rarely visited, so even that deduction was questionable.

The dead man was not from around here. The soles of his shoes did not indicate rough walking. The polished seat of his pants and coat sleeves to the elbow seemed to indicate some work at either desk or table.

Several things he needed to know. Who was the dead man? How did he get to this part of the country? What was he doing here? Why was it necessary to kill him? And above all, who had done the killing?

People had warned him to be careful, and Billy had said somebody seemed to be watching him. Billy was only twelve, but Billy missed little that went on around town and a small boy was often ignored. It also meant that he must not be seen talking to Billy or the boy might be endangered.

Where to begin? The answer was simple. He had the man's clothes. He had gone through them once, but he must do so again, with more attention.

Borden Chantry went to the desk drawer where

he kept Wanted sheets sent by other jurisdictions. Idly, he leafed through them, not hoping to discover a familiar face but to be nudged into thinking of something that would help. Many of the posters were of men or women not likely to be found in the West--pickpockets usually kept to large centers of population where they could work the crowds, and sneak thieves, too. In a Western town like this everything a body did was open to somebody's eyes.

A safe-cracker now, he might try the bank or Reardon's Corral Saloon where he occasionally kept valuables for people who were briefly stopping in town. The express office was another possibility, but a slim one. A man trying to rob the express office would be aware it was in plain sight of Hyatt Johnson's house as well as the bank.

All in all, this town was not a good place for a criminal to operate. When Monson and Clatt tried to take the bank they had a good-sized gang but a plan that had not included him. Nor had they expected Tyrel Sackett to be in town.

Outlaws were fools to tackle these Western towns, anyway, because every man had a gun and knew how to use it. Not only that, they would use it.

He needed to think, and he did that better in the saddle, but first he would have a look at the dead man's clothing.

Rising to go back to the cell where the clothes had been left he caught a glimpse of himself in the mirror.

He glimpsed a man with a lean brown face, a handle-bar mustache, carefully combed dark hair and quiet eyes. He paused for a moment, regarding himself speculatively. What would people think of that face back in those Eastern states? There were outdoorsmen there, of course, so in the country, at least, he would not appear strange.

He shrugged, looking away. He had never thought much of how he looked at any time. Mirrors were not found on the range and until he married Bess he had never owned anything beyond a piece of broken glass he used to shave with. If he went east he would be wearing a collar and tie most of the time, he supposed.

Again that question: What could he do? What work could he find that was within his range of abilities?

The suit taken from the dead man lay on the empty bunk in the nearest cell. He stared at the nondescript jacket and the shirt with the soiled collar. It was not much for a man to leave behind.

Of course, he had come too late. The killers had been through the pockets before he saw the man, removing everything that might offer a clue, and also whatever money the man had on him. Maybe there was nothing here. Maybe they had cleaned him out so thoroughly there would be no clue.

Borden Chantry pulled over a chair and sat down facing the suit.

After he had examined the clothes he would have Big Injun beat the dust from them and collect it. He did not know if that would help or not, but he presumed there might be some indication of where he had worked or lived.

The suit was several years old. The inside of the right coat pocket, particularly around the top edge, had a dark stain which might be ink. There had been ink on the man's hands, washed off carelessly but still ingrained in the wrinkles and under the finger-nails.

The same was true of the right pants pocket. So the man had worked with ink or used it somehow enough to stain his hands and clothes.

A printer? Perhaps. Borden Chantry did not know much about the activities of city men beyond the usual sort of thing. Yet this man, an untidy one, had undoubtedly worked with ink.

There was no label on the clothing. The buttons were of bone, and of a common sort. He had picked up the coat when he heard a light step in the office, and then a woman stood in the door of the cell.

Unreasonably, the first thing he thought of was his gun. The thong was over the hammer.

Then he chuckled. Such a thought! For this was no outlaw, it was a woman, and a damned good looking one into the bargain.

"Howdy, ma'am." He put the coat down and got to his feet. "I wasn't expecting visitors."

"And I thought it was about time a new resident became acquainted with the town marshal. I am Zaretta Clyde, how do you do?"

"Of course, Miss Clyde. If you would go back into the office--?"

He folded the coat and put it down on the bunk. When he followed her out he turned the key in the door.

"You lock your empty cells?" She was smiling at him. "Or is there a ghost in there?"

"A ghost? Come to think of it, there's two ghosts. One is of the murdered man who wore that suit, the other is his murderer."

She smiled again but her eyes were cool, measuring, studying him. "You mean the murderer is dead?"

"Not yet. But his shadow is somewhere close to that suit and when I'm through with it, I'll find him."

Her smile was gone. "You are confident, Mr. Marshal." She sat down in a chair.

He shrugged. "I'm really not much of a marshal, Miss Clyde." He waved a hand to indicate the town. "But the folks out there know me and are comfortable with me."

He glanced at her again. "I have been meaning to run out to see you, but you've beat me to the punch. Same idea, getting acquainted with folks new to the area."

On the desk lay the sheaf of the Wanted circulars. She glanced at them. "How interesting! Do you get those all the time? I mean is there one out for every criminal?"

"No, ma'am, just for those wanted for some reason. The marshal who was here before me kept 'em all, so we've got quite a library." He glanced up at her, smiling. "When I'm settin' around doing nothing I kind of leaf through them. Keeps me up on what's happening."

"But aren't most of them out of date?"

"A criminal is never out of date until he's dead. Mighty few ever go straight, so the law is always on the look-out. Of course, in a town of this size we never see the fancy big city crooks.

Crime here is mostly local, unless it's something like that Monson an' Clatt outfit."

"I hadn't heard about that."

"Happened before you came. Organized gang tried to rob our bank, but they didn't quite make it."

"What happened?"

"Two of them went to prison, got twenty years apiece. We buried the other five yonder on Boot Hill."

Zaretta Clyde shivered. "I'd heard the West was violent, but--"

"No more than back east. It's just more out in the open, like. I represent the law here, but every man an' woman in town takes pride in the place and none of them want folks makin' trouble. That Monson an' Clatt outfit now? Most of the shootin' was done by citizens."

He paused. "You've got a nice place out there, Miss Clyde. Are you plannin' to run cattle?"

"Horses, I think, but that's not the reason I'm here." She smiled at him, and it was a lovely smile. "Doctor's orders. He said I must live where the weather is dry."

"Sorry to hear that, ma'am, but you've got it here. Last few years we've had a spell of dry weather." He shrugged. "It's partly what did me in. Drought first and the grazin' was bad for my stock. Winter came on with them in bad shape and it wiped me out. Wiped out some others, too, but most were in better shape financially than I was."

She got up from her chair. "It has been nice talking to you, Marshal." She paused. "How is the restaurant here?"

"Can't be beat. Ed was an ol' cow-camp cook, an' most folks think that's all he was, but as a matter of fact, Ed was raised to be a chef in one of them fancy hotels. He got his trainin', worked some an' was doin' well, then he had the same trouble you've got, I guess. He had to come west for his health. He fell in love with the country an' stayed.

"He cooks reg'lar for those who like it that way, but ever' now and again he does somethin' fancy. My Bess, she's my wife, she takes to his fancy cookin' so ever' once in awhile he fixes somethin' special for her."

He was standing. Big Injun was outside the door, looking in. "You go along down there and tell Ed I said he was to fix you something special. You have any favorites, you tell him. Nothing he likes better than to throw together something for the women-folks. Most of us are steak an' potato men, or steak and beans."

When she had gone, Big Injun came in. He was well over six feet and despite his age the two braids that hung over his shoulders showed only a few strands of gray.

"Hitchell. He buckboard back of store. Buy many t'ings inside."

Borden Chantry thought for a minute and then he said, "Maybe if you wiped out his buckboard he'd give you two-bits," he suggested casually, "wiped it out with a sack, an' bring the sack to me. If he gives you trouble, tell him Ed pays you." A muscle twitched in Big Injun's cheek; it was what passed for a smile. The man had no interest in impressing anyone, but he was no fool.

Borden dropped into his chair. What did Alvarez know that he did not? The Mexican was his friend, and he had warned him. Time, too, had seemed a little nervous. Saloon-keepers often knew things or heard things others did not, although sometimes they were only whispers of things. Unless he was wise and kept his ear to the ground, too often the last to know was the town marshal.

Why would somebody watch his home? Was somebody scared because of something they thought he knew, or might know? Was that why Zaretta had visited him today? The trouble was, he didn't know anything. He didn't know if there was danger, or where it might come from.

CHAPTER 5

Borden Chantry returned to the cell where he had left the dead man's clothes. Seated again, he examined each article of clothing with care. On the vest now, he turned it over in his hands. That third button looked different. Obviously the original button had been lost and replaced with another. It was likely that the dead man had done the sewing himself. He had taken several turns of the thread, using more than was necessary. He had known little about sewing.

The button itself was not even bone, but some sort of metal of an almost identical color with the other buttons. Something was printed on the back. He rubbed the dirt from the button, some of it alkali, and cleaned it off. Gundy Min.

Gundy Min? What the Hell did that mean? Was it

the name of a company? He doubted that. Or an
organization? The button must have been one
immediately available, and perhaps from another
suit or buttons saved for an emergency.

In one of the hip pockets of the pants he
found some broken leaves; evidently dried leaves
had gotten into the pocket when the body was
dragged along the ground, for there was some
earth along with the leaves. Carefully, he put
them in an envelope with some of the sand and
earth and marked it as evidence.

Replacing the suit, neatly folded on the bunk,
he left the cell, locking it behind him.

Gundy Min? The name meant no sense.

That is, it made no sense to him. Obviously,
it would have made sense to the button
manufacturer or to whomever the original garment
had belonged. Idly, on a tablet, he scratched out
diagrams and drew pictures, always thinking,
wondering. He wrote Gundy Sunday, Gundy
Mundy . . .

He tore off the sheet and stuffed it into his
pocket. Irritably, he got up and went out on the
street. Kim Baca was just coming in and Borden
said, "I'm going for coffee," and started down
the street. At the post office he stopped
abruptly, then went in.

Nobody was around. The mail distribution had
been hours ago. Behind the wall of post office
boxes he could hear Priscilla's pen scratching.

"Well," he said aloud, "somebody is working,
anyway."

Priscilla pushed back her chair and came over
to the window. "I am not working, Borden. I am
writing to my sister."

"Ever hear the name Gundy?" he asked.

"No, I can't say I have." She brushed the question aside. "You had a visitor this morning. That Clyde woman."

"Nice-looking woman," he commented. "Just wanted to get acquainted with the town marshal."

"You wait until I tell Bess about that!" Priscilla teased.

"She seems all right. Get mail here?"

"That's her business, Marshal. Business mail, all of it--brokerage firms, seems like." She paused. "Must be an orphan or something."

"Why do you say that?"

"No personal mail. Women-folks like to keep in touch. Most of us write to a sister, mother, aunt or maybe an old friend. She never gets any mail like that."

Or, he thought, she gets it somewhere else, some other post office or maybe--

He shook his head. That would be unlikely, he thought, but possible. "She invite you for tea?"

He was startled. "Me? I'm not a tea drinker. Bess is, but not me."

"She's invited Hyatt. Elsie Carter told me she over-heard it. Right in the door of the hotel. Invited Hyatt and he went, too."

"Well, why not? She's an attractive woman and a woman's company might do Hyatt some good."

He turned toward the door but she stopped him. "Marshal? You be careful, I've got a bad feeling about things."

He nodded. "So do I, Pris. Worst of it is, I can't think of any reason why I should feel that way."

"I can," Pris replied. "I've seen it happen,

Marshal, but not always the same way. Maybe
somebody in town knows something, or gets a hint
of trouble in his family or close by. So he gets
watchful and doesn't talk as much. Somebody else
notices it, maybe without even thinking of it,
and begins to feel the same way. First thing you
know a lot of people are on edge. There was a
time there before you solved that Sackett killing
when folks were right suspicious of each other,
and nobody wanted to talk about anything." She
paused again. "It's like that now, Marshal. You
be careful."

Borden Chantry walked back to the street and
stood at the corner of the post office building.
Between that building and the cafe there was a
space maybe forty feet wide and he could see his
own home, his corral and barn. Nothing was
stirring there. Through the leaves of the big
cottonwood he glimpsed the pile of ties Billy had
spoken about. He scowled, then shook his head.

He went into the cafe and Ed brought his
coffee. He curled his fingers around the big cup,
the heat seeping into them. The smell was
comforting.

Suddenly the door opened and Turren Downer
came in. He was a broad, powerful man with big
hands and shoulders, thick, curly bronze-like
hair and a square jaw. He glanced over at
Chantry, then at the badge on his vest.

"Marshal, is it? I heard you were marshal but
couldn't believe it." He walked over and drew
back a chair, sitting astride of it and leaning
his arms on the back. "Heard you killed Boone
Silva. Down the country where I was folks were
almighty surprised. They'd have bet Silva would

take you without turnin' a hair." He grinned. "I
could have told them different. I mind the time
we were roundin' up strays over near Lone Butte
an' you killed that rattler. He never got
finished with his rattle before you shot his head
off. I told myself then I'd never get into a
shoot-out with you."

Borden Chantry shifted a little in his chair.
He did not like talk of such things. Especially
talk about himself. He was a modest man and it
all made him uncomfortable.

"Who you ridin' for, Turren?"

"On the loose. Saved up a mite and I'm sort of
lookin' around." He wiped a hand across his face.
"Time I shaped up. I'd like to get me a place of
my own and go to raisin' stock. You don't need a
deputy, do you? I might do all right in your line
of work."

"You might, at that." Chantry smiled at him.
"You'd have to lay off the hooch. Folks don't
take much to having a lawman who hits the
bottle."

Downer nodded. "You'd not believe it, but I
haven't had a drink in two months. Fact. Amazes
me, but it's so."

Downer got up and swung his chair back into
place. As he turned away, Borden Chantry said,
"Turren? For old times' sake? Be careful."

Turren turned sharply around and seemed about
to speak, then turned back to the door. As he
reached it he looked back again. "I'll do that,
Bord, an' you do the same."

Borden Chantry shook his head. The Turren
Downers of the world he could handle; the trouble

was with things like this murder he did not know
where to begin.

Drowned in shallow, alkali water, and there
were a couple of dozen places in twenty miles
where that might happen. After rains, anyway.

So what did he have? A body to be buried in an
unmarked grave, an old suit of clothes and a lot
of suspicion. Zaretta Clyde had just added to
that suspicion. She had occupied that ranch
property for several months now, so why take this
time to come in and get acquainted with the town
marshal? Why not before? Months ago? Was she
trying to find out what he knew?

Borden tasted his coffee and put his cup down.
Let's suppose, he suggested to himself. Having no
evidence, let's speculate a little. Suppose
somebody has a nice little criminal operation
going. What it was didn't matter for the moment.
Suddenly, for one reason or another, one of their
number gets killed? Or maybe he was not one of
them but just somebody who knew too much?
Suddenly the lid was off and the operation was in
danger.

But what kind of operation? Operated by whom?
The line of thought intrigued him. It was the
only solution that occurred to him to account for
the body being found where it was, an obvious
attempt to dispose of a body without risk of
discovery.

Had it been murder by a traveler or even
someone local, a murder for robbery, jealousy or
what not it was unlikely the body would have been
moved but left beside a stage trail or the
railroad. A body found under such circumstances
would certainly require investigation but would

not have aroused the attention this one had. Somebody had tried to be too smart.

Rain had washed away any tracks near the body. He repeated that to himself then stopped. Near the body? What about further away?

I'm not cut out for this job, he told himself. Any fool would have considered that possibility and looked further away from the body. Horse or human tracks could well have been erased by the rain, but what of buckboard tracks? Places where the narrow wheels had cut through drifts of sand or over embankments.

A dead body was not the easiest thing to load on a horse, and that was given the fact that you had a horse who would stand for it all. A Western man might tie a body securely enough so it would not fall off, and some others might too, but it would not be easy.

From the first he had assumed a buckboard was used. Why, he asked himself, had he accepted that idea? Because it was the easiest way to move a body across country? Or because there had been no abrasions on the skin where a rope might have been tied? On a couple of occasions he had tied unconscious men into their saddles. He was a big man, considered unusually strong, and it had not been easy, and difficult if the horse side-steps. A body, dead or unconscious, is awkward to handle, being both limp and heavy.

Was that the only reason why he had so quickly accepted the idea of the buckboard? Suppose, just suppose he had unconsciously seen something that because of more immediate concerns did not register consciously?

Just so he might have passed over tracks or

indications because he was not looking for them
and because he was watching the buzzards or at
last, the body. With his attention focused he
might have over-looked much.

So what to do? To ride back, to swing in a
large and then a larger circle about where the
body was found, and to particularly observe those
places in which a buckboard might most easily be
driven. He doubted if the man he sought would
have been thinking of hiding a trail. His
attention would have been on getting the body to
a place where it might be dumped and getting away
without being seen.

Tomorrow. He would ride out tomorrow and look.
He put his cup down and got up but as he did so
the thought flashed through his mind.

He would be riding alone, away from observers,
and if anyone did want him dead, their
opportunity would be perfect.

A man alone on horseback in empty country
makes a nice target.

CHAPTER 6

The roan he was riding was range-bred from
mustang stock crossed with a Morgan stud, and it
was a stayer, a horse who took to wild country
and rough going. He started off to the west but
when well away from the town and seeing no one on
his back trail he swung toward the south. He took
his time, stopping occasionally to give the roan
a breather and to check behind him. Only when he
was sure he was not followed did he turn toward

his ranch and the place where the body had been found.

He was under no illusions. Whoever had killed would kill again if he believed himself at risk. The loneliness and the quiet gave him a chance to think, and slowly, for he was a slow-thinking man, he turned over all aspects of the problem in his mind.

Why had the man been killed? Over a woman? That seemed doubtful, although possible. Over money? Possible. Or had he known too much? Unlikely, although it was possible the man was engaged in something illegal. He was not a horse or cow thief, the first two possibilities in this country. He might be a yeggman preparing to rob the bank or the express office. As it happened that was one aspect of crime about which Borden Chantry knew something.

Long ago, maybe ten or twelve years back he had worked on an outfit with a yeggman who had gone straight. Well, he had gone straight for awhile. Chantry now knew that the man had told him all he did in hopes of recruiting Chantry into helping him, explaining in detail how yeggs operated and how easy it was to not only live off the country but to pull off a big one.

Could it be that? It was something to keep in mind, at least. Again and again he checked his back trail but saw no evidence that he was followed.

Or were they simply waiting for him?

He circled warily, taking his time, studying every aspect of the terrain. He was west of the place where he had found the body when he saw it.

A narrow cut in a small drift of sand, such as
might be made by the wheel of a buckboard.

For several minutes he sat his saddle studying
the angle of the cut and looking for some sign of
the other wheel. He saw nothing so slowly he
began to back track. It was over a hundred yards
before he found another track but this time it
was double and there, under a bush, was an edge
of track that might have been made by a horse's
hoof.

Four hours later he had tracked the buckboard
almost a mile. Rain and wind had obliterated most
of what might have been a good trail, and he
found nothing with which to identify either the
buckboard or the horses. The one clue with which
he was left was the direction from which the
buckboard had come.

The buckboard had come in from the east. Of
course, it might have circled around but he
doubted it. Whoever the driver was he would have
wanted to be rid of that body as soon as
possible. No doubt it had been covered by a tarp
or some such thing, but the driver would not have
wanted to be seen, and to have met anybody would
have demanded some sort of an explanation.

How long would it have taken? At best, over
this terrain the buckboard could have averaged
three miles an hour, and he would be traveling by
night.

Borden Chantry considered that again. Probably
by night. He might have chanced the daylight
hours, trusting there was no one about, but the
risk would be great. Unless, of course, he was a
man not of the country. A stranger might have
believed this empty looking country was really

empty and not realized that occasional cowboys might cross it at any time.

There was a point here that disturbed him. All the evidence inclined him toward believing whoever left the body was a stranger to the area, except for the place in which the body was left. Or had it been simply chance? Simply an accident as to his choice?

"Bord," he said aloud, "you just ain't cut out for this job."

The sky was impossibly clear, and in the far-off distance he thought he could see the Spanish Peaks. The wind stirred the bunch grass and a tumbleweed left its resting place and rolled over, then again. He took off his hat and let the wind cool his brow, stir in his hair. "I'll miss this country," he spoke aloud again, and the roan twitched an ear.

He rode east, seeing no further sign, considering the nearest road over which the buckboard must have traveled. Thinking of that, he remembered Mable.

She was an Indian woman who lived on a lonely ranch with her two daughters. As a younger man he had worked with her husband, punching cows. A few years later Jacob had been killed when a horse fell on him. Several times while the girls were small he had taken sacks of groceries by the ranch, never stopping long, just dropping them off with a tip of his hat.

Mable, who lived on a low knoll, kept a few sheep, a couple of milk cows and some other stock as well as a few cow ponies. If anything was happening within miles, the chances were that Mable knew of it. Whether she would talk or not

was another question. An Indian might simply not
be concerned with certain things, and they were
not as loose-tongued as a white man.

He rode across the mesa toward Mable's ranch,
in plain sight for well over a mile, and he took
his time. When he reached the ranch there were
three ponies in the corral but no one about. He
stepped down from the saddle and led his horse to
the creek for water. It was not considered polite
to ride right up to the door, and he was giving
them time. Finally, he tied his horse at the
corral and removing his hat, walked over to the
door.

Meralda came to the door. She was about
fourteen, he figured, and bright-eyed and pretty.

"Howdy, ma'am," he said, smiling, "I'm a
stranger hereabouts and was wondering if you had
coffee on?"

"You're not a stranger! You're Mr. Chantry.
Will you come in?"

He ducked his head and stepped in. Mable was
sitting near the stove, mending a dress with a
torn sleeve. Felicia, the older girl who was
seventeen now, went to the stove for the coffee
pot. She was a quiet, serious girl, not as
attractive as Meralda, but he remembered she had
done well in school.

"Passin' by," he explained. "Wondered how you
getting on?"

"It is a good year for the sheep," Mable said.

He accepted a cup of coffee and relaxed. They
talked idly, with long periods of silence. He
knew they knew he wanted something and were
waiting.

"Not many people out this way," he suggested.
"Have many visitors?"

"No."

"I've been looking around," he said. "Somebody
in a buckboard, three or four nights ago."

"We want no trouble," Mable said.

He could not honestly say they would have
none, and simply sipped his coffee and waited.

"At night there is no travel," Felicia
commented. She gestured, "It is a road that comes
here, and goes on to Old Mike's."

And Old Mike had been dead for these past ten
years, he reminded himself.

"The buckboard would go out and back," he
suggested. "Twice along the road."

The coffee was good, the way he liked it, the
way Jacob had liked it.

"Sometimes the dogs bark," Mable commented.

"Dogs are like that."

"They barked when Hitchell come by. He was
with a big old man. They drank coffee, and the
big old man wanted to pay. He say 'I 'spect you
can use this.' He put ten dollars down.

"I tell him keep his money."

"Mr. Hitchell tried to stop him," Meralda
said.

A stranger, looking around, might think they
were poor, but such was not the case. Indians
lived the way they wished to live, and to many
the old ways were the best ways. Chantry was not
sure they were mistaken, but even if there had
been a bad time after Jacob died, Mable now owned
over a thousand sheep. Hitchell would know that,
a stranger would not.

Felicia refilled his cup. "Hitchell come this way often?"

Mable shook her head. "Never before."

"The big old man," Meralda said, "kept looking toward the road. Maybe he expected somebody."

Or maybe he wished to see how far away it was, and if they could hear somebody passing. Why would Hitchell come unless something bothered him? His cattle rarely drifted this way, for there was water and grass closer to the southeast.

He finished his coffee. "Thank you." He took up his hat. "I'll be riding on." He paused in the door. "I miss Jacob."

Mable looked up. "Me, too."

He went out to his horse and gathered the reins, taking his time. Felicia came to the door, then walked over to him. "Four nights ago, the dogs bark. It is somebody on the road. Again, before daylight, they bark again." She paused. "Now they are with the sheep. Tomas is with them, too." Again she paused. "They are not foolish dogs."

He swung into the saddle. "Thank you, Felicia, and thank you for the coffee."

He turned his horse away and headed for the road. When he reached it he hesitated briefly, then turned back the way he had come.

Hitchell again? And a big old man? Now who would that be? Somebody who did not know Mable. Somebody not from around here.

It was long after dark before he stripped the saddle from the roan and spilled some oats into the bucket. He stepped outside the shed, still standing in the shadow and looked toward the pile

of ties. He was some thirty yards from the house
and the yard was in shadow except for one place
of about thirty feet which lay bathed in pale
light. If they were scared, as Billy McCoy
believed, were they scared enough to risk a shot
at night in town? Had it come to that?

He doubted it. He reached the light spot and
crossed with quick steps. He must remember. It
would not pay to take chances.

Tom was already in bed, but Bess was up,
reading. "How's Quentin Durward coming along?" he
asked, as she put the book down.

"You'd like it," she repeated. "You're riding
late."

"Stopped by Mable's," he explained.

"How are the girls?"

"Gettin' prettier by the minute. At least,
Meralda is. She's doing well in school, I hear."

He sat down, suddenly tired. Bess put food
before him and he realized he had not eaten since
rising. "Anything happen in town?"

"Priscilla was by, looking for you."

"She came here?" Priscilla did not often leave
Main Street.

He took his watch from his vest pocket. It was
almost ten, too late to see her now. It was an
early to bed, early to rise town and most of the
houses were already dark.

Moreover the last thing he wished was to call
attention to Priscilla. As postmistress he could
see her at any time but if she called at his home
or he at hers at this hour there would be comment
which might alert the very people he wished to
find.

Bess left for bed and he finished his small

meal, took the dishes to the sink and spilled
water over them. Turning, he cupped his hand over
the globe and blew out the light. Sitting down at
the table he pulled off first one boot and then
the other, with a slight jingle from his spurs.

He leaned back in his chair. It felt good just
to sit, to relax. Now if he could just--

Something moved in the darkness outside. He
sat very still, every sense suddenly alert. It
was a man, rising from behind that pile of ties,
a man who seemed to be staring toward the house.
Then slowly, he moved off.

For an instant Borden Chantry thought of
following, but by the time he got his boots on
the man would be gone.

There were other ways--there had to be other
ways.

CHAPTER 7

He awakened at the first gray light. Borden
Chantry had worked cattle too long to not awaken
before sun-up, yet on this morning he did not
immediately rise. Instead, he lay quiet, staring
up at the ceiling.

Suppose Billy was right and they were running
scared? He had done nothing to frighten anybody
except to find the body.

It had not been intended that the body be
found, but might there not be a reason why it
must not be found _now_? Suppose, just suppose, the
reason for taking the body so far was that it not
be discovered at once? Suppose other plans or
actions depended on not stirring up any dust?

He could think of no other reason why they should be alarmed. Possibly something was happening or about to happen that demanded no suspicion be aroused?

Suppose, and he was stretching the point, only a few weeks or days were needed to complete whatever it was?

The dead man was an Eastern man, so probably any crime he would be associated with would be known in his part of the country? The dead man had not been a cattleman or a sheepman, and had no indications of being interested in mines. So what remained?

Land? That did not make sense, either. Land was a drug on the market as he had reason to know.

Borden Chantry sat up as carefully as possible and swung his feet to the floor, reaching for his socks. He dressed quietly, not to awaken Bess, and tip-toed from the bedroom in his sock feet. By the time he had slipped on his boots sunlight was coming through the curtains of the kitchen windows.

He made coffee and sliced some bacon into a frying-pan, thinking all the while.

Hitchell? What did he know about Hitchell? He cut several slices of bread, toasted it lightly and carried it to the table with the bacon.

Hitchell had ridden on the last round-up before he, Borden Chantry, had gone bust. He had been repping for his own ranch and several others down that way, and he had been a fair to middling cowhand. Slowly, he dredged his memory, making little notes on a tablet as he did so. That must have been four years ago and it was the first time he'd seen Hitchell, a well set-up man on the slim side, who looked like he'd been sick.

Now why had he thought that? He looked pale, like he might have been in a hospital. It was easily seen because in that bunch they all had been burned brown by the sun, or red like Pat Costigan, who just burned as many of the red Irish do, and never got tan.

He had repped for Rocky Wade's Four-Forty-Four outfit, too. Rocky ran a lot of cattle down in New Mexico, just below the line.

He looked down the railroad tracks toward the station. Harold Cuff was sweeping off the platform. Chantry considered him. Cuff talked a lot, but he knew a lot, too. Suppose despite all his talking there were things he never discussed? Perhaps because he did not consider them news? Or just from some reserve? He talked largely of things everyone would soon know, but what else was there?

Cuff was the dispatcher, and he would know when trains were coming, where they stopped, where they were side tracked. It might be worth talking to Cuff, or listening to him, a little push here and there, maybe.

He had no idea how a real officer investigated, yet a few things must be done. He must try to discover the identity of the dead man and just how he had arrived in the area. He had to have known someone here, yet Chantry was positive that the dead man had not left the train in town. There were sidings where trains occasionally stopped, however, and one was near Zaretta Clyde's. Her visitors rarely left the train in town. Had the dead man been one of them?

He shook his head. The man was too untidy. It was unlikely such a man would be accepted socially by the Clyde woman, who was if nothing else, fastidious. From all he could see and learn, she herself was always neat and nicely gotten up and her place was a ranch with everything in place. Still, there could be a connection. What was Nathan Johnson doing, if anything? Attuned to the political winds as he was it was unlikely he would miss the chance to crack this case, especially if it looked like it could gain him attention. The more Borden Chantry thought about it the more certain he was that he had stumbled into something important.

He put on his hat and left the house, strolling down to the depot. As he walked by he noticed the pile of ties again. There were tracks around, some scuffing of the ground. Harold was working his key rapidly and Chantry merely nodded, walking on by. Several packing-cases lay on a baggage truck, all marked for the general store. To take time to look around would also let people in town know he was curious, for little passed that was unobserved.

He was turning back when he saw the suit-case. It was battered and old, standing in a corner of the baggage room. He walked over to it, a well used suit-case, bulging with what it contained and tied around the middle with a heavy strap.

Harold Cuff came out of his office. Today he was wearing his green visor and bright red sleeve garters.

"Found it, did you? I was fixin' to call you, Marshal. That there bag showed up on the night train about five, six days ago and as it seemed to come from around here, the boys put it off to be claimed."

"What do you mean 'it seemed to come from around here'?"

"Bob Neighbors, he's conductor on the night run, he said they found the bag settin' just inside the door on the one passenger car, except there was no passenger."

He studied the suit-case thoughtfully, then he said, "Harold, where'd your train stop that night?"

"Usual. They came out of Trinidad on time, made it in to here on time. No problems."

"No stops?"

"Well, there was one stop, that siding near Iron Springs, name skips me at the moment. There was a signal there to pick up somebody but nobody showed."

"Could that suit-case have been put on then? By somebody who might have planned to get aboard?"

Cuff shrugged. "It's possible, but Neighbors didn't mention that he saw anybody, and he looked around."

"Harold, I'm going to take that suit-case as evidence. If anybody shows up to claim it, send them to me."

"Glad to be rid of it. Sure, take it along. You just sign a release here, for taking unclaimed baggage."

Suit-case in hand he walked back home. So far as he could see he was unobserved, but knowing his town he doubted it.

Borden Chantry sat down in his kitchen and looked at the suit-case, but he was not thinking of it, but of the problem itself. Possibly, the man had gotten his suit-case aboard and gone back to the ground for his carpet-bag, which had been found beside the body. At that moment something prevented him, or perhaps the train took off with him left on the ground?

What if the man was involved in something and wanted out, either scared or felt he was being cheated, perhaps. If this suit-case was his, and the circumstances seemed to fit, he had evidently planned on catching the train out of town where he would not be seen, and had gotten far enough to get his suit-case aboard, and something or somebody had then prevented him from following.

He knew the siding, and had loaded cattle there once, several years ago. That had been his first shipment of beef from the ranch. Just one car-load, but his first income.

Suddenly, he was worried. Suppose someone had seen him bring the suit-case home? Might they not try to recover it? And that would put his family at risk.

Going to the shed he got a couple of grain sacks and brought them into the house. Bess was away, shopping for groceries he suspected, so he unstrapped the suit-case. It was not locked, and contained some clothing, some papers, and a small roll of tools of some kind. Without taking time to examine any of it, he transferred the stuff to the grain sacks and carried the lot back to the shed where he left them in his small tack-room under the saddle given him long ago by the former marshal. Bundling up some old clothes he packed them into the bag, replaced the strap and carried it to his office, walking past the restaurant and

the post office to the office. He wanted to be
seen carrying the suit-case.

Ed was sweeping off the boardwalk. He glanced
at the suit-case. "Leavin' town, Marshal?"

"Unclaimed baggage. We'll hold it until
somebody claims it."

Elsie Carter, who kept the hotel, was emerging
from the post office. "I hope you don't have to
hold it as long as I've held some. One man stayed
three days in the hotel and skipped without
paying. All he left in his bag were some old
newspapers and a couple of bricks. He hadn't
figured on paying at all."

"Somebody will show up. If they can identify
it and will sign for it, they can have it."

He walked to the office, feeling pleased. The
town now knew he had taken a suit-case to the
marshal's office, and that it was not in his
home. He doubted if there would be inquiries. In
fact, he doubted if the murderer or murderers
knew there was another suit-case.

Kim Baca was in the office. He glanced at the
suit-case and Chantry explained, then Baca
commented, "Something's stirring, so watch your
step. Rowan MacAdam is in town."

Borden Chantry sat down in his swivel chair.
"Rowan MacAdam, here?"

Rowan MacAdam was a gunman who had fought in a
couple of cattle wars down New Mexico way. He had
done some shooting there and had been in a couple
of gun battles up in Montana.

Why was he here? This was cattle country but
it was the slack season. Anybody in his right
mind would know that cattlemen were not hiring at

this time. But then, MacAdam had been hiring his gun lately.

"Leave him alone, Kim. He may just be passing through, and we've trouble enough. That is, as long as he minds his own affairs."

"Suppose he's here to get you? He wouldn't be the first."

"Leave him alone." Borden stared out the window. Bess was probably right. Maybe he should get out of this country, as he certainly did not want to be shooting it out with would-be killers all the time. He wanted the quiet life: his ranch, his cattle, Bess and Tom. That was all he wanted, all he needed. No, he told himself, you need money to start ranching again.

He got up and walked to the door, looking out upon the street. For the time being this was his town and he wanted no harm to come to it. As he stood looking absently down the dusty street his thoughts worried over the problem of the dead man.

He would return to Harold Cuff and after him, to the train crews. Someone must have seen the man at some time.

"Kim? I'm walking down to Ed's. I need some coffee. I've got a couple of ideas and they need nourishment."

Nathan Johnson was in the cafe, drinking coffee with Judge McKinney. Both looked up, nodding as he entered.

"Join us?" Nathan suggested.

"Another time, Nathan. I've got some studying to do."

"Anything on the dead man?" Johnson asked.

Chantry shrugged. "He was in your territory,

Nathan. I'll do whatever's necessary for Thursty,
but I've enough to do right here in town."

He dropped into a chair and Ed brought over a
steaming cup of black coffee. He was hardly in
his seat before the door opened and two men came
in. The first one, he knew at once, was Rowan
MacAdam. He was a couple of inches shorter than
Chantry's six feet two, but probably just as
heavy. He spotted Chantry at once and walked
over.

"Marshal? I'm Rowan MacAdam."

"Sorry, I didn't get the name? What was it?"
Chantry looked up blandly.

"MacAdam! Rowan MacAdam." He spoke the name as
if he expected it to be greeted by a roll of
drums.

"Nice to meet you, Mr. MacAdam. We've a nice
town here. Not very busy right now, but things
will pick up. If you're thinking of going into
business we could use a harness shop. Saddles,
bridles, that sort of thing. We always welcome
new folks. In fact right down the street we've a
fine new church, and our school is a good one. Do
you have children, Mr. MacAdan?"

"MacAdam," he said, "Rowan MacAdam." Then he
added, "No, I've no children."

"It's too bad, children can be a comfort. Fine
thing, watching some nice youngsters growing up.
Too bad, a man your age--I had a black stallion
one time. Never could sire a colt. Tried again
and again. Finally had to sell him, but he did
make a good draft horse. Spent the rest of his
life pulling a dray, I imagine he was happy."

He shook his head. "Don't feel bad about it,
Mr. MacAdan. You're a young man yet." Chantry

could hardly force back laughter, but if he laughed now someone might die.

MacAdam was growing angry. "What the Hell are you talkin' about? I said I was Rowan MacAdam!"

"Of course. No need to be upset. Everybody has their problems." Chantry gestured to a chair. "Set down, won't you? You'll feel better in a few minutes."

"I feel all right! There's nothing wrong with me!"

"There! See? You're feeling better already. Altitude sometimes has that effect on people. Will you have a cup of coffee? Ed here makes the best, believe me."

"No, I won't sit down! What are you, some kind of a fool?"

Chantry nodded, seriously. "Yes, that could be it. Each of us is a fool in his own way. I in mine, and you in yours." The time for this foolishness was nearly over. "If you're going to stay in town, Mr. MacAdan, I suggest you hang up that gun. It's a good way to get into trouble around here. The people of our town," he gestured, "no longer accept that sort of thing.

"In fact." Borden Chantry's gun was in his hand. "Maybe I'd better hold those gun belts while you're in town. We wouldn't want anybody hurt here. It gives the town a bad reputation. You just unbuckle very carefully now, very carefully, and when you're ready to leave town, just drop by the marshal's office and I'll give them back."

Rowan MacAdam froze, then he fumbled at his buckle with nervous fingers, and handed the belt to Chantry. Blindly, he turned toward the door.

There he stopped. "Damn you," he said, "how the Hell--?"

"I offered you a cup of coffee, Mr. MacAdan."

"To Hell with you!" MacAdam said, and stumbled into the street.

For a moment there was silence in the cafe, then Nathan Johnson said, "Bord, do you know who that was?"

Chantry glanced around. "I know who he thought he was."

CHAPTER 8

He sat down and Ed brought him a fresh cup.

Nathan Johnson crossed the room and straddled a chair. "This murder, Borden. I could use your help with it."

"It won't be easy," Chantry agreed. "I don't envy you."

"You're not working on it?"

"Just keeping an eye on things for Thursty. He'll be back soon. You need to talk to Doc, and I'll write out a description of what I saw when I found the body."

Nathan talked awhile then wandered back to his own table and Borden Chantry stared out at the sunlit street. The first clue he had was that somebody did not want the body found at any time soon. He could not escape the conclusion that time was a key element here. Something else was nagging him, too, and he could not figure what it was. It was irritating. What had he missed? It was something, he was sure, that happened today.

So what had happened? The only thing out of

the usual was the unclaimed suit-case and he had
not examined it.

Yet he had emptied it of a bunch of
nondescript clothing, some tools, what else he
did not know. There might be a clue there.
Slowly, he tried to examine every minute of the
morning, among the odds and ends of rumpled
clothing--

He scowled. There had been a spot of blue,
blue ribbon. Now what the devil was a man like
this one doing with blue ribbon?

He walked back to the house and got out the
two sacks. The spot of blue was as he had
recalled a strip of blue ribbon, wrinkled at a
couple of points where it had been tied.

"Bess? Why would a man as untidy as this one
have such a ribbon?"

"He probably received a present from his lady
friend. That's been tied to something, some small
box. Maybe he was sentimental. Maybe he just
neglected to throw it away."

Wrapped around something, a small package of
some kind? Who knew about packages? Priscilla
knew. Borden put the ribbon in his pocket and
walked back to the restaurant. The post office
was not open yet so Pris would be unavailable. He
would have another cup of coffee and do some
thinking.

Except for the dead man there had been no
crime, nor even rumors of one. There was just
that veiled feeling of uneasiness about a town
small enough to be sensitive to such things. He
was still sitting there thinking when two men
came in; one was the stranger he had seen in the
saloon, a man with a bit of a sun-burn. As the

man crossed the room to sit down, he almost
stopped, staring at Chantry, then hastily turned
away. As soon as he was seated he whispered
something to his companion.

Borden was puzzled. Both men had seen him
before and pointedly ignored him, yet now
something arrested their attention. Self-
consciously he shifted his coat, drawing it
closer about him and his fingers encountered the
blue ribbon. It had not been completely stuffed
into his pocket.

So? Was that it? Why? What could it mean to
them? Yet even as he considered that a small bell
of warning sounded in his skull. They recognized
his clue, if it was a clue, and it had caused
them to worry, perhaps to fear. That might mean a
cause to kill. He must be very careful.

One of the men got up and left the restaurant,
mounted a horse outside and rode away up the
street.

He finished his coffee. Pris should be open
for business by now. He got up and went out on
the street. One of the two horses was gone but
the remaining one carried Hitchell's brand.
Borden walked up to the post office. The crowd
that came to pick up mail had gone, and Pris was
alone.

"Pris? I can use some help."

"I could use some, too. You'd think it would
be easy in a small post office like this but
there's always something more to do. What can I
do for you, Bord?"

"Bess tells me this was probably tied around
some small package and so I--"

"Terlandra."

"What?"

"Terlandra. That new girl Mary Ann had. Only lasted a couple of months although she was one of the prettiest girls this season."

"What about her?"

"She used to get those little boxes, about three inches square, always tied in pink or blue ribbon, but tied up tight under the ribbon. Looked like some admirer was sending her jewelry or something."

"Notice where they came from?"

"Denver. Some place on Larimer Street."

Bord walked to the window and looked down the dusty street. Now he had a lead, at least. He must talk to Mary Ann but not now. He did not like to be seen going to her house in the day time, and of course now there was the added reason that they would be watching.

The worst of it was he did not know what he was looking for. What was going on? If, as he suspected, time was all important, how much time did he have? Now they knew he was alert, that he knew something was in the wind, and they would be inclined to believe he knew more than he did.

Borden Chantry walked back to the cafe. It was time for some serious thinking and he must alert Kim Baca and Big Injun. And Bess, most of all Bess.

The sun-burned man? He heard him called by name, but what name? He searched his memory and after a bit it came to him. Somebody, somewhere had referred to the man as Ringwald, but that helped him none at all except to put a name to the man.

He finished his coffee and walked back up the

street to the office. Kim was at the desk, his
feet propped up reading a magazine.

"Kim? We've never talked much about Hitchell.
Know anything?"

"He's done time, if that's what you mean. Did
a couple of years for stealing a saddle.
Personally, I never believed he did it, but he
was convicted."

So that's why he was pale. And Ringwald? Might
they have met in prison? Was that why they had
come here in the beginning?

But that brought him no closer to the crime,
if crime there was. The killing might have been
some simple drunken disagreement and nothing
more.

Yet it was more, and he knew it.

It was after nine before he crossed to Mary
Ann's back door. He was the only man allowed to
enter there so the girls knew who he was. Mary
Ann came down and poured tea. "I know coffee is
your drink, Bord, but tea is all I have."

"I drink it now and again, with Bess."

She glanced at him. "I miss that, I really do.
I miss talking with women other than the girls.
You'd not think I'd admit that, but it's true.
I'd not say it to anybody but you."

"I know. Life takes us down strange paths,
sometimes. I never figured on being the law."

"What is it, Bord? How can I help you?"

"You had a girl named Terlandra?"

"Yes, but not for long. She didn't fit in--she
was a snowbird. You know, on cocaine. I can't put
up with that, and never have."

"But she was here for awhile?"

"She was liked, and she was prettier than

most. She could talk to anybody and would. I was inclined to over-look her using the stuff until I found she was peddling it, too."

"What was her source?"

"Denver, I think?"

He took the blue ribbon from his pocket. "Ever see anything like this?"

"Often. Terlandra used to get little packets from Denver, always tied with pink or blue ribbon, like gifts. She had only one steady customer of whom I know, a fellow named Wiemer, Harry Wiemer."

Borden described the dead man. "Is that him?"

"Sounds right. He was an untidy little man and I didn't want him around. You know how it is, once they're into coke they lose interest in women, and you can't trust them anymore. They'll lie, steal, anything just to get the stuff." Mary Ann paused, sipping tea. "That's probably what happened to her."

"What happened?"

"Terlandra was murdered. Not over a month after she left here. Less than a month, in fact. She was back in Denver. Probably by one of those she'd been selling drugs to."

Murdered? By someone she had been selling drugs to or because she knew too much? Harry Wiemer? Where had he heard that name? The dead man had been killed and Terlandra also, but why?

"I need to know all I can about her. I'll trust you to say nothing about that, Mary Ann."

"I don't know anything else, Bord, except that the last time he came here they had a fight. She was furious with him about something and he with her. I heard them arguing, something about money."

They talked for a few minutes and then with the light out he eased himself out the back door, moved quickly to one side and waited, listening. Had they followed him here? Two dead, so they were not playing games. Not for a minute did he believe the two killings were unrelated, but how? Why?

Bess was already in bed and asleep when he eased himself into the dark house. The coffee was still on and he poured a cup and sat down by the window. Harold Cuff was working late. Bord liked it because the light from the dispatcher's office was bright and friendly. It also gave him some light almost as far as the pile of ties.

Arguing about money? He understood that dealing in drugs, even with few laws to restrict them, was a cash on the barrel-head business, so what could be wrong?

Had Wiemer tried to short her? There must have been something wrong about the pay-off, something wrong about the money.

He put his cup down suddenly. Wrong about the money?

CHAPTER 9

Three men sat in the living room of Zaretta Clyde. The big old man sat on a sofa facing the door, Ringwald and Hitchell half-faced him, both nervous. The big man was truly big; he was also not that old. At fifty years he carried the look of a man of thirty, and the body of one. He was also mean, difficult, and uncommonly shrewd.

What his name had been in his early years had been forgotten, left behind when he led an escape through the abandoned sewers of the old prison. He was now known as Lev Larson. Nobody liked him but many needed him, for whatever involved his interest went down well. He had a reputation for success. In the world of crime there is no better name to have.

Rumor was that he had millions stashed away, just where or under what name nobody knew. It was also understood that if you crossed him you were in trouble, the worst kind of trouble.

As he looked out at the yard the gate opened and Turren Downer rode in. Lev sat up, irritated. "Who the Hell is that?"

Hitchell said, "Cowpuncher, a tough man. I think he's sweet on Zaretta."

"Tell her to get rid of him."

Ringwald shook his head. "No can do, Lev. Zaretta does as she pleases and you know that. You cross her and this whole shootin' match is gone."

"We don't need any nosy cowpunchers floating around."

"Better leave him alone, Lev. He doesn't know from nothing and Zaretta's happy."

Lev shifted his big body irritably. He did not like to be crossed and the presence of the big cowboy looked like trouble. "I'll handle it," he said.

Ringwald looked over at Hitchell and said, "There's the other thing. That blue ribbon now. Looks like that town clown is onto something."

"Don't sell him short. Borden Chantry is no
fool. I've worked with him, seen him operate,"
Hitchell said.

Lev Larson snorted. "Smart? Some hick-town
copper? He's no problem. Before he figures which
end is up we'll be long gone from here."

He glanced around at Hitchell. "If he worries
you boys, take him out."

Hitchell shifted his feet, stared at the toes
of his boots and said quietly, "Leave him alone,
Lev. He's a bad man to trifle with. Nobody
dreamed Lang Adams was involved in that Sackett
murder, yet he figured it out and nailed him.

"The best thing we can do is what you've
always said, keep our heads down, pull this off
and you guys can get out of here."

There was silence in the room and then Larson
said, "That Zaretta woman's gettin' too big for
her britches. Needs to be taken down a notch."

"Don't try it, Lev." Ringwald's voice was
sharp. "She has the connections. If she tells the
Chinese it's no go they'll fade out like they'd
never been and we've shot our wad."

Lev Larson sat up irritably. It was true, too
damned true. Everything depended on Zaretta, and
none of her clients wanted anything to happen to
her. Her finger was in too many pies.

He sat very still, looking out the door. The
big cowboy was tying up his horse at Zaretta's
rail, but he was not thinking of that.

No more than ten days now, if all went well,
and he would be holding more than a million
dollars. It was the biggest job he had ever
pulled off and he could not have done it without

Zaretta Clyde. He had gone to her with the idea and she had helped set it up.

She had known about Hitchell and his lonely ranch. She had known where to lay hands on Wiemer, who was the best there was, and she had known where and how to arrange for the buyers. Yet it had turned messy and he did not like that. First Wiemer and then that woman. Even that went off smoothly, at least until Ringwald spotted that blue ribbon. The hick cop seemed to have established a connection. But had he, really?

Zaretta was getting her hooks into that new county sheriff, Nathan Johnson, but Chantry was not sharing ideas with him, and Johnson did not believe Chantry knew anything. Still, the blue ribbon? Was it simply a coincidence? Lev Larson did not believe in such things. Everything had a meaning, a connection.

The sun was setting over the mountains to the westward--he had not seen the mountains but had been told they were there. Denver was out there somewhere, but Lev Larson was an Eastern man, and occasionally a mid-western man. Until now he had never been west of Kansas City.

Lev Larson did not like dealing with Zaretta Clyde. He had nothing but contempt for women and believed her much over-rated. He was a brutal, self-contained man who knew what he wanted and how to get it. He had developed this deal himself and then suddenly he found he needed somebody with connections, and Zaretta had them. She knew people he needed or where to find them; she was respected in certain major seats of power that even Lev Larson hesitated to challenge.

Ten days. He could sit tight for ten days.

Even if the hick cop was onto something there was small chance he could put it together in time. The deal would be consummated and they would scatter to the winds.

Lev Larson had no love for anyone. He wanted to get his money and get out and he was covering all his bases. Where there was money there were people hungry for it, and he knew somebody was probably plotting to steal his end. Well, he was ready. He trusted no one.

That big cowboy out there? Was it that he was in the way, or simply because he was big and looked like a fighter?

Lev stirred irritably. He did not like waiting. If the Chinese were coming, why didn't they come? Why so precise about the date? One particular old man had to view the merchandise, that was it. Everything hung on his word.

Lev had been warned. "Don't try anything funny. The Hop Sing Tong has hatchet men everywhere and they'll nail you, but good. They give their word, and it will be good, but they don't stand for any fancy foot-work."

Lev did not plan on any. He liked a clean deal himself. That was one of the things he liked about this from the first. It was clean. In and out, a big take, and everybody gets lost.

Never a patient man he was doubly impatient now, and staring at the big cowboy's horse made him more so, yet he had to confess the deal had gone together like clock-work, fully as much because of Zaretta as he himself.

They made a team. He had to admit that, reluctant as he was to do so. This was the big one and hopefully the last one. A pitcher could go too often to the well, his own mother had taught him that, and except for the first time his skirts were clean. He had escaped, changed his name and grown bigger, no longer resembling the man who had been imprisoned. One of the men had died in that sewer and they believed it had been him, so his escape was clean and clear.

Lev Larson watched as the big cowboy came out and stepped into the saddle. He could handle that. He would get Turren Downer to pick a fight with him, then he would be in the clear with Zaretta, and after that he would decide about that two-bit country marshal.

He had to admit the accommodations were good and the food was excellent. Everything Zaretta Clyde did was out of the top drawer.

He watched the cowboy ride down the hill. He would be a charger and a swinger, made to order for Lev. Larson smiled. At least he could take his mind off the waiting, and he would teach Zaretta a thing or two.

If her man started the fight, what could she say?

Lev Larson watched the sun set without thinking of it. His mind was on Turren Downer and what he would do to him. The man was known as a fighter, so was vulnerable--that he got into a fight would surprise no one. Lev had whipped a number of the top professionals but had found easier ways of making a living than bare-knuckle fighting. Yet he liked fighting and he was so much better than anyone he had met that he had no problems. Moreover, different than most fighters he liked punishing his opponents. Many times when he could have scored early knockouts he had

deliberately refrained to keep his opponents
trying so he could administer a more thorough
beating.

Ten days might not be too long after all. If
he couldn't trap the cowboy into a fight he might
get that nosy small town copper; either would be
fun.

He went back into his room and began leafing
through magazines that lay on the table. There
was a stack of old Police Gazettes with fight
stories and illustrations on the well known sheet
of pink paper. Occasionally he came upon old
references to himself under one of the several
names he used when fighting.

Often he had been imported into some small
town or city by gamblers wishing to make a
killing. He would work up a match with some local
champion. He usually wore shabby, loose-fitting
clothes that displayed none of his Herculean
frame.

He discovered he could make more money working
as such a "ringer" than with regular boxing
matches. Only once had a gambler tried to short
him. After word got around as to what happened to
the gambler it never happened again.

Sitting alone he thought about all aspects of
their deal. It still looked good, despite the
necessity for the killings. Hitchell worried him
a little. The man was not really a criminal
although he had done time, and Lev did not trust
an honest man.

And those Indian women? Had they heard
anything? Had they talked to that country
marshal? Did they know anything to tell him?

Borden Chantry. That was his name. If he

wanted a fight he should pick one with him, put him out of action for the next ten days, but how did he do that without getting arrested?

He went to his luggage and opened a specially built leather case which contained two fifty pound dumb-bells. Getting them out he went to work and worked for a solid hour, then sponged himself off and went to bed. It was a three-times-a-week ritual, and he never missed.

He walked and climbed at every opportunity, wanting to be always ready. It had become a long established habit which he never ignored.

Ringwald stood by the window looking down at the lights of the town. It wasn't much of a place, yet people seemed contented and it was a supply point for a good stretch of country in every direction.

He glanced around at Hitchell. "Lived here long?"

"Most of my life."

"Do they know you did time?"

"I doubt it. That was in another state. Baca might. He's that deputy marshal Chantry has. Used to be a horse thief and has connections everywhere, both sides of the law. Folks like him."

"How'd you get into this?"

"Zaretta knew about me and she sent a couple of men to talk to me. The way they talked I had to listen. To be honest, I wanted no part of it.

"I'll admit it looked good for me. They built that barn to work in, they bought me enough cows so I'd look legitimate, and laid in more supplies

than I'd ever seen before. I figured, What the
Hell? They'll finish what they're doing and I'll
be left sitting pretty."

"Zaretta will remember. She makes her living
knowing about people like you."

Hitchell stared gloomily down the street. He
liked this town and the country around. He had
friends here. He had never wanted to be rich,
just comfortable.

Ringwald looked down the dark street, only a
few lights showing. He would like to be down
there now, just having a drink, and no worries.

It was a strange thing. The biggest deal any
of them had ever cut into and yet all of them
were edgy, and he for one was like Hitchell--he
was running scared.

CHAPTER 10

Borden Chantry was feeling better about the
situation. Things were beginning to fall into
place. What was coming off he did not know but he
suspected, and he now knew why Wiemer had been
killed and probably why Terlandra had been
murdered.

The trouble was he did not know who all the
players were in the game. Ringwald and Hitchell
were involved but beyond that he knew nothing.
Perhaps Zaretta Clyde was, but he had no
evidence, only that she knew them and some of
them were staying at her place. But others had
stayed there also, before this. There was that
big older man, too, Larson was his name, but his
connection was doubtful. So far he had seen no

more than a nodding acquaintance which would be natural with men staying at the same hotel or boarding place, if Zaretta's place could be called that.

Ringwald and Hitchell were small figures on the board if he was guessing right. Any move to grab them would not only tip his hand but would give him nothing. He must know what was coming off and who was holding the reins.

Who were the top men in the game and what were they waiting for? If they were waiting. He had guessed that time was the key element, but why? Was somebody coming to make a pay-off? If his own timing was off he might miss on everything and the killers might escape him and suddenly all would be gone.

He doubted that Turren Downer was involved. Turren was Western. He was big, strong and tough, a mean fighter and a good one, and if he got into trouble it would be from brawling, a gun battle or something of that nature. He was not a criminal as such. Of course, he had now done time and there was no guessing what connections he had made in prison. That would have to be considered.

When he walked in the door Bess was putting supper on the table and Tom was deep in a book, as usual. He looked up quickly. "How'd it go, Pa? Are you any closer to those men?"

"A little. I believe I know what's happening, and some of those involved, but I can't talk about it now."

Tom was full of questions but he knew his father well enough to know that he had said all he was about to say.

"If we go back east will you be an officer?"

Borden shook his head. "How could I be? I won't know the country or the people as I do here. I'm not a good officer, Tom, I just know this country and use a little common sense."

"Everybody says you're the best."

"That's nice of them, but enough of them didn't think so to re-elect me as sheriff."

"Are we going east, Pa?"

"When I figure out what's happening here we'll decide. I don't know how I'd make a living, son. All I know are horses and cattle."

Tom was silent. His mother's desire to go east and to have him in school there had blinded her to reality. Tom loved his father and knew that here, in the West, he was an important man. Back east that would simply not be true. Yet he himself wanted to go east, and to attend Eastern schools.

He had sneaked back on the street the day the outlaws Monson and Clatt's gang had tried to rob the bank, and he had overheard Time Reardon, no friend of his father's, say, "He's one of the very best. Whatever you do, don't low rate Borden Chantry. With a gun in his hand he's as good or better than anybody I've ever seen."

Tom was fiercely proud of his father yet he had a pen pal in the East who scoffed at the idea there might be such men. Gun-fighters and cattlemen were the stuff of romance. A lot of people believed that and Tom knew enough to know that having survived gun battles and having once built a ranch would do his father no good back there.

Sometimes he was jealous of his friend, Billy McCoy. He felt Billy was closer to his father

than he was, yet he could understand why: Billy
was part of this place, a boy at home in the
harsh Western landscape just as his father was.
He himself had been raised to think like his
mother and, despite the influence of his father,
he had taken on much of it, partly through the
desire for a broader, deeper education.

Billy McCoy had his own ideas about those pink
and blue ribbons. He had seen them in the rubbish
thrown out at Mary Ann's where the girls
sometimes fixed meals for him. He had seen them
and decided where they came from before Borden
Chantry had. People talked a lot in front of a
youngster, taking it for granted he did not
understand. Or that he was not paying attention.
No matter how busy or absent-minded Billy
happened to be he was always paying attention.

Sitting in the kitchen by the window, but just
far back enough not to be a target, even though
it was early, Borden Chantry went over the few
items he had in his mind.

Harry Wiemer had incurred somebody's anger,
enough so they wished him dead, and he was dead,
his body left so hopefully it would not be
immediately discovered.

How had he incurred the displeasure of those
who killed him? And why had it been necessary to
kill Terlandra as well?

Something had gone wrong, if Chantry was
surmising correctly and there had also been a
difficulty between Terlandra and Wiemer.

What had happened?

There had been a dispute about money. Had he not paid? Or had he not paid enough?

He certainly had paid or she would not have delivered. And for the same reason he had probably paid enough.

Harry Wiemer was a man who dealt with ink. An engraver? There had been a dispute about money. Suppose it was counterfeit? Suppose he had unwittingly or on purpose because he was short paid Terlandra with a phony bill and she had passed it on to her people? She would be in trouble and he would be in trouble with Terlandra.

And perhaps with his people?

Somebody had built a mighty fine barn for Hitchell. Suppose that barn had been used to make queer money? Suppose it had been made and was awaiting shipment?

To whom? Where?

Suppose that was the time element?

It was a lot of supposing with very little concrete evidence. He had seen no counterfeit money nor had he heard of any. Suppose that was the idea? Counterfeit money made in the West but for shipment elsewhere? Far from its point of origin?

And suppose in his need for cocaine Wiemer had spent, accidentally or on purpose, some of the counterfeit bills? Bills that weren't his to spend. Even more likely, what if he told Terlandra about the operation? What if they were using some of the counterfeit on the sly to solve some problem that she might be having?

COMMENTS: Louis started planning this sequel to *Borden Chantry* in 1987, around the same time he began laying the groundwork for his memoir, *Education of a Wandering Man*. Although he had been plagued with heart issues and pneumonia throughout the year, it was only around January of 1988 that doctors discovered that both were caused by the lung cancer that eventually ended his life.

The chapters you have just read were written during a time when he was on oxygen and often dealing with the aftereffects of chemotherapy. I fear that even though I have done some judicious editing, you can still tell he was not as focused as usual.

Whenever Louis L'Amour characters sit around drinking coffee and asking themselves questions about what is going on, that is actually Louis trying to figure out what he wants to do with his story. In fact, you can pretty much bet that he either had just returned from doing the same thing himself or was about to go get himself a cup.

By the end of Chapter 8, he was still struggling to raise the stakes, get all the pieces in place, and keep the plot moving. However, it is interesting to see that shifting the point of view to include the bad guys sort of gave the story a second wind.

Writers of mysteries often face a problem where their detectives, especially if they work in law enforcement, have to be reactive rather than proactive—that is, unless enough momentum has been built up and a good chain of evidence created. Since Lev Larson, Zaretta, Ringwald, and Hitchell are the ones actually driving the story forward, shifting to scenes that included them added an energy that even Borden seems to feel is lacking. It also allowed Louis to live inside those characters for a while and figure out what they had done and what they would do in detail.

The other element that shows up while we are dealing with the criminals is the possible involvement of a Chinese Tong. Tongs are sworn brotherhoods or secret societies that often have political goals (in the last sixty years many have been pro-Taiwan, pro-Kuomintang, or anti-Communist groups), but that have also been tied to organized crime. Chinese criminals would have been an excellent way to dispose of counterfeit money, because they could spend it overseas, using it in places and in ways that would take U.S. authorities a long time to even notice. At the time of our story it would have been nearly impossible to trace.

The Tongs have a bit of a connection to Louis's personal history. It is possible that Dad was exposed to Tong organization or activity, or at least to stories of the Chinese societies, while in the Far East. However, his closest connection to the criminal aspect of the Tongs was in Arizona. Louis was an eyewitness to the escape of five "Bing Kong" Tong assassins after they killed a member of the rival "Hop Sing" Tong, the owner of a restaurant in Kingman. Having just returned from Asia, Dad had enjoyed a number of conversations with Tom King, the murdered man.

Also of interest is Dad's mention of "yeggmen," a type of criminal that I imagine he got to know while hoboing around the country. Yeggs were itinerant crooks who were reputed to "peel" their way into vaults with a single jack and chisel, or an axe. They might also boil the nitroglycerine out of dynamite so that they could drip the unstable liquid through a hole in a safe door using a string to guide the droplets into place. Then, wrapping the safe in mattresses, they would hit the door with a sledgehammer to fire just enough of the explosive to break the door free.

One last detail taken from Dad's history is his depiction

of the stifling social atmosphere of small towns. He had lived in, and been an outsider in, many places where people's every action became the subject of gossip. Even I have been in places (as late as the 1970s!) where a local police officer might hesitate to follow up a lead because he feared what being seen talking to a criminal, vagrant, or prostitute might do to his reputation.

There are two generations of notes for this story. The ones that apply directly to the chapters above begin like this:

```
Who? Was he?
Why? Was he killed?
How did he get there?
Who is involved?
What clues?

Ink ingrained in skin of hands
Unlikely if using pen.
Ink on inside of pocket-edges.

Who works with ink?
A printer -

Chantry visits newspaper, watches printing--
    doesn't fit.
```

There was also an earlier concept that led to a very different version of the counterfeit money plot. It all started with the following note:

```
Queer as collateral? Never to be used?
    Perhaps teller used some of it in
emergency?
```

"Queer" in this case is old-time criminal argot for counterfeit money. Louis seems to have been considering a version of the classic bearer-bond con, where millions of dollars in fake bearer bonds are shown to the mark and validated by an "expert" of some sort. Then the con man takes out a loan that is just a small percentage of the value of the bonds, using the bonds as collateral, pretending it's all so he won't have to go through the "trouble" of cashing in the extremely valuable bonds. The con man then disappears with the loaned amount, leaving the mark with a safety deposit box full of worthless paper.

Later Louis expanded those two lines into a pretty complete treatment of the "counterfeit collateral" version of this story.

Borden Chantry Sequel

Hyatt Johnson appears preoccupied and worried. CHANTRY is sensitive to the feelings of his town, is disturbed by some premonition of trouble he cannot understand.

Some time before Chantry has met a newcomer in whom all are interested, a fascinating, interesting man with a couple of men who are his hostlers and guides. The newcomer is planning to invest largely. He will get r.r. [railroad] through the town, and may build a new and better hotel. He looks over the town, buys several lots for which he pays in promissory notes against a large sum of money he has held for him in the local bank. Hyatt has glimpsed this money, but it is being held, not on deposit, but simply held by the bank. Hyatt and his

teller have each signed a receipt for it but
the money is not to be deposited for several
weeks.

Chantry is disturbed by the newcomer.
Although he supposedly knows nothing of the
country he has several times taken the right
turn on the streets and seems to have a
familiarity with the town. Chantry's wife
says he is too suspicious, Hyatt smiles
tolerantly, the saloon-keeper is
noncommittal but, it develops, has invested
no money in the newcomer's schemes. It is
well known that the money is at the bank.
The newcomer has borrowed several sums
against it, for immediate cash needs; it
finally develops that he has borrowed quite
a lot of money from various citizens, or has
obtained the money on false pretenses. An
old man is found dead apparently killed by a
fallen timber, Borden proves such was not
the case. Yet he was a harmless, friendly
old man who has no enemies and no
possessions. Borden is sure it is murder.
But why? Actually it is because he
recognized a scar on the newcomer's finger
and knows him.

The newcomer has been entertaining some
of the big ranchers in town, and also their
cowhands. One young cowhand is found struck
on the head, apparently left for dead, but
he is not dead. Borden takes him to a woman
on a nearby ranch who attempts to nurse him
back to life. He has been struck hard and is
in a coma.

Keeping this man's existence a secret,

Borden hopes to keep him alive and hopes he can identify his assailant. Borden spends time on her ranch, and his wife becomes suspicious. Borden believes the young man can tell who attacked him, and why. He is sure something is wrong and wishes to know, to uncover the mystery.

Boy from the ranch where the man is kept is buying items at the drug store to care for the young man, and newcomer is present; the old druggist asks if somebody has been hurt out that way? Boy says no, just usual stuff they keep on hand, but newcomer's interest is aroused. The body of the cowpuncher has not been found, and this has worried him. [He was left for dead] not too far from the woman's ranch.

Newcomer must find out if puncher is alive.

Meanwhile a rider returns from delivering some horses and is going back out to his ranch. He refuses a drink and in the altercation that follows, is killed in a gun battle. On the surface it is a fair shooting, all agree the puncher was armed, that he had an even break, but the henchman of the newcomer who killed him is obviously a deadly man with a gun.

Slowly Borden begins to tie things together. He believes there is some connection between the killings, although there is no outward tie. He is accused of trying to find a pattern as he did before [in the novel Borden Chantry]. One is a simple shooting, another an accident.

Borden goes about his job with the aid of Kim while the town prepares for a big fandango and celebration. There are to be some contests, cash prizes awarded, saddles, etc. and all the cowpunchers want to compete. An attempt is made to murder puncher in coma but he comes out of it, explains that he had gone up a draw where there were always cattle and there were none. He was studying tracks when slugged by a strange puncher who said "he was looking for strays." Kim comes in to report there are no cattle, the range has been swept clean. Borden and Big Injun trace lost cattle to a distant valley where the cattle are held . . . several thousand head. Perhaps with Indians to help they move cattle to reservation or--?

Return to find big fandango going on, everybody enjoying themselves.

Hyatt obviously concerned; several others seem less than happy and it appears two or three citizens have compared notes and found all are holding notes from newcomer. Some have sought assurance from Hyatt, yes the money is still there. Then he becomes disturbed and Borden puts two and two together and goes to him with a suggestion he check the money. It is counterfeit.

One of the girls on the "line" has given Borden a clue without realizing it, when she mentions one of the newcomer's followers reminds her of a man she knew who is now dead. Borden has routinely checked the name, discovers the man is now in prison for

counterfeiting. He supposedly had been
working hard at making money before arrest
but it was never found.

Or . . . the murdered man had a packet he
would not let out of his sight. Man was very
jumpy at night. Thought he was followed.

Murdered man spoke of his old outfit in
Civil War. Borden writes to Washington for
info on outfit. He finds it had engaged in
counter-guerilla action, including break-up
of gang of counterfeiters. Equipment never
found.

So, the newcomer murdered man with
plates, made large amount of queer. Sells
some, but due to fatal flaw in plates it
cannot be passed . . . some other way of
using it must be found.

Newcomer hates town, because of something
that happened to his father. So he and his
followers loot the town of money and the
range of cattle wanting to effectually
destroy it.

An earlier cash payment to a creditor has
been held up so it would not be discovered
that the money was counterfeit.

Borden kills gunman in a shoot-out and
proves to newcomer his father was not framed
but caught in the act.

Additional, though somewhat cryptic, notes on the plot
read:

Con man using counterfeit money--Has left
bad [bag?] containing $100 bills & [a few]
gold eagles . . . This is left at the bank

as surety to impress. Bag locked.-First he
uses real money, deposits, withdraws
deposits--leaves bag. He has successfully
passed himself off [as] an investor--in
land, cattle, mines.-Man has left large amt.
in bills in bank to be deposited
later.- . . . banker will over-extend
counting on big deposit.-Draws on other
money left at store for supplies, cattle. He
buys much on credit due to money left.-He
plans to loot town, milk it dry of
cash.-- . . . everybody seem[s] to profit.

It is interesting to follow the evolution of this plot from
these notes, which explore a con game that relies on the
townspeople's naive belief in the money a man supposedly
has in the bank, to the concept of selling imperfect counterfeit bills to a Chinese gang that may circulate them overseas. Clearly the latter version is more sophisticated and
more in line with Louis's desire to free the Western genre
from its traditional conventions and connect it to the rest of
the nineteenth-century world. The Chinese experience in
the West was something that Dad always wanted to deal
with but never really got around to. As with many subjects,
it was really just a matter of having too little time.

In other notes Louis left behind, he mentioned that he
was interested in using the fact that there are "two sides of
the street, or an end of town [that separates classes or eth-
nicities or both]." He wanted to "have a poor woman speak
longingly about the quality and style of the prostitutes'
clothes." The "scarcity of Indians on the plains" was something else he wanted to comment on, as opposed to the
"great village referred to in Spanish accounts." This may be
a note regarding the spread of disease that occurred after
contact with Europeans and the other pressures on the Na-

tive American population. "Cover some of plains Indians activities before white man" is also a note in this section. Obviously, Louis had some social and cultural commentary in mind.

Reading through this fragment and the original novel, *Borden Chantry*, I sensed something familiar about the contrast in the relationship Borden has with his son, Tom, who is more protected, bookish, and under his mother's wing, and Billy McCoy, who is a rough-and-tumble street kid and operates more in Borden's world. It is quite similar to the relationship that Louis's father, Dr. L. C. LaMoore, had with Jack, a boy that the family adopted. Jack Otto was a scrappy kid from an Eastern orphanage, and Louis occasionally seemed to feel that his father might have liked Jack better than him. The adoptive father and adopted son had a lot in common in their earthy approach to life, while Louis was more intellectual and introverted, a kid more interested in getting lost in a book than getting out into the world. It is ironic that Louis went on to have adventures beyond anything Jack probably could have imagined.

Buried deep in this manuscript there is also a brief moment out of my own past. When Tom Chantry asks, "Pa? Can I ride out there with you someday? I miss the place," it is likely my father was remembering something I had asked about a number of times. In the early 1970s we moved from West Hollywood to a much nicer neighborhood near UCLA. But our old house didn't sell for nearly two years. I was very attached to that place, and the fact that it was somehow still there, that no one else had taken it over and made it theirs, made it harder to give up.

The move occurred just at the time that I made the transition from grammar school to junior high school. I realize today that the few trips I made with my mother back to the old place to clean up this or that or to show the house (I really can't remember what exactly) were like a haunting return to my childhood, a dusty, empty shell of what it once had been.

It's amusing to realize, now that I am an adult, that many years later Tom Chantry would return to the ruins of his old home and be forced to take refuge in a place where he had played as a child. "The Hole," in *North to the Rails*, seems to be a combination of the tunnels through the deep growth of hillside ivy that the neighborhood kids and I used to travel unseen (or so we thought) between the houses on our West Hollywood street, and the small grotto containing a spring that existed on some land we owned in the Tehachapi Mountains of Kern County. Looking back, I wonder how many times my sister and I were, at least partly, the models for characters in my father's books.

Lastly, but perhaps most important, it is worth noting that my father chose to return to this particular story after finishing *Education of a Wandering Man*. He must have been fairly sure that one or the other would be his last book. After succeeding in his long struggle to publish material in other genres, he had clearly decided to try to complete one last, fairly traditional, Western. He knew that this was something his fans would enjoy and, as much as he had planned to write other, more personal, works, I don't think he wanted to give in to any maudlin, self-absorbed acknowledgment that his time was ending. He wanted the last thing he did to reflect his life at its best. He wanted it to be about moving forward, getting the next thing done, and entertaining the people who had supported him for the previous four decades. While I'm sure he wanted to finish this book, I'm actually glad he didn't. There was nowhere he was happier than in the middle of an unfolding story.

About eighteen months before Louis started this draft, and about ten months before he discovered he had cancer, he wrote the following in his journal:

Don't know how much productive time I
have left so must ration my work with more
care. Sometimes I work like I had all the
time in the world. I have 17 books I must
do--34 I'd like to do and more coming all
the time. But I will be 79 next March. Feel
great most of the time and like I could go
on forever . . .

And then:

I am on the verge of becoming a good
writer, all I need is time.

ACKNOWLEDGMENTS

I would very much like to thank my mother, Paul O'Dell (who worked on the earliest incarnation of this book and came up with the title for this entire program), Jeanne Brown, Angelique Pitney, Charles Van Eman, Sonndra May, Daphne Ashbrook, Jamie Wain, Jayne Rosen, Jessica Wolfson, Mara Purl, Cathy Sandrich Gelfond, Trish Mahoney, Jordan Ladd, and Paula Beyers for all their help and the sorting and transcribing of the original manuscripts.

On the publishing end of things kudos go to the great Stu Applebaum, Gina Wachtel, Ratna Kamath, Nina Shield, Elana Seplow-Jolley, David Moench, Colleen Nuccio, Joe Scalora, Cynthia Lasky and her crack team, Scott Shannon, Matt Schwartz, Paolo Pepe, Scott Biel, Heidi Lilly, Ted Allen, Larry Marks, Bill Takes, Libby McGuire, and Gina Centrello.

Too rarely thanked in the acknowledgments sections of books are the people who create audiobooks, in this case Penguin Random House Audio. To remedy that, I wish to offer my sincere gratitude to Amy Metsch, Orli Moscowitz, Katherine Punia, Heather Dalton, Sue Daulton, Alexis Patterson, Nicole Morano, Laura Wilson, Kaitlyn Robinson, and their fearless and wonderful leaders Amanda D'Acierno and Nina Von Moltke.

In addition, I would like to thank Universal Studios for allowing us to reprint *The Jade Eaters* and Michael Allen for giving me his take on music history, hippies, and cowboys, and to recommend to anyone who is interested Kenneth C. Davis's book *Two-Bit Culture: The Paperbacking of America* as a grand source on the history of the mid-twentieth-century book business.